OPERATION NEW BROOM

First edition
published in 2009 by

WOODFIELD PUBLISHING
Bognor Regis, West Sussex, England
www.woodfieldpublishing.com

© Robert C Bertie, 2009

All rights reserved.
No part of this publication may be reproduced
or transmitted in any form or by any means,
electronic or mechanical, nor may it be stored
in any information storage and retrieval system,
without prior permission from the publisher.

The right of Robert C Bertie
to be identified as Author of this work
has been asserted in accordance with
the Copyright, Designs and Patents Act 1988

ISBN 1-84683-080-X

Operation New Broom

*The sequel to
'Under New Management',
'Flagship March' and
'BlueBelles on Parade'*

ROBERT C BERTIE

Woodfield

Woodfield Publishing Ltd

Woodfield House ~ Babsham Lane ~ Bognor Regis ~ West Sussex ~ PO21 5EL
telephone 01243 821234 ~ **e-mail** enquiries@woodfieldpublishing.com

Interesting and informative books on a variety of subjects

For full details of all our published titles, visit our website at
www.woodfieldpublishing.com

Dedicated to the memory of the late Albert Barrett who it was my privilege to call a true friend.

Whatever the situation, he was always there to lend a helping hand.

In Warrant Officer Bill Barrett I have tried to recreate Albert's admirable qualities of firmness, kindness and a sense of humour.

Acknowledgements

To my wife Jean who has done so much to help and support me.

To Viv Allison, who has done so much to spread the word to our RAF and WRAF colleagues.

To all of you who have read the books ... thank you and for all your good wishes.

The Author

Born in 1921 in the West Riding of Yorkshire Robert Bertie's family returned to Lancashire when he was a babe.

An 8th Army World War II veteran, he also served for 23 years in the peacetime Royal Air Force.

His wife Jean was in nursing for 39 years.

In 2009 they celebrate their Diamond Wedding anniversary. They have one son, Robert Ian.

Best Wishes to my Dear Friend Rosemary.

Bob Bertie

2009

CHAPTER 1

Jackson, the driver for all the Embassy's VIPs, was waiting in the arrivals hall at Heathrow Airport to greet Bill and Tommy Barrett and to escort them to the Savoy Hotel, where they would be contacted by the Aljibian Embassy with instructions regarding their arrival at their final destination.

"Look Bill, there is Jackson waving," said Tommy, as she returned the wave.

"It is great to see you two," Jackson said, as he shook hands with Bill then put Tommy in a bear hug. "Did you have a good flight down and how long are you staying in town?"

"We don't know yet. There should be instructions waiting at the hotel."

"They will be in the letter I delivered on the way here to meet you. Here, let me take the trolley, then follow me. I will get you out of here pretty sharpish."

Once settled down in the car, Tommy asked after Joyce, Jackson's wife.

"She is fine," he replied. "She's delighted you're back in town and is very much looking forward to seeing you. So now you are both ex-RAF, I'll bet you will be missed."

"I'll tell you all about it later Jackson … and it is not a very nice tale."

"Do you fancy an evening at the club? The committee and members will be chuffed to see you. Or do you want a quiet night? Or a quiet one with me and Joyce at home? I will pick you up and bring you back to the hotel when you are ready to leave."

"We will see what the instructions in the letter are, then we will take it from there. What do you say to that, love?"

"Yes, that's a good idea," Tommy replied. "But we must pay our respects to the club committee or they will never forgive us. We will decide after reading the letter."

On reaching the hotel, Bill was booked in by a fawning duty manager, who was still under the impression that Bill and Tommy were people of some consequence from their last visit to the hotel.

"This letter was left for you sir, earlier in the day," he said, as he handed over the letter from the Embassy.

Bill thanked him, then both he and Tommy withdrew to a comfortable seat to read it.

"It says we are booked in here for four nights then will be flown by private aircraft to our destination. Meanwhile, tomorrow I have to report to the tailors, a very reputable one I might add, according to this address, where I have to be measured for my uniforms and all the paraphernalia that go with it. The tailor has been instructed on what I will need, so it looks like all I need to do is stand there like a tailor's dummy. And how about this? 'You will also proceed to be measured and fitted out in footwear'."

"I suppose *I* will have to go and get fitted out with dresses etc, from Marks and Spencer's," said a miffed Tommy.

"Don't worry love, we will get you a wardrobe fit for a Queen. It would not do for me to be poncing about in Savile Row attire while you go around flashing your St. Michael's labels. After all, I will need some made to measure shirts, etc, and a good smart suit. So it looks like these four days are going to be rather hectic. Hey come on we have forgotten Jackson."

They went outside and saw Jackson was still waiting in his car.

They apologised for keeping him waiting and told him the reason why. "We have decided to come to your club with you even if it is only to get you more Brownie points for bringing your friends to the club again."

"Thank you, you have no idea the status I now hold since we became friends and I introduced you to the committee. The Club President still bends the ear of anyone who will listen to him about the talk you gave us about the BlueBelles and any visitor to the club is shown their photograph and told its history. You will be surprised how much the membership has increased; as a matter of fact I do believe the membership is now closed. Anyway, enough of that because you will surely get earache as soon as the President sees you. I will not tell him you are coming otherwise it would be 'wall to wall' with RAFA members and boosting his status. Joyce and myself might just as well be on our own because you would be whisked away to be introduced to all and sundry."

"Should we wear our dark glasses and come incognito?" laughed Tommy.

"Tell me Jackson do you have to sign us in at the Club?" asked Bill.

"Oh yes your names will be entered into the visitor's book."

"Would you like another Brownie Point?"

"Everyone helps Bill."

"Then sign us in as Colonel & Mrs Barrett."

"Do you mean that that is your new title?"

"It certainly is."

"Well I hope I am present when he reads the book, 'Colonel Barrett signed in by yours truly', I should get treated to a couple of pints on the strength of that. Shall I pick you up about eight then?"

"Yes, that would be fine."

"Incidentally, what was the reception like when you booked in?"

"Definitely VIP treatment, they had not forgotten us, we are now looking forward to seeing if the treatment has stretched to the room, we will let you know tonight."

As they made their way to the lift the duty floor manager approached. "Your luggage has been taken care of sir…madam."

They thanked him then entered the lift with a smile on their faces.

"Here goes," laughed Tommy as they entered their room then gave a gasp of delight at the décor and furnishings. "They have certainly done us proud this time Bill."

"Hmm! it is alright isn't it?

"Well I like you burst of enthusiasm, I think it is beautiful. See the flowers and bowl of fruit."

"And two more tickets for a West End Show," he said waving them at a smiling Tommy. "Right then, come on let us have a wash and brush up and go and see what they are offering for lunch I am feeling a bit peckish, then afterwards we can have a stroll on Oxford Street and see if we can find a nice dress shop."

"I like that idea pet," she said as she gave him a kiss, "you know I could begin to like you."

"Come on you little minx," he said as he playfully slapped her on the backside "I want something to eat."

Following a nice lunch Bill followed his wife in and out of dress shops which ended with a beaming Tommy loading up Bill with parcels.

Back at the hotel Bill was the captive audience to Tommy modelling her new buys.

"I have made arrangements at the shop for me to receive their catalogues after sending them my postal address of course with a view to keeping my wardrobe up to date."

"My turn tomorrow and I think it is going to be a long tiring day dear."

That evening they received a call from the front desk telling them their car was waiting. Jackson was waiting by the lift to greet them.

"Good evening sir and your ladyship," he said for the benefit of the staff and with a twinkle in his eye.

"Good evening Jackson," they both responded as he escorted them to the waiting car and his wife Joyce much to their delight.

After the greetings and kisses Tommy said to her. "Your husband is a terrible man Joyce but lovely with it. His attitude to us in front of the staff is paying dividends because we are getting the full treatment now and we love him for it."

On arrival at the RAFA Club Jackson duly signed in his guests then seated them at a table before going to the bar for drinks. Quite a number of the members recognised Bill and Tommy and acknowledged them with many greetings of welcome. After a few minutes the club President came scurrying towards them having been informed of their presence. After greeting them and welcoming them to the club he asked Jackson why he had not told him of the visit.

Jackson explained that he could not raise any false hopes because he did not know how long Bill and Tommy were staying in London or if they had the time to come and visit us.

"We are indeed on a very tight schedule Mr President but Jackson has such a persuasive way with him we could not refuse his request."

Bill was interrupted by a committee member who excused himself and whispered in the president's ear. He in turn excused himself and went off with the member.

"He is taking him to see the guest book," said Jackson, "that is going to put him in a flap. There, I told you so, he is beckoning me, this is going to be good and where I am going to earn another Brownie point."

"I have just had this entry in the guest-book pointed out to me Jackson; I hope it is not one of your jokes, if so you will have to answer to the committee for it."

"It is no joke Mr President he and his wife are no longer members of the Royal Air Force. With the blessing of the MoD and permission from a higher authority he is carrying out his expertise with a friendly country and for a starter he now holds the rank of Colonel which is acceptable to our Ministry."

The president shook Jackson by the hand. "Thank you Jackson for lifting the status of this club, all members will be told of this at our next General Meeting, every one of our members will be proud to be associated with this club. When the word of this gets around there will be more requests for membership than ever before."

"You will have to excuse me Mr President I don't want the Colonel to feel he is being neglected."

"Of course not, by the way when we are by ourselves call me Arthur."

Jackson went back with a great big smile on his face.

"You look like the cat that has got the cream," remarked Joyce.

"Better than that," he replied, I have just got a whole bag full of Brownie points from Arthur."

"You mean that you and the President are now Buddy buddies?" asked Bill.

"Call it what you like Bill but it means I will now be just one or two rungs on the ladder below my friend Arthur."

"Does that mean I will be on a par with golf widows in the foreseeable future?" asked Joyce.

"Not at all love I was just joking about Arthur and how serious he is about the status of this club and how he has put over another coup de maitre on the other clubs. Now you two lovely people how long will you be staying in London before you fly off to foreign lands and what is your purpose while you are here if I am not being too inquisitive?"

Bill told him the main reason was to be tailored for his uniform and accessories.

Tommy delved into her handbag and produced the photographs of the Villa they would be moving into to show Joyce and Jackson.

"Oh my goodness it is absolutely wonderful," exclaimed Joyce, "I really envy you Tommy and you say there are servants included. Take a look at these Clarry," her name for Clarence. "We could do with a place like that."

"What would we do in a place like that? It is only for these here senior officers who do a lot of entertaining to keep up appearances, you would be bored to death doing nothing but being waited on hand and foot by servants."

"Chance would be a fine thing," she retorted. "Anyway I can just see you and Bill in there Tommy so take no notice of old sourpuss, that Villa is meant for you and you are going to have a wonderful time living in it."

As the evening wore on various members came and had a friendly word with Bill.

"Well folk I am ready for my bed," said Tommy.

On their way to the exit there were calls of "Goodnight Colonel" from many of the members.

Bill responded with "Thank you and Goodnight."

The President was waiting in the entrance hall to see them off. "On behalf of the club members I wish to thank you for your patronage and what you have done to help make this club *The One* to be a member of. On behalf of the committee and members we would like you to accept and become our one and only Honorary Member."

"Thank you Mr President it is a great honour I would be proud to accept. I will indeed come to visit you as often as I can but you will appreciate that due to the present circumstances I do not know when the next time I will be in London. I will be keeping in touch with our friend Jackson and he will be able to keep you in the picture regarding my movements. Thank you very much for your hospitality and honour you have given me and if ever there is anything I can do for the club please let me know through Jackson. Goodnight Mr President," he said as he shook him warmly by the hand.

"Goodnight and God speed Colonel. Goodnight and God speed Mrs Barrett.

Back in the car Tommy announced. "I thought that was very nice of him."

"What do you think of your honorary membership sir?" asked Jackson.

"We will have less of the sir, Jackson or I will report you to Arthur."

"You mean to say you would drop your right hand man in the proverbial?"

"He would drop his own mother in it given the chance," Tommy said giving a giggle.

"They don't spoil a pair Tommy," laughed Joyce.

"Here we are at the Hotel Splendide, what time do you folk want picking up tomorrow? I suggest 10am because it will be a tiring day for you.

"That would be fine, do you agree love?"

"Yes, are you doing anything special tomorrow Joyce?"

"No, why do you ask?"

"Well there are one or two items I want but I would like a second opinion."

"Oh, that would make a change I would love to."

"Right then that is settled, do you two hear that? So no pulling your faces, we can make all the arrangements tomorrow, you are going to enjoy tomorrow aren't you? I said, you are going to enjoy tomorrow aren't you?"

"Yes Tommy," they answered in unison.

"And you Jackson will make no excuses for Joyce not to come, do you read me?"

"Yes Ma'am I read you loud and clear! Is she the one they call The Rottweiler, Bill?"

"We'll see you in the morning, Goodnight then and thanks for a very enlightening evening. No don't get out of the car we will see ourselves in," said Bill.

The following day they were informed by the front desk their car had arrived. Jackson was waiting at the lift to greet them. "Good morning sir…madam."

"Good morning Jackson," they replied with a wry smile.

As they got in the car Tommy was asked. "Where do you ladies want dropping off? We cannot pick you up because we will not know where to find you."

"I suggest you boys go your own way and when Joyce and I have finished I will take her for an afternoon tea at the Savoy. You Jackson can bring my husband home sober and in a good mood and collect your dearly beloved. I would like you to stay by his side while the tailor does his stuff because he has the attitude of anything will do. I do not want him looking like he has got his clothes from some second hand shop so bear that in mind the pair of you. Jackson, you are his minder just make sure you mind him."

Joyce was curled up listening to Tommy laying the law down.

The men folk were speechless.

"If that has sunk in get this car moving or you will be getting a parking ticket."

Jackson looked at Bill, gave a couple of weak barks while Bill just raised his eyes heavenwards.

"Where are we going Joyce?" asked Tommy.

"Oxford Street please driver," Joyce politely requested.

"Very good Ma'am," was the reply.

When they arrived there Jackson got out of the car and opened the doors for the ladies to get out. "Have a nice day shopping ladies."

"Thank you Jackson," Joyce replied placing a shilling in his hand.

"That is from both of us," Tommy said with a condescending smile as she and Joyce walked off arm in arm having a good laugh.

"What are those two like?" asked Jackson. You know I have not seen Joyce act like that since we were courting and you know something, I like it."

"And I have never seen Tommy act like that before we met up with you two. There must be something that has brought out characters in them both that must have been hidden for quite a long time."

"Here we are sir at your favourite tailors. A word of advice, if you feel enough is enough while you are being measured up think of the mayhem those women of ours might be causing on Oxford Street, that should make you feel better."

When they entered the shop they were greeted with a friendly smile and "Good morning Gentlemen what can I do for you?"

"I am Colonel Barrett and this is my batman Jackson."

"Ah yes of course I have the necessary instructions concerning your uniform fittings Colonel if you will please step this way into the fitting room where we can have privacy while I carry out the measurements."

They entered a room to see a younger man sat at a table. "This is my associate who will make a note of the measurements as I take them. Please remove your coat Colonel."

Bill did as he was told and threw it to Jackson. "Take hold of this Jackson."

"Yes sir," answered Jackson. The twinkle in his eye said everything.

The tailor concentrated on what he was doing, shouting out the measurements as he took them. On completion he said "That takes care of that. All we need from you now are the descriptions of your decorations. We will dress you, Colonel, from top to toe, although you will have to go next door for your footwear. I will then need you for a fitting tomorrow at 11am."

Bill shook his hand and thanked him. He then beckoned to Jackson who then helped him on with his jacket.

Next door at the shoe shop he introduced himself and was told he was expected.

"If you would please take a seat Colonel, I will measure your feet then bring out the range of shoes you have to be fitted with … and it is quite a range, I must say. A shoe for every occasion in the terrain and climate you are going to."

Bill was gobsmacked to see the array of footwear he would need, ranging from desert boots to evening shoes. "Do I have to sign for these?" he asked.

"No sir. Everything is taken care of. They will be delivered to the Embassy."

Bill shook his hand and thanked him.

When they got outside, Jackson exclaimed. "Bloody Hell! What is that lot going to cost?"

"Put it this way old friend, I would hate to have to foot that bill. If it is all going to the Embassy it must come under diplomatic baggage; that is why we are travelling by private aircraft. Wait while we tell the girls; they will not believe it. I still cannot come to terms with it. Do you fancy a bite to eat? I am feeling a bit peckish. I could just go for some home cooking."

"I will take you to a smashing little restaurant where all their food is home-made. I take Joyce there quite frequently. It makes a nice change for her and she does like it."

"We go on condition that it is my treat."

"I will not argue with you Bill. If you can afford to buy all that load of paraphernalia you can afford to treat me to a meal."

"If only…"

The girls were relaxing in the lounge of the hotel after what Tommy called a very good morning's shopping when she saw Bill and Jackson enter the hotel. "Hello, here come Don Quixote and Sancho Panza looking very pleased with themselves. Come and sit down and give us your report," demanded Tommy.

"There is nothing much to tell," answered Bill. "Is there Jackson?"

"Then why is he spluttering? What have you been up to Bill Barrett?"

"The wardrobe he has been issued with will be following you in a cargo plane. Will you believe me if I tell you he has been kitted out with a full wardrobe? And he took it all in his stride. He even introduced me to the tailor as his batman. Well, it wasn't really an introduction, he just said 'and this is my batman', threw his jacket at me and told me to hold it."

"And what did you say to that?"

"Yes sir."

They all could not help but burst out laughing.

"Bill Barrett you are an evil so-and-so! Poor old Jackson. Let me apologise for his behaviour."

"Well, I had to put up a front, hadn't I, to earn some respect? By the way Jackson, don't forget I will want you to hold my jacket again tomorrow at the fitting. Did you have a good day dear and did you both enjoy your tea and sticky buns? We lunched at your favourite eatery Joyce and by gum but their home baked cooking is good. You would have enjoyed it Tommy. If we have time, Jackson might take us all there."

"Oh you would love it Tommy," said Joyce. "It is a darn sight better than any hotel food. Try your best to find the time to go."

"Come on old girl it is time to go. I will pick you up in time for the show, about 8pm. that Okay?"

"Fine. Ta-ra for now."

The following morning Jackson arrived to take Bill for his fitting and handed him a letter from the embassy, which he opened and read.

"I'll not be a minute. I need to see Tommy and we will have to take that lunch today. I will explain when I return."

"We are having that lunch today, love. I have just had a letter from the Embassy. We have to be at the airport by 8am on Friday and the only thing we are allowed to carry is our hand luggage. The rest of the luggage has to be given to Jackson by 9am and taken to the Embassy, where it will be transferred to the aircraft."

"Well you go down and explain to Jackson while I get myself ready."

Bill explained to Jackson what was in the letter and why the change in plans.

"It looks like I was right then Bill, they must be going under diplomatic baggage. Hey-up, here comes the Rottweiler."

"Good morning your Ladyship," greeted Jackson. "My word, you are looking very smart and chic."

"Bloody creep."

"Thank you Jackson, that is the first nice thing that has been said to me this morning. Now what is the programme? That is if mastermind here has made one. I suggest you drop us off at the tailors and while I am supervising this so-called fitting I expect you, Jackson, to go and collect Joyce, having told her the change in routine then come back in about an hour to pick us up. Any questions? No? Then let's get this show on the road."

Jackson held the car door open for Tommy to climb in then gave Bill that 'God help you mate' look. When he got into the driving seat Bill leaned over and murmured, "That is called the H.P.C."

"What is the H.P.C.?" Jackson asked in a loud voice.

The voice from the backseat boomed. "It is the Henpecked Club and he is a fully paid-up member."

Jackson roared with laughter. "You poor sod! I am not surprised. Here we are Ma'am," he said as he got out and opened the door for her. "Yes Ma'am, I will return in one hour's time. Good Luck Bill," he said meaningfully.

When Tommy had been introduced to the tailor he led them into the fitting room and, apart from a few little minor adjustments, everything was pronounced perfect. "Be assured Colonel, you will not find a single fault with any of the items because if you did it would be a very big black mark against our reputation, consequently our business would suffer. On completion this order will be sent to the Embassy. Thank you Colonel, and I wish you the best of luck in your new venture."

Exactly to the minute, Jackson and Joyce arrived. He got out and opened the car door for Tommy. "Everything go alright, Bill, with the fittings? No complaints I hope?"

"For your information Jackson, I never said a word, so you can wind your neck in."

"Sorry Ma'am, I meant no offence."

She nudged Joyce. "Never mind your twittering, get going, you have two famished ladies back here."

Bill and Jackson looked at each other with a resigned look of 'we just can't win'.

At the restaurant they were unanimous in declaring it was a lovely meal and well worth the visit. Of course the two men argued over whose treat it was. Tommy decided on the flip of a coin. Heads Bill tails Jackson. She then flipped it in the air caught it and turned it over on her wrist, lifted her hand and declared 'Heads'."

"I think it should be the best out of three," objected Bill with a grin.

"Are you objecting to my decision?"

"No pet."

"Then stop moaning and pay up."

"I suggest," said Joyce, "we all go back to our place, I will make us a nice cup of tea and we can relax and have a good chat because it is going to be a long time before we see each other again."

"I second that," smiled Jackson. "And I third it," beamed Bill.

"This man is suffering from sun stroke and he hasn't even got there yet," said Tommy shaking her head in bewilderment. They left the restaurant laughing.

"You are going to have to return here and apologise to those good ladies or you will get barred. Jackson."

"I second that," agreed Joyce.

"Alright, then I will third it," spluttered Jackson as he doubled up laughing.

The afternoon went well they had a good chat telling each other's life history, Jackson reminiscing about his RAF service exchanging experiences with Bill.

"What is your programme tomorrow?" asked Joyce.

"Well we have to pack all our luggage except carry-on bags for the aircraft, Jackson is collecting them tomorrow morning to take to the Embassy; afterwards we will just stroll round seeing the sights."

"I will be coming with Clarry to the airport to see you off."

"I think we had better be going and get stuck into packing our gear. It will be easier to pack the cabin bags and what is left over gets shipped off."

"Come on then I will run you back," said Jackson. "Would you like me to take you for a spin tomorrow, it would be no trouble."

"No thanks Jackson we want to browse around giving us something to remember what England is like when we are baking in the sun and sheltering from sandstorms and thinking of you back home starved for a bit of sunshine. We will keep in touch and let you know how much we are suffering."

"Here we are, I will be here about 9am. Bye for now."

"I suggest we have an early dinner then get busy with the packing, have a relaxing evening with a drink or two from the mini-bar and watch a bit of television. What do you say to that Bill?"

"It suits me fine."

At 8am the following morning Bill answered the telephone. "The front desk here sir, your chauffeur is here for you."

"Thank you. Would you be so kind and send up a Bell Boy to take three pieces of luggage to the car please?"

"Our pleasure sir."

Bill went down with the Bell Boy to see Jackson.

"Good morning Jackson how are you today?"

"I am fine sir," he replied as he took charge of loading the luggage. "Is her ladyship well?"

"Thank you," said Bill, giving the Bell Boy a tip. "Yes she is fine; can I come with you to the embassy? I would like a bit more information of the procedure we have to go through at the airport I have a feeling it will be no ordinary run-of-the-mill check-in."

"I think you go to a special VIP check-in, because your flight will not show with the normal flights and I do know you wait in a VIP lounge. I have to drop you here because I have to report to a different part of the embassy."

You go through that door to the reception desk state your identity and the reason you are here, I will wait for you outside after I hand the luggage over."

After checking in Bill was escorted to see one of the embassy staff who greeted him with "Good morning Colonel Barrett please come and sit down. Have you a problem I can help you with?"

"Yes, I would like clarification on the procedure I have to go through at the airport, at present I know nothing."

"There is no problem Colonel there will be a member of our staff waiting for your arrival and he will guide you through the formalities. On boarding the aircraft you will find other personnel returning to Aljibia from whatever business they have had here or in neighbouring European countries."

"That is interesting maybe I will get to know a little about Aljibia from them. Now what happens about my luggage when we arrive?"

"Everything is taken care of Colonel you will not see your luggage again until it arrives on your doorstep. There you will be greeted by your own personal Chef and housekeeper normally a husband and wife team who reside in accommodation attached to your residence. You will also find a large sealed envelope which contains plenty of advice for you and Mrs Barrett please study it very carefully Colonel it is very explanatory and you will also find it very interesting. Incidentally, there is a very good Ex-Pats Social Club which puts on a variety of entertainment and other social activities. One class which I am sure you and your wife would attend is Learning Arabic."

"Thank you, you have been very helpful indeed."

"Thank you Colonel for joining us, I hope you find our country and our people friendly and hospitable. Good luck. By the way I hope you and your wife are up to date with your inoculations."

"Indeed we are."

"Well, did you find everything you wanted?" asked Jackson as Bill climbed into the car.

"I did and more besides." He then told him what he had learned.

"Well they don't do things in half measures, I hope you both settle down to it quickly, if you get any problems send for your right hand man...your batman. Do you and Tommy still want to stroll around the city then?"

"Yes thanks I think she wants to use it when she is feeling nostalgic. We will see you in the morning though and we will definitely keep in touch."

"Here we are back at the hotel, see you tomorrow Bill, ta ra."

"Where on earth have you been until now? I have been worried sick not knowing if something had happened to you."

"Sorry pet I jumped in the car and went to the Embassy to find out the procedure at the airport. Sit down while I tell you what I have been told. I had an interview with a very nice chap who told me"...When Bill went into detail of what he had learned Tommy got quite excited."

"I wonder what nationality the Chef and his wife are and if we will be compatible?

Oh Bill I do hope they are nice people."

"Do you know we have had no breakfast yet? Come on I have just realised I am hungry," announced Bill as he made his way to the door.

At breakfast Tommy was still twittering on about the Chef and his wife.

"For goodness sake stop your moidering. We will know soon enough. If you don't like them you can ask Mr Aziz if you can import someone of your own choice."

"Don't be so facetious William, it doesn't become you."

"Have you any preference to where you would like to go today?"

"If you don't mind I would like to spend a bit more time in Harrods, dear, and then a casual stroll round some of the big stores."

"If that's what you want then let's get going ... we have a lot of ground to cover."

"We can have a spot of lunch when and where we fancy."

And so it was – a sprightly Tommy dragging a foot-weary Bill from one establishment to another.

After collapsing on the bed at the hotel, absolutely shattered, he was roused by Tommy handing him a drink. "Have you enjoyed today love?"

"Uh-huh."

"I am so pleased we can look back on our last day in London with fond memories because it will be some time before we can enjoy it again."

All she got in reply was a snore!

Very well Mr B. What's good for the goose is good for the gander she muttered to herself, then promptly laid herself on top of her bed and joined Bill in the land of Nod.

A couple of hours later she awoke looked at the time and turned to Bill, who was still fast asleep. "Come on Noddy," she said, shaking him vigorously "Wakey Wakey it is time for 'din-dins'."

After a couple of grunts he stuttered, "Wha... what's the matter?"

"If you don't want any dinner go back to sleep and I will go down on my own."

"Has it got to that time already?" he said, as he swung his feet off the bed. "You are not ready for going yet are you?"

"Not quite. I am just off to the shower and by the time you have shaved I will be finished, so come on, chop-chop!"

When they had ordered their meal Tommy said. "I am disappointed with this hotel."

"Why has somebody rattled your cage?"

"Don't get me wrong, nobody has upset me. This is supposed to be a very high class hotel with people of the upper crust patronising it and in both of our stays here I have never seen one notable or celebrity. Do you think we have frightened them away?"

"You may have a point there. Word must have got round that the Barretts are in town."

"Silly beggar!"

And so their stay at the Savoy Hotel came to a close as they responded to Jackson's greeting of...Good morning sir... your ladyship."

"Good morning" they said to a waiting Joyce... "To the airport please Jackson."

"Yes Ma'am."

CHAPTER 2

At the airport Jackson said. "We will not come inside the terminal building with you but say our farewells here."

There was an awkward silence, broken by Tommy, who grabbed hold of Jackson in an embrace saying, "Come here you lovely man, give me a hug!" Bill embraced Joyce and there were tears from the ladies.

Bill and Jackson shook hands warmly, Bill thanking him for their hospitality. They all promised they would keep in touch.

There was a slight choke in Jackson's voice when he told them. "Right, off you go, God speed and a safe journey. As soon as you can, let us know you are safe and well and we hope everything goes well for you."

At the terminal entrance they turned to give a last farewell wave.

Inside the terminal they were approached by a smartly dressed young man who asked if they were Colonel and Mrs Barrett. He shook hands and asked them to follow him then took them to a special check-in desk reserved for VIPs. After the formalities he took them to the VIP lounge and told them they would be escorted to the aircraft when the time came. "In the meantime, please make use of all the facilities."

They found comfortable seats and were approached almost immediately by a female steward who asked if they would like any refreshments. They both requested tea. As they sat drinking it, they looked around at other passengers, wondering which of them would be travelling companions. Looking at the video screen it showed their flight to Aljibia was scheduled in another two hours. While they were still playing the guessing game they were approached by a very smart lady who looked to be about their age group and was sporting a sun tan.

"Please excuse me asking, but are you bound for Aljibia?"

Bill got to his feet. "Yes we are. I am Bill Barrett and this is my wife Tommy."

"I am Ella Whittaker. My husband is a doctor at Aljibia. Please may I join you?"

"Most certainly. We have been sat here looking for a friendly face and trying to guess who our travelling companions could be. I have been contracted to teach the servicemen and women drill and to build up their characters."

"Then you are Colonel Barrett, whose name at present is on everyone's lips. Your reputation has preceded you and you are held in high esteem by high authority. May I be the first to welcome you to Aljibia." She shook him by the hand.

"That is the last thing I wanted, a reputation to live up to! I wanted to make my mark my way. I do not want to step on anyone's toes or be the cause of any animosity. I just want to do what I am being paid to do and work side by side in harmony with my peers. Shall we talk about something more pleasing, such as you giving Tommy some advice of what to expect and what she should avoid. You can appreciate that as newcomers we will be like fish out of water. There is one thing I would like to know... the ex Pats Social Club, is it for all ranks?"

"Yes, we do not draw a line between us and them. Does that please you?"

"It certainly does. I was dreading I would be forced to attend an Officer's Club. You have no idea what a relief that is to me."

"Now let me see if I can relieve you of any worries Tommy. How did you get the name Tommy, if you don't mind me asking?

When it was explained to her she said. "But of course, Tommy Atkins. My husband was called Ticker at school, but Tommy I think really suits you. He said he felt like a walking time bomb." That caused them all to laugh. "You will have about a week to acclimatise to your new surroundings before reporting for duty. During that time I would like to give you a guided tour of our locality and introduce you to a few people who are worth knowing."

"That is very kind of you, if it is not too much trouble or interfering with your normal routine we gratefully accept your offer."

She laughed. "I am just a housewife who is always on the lookout for something of of interest to do to stop the boredom."

"Do the married families hold dinner parties?" asked Tommy.

"As a matter of fact some do, the ones who do have a roster and take their turn at holding one but it depends on bums on seats and if they have the room to seat everyone, but it does sort itself out and nobody gets uptight. The dress is not formal but we like to go dressed decently. It gets very interesting at times especially after a few glasses of wine then you hear some very interesting experiences."

"It sounds fun," responded Tommy.

They were interrupted by an announcement to board the aircraft.

"What is the seating arrangement?" asked Bill.

"They are all double seats and you can take your pick except when it is carrying a lot of passengers then they are allocated. There are a very few today so we can sit close together and carry on chatting, just follow me." When seated Ella sat behind Bill and Tommy, there were about twenty other passengers mostly men of various nationalities and three other women. Some of those men are engineers I think the women are teachers. Perhaps they are from Dubai because we do stop there. I say Tommy, if Bill does not mind would you care to sit with me then I can give you more information about where you are going?"

"Do you mind if I sit with Ella Bill because she has lots more to tell me?"

"Away you go and get all the gen you can, we are very fortunate to have met her."

The Captain of the aircraft introduced himself and his crew and told them it would be a six hour flight to Aljibia stopping at Dubai to off-load some of our passengers and picking up two more plus more cargo.

When Tommy changed seats the questions and answers began. "What is worrying me most Ella is if the Chef and his wife or housekeeper and I are not compatible, I do not like the word servant, so what do I do about it?"

"To put your mind at ease they will have been well vetted and hand picked especially because of your husband's rank and status. Believe me the rank of Colonel is very high in the pecking order here. A word of warning, do not be surprised to find a number of ladies who want to be your friend because of that."

"I am going to find that difficult trying to distinguish the genuine from the non-genuine"

"Yes I agree, you will have to rely on your woman's intuition.

"Ella, will you be my mentor?"

"Now how do you know I am not one of those I am warning you about?"

"Woman's intuition Ella." They both laughed and clasped hands.

"Of course I will Tommy. Ah, here comes the stewardess with the luncheon menus."

"Then I had better go back to my seat."

"Hello love are you all genned up and do you want the window seat?"

"I have come back because the luncheon menu is coming round and I want to sit with you while we are eating and I can feed you the info' I have been given up to now. "Thank you," she said as the stewardess handed them a menu. "This looks very nice Bill." They made their choice and while they were waiting for the meal she gave Bill the details Ella had given her. "So you see my darling you are now a person of some consequence."

"Well I hope I can handle it."

After a superb lunch they settled down on the reclining seats and had a snooze. They were wakened by a voice announcing that seat belts were to be fastened.

"It looks like we are arriving at Dubai," said Bill.

The voice continued. "We will be on the ground at Dubai for about one hour, if any passengers wishing to stretch their legs in the airport please listen for the announcement to re- board your aircraft."

"Do you fancy stretching your legs Bill?"

"No I am content to stay here."

"Are you coming Tommy?" asked Ella.

"Yes I will come with you; you don't mind Bill do you?"

"Go ahead it will be company for Ella." He then sat at the window watching the activity surrounding the aircraft and the two new passengers boarding who looked like a married couple.

When the girls returned Tommy sat with Bill and told him about the shops and what lovely a place it was.

Meanwhile Ella stopped to speak with the new passengers until she had to take her seat for the take-off. "The couple I just spoke to are school teachers in Aljibia," she told Bill and Tommy "and they are very nice people, I will take you and introduce you to them when it is safe to leave our seats Tommy."

The Captain made an announcement. "Ladies and gentlemen we will be landing at Aljibia in two hours time; we are also two hours ahead of Greenwich Mean Time so please adjust your watches, thank you."

"Come on Tommy," Ella led the way, "Tommy I would like you to meet Joan and Robert Sanderson. This is Tommy Barrett who is just coming to join our community along with her husband Colonel Barrett." They shook hands and pleasantries were exchanged. After a few minutes of conversation Tommy asked to be excused, I have been neglecting my husband on this flight to sit with Ella who has been giving me plenty of information of what awaits us at Aljibia; I look forward to seeing more of you when I settle down."

Tommy rejoined Bill and they browsed over the information Ella had given Tommy.

"Ask Ella if she is being met at the airport."

"Why?"

"Because we can give her a lift if she is not being met."

Tommy turned round and asked. "Ella, are you being met at the airport?"

"No I have to get a taxi, John could get a call-out and we decided to save any mix-up a taxi would be the best bet."

"We will be met so you can come with us and you will be dropped at your door."

"Thank you that will be wonderful," she leaned forward and thanked Bill, "you are very kind."

"It is our pleasure Ella, he replied."

"Here is the stewardess with the dinner menus," Ella informed them.

When she took Bill and Tommy's order Tommy asked if she could keep the menu and explained to the stewardess "The menu looks so inviting I would like to use it when I throw a dinner party."

"Of course you may madam and I will see if I can find you any older ones."

After the meal and the dishes had been cleared away the stewardess returned with three more older menus." Here you are madam with our compliments, one was for the outbound flight and two were from the previous flights."

"Thank you very much that is most kind of you replied Tommy."

"At the airport we disembark at the VIP part of the terminal building, "Ella informed them. "All you will need to show at immigration are your passport and I.D cards. Customs are not strict with the VIPs."

"Our luggage is being delivered to our house, have you any?"

"Two suitcases but it will only take a few minutes to collect. Whoever is meeting you will be there with a name-board."

"Here we go seat belts fastened, isn't it is fascinating seeing all the lights from up in the air Bill?"

As the undercarriage hit the runway Bill exclaimed. "Right bang on time."

They thanked the stewardess as they disembarked and headed for Immigration with Ella leading the way. There they were treated with respect and courtesy.

They went with Ella to collect her luggage and Bill took charge of the luggage trolley and followed Ella to passenger reception.

"There you are Bill there is your chauffeur holding up your name board."

Bill approached him and the chauffeur who was in military uniform and wearing Sergeants chevrons jumped to attention and saluted when Bill identified himself. He acknowledged the salute and told him we would have an extra passenger and you would be given directions where to take her."

"Very good sir," he said in perfect English. He then opened the door to let the ladies climb in. "Sir?" he questioned.

"No I will ride in front with you, you don't mind do you?"

"Not at all sir," he replied giving a huge smile.

Bill helped by carrying one of the cases to the boot.

"Now Sergeant, what is your name and what is your trade in the military?"

"I am called Fred sir, that is not really my given name but it is much easier to say by non-Arabic people. I chose it myself. My basic trade is a Driver sir, but I am specially qualified to chauffeur VIPs like you and I have been detailed to be your permanent chauffeur sir."

"Now I like the sound of that. I pride myself on being an excellent judge of character and I can only say this, welcome aboard Fred but of course you realise I will be formal when and where it is needed."

"I understand sir and thank you."

Bill spoke over his shoulder. "Mrs Whittaker, will you give the sergeant the instructions as to where you would like him to take you?"

"How far from the airport is the accommodation for us ex-pats Fred, and do we all live in the same area?"

"It just about half an hour's run sir and, yes, the ex-pats are all accommodated in the same area, and I may add it is a very salubrious area, as Mrs Whittaker will confirm."

"What I would like to know now is how do I contact you when I need the car, where do you garage it and where are your quarters?"

"Excuse me sir, we are coming to Mrs Whittaker's residence, which one is it Ma'am?"

"The third one on the left Sergeant, here we are, thank you."

"I will be in touch with you Tommy. Here is my card if you want to talk to me. Bye for now and thank you Bill for bringing me home."

Fred had already unloaded the cases and carried them to the front door where he rang the doorbell. As Ella got to the door her husband appeared. She grabbed him by the arm and pulled him towards the car. "I want you to meet Colonel and Mrs Barrett, John, who brought me home. I will tell you the tale later. She did the introductions and John thanked them for bringing Ella home. "We will not keep you but we will get together soon to get to know one another better."

"Right Fred, take us home please, is it far from here?"

"No sir only a few hundred yards. When you want me I am on the phone. All the instructions you need are in the instructions envelope you will find at home. The car is garaged in the motor pool and I live in Sergeants Mess accommodation. If I do not answer leave a message on the phone, I carry a bleeper, which tells me I have a message from you and I get to my phone as quickly as possible. There is a phone in this car which is also linked to my phone and I will never be far from either phones, that is my job."

"Thanks Fred, that is good."

"Here we are sir, this is your residence, the lights are on, that means your housekeeper will be waiting to greet you and provide you with a meal. In about one hour you should be receiving your luggage; do you wish me to stay to help in any way sir?"

"Yes, we would like you to stay and have a drink of tea and a bite to eat with us, but if you prefer to call it a day that is your choice."

"Well, I am partial to a drink of tea, thank you sir."

"Good man. Now let us go and meet our staff."

The Chef and the housekeeper were there waiting to greet them. Bill immediately went to them, shook the Chef's hand and said, "I am Colonel Barrett and this is my wife Mrs Barrett. Tommy shook hands with him and Bill asked him his name.

"Thomas sir, and this is my wife Leila."

Bill shook her hand and said what a pretty name. Tommy then shook her by the hand and also paid a compliment about her name.

"Then we make two nice couples, don't you agree Sergeant?"

"That thought was running through my mind as I stood here watching you introduce yourselves."

The faces on the Chef and his wife showed delight at the informality of Bill and Tommy.

"Would you like a drink and something to eat Ma'am," Leila asked.

"Yes please Leila, Tea, and would you please make some sandwiches of your choice Thomas for the three of us? I will go and have a look round while you chat to Fred."

"Tell me Fred, you are my chauffeur and does that include my wife? For example, if I am tied up at work and the car is lying idle, could she use you with the car to go shopping for instance?"

"Yes sir, there is no problem there, but if I am out with her wherever she wants to go and if the car phone rings then I must report to you immediately and she must either return with me or find other means of getting back home."

"Thank you Fred, we would not dream of abusing that privilege. Thomas and Leila I understand they are vetted and handpicked. What would happen if we found we were not compatible?"

"You would need to see the Families Co-ordinator to solve that problem sir and if there was a serious problem they would be taken off the list."

"You mean their employment would be terminated?"

"Yes sir, if it was their fault. I know Thomas and Leila personally and you can take my word for it sir they will serve you well."

"Ah, here come the sandwiches and tea, along with my wife."

"Leila has been showing me round the kitchen and I know where everything is and how everything works when we want to use it. Come on Fred, don't be shy, tuck into theses sandwiches, they look delicious. Mmm, they taste delicious," she said, as she took a bite. "Excuse me a minute, I want to see Leila." She went into the kitchen. "Your sandwiches are excellent Thomas, thank you. Now you both can go home. You have been here long enough to see to our needs and we appreciate it. We will be pottering about for a good while yet, so leave everything and go home, we will clear everything away, but first I would like to know what time you start your duties in a morning or do you not have a set time?"

"We come in at 6am Ma'am, or when you tell us."

"The Colonel will not commence his duties for a few days, so I suggest you come in at 8am until I tell you any different."

"Thank you Ma'am," they both replied, "and if at any time you want either of us we are connected to you by intercom, the phone is there on the wall."

"Right, then off you go and thank you once more. Goodnight."

"Goodnight Ma'am."

"What have you been up to?" asked Bill, when she returned to the lounge. You are lucky because we have saved you some sandwiches."

"I have just sent Thomas and Leila home because they have been so good to us. Incidentally, you and I are washing up and if you have finished Fred you can go home too."

"But I can stay and help you with your luggage Ma'am."

"Fred, Go Home! The Colonel may be in charge out there but I am in charge here. Besides, he is not helpless. He can still carry cases."

"You had better obey orders Fred. She is very good at giving them, being an ex-Flight Sergeant."

"In that case sir I had better leave. Being put on what you call 'jankers' on my first day of duty I would never live it down." They had a good laugh at his response. "Goodnight sir ... Ma'am." He responded with a salute.

"Goodnight Fred and thank you for taking good care of us."

A few minutes after he left the door bell rang; Bill opened it up to see a smiling Fred.

"Your luggage sir."

Bill and Tommy burst out laughing. "Come in. You were determined you would assist with it."

He was followed in by another man carrying cases who asked. "Will you please check you have got everything sir and sign for them?"

This they did then thanked Fred with Tommy asking him "*Now* will you go home?"

"Yes Ma'am," he said with a salute and a big grin. "Goodnight."

When they were alone Tommy said. "Aren't we fortunate to have three lovely people who I know are going to take good care of us?"

"We are indeed, if you give respect you get respect and I think we have hit the jack-pot."

"Now here is what I suggest Bill. We do the washing up, leave the cases until morning have a good look round then with a brew we can have a shufti at what is inside that big envelope, we should be ready for bed then. Do you know Thomas and Leila report here for duty at 6am each morning! I told them that until you commence your duties they can report in at 8am."

"Good thinking pet they deserve that, let them take it easy while they can because we do not know what is round the corner."

"Come on let us get stuck in to the washing up," coaxed Tommy. She then showed him the well stocked Fridges and Freezers. We do not need to go super market shopping for some time yet I will take Thomas with me when I do have to replenish the food. That phone there on the wall is an inter-com to their living quarters, that is very handy." When everything was washed and put away Tommy got two beakers out ready for the brew they would be having later. "Come with me now and I will show you around, I had a quick look earlier. How do four bathrooms and four bedrooms strike you with four walk-in showers with the master bedroom en suite? I am going to have a lovely soak with all those lovely lotions, potions, shampoos and scents to choose from."

"And I am going to enjoy a damned good shower."

CHAPTER 3

The following morning Leila knocked on the bedroom door and entered on command bearing a tray containing a tea pot with all the trimmings.

"Thank you Leila that is very kind of you."

"Shall I pour Ma'am?"

"No I will do that when sleepy head returns to the land of the living."

"What time would you like breakfast Ma'am and what would you like?"

"I would love a small orange juice a poached egg and this is where we come to the tricky bit, we do not want to offend your religion but are you allowed to come in contact with bacon?"

"Leila laughed, that will be no problem Ma'am."

"Then I will have two rashers well cooked but not quite to the crispy stage white and brown toast and marmalade."

Bill who had surfaced in time to hear what was being said. "Good morning Leila, I would like a grapefruit juice, two fried eggs, fried tomato and three slices of bacon not quite crispy, white and brown toast and marmalade please."

"Oh please, I will have fried tomato too Leila thank you. What time do you want breakfast? She asked Bill.

"What time is it now?" he asked.

"How about 9am then?"

"Thank you that will be fine I will lay the dining room table."

"No Leila would you mind if we had it in the kitchen at the moment it would feel more like home. Unless of course you and Thomas would rather we ate breakfast in the dining room?"

"We would be delighted to have you in the kitchen I know Thomas will like it as much as me and we will take it as a compliment. In such a short space of time you have made us feel like we belong to your family. Never before have we had that experience and privilege and we like you for it." Before emotion took over she gathered the tray and left quickly.

"That was nice don't you think Bill? It looks like we have got ourselves a new family."

"The more the merrier."

When they walked into the kitchen they bade good morning to Thomas. "Are you going to have a busy day slaving over a hot stove? That is the usual excuse I get from my wife."

Both Thomas and Leila laughed. "I don't think so sir; you are not the kind of couple who would take advantage of a poor hardworking and downtrodden man."

"Then I will make you an honorary member of my HPC."

"Thomas looked puzzled and asked. "What kind of club is that sir?"

Before Bill could answer Tommy butted in. "It stands for The Hen Pecked Club Thomas." Seeing that he did not understand she explained its meaning."

He moved quickly from the stove because he could not stop laughing and everyone else could not help but join in laughing with him. "Oh Mrs Barrett that is the funniest thing I have ever heard." he said as he carried on laughing as he cooked"

"I will give you something else to laugh at if my breakfast is not in front of me in one minute flat, I will make you a full member of the HPC."

Leila showed her support for Tommy by clapping her hands enthusiastically.

"Do you hear that Thomas? We are now both in the dog-house." Bill got up from his seat went over to Thomas and shook his hand. "As a fully paid up member I welcome you to the HPC."

To the accompaniment of Leila's laughter Tommy called to Bill. "Come and sit down and eat your breakfast."

Much to the delight of Leila he responded with. "Yes Ma'am."

As they sat drinking their coffee Tommy said. "We will be busy especially this morning Leila unpacking our cases and we do not want to get in the way of your work schedule."

"If you will give me a little time to clean and tidy your bedroom and bathroom first I can then carry on as normal."

"Good, we will stay in the lounge until you have finished."

"I will go and get the paper work Tommy then we can go through the instructions again while we wait," said Bill.

When he returned with the instructions Tommy asked. "What are we going to do about the banking because I will need house keeping money and also be able to go to the bank on my own when I need more?"

"That should not be a problem we can make out a joint account so we will need to go to the bank and see the manager, it should be simple enough because it states here that an account has already been made out in my name, so we already have money in the account. We must ask our housekeeper how far we are from the city centre and if it is only a short way we can have a stroll and have a look around. It says here the currency is the Aljibian dollar and the rate with our pound is pretty good."

"Here comes Leila."

"I have finished you rooms Ma'am if you want any help just call me."

"Leila, how far is it to the town or city centre is it near enough for us to walk there?"

"It is about three kilometres Ma'am Thomas will run you in if you like."

"How far is three kilometres Bill?"

"About three miles much too far for us to walk in this heat, I will get Fred to run us in on Monday. Thanks Leila, we will make a start on our unpacking now."

Fortunately they had a walk-in wardrobe so there was room enough to hang all their clothes comfortably.

"Do you fancy a brew Bill?"

"I could murder one, while you are there see if they have any beakers as opposed to little cups."

Thomas was sat at the table deep in thought staring at some sheets of paper and tapping the end of a ball point on the table. When Tommy entered the kitchen he jumped to his feet.

"Sit down Thomas what are you doing?"

"I am trying to sort out a menu for this coming week Ma'am."

"How far have you got, can I see it please?" She sat down and browsed through the menus, "it looks very good Thomas I hope it tastes as good as it looks. By the way can we have our tea in mugs please? I think that is the name for them in Arabic. I would like two, one for me and one for my husband because we prefer to drink from them as opposed to cups we enjoy our tea better, it is the habit we picked up from our service days. Would you be so kind and make us what we term a 'brew'?"

Just then Leila entered. "Will you make a brew for two in mugs Leila?" asked Thomas."

Tommy explained about the brew.

"Talking about food and menus Thomas, when I settle down I will teach you how to make some of our favourite local English dishes my way."

"Thank you Ma'am I would like that."

"Is the pool safe and clean for use Thomas?"

"Oh yes Ma'am a man comes to check it very often it was drained and cleaned ready for your arrival."

"Good, I think we will try it out this afternoon. Are all the people living in this area in the military?"

"No, people each side of you are civilian airline officials, others are civilian employees on the military base and of course others are senior Air Force Officers. Junior Officers live a little further away, perhaps just less than a kilometre."

"Are any English news papers available?"

"There are but they are usually one to two days old, we have a local daily newspaper which covers both local news and foreign news. Europe gets a good coverage I think you would like that newspaper; it is printed in both Arabic and English. I will bring you one tomorrow and if you like it I will order it for you."

The afternoon was spent in and out of the pool and topping up their Caribbean sun tan.

"Please take care Ma'am the sun gets very strong and drink plenty of liquids," Leila warned as she served them cool drinks.

"Leila, you and Thomas speak excellent English and I am curious with those qualifications you a housekeeper and Thomas a Chef have you, how can I say it without offending you not being able to get better employment?"

"English is our second language here in Aljibia but to get better jobs we need higher qualifications but unfortunately to get those we need a very good bank balance. My parents paid for my training to get a degree in housekeeping that is what I wanted. It got me employment with this organisation and I love it. Of course every situation is not the same and neither are the people but when you and the Colonel came along and made us feel like family it seemed all worth while and too good to be true."

"I know the feeling Leila I worried all the way here praying that we would be compatible and my prayers were answered. My husband has a saying…Treat a person with respect and they will return that respect"

That evening while Bill was studying his Arabic phrase book Tommy sat down at the writing desk and began to write letters to Jackie and Viv. In each letter she told of the happenings since they were waved off at Leeds Airport and how they were getting acclimatised before Bill reports for duty.

"We will have to go into town on Monday, to the post office to post these letters besides going to the bank then a shufti (look) round the shops.

Bill looked at her in amazement. "You have been studying the phrase book on the quiet you crafty devil haven't you?"

"Aiwa" (yes) she replied "I must hand it to you, you are doing very well."

"Shukran" (thank you) was her response giving him a 'whose a clever girl then' look. "I wonder when Thomas and Leila have their time off, I must ask her bukra (tomorrow)," she said still showing off her language skills. She carried on writing letters to Bill's sister Nessie and to Joyce and Clarry Jackson. There that is my letter writing done for now and I have written to our friend Jackson. How are you getting on with your Arabic have you learned anything?"

He replied with a "La (No).you will have to give me a few lessons."

"We will do better than that, we will join a language class as soon as we get ourselves organised."

Sunday morning saw Leila wakening them both with a mug of tea.

"Tell me Leila, when do you take time off? You cannot work seven days a week without a break and when do you find time to do your personal shopping?"

"Thomas and I would ask your permission, there are no set days for us we only take the time off when it is convenient to you."

"Then I suggest we start today, I will be down shortly and I will get any instructions from Thomas about what he was preparing for us today then you both take today off but that is only a suggestion you may want another day. In future Leila if you give me a days notice we will take it from there."

"Thank you Ma'am I will have a word with Thomas."

When Tommy went down to the kitchen Leila said. "We have decided to stay today because it will be very quiet in town but we would like tomorrow off instead because we can do so much more."

"That is no problem Leila it is going to be a very quiet day for us too. Ah here comes sir you are just in time for breakfast."

"Salaam alekum (peace be with you)." greeted Bill.

"Wa alekum es salaam (and upon you be peace)." replied Thomas and Leila smiling.

"Well who is the clever boy then? Asked Tommy.

"I just looked that up in the phrase book before I came down," he said grinning.

While they were eating their breakfast Tommy asked Bill what they were doing today.

"I think I will get my uniform from the wardrobe and press it into shape because it is creased from being packed in cases with the rest of my clothes; in fact all my clothes need to be checked out and today is ideal for doing that."

"No sir," stated Leila, "that is my responsibility as house keeper I take care of the wardrobes."

"Thank you Leila that is the best bit of news I have received today. Talking of news I thought you were bringing me a copy of the local paper to read Thomas."

"I have sir but I left it in my house Leila will bring it."

Later in the morning while they were having a brew sitting in the lounge they heard the doorbell then voices. Leila came to tell them that Doctor and Mrs Whittaker are paying a courtesy call.

"Show them in please Leila"

They rose to greet Ella and John with handshakes and "How nice of you to call on us. Would you like a drink? We have just had a brew," Tommy said as Leila collected the mugs.

"I will have a soft drink please," said Ella.

"What about you John?" asked Tommy.

"A soft drink will do fine thanks."

"Sit yourselves down and I will see to your drinks," Tommy said as she left to tell Leila.

"Well Bill have you settled in?" asked John.

"At present we are doing fine all due to our housekeeper who with her husband have made us feel right at home and we are learning every day. Isn't that right?" He asked Tommy as she came back into the room.

"Leila will be in with the drinks in a minute. Yes I heard the last bit as I came in, they are both wonderful and we get along fine with them."

"I told you your fears would be unfounded about them," said Ella.

"Have you ventured into town yet?"

"No we have got on with settling in and sorting all our belongings out and finding the right places to store them. Yesterday afternoon we just lazed by the pool and topped up our sun tan a little. Tomorrow Bill's chauffer is taking us into town we need to see the bank manager and visit the Post Office then take in the shops and sights."

"If you would like a personal guide I can come with you if you like to show you the best places to shop."

"Thank you Leila," said Tommy as Leila served the drinks to the guests.

They carried on chatting trying to give Bill and Tommy as much information as they could.

"What can you tell me about this Ex-Pat Social Club John?" asked a curious Bill.

"Membership costs you twenty Aljibian Dollars per person per year. The wet bar is extraordinary and it stocks drinks from anywhere, you name it and you have a very good chance of getting it. The building itself is very nice and it is absolutely squeaky clean there are different lounges all with waiter service, two games rooms, a library and a snack bar. The members are of different nationalities and it is very democratic,

Rank and social status you leave behind when you walk through the door."

"That sounds like my cup of tea I will go along with that what say you Tommy?" Bill asked.

"It sounds lovely," answered Tommy, "is it far?"

"No just a ten minute stroll from here would you like us to take you there this evening then you can enrol for membership?"

"Yes please," was the answer from them both, "we will look forward to that.

What is the dress by the way?"

"Clean smart casual. Right then we will be off and will call on you about 8pm."

On the way to the club the residences of senior officers of the Air Force were pointed out. "There is the club," John said pointing to a very imposing building.

"Oh it is only a short walk from our Villa," exclaimed Tommy "we don't need to use a car."

Bill and Tommy were introduced to the club secretary and the formality of enrolment was carried out.

"Welcome to the club Bill and Jean I am sure you are going to enjoy your stay with us for we are a very friendly bunch."

As he spoke a member with a bit too much drink inside him came and put his arm round Tommy spouting "All new female members are duty bound to give me a kiss."

"Here, we will have less of that Cartwright, apologise to the lady."

"I have something you will appreciate more than a kiss," said Tommy.

His big grin turned quickly to tears when he received a knee delivered with great force into his groin putting him on the floor writhing in agony.

"Do you have a garbage can handy Mr Secretary?" she asked.

There came a round of applause from members who had witnessed the incident. The secretary apologised for the disgraceful behaviour, "rest assured Jean the committee will have him on the carpet. But please do not place the rest of our members in the same category."

"I would not dream of it."

"Perhaps we can now take a seat," suggested John "or would you like a guided tour of the club first?"

"A tour please John, we would like that." As they went from room to room they were introduced to members. One lady congratulated Tommy with…"Well done. He has had that coming to him for a long time."

When they had sat down and ordered drinks from a waiter, John asked. "Well, what do you think of your club?"

"I am very impressed," replied Bill.

"And I think it is lovely and well worth patronising," added Tommy.

"Going back to that incident John, do you know anything about that Cartwright chap?" Asked Bill.

"Not professionally but I believe he is one of these 'God's Gift' to women so he thinks, he happens to be a Captain in the Air Force so your paths are going to cross again."

"Have you any idea what he does?"

"I think but not sure he has something to do with recruits."

Tommy saw a flicker of a smile cross Bill's face. I have seen that expression before she said to herself and it is heaven help Mr Cartwright.

"Where is your surgery John and what does your practice cover?"

"I have a surgery in town and one on the Air Force base, but I am just one of many practitioners Arab and Europeans."

"Then you must be a very busy man," added Tommy, "What will you give Cartwright if he comes to visit you, an X-Ray or crutches?"

"I think an entry in a one hundred yard sprint would be more appropriate," he said with a chuckle. How is your knee by the way Tommy any after-effects?"

"No, I used the fleshy part of my knee, if I had used the kneecap he would have needed a stretcher, so he got off lightly apart from a little discomfort and a few tears."

"That will be the main topic in the club for a little while now, especially amongst the ladies," Ella said with a chuckle.

"Where do you have your visiting cards printed Ella? We will certainly need some especially with the phone number included."

"You do have a phone book but obviously it cannot be up to date, you will receive an update pretty soon. The printers will be one of the first places I will show you so formulate one and by the time we are ready to return home your cards will be ready to collect."

"Thanks Ella we will use yours as a guide and what time shall we pick you up tomorrow?"

"10 o' clock will be fine."

When they were saying their Good nights Bill spoke to John. "Whenever you want company to go to the club John give me a call."

"And if you want a bodyguard John call me."

"I will do just that Tommy, Goodnight," he said as he left laughing.

CHAPTER 4

When Fred, Bill's chauffeur arrived he greeted them with a salute and "Good morning sir."

Bill returned the compliment. "Morning Fred, round to Dr. Whittaker's villa to pick up Mrs Whittaker then to El Medina." (City)

As Ella got into the car she asked Tommy. "Aren't you wearing a sun hat dear? You do need one to prevent sun stroke, you know the sun gets rather fierce especially at noon that is when it is hottest."

"I have not got one Ella."

"Never mind we can pick one up for you from a store."

"Where do you want to go sir?"

"Park-up somewhere in the city centre where it will be easy to find you because we will be having a good shufti round the shops."

When they had parked-up Bill asked Ella. "Are you familiar with this area?"

"Oh yes it is very close to the main shopping area, I know where we are, trust me I will not get you lost," she said with a chuckle.

"Are we staying here for lunch?" asked Tommy "because if we are we can give Fred an approximate time to pick us up here then he can return to base instead of getting bored waiting for us all day. Are there any nice restaurants you can recommend Ella?"

"Yes indeed, there are some very nice ones which serve a European cuisine."

"That settles it then. Shall we say around four o'clock, is that convenient for you Fred?"

"Yes Ma'am, any time you wish, I will be here at the time you stated."

"Come Ella lead the way to the main bank."

When they entered the bank they were approached by a young man who asked if they were English, when this was confirmed he asked if he could help.

"I would like to see the manager if that is possible please?" asked Bill.

"Can I ask your name please sir?"

"Barrett, Colonel Barrett."

"If you all would take a seat I will go and inform the manager."

Very soon the young man returned with the manager in tow who came forward with outstretched hand and introduced himself as Mr Haddad.

"I am Colonel Barrett and I understand I have been given an account with your bank."

"Come with me please."

"I will stay out here," said Ella.

Mr Haddad clicked his fingers at the young man and told him to get some refreshments for the lady."

Bill and Tommy followed him into his office where Bill's account and other monetary matters were explained to him.

"I would like my account changed to a joint account with my wife and I would like cheque books for each of us."

Haddad pressed a bell push and a young man entered. Haddad spoke to him in Arabic, obviously he was his PA. He nodded then left the room.

"Excuse me Mr Haddad but I am at a disadvantage in as such I do not speak or understand Arabic. Your advantage is that English is your second language consequently I find it most impolite for you to converse in Arabic in my presence."

Haddad was most profuse in his apologies. "I was ordering my personal assistant to bring in the necessary documents for you to sign concerning your joint account Colonel."

"And when can we expect to receive our cheque books Mr Haddad?"

"I will have them delivered to you tomorrow by a special courier Colonel."

The joint account documents were filled in to everyone's satisfaction.

"Now Mr Haddad I would like to withdraw some money."

"That is no problem Colonel, tell me how much you want and I will have it brought to you."

Tommy and he decided on the sum they wanted and told Haddad who explained the various values of paper money and coins. Between the three of them they sorted out the amount in various denominations. When they got up to leave Bill held out his hand and thanked Haddad for his help as did Tommy.

"I am sorry about my bad manners Colonel...Bill interrupted him.

"Forget it Mr Haddad I have; besides it is now history."

He personally escorted them from the bank with a handshake and. "Please enjoy your stay with us in Aljibia Colonel and you too Mrs Barrett."

"Come on let us go and purchase a sun hat for you Tommy and you need one with a wide brim insisted Ella who then steered them round the shopping area telling Tommy the best places to shop gained from her own experiences. The highlight of the day for Tommy was the huge supermarket; she had never seen anything like it before.

"There is just about everything we need and more besides. I could spend a full day looking round here Ella."

"They have a very good restaurant here on the top floor if you are ready for lunch and they do a European menu too."

"I am, how about you Bill/"

"Well I am certainly feeling a bit peckish."

"That means you are hungry. Lead the way Ella"

"Lift or escalator?"

"Escalator then we can look around us as we go up."

They were really impressed by the standards in the restaurant, the food and service was excellent. They continued to tour the main shopping area then went to collect their calling cards from the printers.

"You Ella have the privilege of receiving our very first card."

"Then I will keep it as a memento for when we return to the UK."

"You are not going back soon are you?" asked Tommy.

"No we have another eighteen months left on our contract."

"Do you think you will extend it?"

"Who knows?"

When they got back to the car park they saw that Fred was there waiting for them. "Have you had a good day ladies?" He asked "And I like your hat Ma'am."

"We have indeed and thank you Fred," she replied, "it has been an eye opener for us both not realising or expecting to find such an up to date city."

"We surprise all the foreign visitors who never expect that we are capable of matching anything in Europe or the Americas. Another thing you may not have noticed which is prevalent in many Arabic countries, there are no beggars on our streets."

"That can only mean that the people are treated well. We can learn a lot from your people Fred," said Bill. "Here you are Ella, home sweet home and thank you for today no doubt Tommy will call for you to take her shopping again quite soon."

"It will be my pleasure Bill I have enjoyed and been glad to accompany you and will look forward to another trip with you Tommy but it will be a Girlie outing."

"Then I shall ask Fred to chaperone the pair of you to keep you out of mischief."

Fred escorted her to the door, she then waved them off.

"What a delightful day we have had and thank you Fred but would you like to come in for a drink before you leave?" asked Tommy.

"No thank you Ma'am I have a little job to do before I finish."

"We won't need you again today Fred unless we have an emergency, so go back and put your feet up."

On entering the villa Leila came from the kitchen to ask if they would like a brew. "Yes please Leila we will be with you in a few minutes we will have it in the kitchen then we can tell you how much we like your wonderful city."

They made the most of the rest of the week getting acclimatised to their new surroundings, spending some time by the pool and taking trips into the city and meeting more people through John and Ella at the Club where they learned that Cartwright had been banned for a month by the Club committee. Bill also rang the Station Commandant's PA to request an interview regarding his reporting for duty. He was told to present himself at the PA's office at 09:50 Monday morning. He then rang Fred his chauffeur to ask how long it would take to reach the Commandant's office from the villa.

"No more than ten minutes sir."

"Good, then pick me up at 09:30 Monday morning."

"Leila, Monday morning will you bring early morning tea at 6am, we will breakfast at 8am please?"

CHAPTER 5

At 6am Leila took them their early morning tea. "Would you like me to run a bath for you sir?"

"No thank you Leila I will shower."

After breakfast it was time to don his uniform, when he was fully dressed Tommy asked Thomas to take a photograph of the pair of them. When Fred arrived Tommy asked him to take photographs of the four of them in a group much to the delight of Thomas and Leila.

"Right then I will be off and report for duty." He then gave Tommy a kiss.

"You look so smart and I am so proud of you," Tommy said as she returned his kiss.

Fred saluted as he held open the rear door for Bill to enter. Returning his first official salute he said. "I would rather be in front Fred but being my first day I had better stick to protocol."

He was then waved off by Tommy, Thomas and Leila.

"What can you tell me about the Commandant Fred?"

"He is elderly he likes things done right and frowns upon incompetence. He is a likeable man and fair with his judgement."

"I presume he is an Arab but how does he react to all us ex-pats?"

"He has his preferences naturally but he does respect the mature Brits'. I also know your arrival has been looked forward to for some time especially by me when I was chosen to be your chauffeur."

"I am glad you won Fred. Tell me this, Mr Aziz, I know he is of some high authority but how high is he in the pecking order?"

Fred laughed out loud. "You are right there sir he just happens to be at the very top of the pecking order as you call it, he is The Emir of Aljibia. Have you met him sir?"

"I certainly have and what a grand gentleman he is, he enjoyed the chat he had with my wife and always sends her his regards in any correspondence we have had from him, she will be thrilled to bits when I tell her."

"Well sir you are likely to see more of him because he visits the Station quite often especially when he uses his aircraft and the Commandant is a relative of his."

When they were stopped at the gated entrance to the station Fred spoke to the guards in Arabic who immediately jumped to attention and saluted. Bill returned the salute. They then carried on to the Station's Headquarters.

"What is his PA like Fred?"

"He is a young officer, friendly and very efficient, I think you will like him sir his name and rank is Major Khaleel. You will see his name on his office door l will stay in the car to wait for further orders."

Bill entered through two sets of double doors which opened on to a wide corridor that led him to the centre of the building sporting a running fountain and the roof was a cupola of stained glass which filtered the strong sunlight. Four corridors branched from its centre showing many doors most of which held name plates. While he was contemplating which corridor he should take a young man approached and asked. "Can I help you sir?

"Yes please I want Major Khaleel's office."

The young man took him to the first corridor and told him where it was.

He knocked on the door and a voice called "Come in."

When he entered a young officer sprang to his feet from where he had been sitting behind a desk. "Colonel Barrett, please come and sit down, I am Major Khaleel private secretary to General Mahmood."

Bill offered his hand and said. "I am very pleased to meet you Major."

"You are very punctual sir."

"I almost was not because I was lost when I first stepped into this lovely building a young man guided me here to your office."

"The Major laughed. "That always happens to strangers. We have been looking forward to you joining us, the word is that you are the man to take our problem by the scruff of the neck and turn it into a force we can be proud of and other countries to envy. Now since your arrival has everything been to your satisfaction?"

It certainly has we are very impressed with our accommodation and our housekeepers, I do not know where you produced them from but they are the icing on the cake for us. Everyone is so kind and helpful although we had a little unpleasantness in the Ex-Pat's Club."

"Tell me about it sir."

When Bill told the tale the Major frowned. "That is something we will definitely not tolerate, I will deal with that shortly."

"Look, please leave it with me to deal with because he is my subordinate I am given to understand and apart from that scuffle there is something about him which tells me that he is not a fit person to handle recruits. I am not vindictive Major and it is not retaliation, there is something about that man that will be detrimental to my teachings."

"I understand Colonel, your record and can I say fame has preceded you, you have our backing all the way. Now I think it is time we saw the Commandant, you will find a good man who does not suffer fools. You can talk to him and he listens and all he asks for besides doing a good job is loyalty. Incidentally I will say nothing about Cartwright he is in your hands. When your interview is over come back here and I will take you to your office and introduce you to your PA."

The Major knocked and entered announcing, "Colonel Barrett sir."

Bill saluted smartly. He saw before him a middle aged man dark hair turning grey with a happy smiling face who came forward with outstretched hand saying. "It is a real pleasure to meet you Colonel after all I have been told about you. Welcome to Aljibia."

"Thank you sir it is my pleasure and I am looking forward to becoming a member of your team."

"Can I offer you a drink Colonel?"

"I would like a nice cold soft drink please sir I have not got quite used to the heat and I find myself constantly thirsty at the moment."

"You are very wise to drink a lot to keep dehydration at bay." He pressed a buzzer and spoke into the mouthpiece.

They spoke for a while talking about England and the Royal Air Force and the role he had played at RAF March. "Obviously your instructors and I differ with the training methods but I have been brought here to do it my way. Therefore I am anticipating having to make a few drastic changes. I do not want to be dubbed 'A new broom sweeping clean' but changes are inevitable sir."

"Colonel you are completely in charge and responsible for recruit training, I would like to be kept in the picture regarding the changes and when you want to implement them we will talk them over and you can contact my PA for an appointment anytime."

"Thank you sir and do you have a steady flow of recruits?"

"We certainly do there is no shortage where they are concerned."

"Does that include females sir?"

"Yes, our service is very popular with our women Colonel."

"And do I have any jurisdiction over them if so in what capacity?"

"He laughed. Colonel as I have already told you, you are in sole charge of ALL trainees, NCOs and Officers of both sexes can you handle them?"

"If I can't sir you can kick my backside right through your entrance gates with my blessings."

"Colonel I can see you and me getting along fine I like your sense of humour I was forewarned that I was getting a loyal no nonsense straight talking person with a good sense of humour and your reputation does you proud. Go now and report back to my PA, I have enjoyed our introductory chat Colonel. He rose from his chair held out his hand and said. Welcome aboard Colonel Barrett and I mean that with all sincerity."

"Thank you sir I promise not to let you down." He then saluted and left.

"So how did you find our Commandant Colonel?"

"He is a good man I like him very much, he made me feel at ease immediately, you are very fortunate to have such a good man at your head and I am pleased to be able to share your good fortune."

"Right then come, I will take you to your office where your PA awaits you." He took him to the second corridor and pointed to the first door at the nameplate which read Colonel William Barrett. They went to the second door which read, Miss Barbara Battle PA to Colonel William Barrett.

Bill gave the Major a puzzled look. "Are my eyes deceiving me Major?"

"No sir this was the Commandant's special surprise for you."

A big grin appeared on Bill's face. "Then let us go and meet her."

The Major knocked on the door and entered followed by Bill his face wreathed in smiles. Colonel Barrett it is my very great pleasure to introduce you to your private secretary Miss Barbara Battle."

Bill saw before him a middle aged lady of medium height brown hair and dressed very smartly. He came forward with outstretched hand. "What a lovely surprise and I am so happy to meet you Miss Battle."

"The pleasure is mine Colonel." She replied in a soft voice."

"I will now leave you to get to know each other Colonel, Miss Battle will take over now and show you the ropes," he said smiling.

"Thank you for everything Major I will thank the commandant when I have the pleasure of seeing him again but this surprise is the icing on the cake."

When the Major left Bill faced his PA and said. "Miss Battle, would you be offended if I call you by your Christian name?"

"Colonel I would be delighted."

"Good, show me my office then we will have a drink of tea and get to know each other while we drink it. What do you say?"

"I think you are a mind reader Colonel."

"Do you have the facilities for brewing tea etc?"

"I have seen to that and we also have a fridge' for cool drinks."

Have you got cups or beakers, mugs as they are called here as well as at home?"

"I am afraid not, we only have dainty china cups and saucers."

"Then that will be your first assignment Barbara or would you prefer a cup?"

"I was weaned on a mug Colonel and I am looking forward to that experience again, you know the thoughts of it give me a feeling of nostalgia."

"So that gives us something in common to start with. Shall we now go and let you introduce me to my office?"

They went through the connecting door and Bill was amazed to see the size of it. There were settees, easy chairs, a huge desk with an array of instruments and telephones. Another door led him into a toilet and shower room with hand basin, towels, soaps, and toiletries littering the shelves. "I am gob smacked Barbara this is simply amazing. Now what are all these gadgets on the desk?"

"Everything an executive needs, all at your finger tips. I will go and make a brew as you call it then we can talk sir." When she returned with cups and saucers plus a tea pot she said. I am sorry sir you will have to use these if you want a brew, I will have mugs for you in the morning. Incidentally do you like a biscuit with your tea?"

"None in particular but I do like the odd chocolate biscuit. Now tell me about yourself and how you came to be here as a civilian."

"I went to university in England of course Oxford to be precise to study languages. I am fortunate to be able to pick up a foreign language with ease consequently I graduated with an honours degree in French, German, Italian, Spanish, Russian and Arabic. I got employment as an interpreter with the United Nations where I stayed for a few years. I then wanted to spread my wings and someone told me about language teachers needed here in Aljibia. I applied for and got one of the posts and taught here for three years. Then I was approached to see if I was interested in becoming private secretary to an English Officer. I thought well that is a different challenge so I applied and got the situation. Major Khaleel took me under his wing and put me through some intensive training to qualify as a PA. Shall I pour you another cup sir?"

"Yes please. You are a very remarkable woman Barbara Battle and somebody up there," he pointed a finger skywards, "must like me because I am a very lucky man to have you in my corner." He lifted his cup and announced. "Here's to a long and happy friendship."

"Thank you sir I think we are compatible."

"You know I am feeling peckish, is there anywhere around here where we can go for lunch?"

"Oh yes we have a lovely restaurant in a different part of the building and we do not have to pay for the meals."

"Then will you have lunch with me and show me the ropes please."

"It will be my pleasure sir."

"Are there any restrictions of any kind?"

"Non whatsoever it is very democratic."

"I have just remembered I have left my chauffeur outside waiting for instructions from me, I must go and tell him I will not need him until I am finished for the day."

"I will go sir, what is his name?"

"Fred."

She approached the car and rapped on the window. When it was wound down she asked. "Are you Fred?"

"Yes Ma.am" he replied.

"The Colonel sends his apologies for keeping you waiting you can stand down until he finishes his work then he will then phone you."

"I will do that and thank you Ma'am."

When she returned she asked. "Are you ready for lunch sir?"

"Lead the way Ma'am. I say, these corridors are like a maze and very confusing, there are not even any street names to direct one."

She laughed, "You will soon get used to that you will be running around these corridors blindfold. Here we are sir this is what I call the Luncheon Box."

He gazed around taking in the splendour of the place. "And you call this a lunch box, the Savoy in London does not even compare to this lavish set up."

"Table for two Ma'am?" asked a waiter dressed immaculately in whites.

"I would like one where we can observe the rest of the diners discreetly."

"But of course, follow me please."

She thanked him. "This will be fine." Bill looked at her with a puzzled look. "It is because I want to point out personnel to you who you will have contact with."

"Oh I see," he said smiling. "My mind is so full of the grandeur I have to get used to sorry my brain is still in bottom gear."

Barbara was still laughing when a waiter brought menus. "Wine sir? She looked across to Bill and he shook his head. "Water please."

They then ordered from the menus which were written both in English and Arabic. "Can you read the written Arabic?" He asked of her.

"Not as well as I would like but I can when it is written in our style. While they were waiting for the meal to be served she began to point out various characters to him. See that Captain who has just entered, he is one of your staff."

"Captain Cartwright," he said.

"Then you know him, do I discern a note of bitterness in your voice sir?"

"To my misfortune," he replied. He then told her what had happened at the Ex-Pat's Club.

"That was disgusting but full marks to your wife she deserves a medal."

"I am not a vindictive man Barbara and I will not use that incident as a lever, but his body language tells me that he needs watching. I will just say, watch this space. Ah! Here comes our lunch, let us enjoy it."

Over coffee he asked. "Where do we go from here to kill the time?"

"There are various games room, a Gym, a library, and a reading room. An indoor garden where one can sit, relax and meditate. Various TV lounges with programmes that cover the world, you name it sir and you will most likely find it."

"What about a nice quiet lounge where we can sit and talk? You realise it will be mostly shop talk because I want to find out as much as I can and as quick as I can about this Station and the people who run it."

"If that is what you want I am agreeable I will try my upmost to answer your queries."

Walking through the tables to the exit they were confronted by Cartwright who jumped up from his table. "Colonel I am Captain Cartwr...at this point Bill interrupted him. "Come and see me in my office and we will talk about it."

"But I only...this time Bill turned to Barbara. "Obviously he does not understand me Miss Battle perhaps you can translate to him in whatever language he understands to report to your Office at 9am prompt tomorrow morning."

"Very good sir."

Bill then walked away with a big smile on his face.

When Barbara caught up with him she laughed and said. "You are a wicked man Colonel Barrett and I do not know how I refrained from bursting out laughing."

"How did he take it?"

"He was speechless, then when he realised what you had said he spluttered 'The bloody man is mad.' He then sat down and I left him staring into space."

"Then we should have an interesting day tomorrow Miss Battle, come on lead me to this quiet lounge."

Looking round he saw numerous settees for two and three people, lots of easy chairs and coffee tables. They chose chairs facing each other.

"Can you tell me anything about the female officers in charge of the female trainees because they too come under my command and I have not seen any of them yet?"

"There is a Captain in charge with a Lieutenant as second in command. They are Arabs but they lack experience and authority, consequently the recruits are ill trained."

"It looks like I may have a problem there. Look, can you put together a list of all NCOs and Officers with their qualifications, if any, including both sexes please?

"I will soon give you the lists when we get back to the office sir."

"Excellent we may have time to study them between us before we finish for the day, what are the working hours?"

"In summer it is usually 7am until 1pm. winter it is 8am to 5pm of course it depends on commitments. I suggest we return and make a start sir." She laughed when he replied, "Yes Ma'am."

"Give me a buzz if you want any help he said laughing as he entered his office."

He busied himself exploring his office and familiarizing himself with all the gadgets. *Tommy will never believe me when I tell her he said to himself.*

After an hour Barbara entered with two sheets of paper. "Here you are sir these are the lists you wanted."

"There are not many are there? That is the reason I assume why the standard is so low and why I have been recruited to rectify it. Look at this, sorry grab a seat now we can have a good shufti at these names. See, the two female officers have had no training to teach recruits; they are office workers. They have one Sergeant who trained to be a stewardess she must have failed the course so she wound up training recruits. Now what about the men? let us start with Captain Cartwright, he served a short term engagement with the RAF. That tells me nothing.

Lieutenant Smith also served a short engagement with the RAF. What a mess surely they could have chosen someone better then those two. I am not satisfied because it just does not make sense to me. No wonder the Emir said 'We need you Mr Barrett'.

"Are you friendly with the Emir, sir?" Barbara asked.

"We have met two or three times, I had the responsibility of training his son prior to him going to RAF Cranwell." He has a soft spot for Tommy."

"Who is Tommy sir?"

"Sorry, I didn't tell you she is my wife."

"Your wife is called Tommy?"

"Don't let your mind run wild Barbara. Her maiden name was Atkins and you should know that anyone with that surname whatever their Christian name always get tagged with Tommy after World War one Tommy Atkins. Now has your mind got back into neutral?"

"I am sorry sir but it really did come as a shock."

"Silly Billy," he said as they both laughed about it.

"I am going to have a word with the Major will you ring and ask him if he is free for me to have a word with him?"

She rang then told Bill he can go round right away.

"Come in" was the answer to Bill's knock.

"Hello Colonel" he said as he rose from his seat in respect. "Are you settling in alright?"

"It could not be better because I have got my teeth into something I am definitely not happy about. Before we go into detail I would like you to do me a favour."

"If I can it will be my pleasure sir."

"I think you and I respect each other and on those grounds I would be very happy for you to call me Bill and here is my hand on it."

The Major shook it and said. "Thank you Bill it is my pleasure and my English name is Eric," a firm and warm handshake sealed the bond.

"Take a seat Bill and we will try and sort out this problem." "I have checked the records what bits there are of Cartwright and Smith all I read was that both held a short engagement in the RAF, but there is something missing and I want to clear up before I go for the jugular vein."

Eric burst out laughing. "You English, I love your sense of humour and I am going to learn a lot of it from you Bill. You are a smart man and I give you credit for spotting the flaws in the reason Cartwright and Smith have been allowed to stay here and we have been waiting for the opportunity to terminate their contract. We thought that incident with your wife would have been enough unfortunately it was not. Cartwright is the dominant figure of the two, he shouts and Smith jumps through the hoop. We got the pair of them through the recommendations of an ex RAF Warrant Officer called Barnes. We soon got rid of him because he had no respect for our people."

"Correct me if I am wrong Eric but does the name Sam Barnes ring a bell?"

"That's the man Bill do you know him?"

"He was an old adversary of mine; he was the most obnoxious person you would never wish to meet. He was made to drop down a rank to Flight Sergeant with the proviso he applied for his discharge otherwise he would have been court-martialled and discharged with ignominy and the loss of his service pension."

"Isn't it a small world," said Eric in amazement.

"Have you got the names of the RAF Stations where those two were stationed?"

"Yes, here we are RAF Saltash and they were both store men, Cartwright a Sergeant and Smith a Corporal."

"Got em' said Bill gleefully. Now comes the difficult part of the plan and that is replacements for them and how they are all tied in with Aljibia. It smells fishy Eric.

"Have you got any thoughts Bill?"

"I have but it would be very tricky what I would propose. Eric, can I put pen to paper of the ideas that are running through my head for you and me to go through it minutely before you think it is worth submitting to the Commandant."

"Go ahead Bill you have raised my hopes."

"I have a friend in the RAF who has a friend at RAF Records and through him I could possibly find out about Cartwright and Smith. Can I ring him from here to ask if he can find out for us?"

"Of course, just keep me informed please."

"Now the other thing Eric, I want the two female Officers withdrawn from training the female recruits, I see that with their qualifications they would be out of their depth training puppets. There again we would need qualified replacements. Eric the training programme is in a mess and I have not even seen it in action. To put it bluntly there are no qualified instructors to teach them and if I want to earn my salt and train your recruits to the standard the Emir requires. I must be drastic and start from scratch and if my plan is accepted by all parties then we will be in business.

On returning to his office he told Barbara what had gone on, I now need your help to contact an RAF friend who can help get the service records of those two characters."

"Give me the phone number and stand by."

"The person you want is Warrant Officer Shaw."

After a short wait she held up a thumb. "Warrant Officer Shaw speaking can I help you?"

"Will you hold the line please to receive a message from Colonel Barrett?"

Bill heard the shout of "Put him on, put him on."

"Hello Roy how are you old friend?"

"Bill I can hardly speak I have choked up, this is wonderful."

"Hang on a minute Roy and calm down. I need your help on a very delicate matter; I am speaking from Head Quarters here. Getting to the point, will you find out as much gen as you can from your friend at Records Office on a Frank Cartwright and Henry Smith? They both worked in the stores at RAF Saltash I cannot give you any dates but it will be within the last two years and they were on short term engagements. I think they are protégés of Sam Barnes, yes he is behind it. I am not allowed to disclose this number but shall I ring you tomorrow about 14:00hrs. Your time, we are two hours ahead of you. Yes we are very happy here, speak with you tomorrow try your best for me cheers Roy. If anyone can find out for me Barbara he can. Tell me what I should do to ring him from home because when I tell Tommy she will want to ring her service friends actually the friends are ours. Roy was my best man at our wedding. I think I will leave seeing Cartwright on hold for a short while, so when he turns up tomorrow tell him I am too busy to see him. I think it is going home time now, will you ring Fred I am ready for home please? Do you want a lift home Barbara?"

"No thanks I have my own car by courtesy of the firm"

"How did your first day go sir?" asked Fred when Bill got into the car.

"Much better than I expected Fred. I have an excellent private secretary she is the one who gave you the message, I am sorry I kept you waiting all that time but I had interviews with various people the longest being with the Commandant, I must say he is a good man and we got on well together. Now I will have to relive it all again because my wife will want to know every single detail. Here we are home sweet home thanks Fred 8:30am pick up please."

Tommy greeted him with a kiss. "Would you like a cold beer to help you relax and wind down love? We are not going to talk shop until we can relax after dinner which will be around six o'clock."

"I will have a shower and change my clothes so that Leila can smarten them up in her own time, I will wear my second set tomorrow. After my shower I can sit awhile and enjoy that beer and listen to what you have been doing today that will help me relax."

When he came for his beer Tommy said. "I will go and ask Leila to bring it," In the kitchen she told Leila then asked Thomas if everything was under control.

"Yes Ma'am," he said with a grin, "it has a good smell with it."

"There is a good smell coming from the kitchen each time you open the door."

"Yes there is," she agreed "it smells like chef is doing us proud today."

"Now what have you been doing with yourself today?" he asked.

"After you left this morning I decided I needed one or two little items so Chef volunteered to drive me into town for them. I also took in the roll of film which will be ready tomorrow. While I am there I can order extra prints to send to our friends and Nessie. Remind me to make a list then I will not forget. The rest of the day I have been giving Leila a hand so we could chat, then Thomas told me about Arabic cooking he is going to teach me the hows and whys of it, it looks interesting."

"It might look it but will it agree with our English stomachs?"

"Unless we try it Bill how will we know?"

"Fair enough I get the point."

Leila came to tell them that dinner was ready.

"We will have it in the kitchen Leila. Can we come in now?"

"Yes Ma'am the table has been set."

They went in and Bill took a good sniff. "If it tastes as good as it smells Thomas I will promote you to be my head chef."

"If he is not head chef what is he now?"

"Second best chef."

"And who may I ask is the present best chef?"

"You are my love." then gave her a kiss much to the amusement of Thomas and Leila.

"For that he deserves a treat don't you agree Leila?"

"Yes Ma'am," she said with a big smile.

"Close your eyes." Thomas then carried the dish to the table. "Open them."

"Well goodness me, it is Cottage Pie and with Parmesan cheese too, now that is what I call a real treat. As he savoured every mouthful he asked. "And have you made this Thomas?"

"Yes sir but only under supervision."

"Well congratulations, my wife and my sister could not have cooked it any better; you have got your promotion."

"He has made one for himself and Leila but they are taking it to their apartment where they can relax to eat it."

"I promise you will both enjoy it," said an enthusiastic Bill. "That was a perfect finish after a hard day at the office."

"If it is sympathy you are looking for, I can give you some. It's your turn to wash up!"

Upon hearing that remark Leila and Thomas just curled up with laughter. "Oh Mrs Barrett, you are both so funny and we do love you both. Please will you stay with us forever?"

Tommy went to her and gave her a cuddle. "We are very fond you two as well, Leila, but there will be a time when we will have to leave and until that time comes we will just have to enjoy each other's company as much as we can. I now suggest we go and have coffee, when you have done what you have to in here you go home and enjoy your husband's new recipe, we will see to the pots. I now have to go and suffer earache listening to my husband's tale of his hard day at the office."

This brought another burst of laughter from Leila and Thomas.

After coffee they settled down and Bill began to tell his amazing story in between constant interruptions from Tommy who wanted to know every minute detail.

"Oh Bill the place sounds too good to be true do you think that at some stage I could have a grand tour?"

"I don't know pet. I will have to ask about that, but I have saved this for last. I have spoken to Roy on the phone."

Here Tommy really got excited. "What did he say? How is everyone? Have they got our letters?"

"Whoa there! Hang fire a minute while I tell you. I was asking him to get me some information and I hope to receive it tomorrow. I am not allowed to talk about personal things but I am getting the phone lines and relevant numbers for us to speak from here."

"Oh you lovely man, you are my favourite husband."

"From how many?"

"We will have to make a list of times and places where we can contact our friends. It is going to be difficult but we can contact Roy and Viv at their offices or the Sergeants Mess, can't we? And even Jackie ... unless old frozen face stops her. I forgot Jackie is on the phone at home, all the better."

"I had better find out the cost of calls from here. We may have to go steady in that respect. Of course, we can give them our home number, that will ease it."

"William Barrett you are turning into a scrooge."

CHAPTER 6

Bill entered his office quietly, buzzed Barbara and asked. "Has Captain Cartwright arrived Miss Battle?"

"No sir he...I think he is here now."

"Hold him there I am coming in. Ah Good morning Captain I do apologise but I cannot hold our interview just yet but please hold yourself available I assure you I will try to hold it later today."

"No problem sir," he said as he saluted.

Bill returned the salute with the famous Officer's salute, a hand casually lifted in acknowledgement.

When Cartwright left, Barbara looked at Bill with surprise. "That was a bit smarmy of you sir towards your favourite enemy."

"All is not what it seems Barbara; I have just put him at ease because he thought he was to be carpeted. Little does he know that if I get the right results from the UK he will not know what has hit him, he could be due for a really rough ride. My gut feeling tells me there is something deeper than telling a few minor Porky Pies. Roll on 4pm then hopefully I will get the results I want. I will now have to put my thinking cap on to decide about replacing the two female Officers Captain Fikriyya and Lieutenant Jamila, I am open to suggestions if you can come up with any bright ideas."

He returned to his office to begin a plan for qualified male and female replacements.

After two hours of thought and deliberation he arrived at a basic plan of one Male Warrant Officer and one Female Warrant Officer two Male Sergeants and two Female Sergeants. Long term contracts if so required from applicants or a secondment for a two year period. It is respectfully requested that the Emir negotiates with the Ministry of Defence to acquire these people otherwise his training programme will suffer. Satisfied with his effort he asked Barbara to type it out as an Official request.

At 4pm he asked Barbara to phone that UK number again.

"Warrant Officer Shaw speaking can I help you?"

"Hold the line please for a message from Colonel Barrett requested Barbara."

"Hello Roy, Bill here how are you my friend?"

"It is great to be talking to you Bill I told Jackie and Viv, they say they have got Tommy's letters and send tons of love to you both. Derwent sends his best wishes and so does your pal Fred Fox we are drinking your health tonight and Fred is paying."

"Thanks to all of you, Tommy is so excited to be able to speak to you from our house phone. Now what gen have you got for me Roy?"

"The Jack Pot Bill, both guys are old DI.s, Cartwright an ex Sergeant who was demoted by our scourge remember and Smith an ex Corporal DI was also demoted. Both were employed as store men at Saltash. Sam was also stationed there waiting for his ticket. Apparently they got together and formed a 'We hate the RAF. society of sorts. I do not know how but Sam was recruited by one of the people at your end and a lot of money changed hands. Suddenly Sam became very important to someone because he fronted the money for those two to buy themselves out, that gen came from an unknown source. Sam obviously got them employment there and the unknown source swears Sam has some kind of serious hold over them. There you are Bill I still have not lost my touch have I?"

"What can I say Roy except one day you will know how much your information has helped this country. I am absolutely proud of you so much so I will buy you a pint when I see you and if my plan comes to fruition it may not be too far away. Thank you again from all the senior staff here. Bye for now I will be in touch, Tommy sends her love to you and the family."

"Well Barbara that is a turn up for the books, I was right with my gut feeling."

"Congratulations sir that is some achievement."

"Stage two will start tomorrow then the dirt will hit the fan. Ask the Major if I can see him please."

"You can go right in sir and good luck."

"You have a smile on your face Bill must be good news."

"We are on the verge of finding out something sinister Eric; tomorrow will be a Showdown at the OK Coral." He then told Eric everything Roy had told him.

"Oh well done Bill that is absolutely great."

"Tomorrow when I will interview those two I would like you to sit in with me, the reason I ask is you will be my witness in support of the recording I will make of the interviews."

"Most certainly I will look forward to that. I will put the Commandant in the picture and he is sure to tell us to go ahead."

"Oh one other thing Eric can you have your security police standing by and for them to make sure two cells are vacant."

"You mean …"

"Yes, my gut feeling tells me we are going to need them. I want Smith in first because he is obviously the weaker of the two."

Back in his office he told Barbara that he wanted Smith first could she arrange that.

"Yes sir Smith at 9am Cartwright at 10am.

"That will do fine Barbara, by the way keep the inter-com switched off, the Major is sitting in with me."

"That makes sense sir will that be all for today?"

"My goodness has it got to that time, please ring for Fred. Time does certainly fly out here especially when we are having fun. By the way, tell me one thing; am I out of order by coming in after 8am?"

"Well put it this way sir most people come in for 8am including the Major."

"Looks like I am setting a bad example I will be in at 8am in future Ma'am."

She smiled then said. "Shall I forward your times forward an hour sir?"

Giving a sheepish look he replied, "Yes please."

"Had another busy day sir?" asked Fred.

"Yes Fred and it will be a busier one tomorrow and so will you because the new pick-up time is now 7: 45am and until further notice it will be permanent."

Tommy was thrilled to bits with Bill's message from Roy especially knowing that everyone had received her letters.

"Why don't you try phoning Jackie about 8 o' clock, if she has been on late duty shouldn't she be home by then?"

"I think 9 o' clock would be a safer time Bill."

"Did Thomas and Leila say how they enjoyed that Cottage Pie?"

"They went mad on it, Thomas has written it into his book of Favourite Recipes."

"What's for dinner tonight anything I know?"

"It is something I don't know either."

"Anyway I must go for a shower and get into some comfortable clothes I will have a beer when I have finished."

When he came in the lounge Tommy called Leila who brought him his cool beer.

"He has not noticed it Leila I told you he would not."

"Noticed what?" he asked.

Leila was giggling at the pair of them.

"Have a look round, I think the beer is affecting his sight Leila."

After much searching his eyes fell on a photograph in a frame stood on a table. It was an enlargement of the one taken yesterday by Fred of the four of them. "I like that he said as he picked it up for a closer look. It is a good photo."

"I got one for Leila and Thomas and some smaller ones for our friends of just you and me," she showed them to him.

"Oh yes they are all very good the family will like them and Jackie will drool over hers."

"Dinner is ready Ma'am."

"Coming Leila, they were thrilled to bits with their photograph I had it framed similar to ours."

"Good evening Thomas I hear you had another busy day acting as chauffeur."

"Good evening sir, it is my pleasure to take Mrs Barrett wherever she wants and she is not a back seat driver because she sits in front with me."

That caused a laugh and Tommy to clap her hands saying. "Well said Thomas."

"Let me know when you want to stay in town for a good while and I will detail Fred to take you. Why don't you take Leila shopping sometime maybe she will introduce you to some of the shopkeepers that Ella would not know of and if you get friendly with them it could be to your advantage."

"What do you say to us two going shopping Leila, you could do yours and me mine and we could leave Thomas holding the Fort.? And he could make us a brew when we return. Would you like to go tomorrow or when would be a more convenient day be for you? Oh my goodness I have just thought of something Bill. We are supposed to buy all the food for our requirements and we have not paid Thomas a single dollar. Thomas and Leila come and sit down with us. Now Thomas tell us please what are we supposed to pay."

"For the running of the Villa is mainly food, our wages are paid by the government. The other main item is your telephone calls."

"How do we pay for the food Thomas surely we don't have to give you cash every time you want to shop."

"I am afraid you do Ma'am because it is your responsibility to shop for the food. I shop for the food that we run out of when you want me to go to town for it."

"Thomas I am so sorry but I must owe you money for the food you have already bought out of your own pocket. Have you made a list of the cost I owe you?"

"Yes Ma'am," he replied as he handed her the list.

"Thomas, are you sure this is only what I owe you, what about all the food we have eaten since we have been here?"

Thomas and Leila laughed. "You received a week's supply of food free on your arrival by courtesy of the system. It was in your information pack Ma'am."

"We obviously skipped over it in our excitement. Leila, you are going to act as nursemaid to me besides your role as housekeeper. I will not be a minute while I go for your money Thomas," She made them both laugh when she said, "that is if I can remember where I put it."

"Almost time to ring Jackie," Bill said to the back of Tommy as she rushed by him.

"Won't be a minute, I'm going for some money to pay my debts."

When she returned he asked. "What debts?"

When she told him he remarked. "That was very kind of Thomas."

When Tommy returned after paying her debts Bill gave her the numbers she had to ring before Jackie's number.

"She then put a finger to her lips whispering, "It's ringing. Hello Mum! "

Bill heard the scream from where he was sitting.

"Are you alright Mum? She is crying she whispered to Bill. She says they are tears of happiness." When Jackie had settled down they had a long and informative chat before Tommy said she must now go. "Bill would like a quick word I will ring again soon, yes I love you too." She handed the phone to Bill with tears rolling down her face.

"Hello Mum how are you, yes I have been listening to Tommy and I cannot add to all she has told you except she really loves it here. Yes I am fine I think we made a good decision to come here, everyone is so friendly. Please give my regards to all our friends we left behind especially Old Mary Brown you can guess what remark she will come out with. Anyway I must go and as Tommy said we will be in touch with you soon, take good care of yourself…love you, bye Mum."

"What news has she got for us and any scandal?"

"My replacement is not liked Jackie said, she is a cocky little madam and a terrible nit picker she is quite beastly to Jackie and Jill. Chef has got to the stage where he will not co-operate with her because she belittles most things that he tries to help the Mess with especially on dining-in nights and other functions. She said that Sqn. Leader Macfarlane is the answer to every WRAF's Prayer. The good news is Graham and Marion have become engaged."

"That is good news, If you are going into town tomorrow get them a congrats' card and send it off while you are there. Do you want Fred to take you?"

"That is a thought Bill, yes, tell Fred in the morning to pick me up about 10 o'clock. I will ask Leila if she would like a ride out to keep me company."

At 6am Leila brought their early morning tea. "Thank you Leila and will you ask Thomas if there is anything he is wants from town this morning I am asking Fred to take me in. Would you like to come and keep me company?"

"Yes Ma'am I would love to."

"I was hoping you would say yes because I want a shop that sells Greetings Cards and I would not know where to look for one and I am sure Fred would not know him being a man. He will pick us up at 10 o'clock."

At 7:45 Fred was there to pick up Bill. "Fred will you take my wife and Leila to town today picking them up at 10 o'clock?"

"Yes sir that is no problem. Will you need the car today?"

"Only when you come to collect me to bring me back home Fred."

CHAPTER 7

Bill looked through the connecting door to Barbara's Office. "Good Morning Miss Battle," When he saw Smith standing there "I will be with you in a few minutes Lieutenant." He went back into his office to wait the arrival of Major Khaleel.

When he arrived they greeted each other and shook hands.

"I had a word yesterday with the Commandant and he is in full agreement with the procedures we are taking."

"Good then I will have Smith in and be free to speak anytime during the interview Eric." He pressed his buzzer, "Send him in please Miss Battle."

Barbara knocked, opened the connecting door and announced. "Lieutenant Smith sir."

Smith marched to the desk saluted then introduced himself. "Lieutenant Smith sir."

"Stand at ease Smith. I have asked you here for this interview to get to know my staff. Would you feel better stood easy?"

"Yes sir."

"Go ahead then stand easy, that is a relief for you I'm sure. Now I want you to tell me in your own words not any of this snapping out answers in military jargon like a machine gun, the more you relax you will find that words come more easily. Tell me about your Royal Air Force service and how you came to be serving the Emir of Aljibia."

"I was a Corporal Drill Instructor in the RAF until there was a structural change in so much as two training establishments were closed down, that left only one which could not absorb any more staff. Consequently we surplus staff were scattered to various units who naturally did not want us but were forced to employ us on any jobs except the ones we trained for."

"How did that affect your rank if you were not Drill Instructing?"

"We kept our rank sir."

"Then what job were you doing?"

"I applied for a storeman's course and until a course came available I worked in the stores for experience."

"That was very commendable of you but while you still retained your rank you prevented a qualified storeman from being promoted to a Corporal."

"My stripes were soon taken from me for that very same reason sir and I was demoted to the low rank of leading aircraftsman then to top it all I was refused the storeman's course. Of course I got very bitter and that is when I met Cartwright who was a Drill Sergeant demoted to Corporal and because he could not pass a storeman's course to the rank of Corporal he was discharged from the service. Fortunately for us there was a Flight Sergeant Barnes storeman who was waiting for his discharge papers. He had been the victim of a senior officer who had victimised him. I don't know how but he promised Cartwright and me if I discharged myself from the service a job Drill Instructing here in Aljibia. We jumped at the chance but had to wait until he had been installed here then he would get things moving for our acceptance. Eventually the day arrived when we were installed here and Sam's contact pulled a few strings to get us the ranks we now hold."

"Do you know the name of this contact?" asked the Major.

"No sir but I would recognise him if I saw him again."

"Did you see him often?"

"About every two months, he would give us a roll of film to take to Sam when we went back to the UK for a little break."

"Was he a photographer?" asked Bill.

"I don't think so it was Sam who was an aircraft spotter and he collected photographs of them. When we went back to the UK for a break we would take them to Sam, it was a good little earner for he would pay us well for the service."

"What was this mystery man's job or where did he work? "He was on the ground staff but I do not know what he did but I do remember him saying to me once. I will have to dash because I have a VIP coming in anytime now."

"When was the last time you saw him?" asked Bill.

"Three weeks ago."

"And did he give you another roll of film?"

"Oh yes, I gave it to Cartwright because it is his turn to take it to Sam."

"Well Lieutenant I am very impressed, you have been very frank about your service thank you. The Major will see you out."

Smith saluted smartly then the Major escorted him out into the arms of the security police who whisked him away quietly and with little fuss.

On his return Eric seized Bill's hand and gave it a real good shake. "Thank you Bill that gut feeling of yours proved you were right."

"Have we more security men in waiting Eric?"

"Oh yes they are waiting for the call, they told me that Cartwright is with your PA.

Excuse me for a couple of minutes Bill I have just thought of something." He left the room but was back in a few minutes with three large group photographs.

"What have you got there Eric?" Bill asked.

"I had a brain wave and thought these might help with identification of our mystery man."

"Are we then ready to wheel the next one in Major?"

"Yes Colonel," he responded with a laugh.

Bill rang the inter-com buzzer. "Has Captain Cartwright arrived yet Miss Battle?"

"Yes sir he is here waiting."

"Then show him in please."

A knock on the door and Barbara entered and announced. "Captain Cartwright sir."

Cartwright entered, saluted then announced himself. "Captain Cartwright sir."

"Good morning Captain, stand easy you will feel better. At last I have managed to get to that elusive interview with you. I apologise for what seems like I have been messing you about."

"I understand sir that these little hiccups do occur at times."

"Thank you Captain. Now shall we get down to business? What I want from you is your service record while in the Royal Air Force up to shall we say the present day. I want you to tell it to me in your own words not the service jargon chattering like a machine gun, just take it easy and start when you are ready."

"I rose to the rank of Sergeant Drill Instructor…he then repeated what Smith had said about Sam Barnes offering him a post.

"Sam said it was a job where I could earn a lot of money and become a senior officer in the bargain. Naturally by having a grudge against the RAF my mind went immediately into overdrive. Plenty of money and a commission promised who wouldn't jump at a chance like that? I accepted but had to wait until Sam had come out here and set it up. Some local serviceman here who I understand had some authority had got Sam a post who in turn managed somehow to get myself and Smith a post here on this station."

"I interrupt here Captain," said Eric, "this unknown serviceman is he stationed here?"

"Yes sir the only thing I know about him is that he has an important job in the airfield area. I do not know his name or his rank but I can recognise him when I see him."

"Take a look at these photographs Captain and see if you can identify him for me."

On the second photograph he spotted him. "That is him sir there is no doubt in my mind, what will you do to him give him a court martial?"

"Well we will have to do something he has been very naughty." That made Cartwright laugh.

"He used to give us rolls of films to take to Sam Barnes, he said they were aircraft photos because Sam was a keen collector and we got well paid for doing it."

"And have you got any films in your possession now waiting to be delivered?

"Not on me sir but I have two in my apartment."

"Well Captain Cartwright you have been very frank and we have learned a lot about you haven't we Major?"

"Indeed we have and we thank you for your help in identifying a naughty boy for us."

"The Major will show you out Captain." Said Bill.

Cartwright saluted did a smart left turn and marched out with the Major straight into the arms of the security police.

When Eric returned he threw his arms around Bill. "Bill thank you very much we owe you a great debt of gratitude for what you have done for us."

"It is only what I am paid for Eric." There are two things left for us to do Eric, one is to sign off on this recording. I will say. "These two interviews were taken by me Colonel William Barrett with Major Eric Khaleel as witness. You can say in English and Arabic, I Major Eric Khaleel sat as witness in the two interviews taken by Colonel William Barrett. Do you agree with that Eric?

"Yes."

They then spoke into the tape recording. They gave it a quick run through to hear if everything was as it should be.

"Now you must take this tape to the Commandant along with the picture of the identified guy. This will now be a job for your National Security people."

When Eric had left Bill poked his head round the connecting door to Barbara's office. "Do you fancy a spot of lunch Miss Battle?"

"Hello sir are you all done and dusted to your satisfaction?"

"I am and I have worked up an appetite in the bargain."

"Give me five minutes sir and I will be ready."

A few minutes later came the voice of Barbara. "Ready when you are sir."

On the way to the restaurant she asked how the interviews had gone.

"I will tell you over lunch," he said humming to himself.

"I don't know about over lunch you sound as if you are over the moon."

He just looked at her, smiled and continued humming tunelessly.

On entering the restaurant the waiter showed them to the same table they had occupied previously. They looked at the given menus and made their choice.

While they were waiting for the meal to arrive Barbara said. "Come on sir I am dying to know."

He told her what had transpired and how they walked into the trap. "In a way I feel sorry for them, picture two young men who thought the service had done them an injustice it would be a natural reaction to feel very bitter. Then along came their fairy godfather offering them the moon on a silver platter but only to use them for his own ends. Who wouldn't have taken this opportunity to grasp this gift? Then the fairy godfather began weaving his evil web and the two lads were too naive to see what they were letting themselves in for. It will result in them going to prison there is no doubt about that. They were duped into becoming couriers for something very detrimental to this country."

"You mean…"

He put a finger to his lips and nodded a yes.

"Well you have certainly made your mark in the few days you have been here and if it results in you going higher up the ladder I am coming with you," she said with a laugh. "I can understand your feelings about those two young men now that I know they have been used but like you said, they will suffer for it. I hope they catch that bad devil."

Around the middle of the afternoon Eric came and informed Bill the Commandant would like to see him. He buzzed Barbara. "I have been summoned to see the Commandant Barbara, see you in a little while."

Eric knocked on the Commandants door and entered announcing "Colonel Barrett sir."

Bill saluted smartly.

"Come and sit down Colonel, I understand you have had a busy day. You sorted out what we thought was a little problem and it turned out to be a major one. Major Khaleel told me that you had a premonition something sinister existed, he said you call it a gut feeling."

"Yes sir I do and it very rarely lets me down. I must point out that Major Khaleel played a major role in the interviews and it was his foresight and quick thinking that the mystery man was identified."

"That was indeed a good result Colonel the man has been arrested, he was the officer in charge of the armoury so what technical data he has stolen and passed on we do not know until we can get the information from him. He will of course be tried as a traitor. I can see in your eyes Colonel you are anticipating what I am about to say. You must appreciate that the laws of most countries differ as do ours and yours and you have to accept that. He will be tried by the laws of the land and yes, if found guilty of treason he will be executed. Those two young men will I am sure receive a light prison sentences they were so naïve. Two rolls of film were found in the search of Cartwright's apartment as he stated, nothing was found in Smith's. London has been informed of the role Mr Barnes played in this scenario and hopefully will be apprehended. A full report of this has been sent to the Emir so we can expect a visit from him soon. I will make sure you are kept up to date with the progress Colonel. He stood and shook Bill's hand saying. "We owe you a great debt Colonel, thank you."

Bill saluted and left. He saw Eric's office door was open as he walked by and he was halted by Eric's shout of "Colonel."

He turned and walked in the office. "You wanted me Eric?"

"I only wanted to ask how your interview went with the Commandant."

"Quite good, he put me in the picture of what was happening. He is a good man Eric and approachable he does listen with interest to what you have to say, I am happy to serve under him. And how are you Eric after today's spy catching?"

"I am still full of excitement and I am learning a lot from you already. You did a wonderful job with those two characters Bill."

"Rephrase that Eric to 'We' did a good job, now don't you forget that. I think you and I make a good team, don't you?"

A still excited Eric came forward and shook Bill's hand. "Thank you Bill."

Back in his office he went to see Barbara. "Everything quiet Barbara any messages?"

"No sir were you expecting any?"

"Not really although once I get my feet under the desk and settled in situ you should be run off your feet."

"I cannot foresee that happening sir we are not in the middle of the hustle and bustle of city life."

"All that will change when I start cracking the whip then you will beg me to get you an assistant."

"You know what they say about pigs flying."

"O ye of little faith! Oh yes, that paper I asked you to type officially will you file it please? I have come up with something that at the moment will be more acceptable; I will let you have it when I have finished it. I will not start now it is time we were not here. Will you ring Fred please and are you all right for transport?"

"Yes thank you sir, my little beauty is running like a dream."

"I will go and see what Tommy has been up to today Fred took her and our house keeper into town to do a little shopping."

"You have a housekeeper?"

"Oh yes and a Chef, they are a married couple and live in an apartment attached to the Villa and they are a lovely couple. Tommy was worried on our way here in case we were not compatible but we are a very friendly household. Thomas and Tommy are happy with the situation they swap recipes. The other day she taught him how to make a Cottage Pie and it turned out a treat, she also told him to make one for him and Leila, they took it to their apartment to eat and their verdict was excellent. He wants her to teach him more English recipes, she is a good cook in her own rights and she got a lot of her recipes from my sister who is one of the good old fashioned cooks. Here is me rabbitting on while Fred is sat there waiting for me. I hope I have not kept you with my ramblings Barbara."

"Not at all, I found it very interesting. Bye, see you tomorrow."

"Sorry to have kept you waiting Fred, how did the day go any problems?"

"No sir they really enjoyed themselves. I will not divulge anything in case Mrs Barrett wants to tell you herself and I do not want to get into her bad books."

"You are being very diplomatic Fred but wise."

"Here we are sir, same time tomorrow?"

"Until further notice Fred, thank you."

Tommy greeted him with a kiss.

"Give me time to shower and change then I will be right down for a cool beer."

When he returned and after a good swig of his beer he asked. "And what has your day been like?"

"Very nice I really enjoyed it; Leila took me to a lot of very interesting shops and where to buy good fresh vegetables a lot cheaper than the big stores. They are very clean too, do you know their food shops are inspected every month. They can fail the inspection once and after that if it fails again the shop is closed down. I got a nice engagement card for Chris' and Marion and posted it. Fred was funny, he kept making us laugh. He stayed with the car while we went shopping. Leila took me to a little Arabic restaurant for lunch." I also bought a few items that Thomas wanted for his larder. Leila took me to an Arab shop where they make very nice light women's clothes. There is a men's tailor where you cannot go wrong Bill for light cool shirts, shorts and slacks it will be worth a look. You can't have too many cool clothes for this climate What say we go and take a look Saturday morning?"

"We'll see."

After dinner when Leila brought in the coffee Tommy told her and Thomas to go home after they had done what was needed to be done. "I will see to these coffee pots, I will dry them and you can guess who will volunteer to wash them."

Leila thanked her and went back into the kitchen laughing.

"I am going to try and catch up on the BBC news. What are you going to do?"

"I will try to catch up on my diary."

"I didn't know you kept a diary."

"I didn't but I am doing now, I bought it in town and thought it would make interesting reading in future years."

"It certainly will, well done you." He tuned in the TV but not many minutes had past before he was fast asleep.

CHAPTER 8

"Good morning Barbara". Bill said when he opened their connecting door. "How are we today?"

"Good morning sir," she replied. "You are chirpy and I feel fine thank you. We have had no messages, no telephone calls and no visitors. I think we are going to have a quiet day."

"In that case I had better find you something to do so put your knitting away and take a message. I would like the names of the Sergeant who is training the male recruits and the names of the two female Officers and Sergeant who are training the female recruits."

"When do you want these names sir?"

"Can you manage them for yesterday please?"

"Ouch! She gasped that hurt; little did I know I was to work for a slave driver."

"Well get on with it or you will working on that project during your lunch break."

He left grinning to himself. When he had sorted himself out he then concentrated on plan 'B' for Drill Instructor replacements. *I request one RAF Sergeant and one WRAF Sergeant from RAF March to serve a two years secondment duty. When they arrive and take over their duties the present Drill Sergeants I recommend to take a three months Sergeant's Drill Instructor' course at RAF March.*

"Miss Battle will you turn this effort into an official request please?"

"Very good sir, here are the names you wanted. Captain Fikriyya, Lieutenant Jamila and Sergeant Anisa. The Male Sergeant is Saleem."

"I shall be checking on the recruit training and introducing myself to these people if anyone wants me."

"Don't forget to take your bleeper with you sir."

"What bleeper?"

Barbara went into his office and opened a drawer.

"There you are sir that is your bleeper; you are required to carry it with you on the station at all times. When it bleeps you read the sender's name who wants you to report to him or her immediately. It will be either myself or Major Khaleel who will use it the most."

"Hm! That is handy, thank you Barbara."

"Is it far to the training area?"

"I suggest you let Fred take you and to show you round the station, I will ring for him. He should be outside in two minutes sir."

When he got in the car Bill said. "A slow drive round the station Fred and point out everything to me then stop at the recruit's training area." When the tour was complete and they stopped where Bill wanted to he stayed in the car watching Sergeant Shaleem drilling his flight. "Have you any idea how long those recruits have been here training Fred?"

"I think about four weeks sir."

"Well they are in a sorry state they are just shambling along instead of marching. "You stay here Fred I may be some time."

He walked over and called. "Sergeant Shaleem."

Shaleem just looked over his shoulder and when he saw it was a senior officer he jumped round and marched over to Bill saluting as he came to attention before him.

"Sergeant if you do not bring your flight to a halt you will lose them."

He turned and shouted 'Halt' in Arabic. He then turned round to face Bill again.

"Are you going to leave them stood to attention or stand them at ease Sergeant?"

Once more he turned away and shouted in Arabic to Stand at Ease. When he turned and faced Bill once more he was asked if he was a qualified Drill Instructor.

"Yes sir."

"How long have you been instructing and how long have you had these recruits?"

"Two years sir and I have had them for four weeks sir."

"Very well show me what you can do and I want to hear all your commands in English."

After ten minutes Bill stopped the display. "I have seen enough Sergeant now I want a word with these recruits. My name is Colonel Barrett and I am your Officer Commanding. I have been watching you make an almighty mess of trying to march and carry out the simple basics of drill. YOU! He shouted pointing a finger at a recruit come out here." The recruit did as he was told. Why were you talking, were you objecting to what I said of you people not having the foggiest idea how to march?"

"No sir."

"Do you see that car over there it is about one hundred metres away, I want you to double to it touch it then double back to me, do you understand?"

"Yes sir."

"Then Move!"

When he returned Bill ordered "AGAIN"

On his return he was told to rejoin the flight. "When I am addressing you, you will keep quiet in future and that goes for each and every one of you, do you understand?"

He got a murmur in return.

"I SAID DO YOU UNDERSTAND?"

"Yes sir," was the response.

"Right then I want you all to listen very carefully to what I am about to say. I will give you three days to improve your drill and if I am not satisfied with you I will personally take charge of you and drill you until the sweat from your bodies form pools at your feet. At present you are a disgrace to your uniform, when I see you again your uniforms will be clean and smartly pressed and that is just for starters. Finally I know you all speak perfect English and as from now you will speak only English in my presence, is that understood?"

"Yes sir" was the unanimous reply.

"Where do the females do their drill Sergeant?"

"On the other side of that building there sir and beyond that is the domestic site."

"Thank you Sergeant, Carry on."

As he made his way to the building he noticed that Fred was following him in the car but keeping at a respectful distance. Good Old Fred, he laughed to himself thinking back to the Astra cinema days when as soon as the name Fred Quimby flashed on the screen the audience as one would shout that time honoured cry of 'Good Old Fred'. He rounded the corner of the building to see and hear a bunch of female recruits with a Sergeant trying to control them with little or no success. He watched for a few minutes then marched forward with determination to sort out the young devils.

He approached the Sergeant and asked. "What is going on here Sergeant Anisa?"

She saluted and replied "I am trying my best sir to get them in order so that I can carry on teaching them drill movements."

Bill moved to the front of the flight and shouted. "SILENCE." The chatter stopped immediately and everyone looked at him in amazement.

"Now that I have got your attention, FALL IN, IN THREE RANKS AND YOU WILL REMAIN SILENT WHILE DOING IT…NOW MOVE!"

Some moved liked scared rabbits others looked disdainfully and shambled into position. *He thought, I think there are a few rebels amongst this lot and that is just what I need to instil my authority over them.* "Have you taught them how to Right Dress Sergeant?"

"Yes sir."

"Well we will see how they shape up. RIGHT…DRESS." It was a sad effort as if they were carrying out the order in slow motion. On the next order of EYES FRONT their head and eyes slowly swivelled to the front at the same time as their right arms flopped down to their sides.

"Do you know what you people remind me of, a bunch of disorientated puppets. You are rubbish, pathetic and you are a disgrace to the uniform you are wearing which looks as if you have slept in it. I will now introduce myself. I am Colonel Barrett your Officer Commanding and if you do not toe my line I will personally run you ragged. Also I should not as a male have to tell you about personal hygiene because from where I am standing I can smell the over use of deodorants, do I need to say more? Tomorrow morning you will parade at 9am clean, pressed uniform, polished shoes and I do not want to see your hair looking as if you have been pulled through a hedgerow, I want to see a flight of young ladies looking proud to be wearing her country's uniform. Sergeant, I will dismiss them for the day then I want you to take me to see your leaders. PARADE…until I see you tomorrow DIS…MISS."

"Your officers Sergeant, do they ever come to see how the recruits are shaping up?"

"If I see them once a week I am lucky sir."

"Then what do they do when they are absent?"

"I do not know sir but this I do know, they spend more time away from the station than they do on the station."

"Are you a qualified Drill Instructor?"

"No sir but I would like to be, I have been standing in doing this job for a year but there is no course I can go on where I could be taught."

"Leave that with me I will see what I can do for you."

"Their offices are in that building sir the Administration Building, the personnel inside who are training staff in some form or another are on the first floor. There are two male Lieutenants, two female Lieutenants and a male Captain in charge of them, on the ground floor are Administration offices."

"Thank you Sergeant Anisa you have been most helpful. One little tip, be strong and firm with your recruits and don't you worry I will back you up and that is a promise."

"Thank you sir," she said as she showed a happier face giving Bill a smart salute.

He entered the building and climbed the stairs to the first floor. He saw a few offices empty of any occupants although there were plenty of signs showing that the occupants were elsewhere. He went towards a room with a partially open door from where voices were coming. Looking inside he saw the voices were coming from a TV set. On entering he saw three men and two women officers watching the TV. He went to the TV and switched it off much to the consternation of the occupants. As one of them jumped to his feet to protest Bill held up his hand and stopped him.

"Allow me to introduce myself; my name is Colonel Barrett your Officer Commanding." Immediately they all rose to their feet and stood to attention. Please sit down," he smiled. "I would like you to introduce yourselves and tell me your status regarding the training of recruits,"

"I am Captain Khatib." I am fully in charge over these four officers."

"I am Lieutenant Yasseen." I am in charge of the data and records of the male recruits."

"I am Lieutenant Habib." I am in charge of the male accommodation."

"And you ladies."

"I am Lieutenant Basma." I am in charge of the data and records of the female recruits."

"I am Lieutenant Fidda." I am in charge of the female accommodation."

"I would now like to know why you have left your offices to watch television, I know it is not your lunch break but I would like an honest answer from you Captain as their superior?"

One of the men spoke to the Captain in Arabic.

"Stop right there Habib. In my presence you will all speak English not only is it discourteous but it shows your ignorance. In this country you are taught English as your second language I envy you for that because when I was a schoolboy only selected schools taught a second language and inevitably it was French, I did not make the grade to qualify for such a school. Put yourself in my position by going to a foreign country and you are amidst some of the natives of that country and they converse in their own language, what would your reactions be?"

Habib immediately apologised. "I am sorry sir it was very discourteous of me, please accept my humble apology."

"I accept your apology in the spirit it was given and to show I bear no ill feeling it is now history and here is my hand on it. Now where were we? Ah, you were about to answer my question Captain."

"Sir, our work load is not enough for us to get our teeth into to give a hundred percent effort. Consequently we find we have a lot of free time on our hands and the Television is our only relief from boredom."

"Thank you Captain, that is a fair answer to my question. "Unfortunately for you I cannot condone that so it means I must put on my thinking cap and come up with a solution to give you something you can stick your teeth into and enjoy doing. If you have anything you would like to get off your chests ideas, grievances or any moans come and see me I will listen to you if I cannot help you I will find someone who can. As for you ladies if you ever want a soft shoulder to cry on you can try mine. Thank you for your time and I hope we can work together."

As one they all stood up and gave him a round of applause.

"Captain, I would like a word in private." When the others left the room Bill asked him. "How often do you see Captain Fikriyya and Lieutenant Jamila?"

"Not very often I'm afraid, sir."

"Tell me about it."

"Fikriyya has an overbearing attitude and Jamila is her poodle. It is sometimes days before they report in here and at times it might be only for an hour or so doing nothing but chat. They do spend a lot of time watching Television sir."

"Does anyone check on the training staff Captain?"

"No sir, you are the first and I cannot remember the last one."

"Little wonder it is in the state it now is. Look, I want you to contact me when they do show up. This is between you and me, tell nobody else."

"You can count on me sir."

Fred was waiting in the car. "Thank you Fred back to base please."

"You have had a busy morning sir did everything go well?"

"Let's say I have left my mark but there still is a long way to go. I will not need you again Fred until home time…I hope."

"Hello Miss Battle I am back, any messages for me?"

"Sorry sir, nothing."

"Then we will go to lunch, are you ready?"

"Give me five minutes sir."

After lunch when they were having coffee in a quiet lounge Barbara asked. "What kind of a morning did you have sir?"

"I found out that to make something out of the dregs of the training personnel I will need to take a course of paracetamols to take on the task ahead of me. There is no way out of this mess unless I am ruthless and get one hundred percent backing, which I have been promised."

"Is it as bad as that sir?"

"Worse if anything. I cannot understand how it has got into such a mess. There is no discipline at all on this station but I will try my damndest to rectify that. I will have a word with Major Khaleel when I get back."

When they returned he asked Barbara to get him an interview with the Major.

"You can go right away sir, he is free."

"You have a problem Colonel; your face gives you away. I am not physic by any means."

"What action would you take, say, for an officer who shirks their responsibility for the people under their command and is continually absent from their place of duty?"

"Is that a hypothetical question Bill?"

"No, that is an incident which occurs very regularly on this station."

"The person would have to appear in front of the Commandant and if it is proved positive he will strip the officer of his rank and discharge him from the service, it is as simple as that."

"Excellent. I am all in favour of that. Captain Fikriyya and Lieutenant Jamila are the culprits. At present they are absent without leave and apparently have been for a few days. I understand from my informant this is a regular occurrence. I am now waiting for a message telling me when they have returned to duty then I will put them under open arrest and confined to camp. Then you will instruct me on the procedure I will have to take."

"You are certainly sorting out the wheat from the chaff Bill."

"And there is still a lot of sorting out to do Eric. Do you know where those two are accommodated?"

"Give me a minute..." he said, as he began looking through some files. "Here we are, they live on camp in the female officers' block."

"Can you find out if they are in the block at present? If not I would like to know the last time they were seen in there. I want to cover all angles Eric then I will be able to tell if they are telling porkies."

"What are porkies Bill?"

Bill laughed. "Porkie Pies is rhyming slang for 'lies'."

Eric laughed out loud. "I like that Bill, it is very funny. Have no fear about back-up; you will get one hundred percent from us."

"Thanks Eric, I will let you know when things start to move."

The following day Bill marched to the drill area to inspect the girl recruits. When he arrived they were stood on parade awaiting his arrival. Sergeant Anisa called them to attention, saluted Bill declaring. "Parade is ready for inspection sir."

"Thank you Sergeant."

Open Order March was given followed by a Right Dress then Eyes Front. Bill and the Sergeant walked slowly along each rank with Bill giving words of encouragement. When the inspection was finished the flight was returned to a normal position then made to Stand at Ease for Bill to address them.

"Good morning ladies I am very much impressed with your turn out and your drill movements. I have been pleasantly surprised because marching here I was wondering what kind of a mess would be waiting for me. You have done Sergeant Anisa proud you have done me proud but most of all you have done yourselves proud. I want you to keep up the good work because at the end of this course you are going to compete against the men recruits to see which team is the best at drill. Do you think you are better than them?"

"Yes sir," they shouted.

"Good that is pleasing to know because I think you will win. What I want you to do is listen and do exactly what Sergeant Anisa tells you. Once you get into the swing of it and work together as a team you will enjoy it. Very soon I will show you a film of young ladies like yourselves who after only three weeks service I trained them to beat a men's team, you will learn a lot from watching that film." He then drew the Sergeant to one side and told her that she was now in full charge of the female recruits.

Two days later he made his way to see how the male recruits had progressed any or none at all. As he approached Sergeant Saleem brought his flight to attention, saluted and reported the flight was ready to be inspected. Bill went along each rank criticizing many of recruits about the state of their uniforms. Finishing his inspection he handed them over to the Sergeant and told him to put them through their paces. After a short while he called them to a halt. "Sergeant that was a load of rubbish you had better pull your finger out and start teaching them properly or you will find yourself lined up with them." He then addressed the airmen. "You have got two more days to improve your performance or I will take over. I also want you to smarten up your uniforms and yourselves because right now you are a disgrace to the uniforms you are wearing. Where are these men accommodated?"

"In a barrack block sir"

"Then march them to it and I will march along with you."

As they marched Bill was shouting at them to swing their arms and watch their dressing. By the time they had got to their accommodation they had improved somewhat. "Stand them at ease then come with me Sergeant, he walked inside the block. "Do they have separate rooms and who is in charge of the block?"

"Yes sir they each have their own room and nobody is in charge" Bill tried a door to find it locked. Go outside and tell the occupant of room one to report to me." Is this your room?" He asked the recruit.

"Yes sir."

"Open it up I would like to see inside."

When he opened the door the stench hit him. Bill stood in the doorway to see the room was in a shambles. "Lock up rejoin the flight and send room two occupant in." His room was just as bad as the previous one. Bill made each airman open his room door only to find each one was as bad as the other. When he went outside he took a few lungfulls of fresh air before addressing the flight. "How you live in a muck heap like that is beyond belief any self respecting person would refuse to let his dog in there, the place needs fumigating and you lot with it. Starting right now you will remove everything out of your rooms, and give it a good scrubbing, floor walls and ceiling, open all windows to help get rid of the smell. Wash the furniture and when you are satisfied with the cleanliness and pronounce it fit for humans to live in there then make a start on the ablutions. I will inspect it tomorrow and if it fails my inspection you will start all over again. Carry on."

Back in his office he asked Barbara where the Medical or Health Centre was.

"Get Fred to take you there sir it will be much easier."

"Get hold of him for me please. I have just tried to inspect the recruit's accommodation but the smell and filth drove me out, I am going to see the M.O. to ask him to fumigate it, I have never seen anything like it."

"Medical Centre Fred."

"You are not ill are you sir?"

"I would have been if I had stayed in the recruits' accommodation any longer. "Here we are sir go straight in the reception desk is on your left."

"Hello, Bill greeted the female receptionist. "I am Colonel Barrett Officer Commanding recruit training; and I would like to see the Medical Officer."

"Sorry sir you cannot without an appointment."

"Then will I get to see him if I return with the EMIR?"

A look of terror showed. "Excuse me," she whimpered as she scuttled off, returning with a pompous looking man who appeared to be very flustered.

"I am Doctor Alam I am in charge of the Medical Centre, how can I help you Colonel?"

"Can we talk in private please?"

"Please, come to my office."

"Doctor Alam I have been sent on a mission to this station by his Excellency the Emir himself, what the mission is, is top secret. During my investigation I had reason to inspect the accommodation of the airmen recruits which I found in a very unhealthy state. I have put them to work to clean the place but I would like from you a man to supervise the cleaning and to fumigate the entire building and individual rooms. I have come to the conclusion that any of the accommodations have never received a health inspection, I would like to put it in my report that an inspection is to be held frequently."

"Yes Colonel I understand the implications that could lead to unhealthy surroundings in service accommodation where many bodies sleep."

"You are right there Doctor Alam there could be an endemic resulting in many bodies but now it has been brought to your attention there will be no fear of that. Thank you for your time and co-operation." He left the centre with a self satisfied smile on his face.

"It looks like you won your case sir."

Bill laughed." You should have seen the panic when I mentioned the Emir. Back to the office Fred I'll see you later." He said still laughing."

"I'm back Miss Battle."

"Did you get what you wanted sir?"

"Yes and more besides." He then told her everything, what had happened."

"Well done sir, at least you have made sure the recruits will now live in a healthier environment."

"Major Khaleel rang asking for you saying he had some information for you."

"You know where to find me Barbara, I shouldn't be too long."

"Well Major Khaleel I believe you have some gen for me."

"Gen sir?"

"An RAF term for information."

"Ah I see, yes I have some gen for you. Those two officers have not been seen for a week."

"They are not on any kind of leave are they?"

"No, leave of any description by officers has to be rubber stamped by the commandant"

"We have got them Eric."

"When you confront them you escort Captain Fikriyya here to my office and get Captain Khatib to escort Lieutenant Jamila. They must not have any contact with each other before seeing the Commandant."

"Good, I am going to find how you deal with situations like this it will be very interesting. There is something I have meant to ask you but something always seems to crop up to take my mind off it. I notice that on this station there appear to be more chiefs than Indians."

"I do not understand."

"There are more officers than NCOs. The lowest ranking NCO is Sergeant. Why are there no Warrant Officers, Flight Sergeants and Corporals? I was given to understand that your Air Force was modelled on the Royal Air Force, it is nothing like it. Any chain of command stops at Sergeant, there are some missing links in that chain Eric and I am not happy about it."

Eric smiled. "It is very similar to your RAF. WAF, Women's Air Force. The reason for the lack of junior NCOs in training is we think a Sergeant has the power of control and a JNCO would be surplus to requirements. Warrant Officers, senior and junior NCOs are qualified tradesmen and you will only find them employed on the airfield and in the clerical departments. When recruits pass out from basic training they are sent to training establishments to be trained for their choice of trades."

"But you have only one airfield and surely you will be overmanned if you are continually training recruits."

"Colonel Barrett, this is not our only airfield," he said with a laugh.

"Well I am glad you have explained the set up here but how it has functioned beggars belief. I wish I could have a free hand in reorganising it."

The following morning he was greeted by Sergeant Saleem with a salute. He took a good look at the airmen who stood there looking smart and clean. "That is what I call a vast improvement, well done. We will now march to your living accommodation to see what improvements have been made there. March them off Sergeant."

When they were halted outside their accommodation they were told to fall out, unlock and open the doors to their rooms and stand by for inspection. When he entered he commented on how fresh it smelled inside. He commenced his inspection with room one .and saw it was still as untidy as it was the previous day as were all the rest of the rooms. "Lock up and fall in outside quickly and without any chatter." He ordered.

When they had formed up outside he addressed them. Your accommodation has the smell of cleanliness while your individual rooms look as if a cyclone has whipped through them. You may be used to living in squalor but you are now serving in the Air Force and I will not tolerate it in any shape or form. As from now you will make up bed packs, place your entire clothing etc in wardrobes and cupboards where they belong, only items of service issue will be displayed and I or my deputy will inspect each room and the ablutions each morning at 9am until further notice or until you can be trusted to keep to my standards."

"Excuse me sir," said one recruit. "What are bed packs?"

"Room one airman," he called. "Go and bring your bed with all the bedding out here, you and you," pointing to two more airmen, "will go and help him."

The bed was brought out to loud laughter from the rest of the flight. "Now pay attention I will demonstrate how to make up a bed pack." There you are and that is how I want to see it when I inspect you tomorrow." He then pulled the bed pack apart and told the three airmen to take it back inside. When they returned he said. "I will give you all fifteen minutes to make your bed pack then stand by your beds for I will be inspecting your efforts, away you go."

He began by inspecting room one. "That is a good effort but try to make it neater.

Stow all this clutter away where it should belong, do it now because I want to make your room the show piece of this accommodation block. He continued to tell the airman what to do to make his room acceptable for inspections. When he was satisfied he asked. "What do you think of it now it is a vast improvement don't you think?"

"Yes sir it is very neat."

"I am glad you agree because the rest of the airmen are going to come and see how I want all the rooms to be like when I come to inspect them. Lock up and fall in outside." He carried out the rest of his inspection before telling each airman to lock up and fall in outside. I think you all have tried hard but you need more practice. When you have finished training for the day you will inspect number one room and absorb in your minds how I want it to be laid out for my inspections. I suggest you help each other because if one person lets you down on my inspection you will receive a collective punishment so make sure that does not happen. My first inspection will be at 9am Monday morning. They are all yours Sergeant Shaleem, take em' away." He returned the salute then marched off.

He made his way to the Administration Building to see Captain Khatib. Startled glances came his way from the four Officers as he passed their offices. The Captain got to his feet from behind his desk when he saw Bill approaching and hurried to his door to open it.

"Good morning sir, please sit down and can I get you a cooling drink?"

"That would be most welcome Captain. Thank you."

He beckoned Lieutenant Fidda and gave her the message.

"There are still no signs of the two Happy Wanderers returning Captain."

"No sir," he said with a smile, "I do not think they will return before Monday now."

"Do they usually stay away so long when they are AWOL?"

"AWOL sir? I am not familiar with that wording."

"Absent With-Out Leave."

"Oh yes, forgive me sir my brain is not functioning as it should do."

At this stage Fidda brought in the drinks and Bill thanked her.

"Thank you sir," continued the Captain "I have no problem as such it is trepidation of what is going to happen to my section here."

"Captain remove any notions from your head that I am going to do anything detrimental to this section. On the contrary, from personal experience I can see ways to improve its efficiency. Have you any objections to that?"

"On the contrary sir I would welcome it."

"And so will your staff when you get it off the ground they will be proud of their achievements and so will you. There is a lot of work to be done initially and it is so simple and rewarding you will wish you had thought about it long ago."

"The way you put it sir sounds as if it will be interesting."

"Believe me Captain it is." He then told him in detail everything about wall charts and their functions, the more he told him the more the Captain was interested. If you have any difficulty in getting the materials mention my name and if it is not accepted drop a little hint that I have been commissioned personally by his Excellency the Emir, which is true Captain it is my secret weapon so do not show surprise when you get the Royal treatment. Also when you do get your materials and are a little unsure of anything get in touch with my PA I will come as soon as I can. Have you lost that trepidation now Captain?"

"I certainly have sir and thank you for what you are doing for us."

Bill shook his hand saying. "And don't forget my secret weapon."

"Thank you sir I will not."

.

CHAPTER 9

When Bill returned to his office he asked. "Any messages Barbara?"

"Nothing at all sir."

"Don't despair very soon I shall expect you to be busy answering calls, I am gradually beginning to make my mark on this station mostly for the bad reasons so watch out for squalls on Monday. Are you ready for lunch I am feeling peckish."

"I am sir and ready when you are."

Just as they were about to leave, Major Khaleel came in all excited. "Good news Colonel the English security people have arrested Sam Barnes at

Heathrow airport trying to flee the country, he is now being interrogated, that is all the gen we have at this moment of time."

"Now that is what I call wonderful news and I will certainly enjoy my lunch today Miss Battle. Thank you Major you have made my day, but what is happening about the three we caught?"

"I think we are waiting for the outcome of the interrogation."

"Come on Miss Battle let us go to lunch, why don't you join us Major?"

"Sorry sir can't manage it today."

On the way to the restaurant he said. "I wonder where he eats because I have never seen him eat in the restaurant."

"Sorry I cannot help you there sir but I can find out for you."

"I don't think so it would be encroaching on his privacy."

Over coffee they discussed his morning's work. She laughed when he told her he had to demonstrate making a bed for the airmen to copy. "They cannot take care of themselves because they have never been taught due to the absence of any discipline. The state in which they leave their rooms an animal would turn its nose up about sleeping there. They will learn, I will make sure they do. The two WAF officers are in big trouble too when they do decide to return from wherever they have been."

"What will become of them will they be disciplined?"

"Most certainly, from what the Major told me the Commandant has the powers to kick them out of the service immediately."

"Then how will you replace them? I do not think we have any WAF officers to do so."

"All I need is one officer a disciplinarian would suit me fine. I wonder if the Commandant can get one posted in from another camp, I will suggest that to him when I see him but it will be after he has dealt with the two Happy Wanderers."

"I don't think they are going be very happy on their return. I wonder if we will get weeping and wailing and the beating of breasts."

Back in his office Bill set about adding to his personnel requirements list an Administration WAF Captain to replace Captain Fikriyya, no other WAF Officer will be required. He took it into Barbara and asked her to add it to the previous list. "I am sorry I cannot find more work for you to do Barbara aren't you bored with having so little to do?"

"I do a little but you must remember the job we both are doing is in its infancy and I have my diary to keep up to date. You are doing very well in the short space of time you have been here consequently if your plans come to fruition then things can only get better. I might add that if one of the Arab officers had been given your post my job would have become absolutely static and I would not have tolerated it for two minutes. You will know by now that our culture when anything needs doing we get on with it right away, while the Arab culture sits back and lets it slide with a 'Bardin Bukra' (later tomorrow) attitude. Yes, I do get a little bored but I intend to stick it out because things are beginning to happen and I want to see the fruits of your labours right to the end."

"What do you do with yourself on a weekend, if you don't mind me asking?"

"It depends on my mood I rest by the pool or visit my teaching friends at the university. Sometimes I will nip off in my car and see some of the country, the people are very nice and they like to chat to you."

"Do you ever visit the Ex-Pats Club for a little relaxation and to wind down?"

"Not very often, I am not a drinking person but I must admit it is a nice place to wind down in."

"Tommy and I have been going with Doctor Whittaker and his wife on a Saturday night and you are quite welcome to join us if you ever feel like it."

"Thank you I will bear that in mind."

"I have my card here somewhere, ah, here it is, anytime you feel like you want a bit of company just phone us to tell us you are coming and we will be only too pleased to see you, if we are not in you can leave a message with Leila our housekeeper. Well I think it is about time we were not here, give Fred a ring please and if we do not see you over the weekend I will see you on Monday."

"Had a good day sir?"

"Not bad Fred I think Monday is going to be a very interesting one. By the way place yourself on stand-by tomorrow morning I think Mrs B. wants to take me shopping for some light clothing to one of your local tailors."

Fred fished in the glove compartment and pulled out a business card. "Here you are sir, if the tailor your wife takes you is not to your liking go to this one; he is a high class tailor and a favourite with our upper class people. Mention that to your wife sir and you know how women react, she will want to go there first, and as you English say 'keeping up with the Joneses'

"Are you a student of psychology by any chance Fred?"

He laughed. "That comes from experience sir. Here we are and I will see you tomorrow, about 10 o'clock sir?"

"Salaam (goodbye) Fred."

"Salaam Colonel"

He entered the Villa to receive a kiss from Tommy. "Have you had a good day love?"

"Not so bad," he replied, "how about you?"

"I will tell you after you have showered and changed and I will have a cool beer waiting for you."

"Ella came round this morning and wanted to know if I would like a trip into town with her, of course I jumped at the chance because I enjoy going there and I had a little shopping to do"

"What did you buy?" He asked giving her a quizzical look.

"Nothing much really, one or two things Thomas wanted and a couple of items for myself, two summery frocks and a swim suit."

"What do you want another swim suit for, what is wrong with the one you have got?"

"Bill, I bought that in the UK and it is not as nice as the ones I can buy here, besides it is rather chic, just you wait till you see it."

"Hmm, what time will dinner be ready?"

"Men!" she said as she stamped off to the kitchen. "Thomas, sir wants to know when he can put his face in the trough."

Thomas and Leila curled up laughing. "Oh Mrs Barrett." Leila said still laughing; you are so funny you always keep making us laugh."

"He can come right now Ma'am it is ready."

"Grub up," Tommy shouted through the door to the accompaniment of more laughter.

Over coffee Tommy asked. "Are we going to do some shopping for you in the morning?"

"Yes, I have already booked Fred for 10 o'clock. Take a look at this card he gave me, he says that all the important people around here patronise this place"

"Then we will make that our first stop."

Bill smiled to himself thinking of what Fred had said.

"Ella told me that John is unable to go to the club tomorrow night and would you mind if she tagged along with us?"

"Not at all, she is very welcome, you had better phone and tell her then after you have phoned her are you going to phone Jackie?"

"Yes, she will be thrilled to bits. I will see to these pots Leila, go on off home and remember it is Saturday tomorrow your day off. Tesbah ala kheir Leila."(goodnight) said Tommy trying to show off a little more Arabic she had learnt.

"Goodnight Ma'am," Leila responded with a smile.

While Tommy was phoning Jackie Bill had switched on the TV and had promptly fallen asleep. Tommy was quick to take advantage but keeping one eye on Noddy in case he showed signs of wakening she carried on chatting to Jackie.

An hour later she said. "I had better ring off Mum, Bill is showing signs of wakening, I will be in touch again soon, our love to you and the family."

"Hello Noddy, welcome back to the land of the living. Jackie sends her love and pleased we have settled down."

"Has she any news for us?"

"Yes, F/Sergeant Harding, you know my replacement, has just received a rocket for making a cock-up of a dining-in night. Roy jumped on her like a ton of bricks and had her up in front of Flt.Lt. Ticker the Mess President. Apparently she is not running the Mess as she should and because of the many complaints against her Ticker referred her to Wing Commander Charles Chaplain who was not happy about the long string of complaints. He promptly got rid of her by referring her to the Station Commander. He in turn sent her to Command HQ and requested the AOC to replace her and guess what; her replacement is an old friend of mine Flight Sergeant Wendy Bertram, we palled up when we met on the same course and hit it off straight away. She has not arrived yet but is expected any day, in the meantime Jackie and Jill are filling in. Oh yes, Joe Franks and his wife moved into our ex-married quarter. Chris' Graham and his fiancée Marion Macken went to Portugal to celebrate their engagement."

"You can bet they will have stayed at the same hotel we all did on Roy's recommendation."

"Marion loves being PA to Sqn.Ldr. Macfarlane she says she is a lovely lady. Jackie says Chef keeps asking after me and to tell you he misses us. She said that all the training staff invariably asks after us and she was thrilled to receive our photos' and doesn't Bill look smart in his uniform. Do you know what the cheeky madam said? If I was twenty years younger you would have had a fight on your hands for him Tommy Barrett. Bless her."

"Aye, they are a good crowd."

"What do you fancy for your supper? You know what I fancy? A cold breast of chicken butty with trimmings."

"That will do me fine love."

"Good morning Fred."

"Salaam alekum (Peace be with you) Colonel…Ma'am"

"Alekum salaam (and on you be peace) Fred" they replied.

"This is our first stop Fred," Bill said with a wink handing him the card that Fred had given him.

"Very good sir," he said with a big smile. "I understand it has a very good reputation, all the well to do people of some consequence go there."

"Really?" asked Bill I was given to understand it was a second hand shop who dealt in hand-me-down clothing."

Fred spluttered and almost lost control of the car.

"Steady on Fred he is just teasing you. Behave yourself Bill you could have made Fred have an accident."

"Sorry Fred."

"Mashy Colonel."

"What does he mean…Mashy?" asked Tommy.

"It means OK/fine Ma'am," explained Fred.

"Mashy," replied Tommy with a chuckle. "I like that."

They came out of the tailor's shop with plenty of buys and left an order for a few items to be tailored. Not all the items were for Bill obviously. They left the packages in the car and went looking around the shops. When they were browsing in a bazaar Tommy saw Leila. She gave a shout and a wave to draw her attention They went towards her and Tommy said, "I am so pleased to have seen you Leila because I want you and Thomas to have Sunday off as well I think you have both deserved it.

"But will you be alright Ma'am?"

"Of course we will I have managed to take care of him before without any help and he has come to no harm. So you and Thomas enjoy your weekend and we will see you Monday morning at 6 o'clock with a brew. Mashy?"

"Mashy." Leila replied with a big smile. "Salaam."

"Are we staying in town for a spot of lunch or going home for a catch as catch can meal?"

"Home, then we can have a lazy afternoon by the pool and you can model your new swim suit."

"Steady boy, I can see a wicked twinkle in your eyes."

"Home Fred," said Tommy then we will not need you for the rest of the day."

"I will get in touch with you early tomorrow to let you know if there has been a change of plans. Mashy Fred?"

"Mashy sir, shukran (thank you)"

That evening in the club they were chatting when Ella said in a half whisper. "There has been something funny happening on the station. You will remember that Cartwright chap, of course you will, well he and his friend Lieutenant Smith have been arrested and I think it is about security. All I know is John had to go and give them a medical examination for when they have to stand trial. Do you know anything about it Bill?"

"Yes Ella I do but I am not allowed to discus it, because I am bound by the Country's Official Secrets Act, sorry."

"I understand Bill I will not embarrass you by asking any more questions. I always thought he was a wrong one and when he assaulted you Tommy I knew I was right. Anyway it will probably make headlines in the local press when the trial starts."

Later in the evening a lady member approached their table. "Excuse me asking Tommy but did you register a complaint when that Cartwright fellow assaulted you?"

"I most certainly did not, why do you ask?"

"That's odd because the fellow has been arrested and taken into custody, sounds fishy to me."

"Well I can assure you it has definitely nothing to do with me." Turning to Bill she said. No wonder I have been getting smiles and nods from other tables they must think that I shopped him. "Take me home Bill that has spoiled my evening."

"Then I am coming with you," said Ella.

"Would you like to come in for a drink Ella?"

"No thanks I will carry on John will probably be home by now anyway."

"We will see you home Ella," said Tommy "won't we Bill?"

"Of course, that is no problem." As they made their way out they bade goodnight in reply to the ones they received. Although in one instance Bill had to take hold of her arm to keep her moving towards the exit when some female said. 'Well done Tommy'.

Outside Tommy said. "Thanks Bill you saved a scene there."

"I looked at your face and thought I had better get you out quick or we three would have been suspended." They all had a good laugh at that remark which calmed Tommy down.

"I am sorry if I spoiled your evening Ella."

"It was inevitable Tommy with everyone not knowing the true facts but putting two and two together and coming up with the wrong answer because of that assault on you by that wretched man."

"Yes I suppose you are right Ella, it is a good job Bill got me out in time or I would have had to do some apologising. Anyway we will say Goodnight Ella I will keep in touch, regards to John."

Back home Tommy said. "I will make some supper, make a brew then we will have it as we watch the Tele' for a bit."

"I'll come and give you a hand. "If tonight's episode is something to go by and they know nothing, we will be in for a rough ride when the truth does come out love. I don't mean that in the sense that we will be castigated it will be just the opposite. Friends popping out of the woodwork, back slapping and we even get invitations by the shipping load."

"Now just calm down and tell me what you are rabbitting on about."

"The reactions when the truth comes out about Cartwright and Smith."

"Bill, sit down, this Cartwright and Smith business, you are involved aren't you? Can you tell me about it?"

"I think you had better sit down because you are in for a very big surprise but what I tell you has to be kept quiet for the time being." He told her how the two men got involved with Sam Barnes."

"Our Sam Barnes? The rotten conniving scoundrel that was him getting his revenge on you and the RAF."

Bill continued with the rest of the scenario. "That is the reason they are in custody awaiting trial."

"And you are responsible for all this coming to light."

"With the help of Major Khaleel."

"I feel over the moon knowing that Sam Barnes is now where he should be awaiting his trial and I hope they throw the key away when they lock him up. Now all is clear what you were rabbitting on about and I can see now what you mean. We will have to go into hiding until the euphoria has died down."

"It will not be as easy as that pet."

Sunday they relaxed by the pool and for Tommy to get her new swim suit admired.

CHAPTER 10

At 6am on the dot Leila wished them a Good morning with their early morning tea.

"Good morning to you Leila, thank you, it is nice to see you back, we will have a chat later."

When they walked into the kitchen for breakfast they greeted Thomas with. "Good morning Thomas nice to see you back on duty. Have you had a good weekend?"

"Yes thank you Leila did all the cooking while I overhauled the car engine."

"So you are a mechanic as well."

"Yes sir, I took a mechanics course in my spare time knowing it would come in very useful for keeping repair costs down."

"You are a wise man Thomas."

"Did you have a nice weekend sir…Ma'am?"

"I missed your cooking Thomas."

"I missed your company Leila."

"The next time you have a weekend off I am coming with you Thomas."

"And I am coming with you Leila and we will go on a spending spree."

Of course these exchanges between Bill and Tommy delighted Thomas and Leila.

"I will show you my new swim suit later Leila when we won't be disturbed."

"Sorry Thomas I have nothing new to show you."

"Bill Barrett, you are telling Porkie Pies again."

"What are Porkie Pies?" Thomas asked.

"It is an English popular saying for telling lies. Sometimes we just say telling porkies."

"You had better get your skates on Bill Fred is here."

"Sorry to leave you folk but duty calls."

"Good morning Barbara" Bill called as he walked into his office. "Have you got any messages for me?"

"One from Captain Khatib, he said I have to tell you the wanderers are back."

"Great some action at last, ask Major Khaleen if he is free for me to see him?"

"He is free sir."

"I will be some time Barbara, I have my Bleep."

"Good morning Eric, the wanderers have arrived. I will tell them they are to be charged with neglect of duty and being absent without leave, will that be sufficient?"

"Yes but bring them here and separate them to avoid any personal contact. I will advise the Commandant to interview the Lieutenant first because she is obviously the weak one."

"I will detail Captain Khatib to escort her and I will deal with Captain Fikriyya. Right Eric I will be on my way."

He entered the Admin' Block and went straight to Captain Khatib's office and explained what role he was to play. "Come with me and I will place the Lieutenant under arrest then you escort her incommunicado to Major Khaleel's office. Open the door for me Captain to make it appear like it is a social visit." This he did and Bill entered and said. "Good morning Lieutenant Jamila I am Colonel Barrett your Officer Commanding and I am placing you under arrest for neglect of duty and with being absent without leave.

Captain Khatib will escort you to Major Khaleel's office. March her out Captain."

He then went to Captain Fikriyya's office knocked on the door and said. "Good morning Captain I am Colonel Barrett your Officer Commanding."

Not suspecting anything she replied. "Good morning sir how can I help you?"

"By getting yourself properly dressed then you will accompany me to Major Khaleel's office. Captain Fikriyya I am placing you under arrest and you will be charged with neglect of duty and being absent without leave, I am also placing you incommunicado. Shall we go?" He took possession of the two office keys and made sure the doors were locked. As they left he saw some smiling faces peering through the glass windows of offices.

At Major Khaleel's office he saw it was empty and presumed that the Lieutenant was being interviewed by the Commandant. "You had better come into my office until you are called for." he said to Captain Fikriyya. He sat her down and asked if she would like a cup of tea.

"Yes please," she replied.

He buzzed Barbara and asked her to make a cup of tea for Captain Fikriyya.

"Thank you," she said on receiving it. "I am impressed by your courtesy and my treatment which you are carrying out in a civilised manner Colonel, a typical English gentleman."

"Thank you I have a favourite saying. Treat a person with respect and they will respond in the same manner."

When the Major entered he told the Captain to accompany him.

She saluted Bill saying. "If I do not have the pleasure of meeting you again Colonel it has been a privilege to meet a true Officer and Gentleman, thank you."

"Well whatever kind of person is she?" asked Barbara who had stayed for security reasons by not leaving him alone with a female. "It was a nice thing to say and I agree with her, you were very chivalrous towards her."

Half hour later the Major burst in. "Have you their office keys sir. They need to get in to collect their personal belongings."

As he handed the keys over he asked. "Are they under escort?"

"Yes, a Major and a Captain from Admin' are doing the honours, females of course he said with a grin. I will give you the gen later."

"It looks like they have got the chop Barbara."

"What do you mean the chop? Surely not…"

"No, nothing like that. I meant they must have been kicked out of the service."

"You men and your service jargon! I have noticed that Major Khaleel has suddenly started using a few RAF words. I wonder who he gets them from?"

"I forgot to tell you but Saturday night in the Club we had to make a quick exit before Tommy blew her top. Apparently the members think that Tommy is responsible for Cartwright being in custody because of when he tried to get fresh with her. As we were leaving one lady even shouted 'Well done Tommy'. it was at that point when I had to grab her arm and bustle her out."

"What is it going to be like when the news breaks on the real reason they are in custody and who was responsible for it.?"

"I hate to think Barbara, I just hate to think. Come on let us go to lunch."

As they walked into the restaurant heads turned with smiling faces, nodding to them as they passed by.

"It looks like it has started already with the WAF incidents. You are going to have to watch your step sir or you could become a local hero."

"That is what I am afraid of Barbara."

After lunch Major Khaleel came to see Bill. "I am sorry Bill but I am not allowed to divulge to you what went on in the Commandant's office. All I am allowed to tell you is they were stripped of their ranks and discharged immediately. They collected their personal belongings then were escorted through the gates of the station."

"No court martial?"

"No sir, it may seem strange to you but we punish strongly anyone who flagrantly breaks our rules and code of conduct and our service men and women are well aware of this. There is nothing unfair about punishing people who do wrong."

"Well said Eric and I am much wiser for it, as we English say, "Point taken."

"Be prepared Bill because I think the Commandant will want a word with you so if you have any plans for the training of the recruits it will be your chance to air them and as you know he is a good listener. The best of luck sir."

"Well Colonel you are certainly living up to your reputation by sorting out two major problems. Now I am looking forward with keen interest to your progress and what you have in mind for sorting out our Recruit Training problems."

"Sir, Sergeant Saleem and Sergeant Anisa are solely in charge of training the recruits. That is not what I want because both of them are far below the standard I require albeit I have helped them to gain more confidence and they are responding very well to my advice but that is not good enough. I want a leader for them, a disciplinarian but not a martinet, a person who understands young people and can talk to them at their own level. My choice sir would be a WAF Officer with a rank that holds some clout behind it and answerable to me. Yes, she would be in charge of both sexes. Then I would like an RAF and a WRAF Drill Sergeant to become seconded to us on a two year secondment. Once they are settled in I would like Sergeants Saleem and Anisa to be sent for three months training to RAF March. With respect sir I would like to add, and make it worthwhile for the RAF personnel to want to come here and I suggest it might be better to have unmarried personnel. The two Sergeants I would like would prove to be a benefit to the training programme in the long term sir by teaching and sharing their skills with other would be Drill Instructors. In the meantime I will continue instilling confidence and advice in the two present instructors."

"Colonel I like your format and the way you are approaching the problem. Actually it is a simple solution that has been staring us in the face and we could not see it. When I report to his Excellency the Emir I am sure he will accept it especially knowing it came from you. He is a very shrewd man and he certainly knew what he was doing when he acquired your services. I will see that your proposals reach the Emir very soon and I will let you know his answer." He rose from his chair and held out his hand. "Colonel Barrett, thank you."

"One other thing sir, if his Excellency approves I would like to recommend the two Sergeants I personally trained who would be ideal for this situation."

"It will be noted Colonel."

Bill gave a smart salute and made his exit.

After leaving Bill went to see Major Khaleel.

"How did the interview go Bill?"

"Great, he agreed with all I asked for and is offering it to the Emir."

"What have you asked for?" He too was pleased when Bill told him. "Why did you not join us years ago Bill? If only you had."

Bill went into Barbara's office only to be greeted with. "You look like the cat that got the cream. That means you have some good news to tell me."

"I have indeed, the Commandant likes my recommendations appertaining to the trainee recruits and he is going to pass them on to the Emir."

"Oh well done sir I am pleased for you, what now?"

"It is playing the waiting game Barbara but I am hoping my team will be in situ not later than in three months time. I hope the two Sergeants I want will be interested, they are young and very bright and I hope to get the chance to recommend them if the Emir approves. Excuse me Barbara I have just thought of something."

He then went to see Major Khaleel. "Eric I have a CD which I always show to new recruits. Have you the facilities to show it to a number of people if so when can you make them available?"

"No problem Bill we have a cinema which can show it and the seating is plentiful. When do you want the show, I can have it arranged say for 10 o'clock tomorrow morning."

"That would be ideal Eric. You might be interested in knowing that the Emir when he was shown it requested a copy. I think it might be a good idea for you to give the Commandant this info' and I would appreciate it if you attended also. I will parade the recruits to see it and anyone else who would be interested will be more than welcome. I can promise you a real eye catcher of a show you will never believe the performance my WRAF recruits put on."

"Your word is good enough for me Bill I will be first in the queue."

Back in his office he asked Barbara to get Captain Khatib on the phone. When his phone rang he identified himself. "Captain this is Colonel Barrett tomorrow morning I want you to shut up shop then be seated in the cinema by 9:45 along with your four fellow officers, good I will see the five of you there."

"Barbara, tomorrow morning we will be shutting up shop and going to the cinema. I want you to take me there to arrive by 9:40am. No I am not giving you the reason why, it would only spoil the surprise. Now will you phone for Fred please? It is home time."

"Has it been a good day for you sir?" asked Fred.

"It has indeed Fred and tomorrow should be an interesting one because I am putting on a film show. I think everyone except the Emir will be there but it won't bother him because he has a copy of the film.

"It sounds interesting sir are you giving any clues as to what it is about?"

"My lips are sealed Fred but of course if you do not turn up I will probably advertise for a more reliable chauffeur."

"You would not do that because I would report you to Mrs Barrett."

"Do you mean to tell me you would pull such a low, underhand conniving trick like that on the hand that feeds you?"

"You have got that all wrong sir it is *you* I will report to Mrs Barrett not the other way round and if you think I will not, try me sir."

"Then I will have you blacklisted. Here we are once again and I will see you tomorrow here then be seated at the cinema by 9:45am. Mashy?"

"Mashy sir," he replied with a grin."

"Hello love," welcomed Tommy giving him a kiss. "Had a good day at the office?"

"As a matter of fact it has been an excellent day, very gratifying."

"Well off you go for your shower and a change of clothes and I will have that nice cool beer waiting for you."

When he rejoined Tommy he asked. "The Sergeants Mess phone at March is it geared up to receive outside calls?"

"Of course it is why, what is on your mind?"

He then told her about the events of the day. I want to get in touch with Sergeant Deacon and Sergeant (w) Dean to see if they are interested in a secondment. If they are I can put their names forward. I could phone Viv and tell her about the secondment then she can relay it to both Sergeants."

"Good thinking dear I will be able to have a short chat with her after you have finished and got what you wanted. Why don't you phone now and ask Jackie or Jill if they will tell Viv to stand by at 6pm their time?"

It was Jackie who answered the phone with a scream of delight when she heard who was phoning. "This is just a quickie Jackie, will you ask Viv Anderson to stand by that phone at 6pm your time I want to speak to her on a matter of some importance. Thank you Mum we will be in touch soon."

"That's that done, now how about something to eat?"

As he followed her to the kitchen he could hear her muttering to herself. 'And how was your day my darling? I do love the way you have a cool beer waiting for me I can't wait to rush home to you.'

He caught up with her and put his arms round her waist and whispered in her ear. "And how was your day my darling?" as they entered the kitchen.

"Behave yourself or you will frighten Leila." who just stood there laughing. "Thomas!" Tommy shouted. "Have you got any Bromide to put in this man's tea?"

The kitchen erupted with laughter, tears were rolling down Leila's cheeks and Thomas had to back away from his cooking stove doubled up with laughter.

"If you have made Thomas spoil my dinner you are sleeping in the back room tonight."

As dinner was being served it was interrupted with bursts of giggling from Leila which affected the rest of them.

"Coffee in the lounge as usual Leila please then off you go home when you are ready, my husband has volunteered to wash the pots haven't you dear?"

"I enjoyed my dinner Thomas, thank you."

The two women just looked at each other and smiled.

At 6pm UK time he rang Viv. Immediately a voice said. "Is that you Colonel?"

"I'll give you Colonel; I should make you stand to attention for that Warrant Officer. It is great speaking to you Viv. Now before I start you can have a chat with Tommy later because this is important, and at present it is top secret." He then explained what his recommendations to the Emir were and why. "What I would like you to do is explain about the secondment to Dot Dean and Alfred Deacon, they are the two I want. They have my word they will like it here and I will be their overall boss. If you can have a word with them now I will ring you back at 8pm your time then you can give me their decision or we try Plan 'B'. After I know the result I will hand you over to Tommy. Oh yes if they have any questions I can always get back to you. Please impress upon them that no-one is to know about this not until it has been finalised. Have you got everything? Good, speak with you later, thanks Viv.... I will just watch a little television before I ring her back Tommy." As he switched on Tommy looked at her watch, *'I'll give him four minutes.'*

Two and a half minutes later he was fast asleep.

At 9:45 Tommy shook him. "Come on sleepy head remember you have a phone call to make and if you are late Viv will put you on Jankers."

After a few yawns and stretches he asked Tommy to get him a cold drink. "Well we will see what the verdict is, fingers crossed pet."

As soon as he dialled Viv answered. "Hello Bill how are you?"

"I have just been woken up by Tommy from having a snooze in front of the Tele.'

"How are things at your end have you got good news for me?"

"I most certainly have."

"They both are very enthusiastic and excited over the project and the first thing I have to thank you for is thinking about them and giving them the first refusal. You should have been here to see their excitement it was a pleasure to see. They realise they will have to be patient but they know with you at the helm they say it will be sooner than later."

"I repeat Viv, ask them please tell no-one or it could cause repercussions and the project sent to the wall this is an opportunity not to be missed. Thanks for everything Viv my regards to the family and the next time you go to the March Hare please put them in the picture. Here is Tommy she can't wait to get on the phone."

"Hi Viv how lovely to speak with you again and I have so much to tell you about life out here it is wonderful I am enjoying every minute." That chat lasted an hour.

"Oh Bill it was lovely talking with her and they do really miss us. She said she has been showing our photo' to everybody and they all commented how smart and dignified you look in your uniform and how well we both are looking. March is not the same exciting station where there was always something happening. Roy is doing his best to keep the Sgts. Mess attractive to the members and their families. Our little lot can't wait for a Saturday night when they can go and have a pleasant evening in the March Hare. Those locals are still barred; Tim and Ann won't have them anywhere near the pub. She says Group Captain Hopwood has made a right good Commanding Officer everyone has a good word for him."

"Yes, he is a good man one who earns respect, I wonder when I get two of his Sgts. if he will accuse me of poaching his staff again I would love to be a fly on the wall when it does happen." He began to laugh. "I can just picture his face."

"If you are ready for a bit of supper I will go and raid Thomas' fridge to see what he has and knowing him we will be spoilt for choice."

CHAPTER 11

"Good morning Fred how are you this lovely morning, have you got your bag of Popcorns ready for this morning's trip to the cinema?"

"Good morning to you sir, you seem happy and cheerful today has Mrs B put an apple in your lunch box?"

"Touché Fred, I see you are also in fine form. Remember this I do not want you doing a runner to the exit when I come round with the hat for contributions to the charity."

"Whose charity would that be sir?"

"A very deserving one Fred...MINE! Watch your driving!" He was still laughing when he got out of the car at his destination. See you later Fred and do not be late."

Fred drove away laughing to himself and shaking his head murmuring, what a character.

"Good morning Barbara any messages?"
"No sir."

He rang the Major to ask if the Commandant would be attending the film show.

"Definitely Colonel he is looking forward to seeing your handiwork."

"Are you accompanying him Eric?"

"Yes, I will be going with him in his car."

"Barbara, I am just nipping over to have a word with the recruits, you and I will make our way to the cinema when I get back."

"Good morning Sergeant Saleem," he replied to the salute, I want a quick word with the flight. You are to be seated at 9:40 at the cinema, the Station Commandant will be present and when he enters the cinema I will call out 'The Station Commandant and you will rise from your seats and stand to attention until he is seated. MASHY?"

"MASHY sir" was the loud and cheerful reply"

"Bill laughed. "Enjoy the show."

He then went to see Sergeant (w) Anisa and the female recruits and told them the same.

"Come on Barbara escort me to the cinema."

Inside were attendants who would usher everyone to seats. Bill had a word with them to make sure they knew the Commandant would be attending.

"Yes sir the seating order has been arranged and we have everything organised."

"Well done I am impressed with your efficiency. I will greet the Commandant outside and you will escort him to his seat. Please seat my Personal Assistant among the dignitaries."

Outside, the recruits were lined up and waiting for the command to enter and did so when he gave the two Sergeants the nod to enter. Everything ran smoothly and soon everyone was seated and waiting for the Commandant to appear.

At 9:55 when the Commandant arrived Bill waited for him to climb out of the car then gave him a very smart salute. "Welcome to BlueBelles on Parade Sir."

"Good morning Colonel, I have been given to understand his Excellency is the proud possessor of a copy of your film."

"Indeed he is sir and it gave him a great deal of excitement when he watched it."

"Then I have something to look forward to Colonel. Come let us go and not keep the troops waiting," he said with a smile.

As they entered Bill shouted, "The Station Commandant". Everyone got to their feet in respect and stood to attention until he was seated.

Bill then went onto the stage to face his audience.

"SIR, Ladies and gentlemen Welcome to BlueBelles on Parade. It is my pleasure and privilege to show you two films of WRAF recruits who I stress had only been training in the Royal Air Force for three weeks. When you see them in action you will be convinced I am telling Porkie Pies. Porkie Pies is one of the English favourite sayings for telling lies, which I am not." The audience as one burst out laughing and made them relax and increase their interest. The first film is a challenge between the boys and the girls. Of course the boys thought it would be a walk over for them because who had ever heard of girls beating boys at drill. He then went into the training methods he applied along with a WRAF Sergeant.

He caused uproars of laughter from his audience who he now had in the palm of his hand when he told them about the Wibbly Wobblies, it was a little time before he could carry on. He got laughter and applause especially from the female members of the audience when he told them about the Battle of the NAAFI and the Knock-Out Kid when she called her adversary the boy who was stripped in the park, Mr Teeny Weenie. Now Ladies and gentlemen we will watch the first film. Entitled BlueBelles On Parade 1. It was the name their Sergeant Instructor gave them.

When the film got to the stage where the very minimum of commands were given there were sounds of ohs' and ahs'. At the end the audience as one applauded and the WAF recruits began to cheer.

Bill returned on the stage. You boys and girl recruits should remember and take note of what can be done with the right training and the will to prove that you also can do what you have just seen. I have a surprise for you because at the end of your course I am proposing a contest between you AF boys and you WAF girls. Now we come to the second film which took place two years after the first contest, named BlueBelles 2. This was an Inter-Service challenge between the Royal Navy, the Army and The Royal Air Force. He went into great lengths to tell them how and why BlueBelles 2 was formed and trained. I will not spoil the show by telling you the result of the competition so we will start the film and I hope you are not too disappointed with the result.

There was complete silence while the Navy and the Army carried out their routines but when the WRAF team came out to do theirs the entire audience began to clap and cheer. As soon as they began silence fell in the cinema but when they commenced their specialised routine there was pandemonium of cheering for the BlueBelles. Then when the result was announced the audience got to its feet to applaud while the recruits continued to cheer. When all the applause had subsided The Commandant rose to his feet and went on to the stage taking Bill along with him.

"Wasn't that a wonderful show? I do not think for one minute that during all that excitement that you realised that Colonel Barrett was the instigator and trainer of all the BlueBelles and I feel privileged and so should every one of you especially the training staff that he is here with us on our team. I think he deserves a round of applause, don't you? He led the applause then shook him by the hand thanking him. I can understand now why his Excellency wanted a copy, what a wonderful achievement for those young girls."

When Bill escorted him to his car he wound down his window and said. "Thank you again Colonel for giving my training staff's morale such a big boost and mine too."

Bill saluted him as the car sped away. He was then faced with the two flights of recruits who were all called to attention as their respective Sergeants saluted Bill and brought spontaneous applause from the recruits. He returned the salute then told the Sergeants to march them off then stand them down for the rest of the day.

Barbara was waiting to accompany him back to the office and as they walked she said. "You put on an excellent show sir your talk had us rolling in our seats it was really funny but informative. I must congratulate you for what you did for all those girls and when they were announced the winners there were more faces than mine with tears of happiness rolling down our cheeks, those girls were wonderful. You and your Sergeant deserved a medal for what you did."

"We were honoured Barbara. I received the Meritorious Service Medal and Sergeant Anderson received the British Empire Medal and promoted to Flight Sergeant, she should have received the MBE for what she did. Anyhow she is now a Warrant Officer and has just been awarded the MBE."

"That is wonderful and if I have done my sums correctly you were responsible for putting smiles on faces. Am I right?"

"I just helped where I could."

"You are a good man Colonel Barrett and I am fortunate to have been chosen to work for you."

"We don't make a bad team Barbara Battle. We'll go back to the office have a wash and brush up then go to lunch. Mashy?"

"Mashy," she replied with a grin.

On entering the restaurant they received polite applause from some of the diners and Bill raised his arm in acknowledgement. "It appears our fame is spreading sir."

"I won't mind so long as they don't bring a candlelit cake to the table in celebration."

Barbara had to cover her mouth with a handkerchief to stop and hide the laugh that was trying to burst out. Please don't start me giggling or I shall have to make a quick exit."

After a good lunch they retired to the quiet lounge with coffee then the questions began to flow from Barbara about the forming and training of BlueBelles 2.

"Tomorrow I will bring my two framed photos of the two teams and I will introduce you to them, then I will hang them in a prominent place of honour."

"And so you jolly well should."

No sooner had they returned to their offices than the Major came bounding in. He grabbed Bill's hand and pumped until Bill told him to let go. "I have never seen anything like that ever Bill, it was amazing I was sat on the edge of my seat as they were going through their special repertoire willing them to out-drill their opponents. Even the Commandant was clenching his fists and urging them on, I have never seen him so excited and it was catching. When the result was announced the Commandant threw up his arms in a congratulatory gesture with many more reacting the same way and you heard the cheering. There could not have been a better reaction if we had been watching it live. Bill, I am so proud to be able to call you my friend."

"Barbara, do you fancy a brew?" I could murder one.

"Be right there in a couple of minutes sir."

When she brought it in he asked. "Where's yours?"

"In my office."

"If you are not busy bring it in here if you like."

She returned with her mug. "I was only bringing the diary up to date and I have not even filled a page with your engagements yet."

"It will come in time but it will probably be later than sooner I'm afraid but do not let it get you down."

"How are you getting on with speaking Arabic?"

"Oh I pick up the odd word now and again but I have trouble retaining it. There is one word I really do like which is Mashy. I think it a great little word which has plenty of uses. Fred my driver gave me that, he is quite a character is our Fred, he teases me as much as I do him."

"He is a special person, obviously you have not been told but while he is with you he protects you, in some way like a bodyguard would and that goes for Tommy also when he takes her anywhere. Obviously when you dismiss him he cannot carry out his duties but please do not give away any clues that you know this. It is just a precautionary measure taken with any VIP worth protecting both you and Tommy come under that category I am pleased to say. I would not mention it to Tommy it may alarm her and it would not do for her to keep looking over her shoulder when she is out shopping, she might forget what she went shopping for," she said with a smile.

"Thanks for that information Barbara it is good to know who one is rubbing shoulders with. I think we may as well lock up and go home now. By the way who does lock-up behind us and opens up for us in a morning?"

"We have a security system in operation twenty four hours a day. Guards check when everyone has left the building. They clear each room individually with the ops' room then that room is locked from there by remote control. That is to make sure no-one enters that room when the guard leaves it. I do not know how many guards carry out the checks but several are given a certain areas to cover and they are held responsible for it. At exactly on time in a morning all offices are opened automatically"

"I call that a very good security system Barbara and you are a mine of information."

After she had gone to wash the mugs Bill sat there and began to think abut the information she had given him. I think, he said to himself there is more to Miss Battle than meets the eye. I wonder if she let it slip deliberately about Fred being a security man to let me know without confiding in me that she is also a security woman seconded to me personally. She seems to know more about security as a newcomer secretary than what I would expect. I will find out for sure sooner or later Miss Battle, I can play the waiting game.

"Ring for Fred please Barbara it is going home time."

"Congratulations sir you put on a very good show for everyone and I was just one who was glued to the screen and jumped to my feet in excitement when the BlueBelles won. You and your Sergeant did a great job, you know it was hard to believe those girls had only three weeks training when you took charge of them."

"Thank you Fred but I forgot to mention that two of those girls had only two weeks training before they joined the BlueBelles."

"I was telling some of my associates about it, they would like to know when you would be running it again because they would like to see it. I am sure if you do the cinema would be full."

"There is no reason why we cannot have another showing Fred and I will let you know when it is convenient to do so, probably when the new recruits arrive."

"Thank you, sir."

"What sort of a day have you had dear?" asked Tommy giving him a kiss.

"Very satisfying, I showed the BlueBelles film and everyone has gone ecstatic over it."

"I am not surprised it should have won an Oscar. Right, shower and get changed and a cool beer will be waiting for you."

"Thanks love," he said giving her a kiss. When he returned he said. "There is a good smell coming from the kitchen when the door opens, what are we having?"

"Just something Thomas has thrown together I understand."

"Well he can carry on throwing it together more often if it tastes as good as it smells. Come on then I can feel my taste buds tingling. Good evening Thomas and Leila."

"Good evening sir, have you had a good day or a hard day at the office? Thomas asked with a grin.

"Excellent thank you and if my meal is not on the table in two minutes I will go back to my office and order a take-away."

"Coming up now sir," he said grinning all over his face.

"I don't believe it, Roast Beef and Yorkshire pudding with all the trimmings." He never said another word until he had cleared his plate. He rose from his chair went to Thomas wrung his hand and gave him a hug. Thank you Thomas, that was wonderful and what a surprise to come home to that meal. Now that has made my day and everything is alright with the world."

"Would you like Apple Pie with custard to finish your meal off with sir?" asked Leila.

"Will someone give me a pinch? I must be in heaven. The whole meal was cooked to perfection thank you both we are very grateful for the care you take of us. I suppose you had a hand in it," he said talking to Tommy.

"I just gave the instructions and Thomas did the cooking, he made enough for him and Leila to try, now shall we leave them to sit down and enjoy it? We will have coffee when you have finished Leila but please, take your time. Just bring coffee for me because in two minutes flat he will be fast asleep after he has turned the Television on."

CHAPTER 12

"Good morning Barbara, any messages?"
"No messages sir but Major Khaleel would like to see you when it is convenient."
"Right I will go and see him now it could be something important."
He knocked on the Major's door and entered to the call of 'Come in'.
"Good morning Bill I have some news you will be interested in. His Excellency the Emir is in London for talks on where Sam Barnes should be tried. On good authority it is a stalemate between our two countries. The Brits' say because he is a UK subject he should be tried in the UK. The Emir insists because he was employed by Aljibia and he committed the offence of perpetrating the security of our country we have the rights to put him on trial, so where is it going to end?"
"Politics Eric, keep well clear of them. Personally from my point of view I think the Emir is well within his rights but I can see a lot of hard bargaining being carried out and there will be no winner. Between you and me Eric I would like him to be tried here, given a thirty year sentence one third to be carried out here and two thirds in the UK. Do you think your people will go ahead and put your perpetrator on trial Eric despite what is going on in the UK?"
"Your guess is as good as mine Bill but whatever happens I will keep you in the picture."
"By the way Eric, has the Commandant made any move to obtaining the WAF officer I requested?"
"I think he is waiting to submit your entire recommendations to the Emir to get his approval but this business in the UK takes priority and I do not think we will get a result until that is settled."
"Good news or bad news sir?" Asked Barbara when he had returned to his office.
"I don't think I can give you a direct answer Barbara."
When he told her the news she replied. "I see what you mean sir, it is stalemate."
"If I am wanted I will be with Captain Khatib I want to see how he is getting on with the project I set him and his staff and yes, I have my bleeper with me." He saw as he walked towards Captain Khatib's office that the four Officers were too interested in what they were doing to notice him. "Good morning Captain," he responding to the Captain's greeting. "How is the project going? I have had no cry for help so I must assume you are having no problems."

"No sir, we are doing very well and we find it very interesting, my staff is enjoying doing it because it has given them something to keep them from boredom."

"Shall we go and have a word and see how they are progressing? Did you have any problems with the store people in issuing the materials?"

"Initially yes but when I used your secret weapon the change was dramatic, I could have had the moon if I so wished."

Bill had a word with the four officers and was impressed with their individual progress.

"You are doing a good job Captain keep up the good work."

"Excuse me sir, now you have got rid of those two WAF officers are you going to replace them?"

"I will put it this way Captain, there are going to be changes and my recommendations have been forwarded to his Excellency the Emir for his approval."

On his way to see what progress the recruits had made he checked on his bleeper which was sounding off and saw he was to report to Major Khaleel. He immediately change direction and reported to his office. "Hello Bill we have just received a signal from the Embassy in London. You are to report there as soon as possible. You are to travel in Mufti but carry your uniform and your stay will be between one and two weeks. RAF March will be included in the itinerary."

"Brilliant, it would be better if I could take my wife with me Eric."

"Leave it with me Bill I will see what I can do."

"It looks like the Emir is going along with my recommendations Eric this visit is going to be very interesting indeed. I will be in my office waiting to hear from you, if not I will be at lunch."

On returning to his office he called Barbara on the inter-com. "Are you ready for lunch Miss Battle?"

"We are early sir!"

"Yes indeed, needs must, so drop whatever you are doing and I will explain over lunch, Mashy?"

He heard her laugh, "Mashy, sir."

They received smiles and nods from other diners as they were escorted to their table. "Looks like we are still the flavour of the month," he said as he sat down while returning a nod. I hope I am still in favour when I tell you that you will be in sole charge of the office for a week or so."

"Why, where are you going?

"Do you remember that nursery rhyme? 'Pussy cat, pussy cat, where have you been?"

"I've been to London to see the Queen," she continued.

"Well substitute Emir for the Queen."

"My words, that is an honour is it related to your recommendations for personnel replacements, or could it be related to your favourite enemy?"

"You mean Sam Barnes? I never thought of that, now you could be right and here is me thinking I was getting the chance to see my friends and I will not know until I get to the Embassy. Ah! But wait a minute, Eric told me I would be visiting RAF March."

While they were having coffee his bleep went off showing Major Khaleel's name.

"Here goes I'll soon find out if it is a Yeah or Nay."

"Come in," said the Major. Unfortunately the news is you are to go alone and you will be travelling by private jet, your ETD is 05:00hrs. All arrangements have been made your chauffeur will pick you up at 03:30 hrs. And you will be met at Heathrow Airport."

"Have you any clues on what this is all about Eric?"

"I think you are going in an advisory capacity Bill for the secondment of the two personnel you want and the training of our two personnel. Now are you clear on everything?"

"I am and thank you Eric for putting me in the picture." They shook hands and Eric wished him the best of luck.

"Barbara, I have to leave you now I have a very early start in the morning and yes, it is about the replacements. So hold the fort until I return and keep your diary up to date. Give Fred a ring please."

"The best of luck sir and I want to see a big smiling face peering through that door on your return."

"To the city bank Fred and make it snappy I am in a hurry."

"I have already been briefed for tomorrow morning sir, would you like me to give you an early call?"

"If you did you would need to wear ear protectors for my reply. Take care of Mrs Barrett Fred and try your best to steer her clear of the clothes shops."

"I will park outside the bank sir and if I am moved on I will come and stand at the entrance."

On entering the bank the same young man welcomed him and asked if he needed help.

"I want the currency exchange counter please."

"Come with me sir." He took him to Mr Haddad's office.

"Ah Colonel Barrett do come in, can I offer you some refreshment?"

"No thank you Mr Haddad I am in a hurry and would like to change some money into pound sterling. He told him how much he wanted and Haddad pressed a bell and an assistant came in.

"He gave him Bill's cheque. "I want that changing to pounds sterling and be quick about it because the Colonel is in a hurry."

It took only a minute or two and he was back, Bill thanked him for his promptness. "Thank you Mr Haddad for your help I do appreciate it." They shook hands and Bill left a beaming bank manager.

"Home Fred and put your clog down."

"What does that mean sir I have never heard that expression before?"

"It means put your foot down on the accelerator pedal, in other words, step on the gas."

"Fred laughed, "Ah, I know what you mean now. You English have some funny expressions but I like them. When I go back to the motor pool I have a laugh with my friends when I repeat them and they see the funny side of them. They will have a good laugh at 'put your clog down'." Here we are sir," he said as he opened the door and saluted. "I will see you in the morning sir."

"Thanks Fred."

When he walked in home Tommy looked at him. "Why are you home so early?" she asked.

"Just give me chance to shower, change and over a nice cool beer I will tell you the whole story."

"Well be quick about it I am dying to know."

When he returned he had a good swig of his beer then began to tell Tommy what was happening. "I am not allowed to come with you then, well I think that is very mean of the Emir. How long did you say you were going for?"

"Anything between one and two weeks but you will not be alone; you have Thomas and Leila to take care of you, Ella and John who will take you to the club if you want. Then of course you have Fred and the car at your disposal so I do not have to worry about how you are coping."

"Yes, I suppose I am fortunate to have friends around me, sorry Emir I did not mean it."

"Come here said Bill giving her a kiss I will phone you to tell you how I am getting on. I expect Jackson will get a shock when he is told to pick me up at the airport. I hope to see our family when we go to March won't they get a shock when they see me turn up. I hope the Emir will give me a little time to see them or it will be a big disappointment for everybody. The only thing I am nervous about Tommy is meeting the AOC because he and Group Captain Pilling were very close and I am wondering if he has taken umbrage with me over Pilling's demotion."

"Why should he? Pilling brought it upon himself treating you like dirt, perhaps Group Captain Hopwood has told him the truth I think you will have him as a champion in your corner love. Think of that old service motto…'Nil Carborundum Illegitimus'."

"I will do just that pet."

At dinner he told Thomas and Leila he would be away for a few days and I am going to miss your cooking Thomas so ask my wife to show you more recipes because when I return I shall expect your culinary expertise to rank among the big names of Haute cuisine."

"I will try my best, sir."

"Good man. Come on love we will go and have coffee then I will get my packing done."

CHAPTER 13

At 2am Leila knocked on their bedroom door and entered, "Your early morning tea sir…madam."

Tommy woke immediately. "Oh thank you Leila." She shook Bill awake to a series of grunts and groans. "Come on Leila has just brought you early morning tea and I mean *early*."

"Give me a minute to come round. What is it?"

"Leila is here with your tea."

He jumped with a start. "I haven't over-slept have I?"

"No, Leila and Thomas have very kindly come to make sure you were up and not leaving on an empty stomach. Your breakfast will be on the table at 3am, now stir yourself."

Leila left the room having a good laugh.

At 3am prompt Bill walked into the kitchen. "Good Morning Thomas …Leila. It is very kind of you both to go to all the trouble of making sure I did not oversleep and leave here without something to eat. It is worth a few hours missed sleep to eat a breakfast like this. Ah, here comes Sleeping Beauty," as Tommy came into the kitchen carrying the tea tray.

"If it was left to your devices you would still be snoring your head off. I will have my breakfast now please Thomas then when we get rid of the lodger we can all go back to bed and get up at a civilised hour." The banter between Bill and Tommy never failed to amuse Thomas and Leila.

The door bell rang at 3:30am Fred was on time. "Come in Fred have you time for a brew? Your boss is still sorting himself out. Would you like a bacon butty to help you on your way? Yes you do. Thomas will you make Fred a bacon butty and a brew I am sure he has had nothing to eat yet."

Bill arrived on the scene to see Fred tucking into sandwiches and a brew.

"What is going on have we opened a home for waifs and strays? I will make sure that feast you are having is deducted from your wages, no wonder I am always skint."

"What does he mean by skint Mrs Barrett?"

"It means Mafeesh Felouse Fred (no money) Mashy?"

"Mashy, Mrs Barrett."

"Are you ready Fred you do realise I have a plane to catch today and not (ba'deen bukkra?" (later tomorrow)

"Aiwa (Yes) Colonel."

"Bye love," he said kissing Tommy, "and take good care of my staff."

"Mashy Colonel," she replied to the delight of Thomas, Leila and Fred.

As they drove off Fred said. "Your staff think the world of you and Mrs Barrett."

"And we are very fond of them Fred, show respect you will get respect in return but apart from that we are very lucky they were chosen for us."

"Here we are sir; I will just park up then take you to your privileged check-out."

When that was done Fred said. "Good luck with your mission sir, I hope everything goes well for you and you come back to us a happy man. Salaam Colonel." (goodbye)

"Salaam Fred."

Bill went through emigration and into the VIP lounge and got himself a seat where he could watch the indicator screen. Looking round he saw perhaps a dozen people who he surmised were fellow passengers and not recognising any of them he picked up a local newspaper and settled himself down to read. At 4:30am all passengers were called to the flight. As he boarded he recognised the stewardess who was on the flight when he and Tommy flew initially from London. He chose his seat away from the other passengers not wanting to become involved if any of them wanted to come and nosey, as he put it. He wanted to run through what might lie ahead and how he would react to any adverse reactions. He was wakened by the Stewardess wanting to know if he would like breakfast. *Shall I or shan't I he mused to himself, well it will be a longish wait until lunch.* "Yes please he answered."

She gave him a menu. "It will be served in an hour's time sir."

"Thank you." *That is good he said to himself I may have worked up an appetite by then.* He chose what he wanted and decided he would have tea thinking that coffee would keep him awake and he had some lost sleep to catch up on. He gave his choice to the stewardess then settled himself down and within a couple of minutes he was fast asleep. A gentle shake of his shoulder woke him to see the stewardess standing there.

"Your breakfast sir."

"Thank you," he replied. He looked at his watch, which read 6:30am. He downed his grapefruit juice in one, Ah, that's better, he then tucked into a good English breakfast. When he had finished and was drinking his tea *he laughed to himself thinking of Tommy's reaction if she had been with him. 'Bill Barrett you are a greedy pig but it shows you have got a very healthy appetite' are you going to have a second helping?* "No! I am not he blurted out aloud."

"I beg your pardon sir."

He looked up to see the stewardess standing there with a hot jug of tea. "I am so sorry I was thinking out aloud."

"Would you like more tea sir," she said with a smile.

"Yes please."

'Plonker,' said Tommy's voice in his ear. He laughed to himself, if only she knew. He soon settled himself down to sleep after his food tray had been collected. He was roused an hour later by a voice announcing they would be landing at Dubai in fifteen minutes. *Good he thought I will go and stretch my legs and get a breath of fresh air.* The voice continued. "Passengers are requested to stay in their seats because we are on a tight schedule and are just picking up passengers." *Ah' well back to sleep Noddy.*

The rest of the flight was uneventful, he passed his time sleeping, making notes and reading the 'In-flight magazine'.

"Ladies and gentlemen we will be landing at Heathrow in fifteen minutes please re-adjust your watches to…10:48am Greenwich Mean Time and please obey the signs, Fasten your Seat Belts."

On landing it was just a formality going through immigration and customs. *I hope it is Jackson who will be meeting me he said to himself* as he made his way to the Incoming Passengers Terminal. He spotted Jackson who was waving. They shook hands and embraced as good friends do.

"Welcome home Bill," said a delighted Jackson, "Gosh it is good to see you again and you looking so well, what does it feel like underneath that fingers down the throat sun-tan?"

"A bit chilly old friend but seeing you waiting to greet me has warmed the cockles."

"How is Tommy?" was his next question, "Joyce and I were thrilled to bits with the photos, my words but you look just the part dressed up in your finery. How long are you staying and is it business? I know I have to take you straight to the Embassy."

"Anything between one and two weeks but it will not be entirely in London and I am now on my way to be briefed. I do not even know where I am staying, any room at your house?"

"You are more than welcome and Joyce would be as delighted as me if you could stay with us."

"Well we will soon know, here we are. Have you been ordered to wait for me?"

"I most certainly have, so don't take all day because I want to know what is going on."

He entered the Embassy and approached reception. "Colonel Barrett" said the receptionist, "You are expected so will you please take a seat, you will be attended to directly."

Very soon the same member of staff who had previously given him the gen on the airport procedures approached with outstretched hand. "How nice to see you again Colonel Barrett we have been hearing of your exploits which have made quite a big impression here at the Embassy. If you will come with me I will take you to see his Excellency." He knocked and opened the door on command. "Colonel Barrett, sir."

"Come in Colonel," the Emir greeted Bill holding out his hand to shake Bill's. "Did you have a good flight?"

"Yes sir it was a very a comfortable one I slept most of the way."

"And how is your lovely wife Tommy? He said with a smile.

"She sends her regards sir, she loves your country and people and I have to thank that very nice Emir for everything he has done for us and she hopes to have the pleasure of seeing you again."

"That is most kind of her. Sit yourself down Colonel. I have much to thank you for, in the short space of time you have been in my service you have been responsible for uncovering a spy network and bringing the perpetrators of my country to justice."

"Excuse my interruption sir but I was not alone in this incident, Major Khaleel played a big part in getting the person who I called the mystery man identified."

"Thank you Colonel that is what I would expect from a man of honour. The other thing I am impressed with is your handling of the recruit training problems. I received your recommendations for improvements and after studying it carefully I agree with it. I have had meetings with the MoD who think your ideas are sound and good for the relationship between our two countries. The Air Commodore of Training Command has been briefed to assist us completely with no obstacles put in our way.

Now that we have the full backing of the MoD, are there any changes you would like to make?""

"No sir, although I would like to take all the training staff back with me but the MoD would chase me out of the country. Do you intend to interview the two Sergeants sir?"

"Yes, I think it only courteous but you will sit in with me."

"Forgive me if I sound mercenary sir but will you make it worth their while accepting? Yes it is a secondment and they can be ordered to come to us but we want staff that are going to be willing and happy to do a good job for us and not under forced medicine."

"I see your point Colonel and understand what you are saying, have you any suggestions of what perks I can give them?"

"Their RAF service pay does not reach the standard of most countries by far and although they would receive overseas pay it would not break the bank. Can I suggest you give them a little bit extra for their pocket, an upgrade to Warrant Officer a courtesy car each and lastly, accommodation they could write home about with pride and become the envy of their service comrades."

"Colonel Barrett I like your attitude towards your subordinates it is very commendable. Now where to hold the interviews? I think we will hold them here on home ground. It is a long way to travel for a few minutes interview besides sparing the airmen having to 'Bull' the place up for our visit I think that is your terminology. I know you would like to see your friends so this is what I propose doing. In two day's time I will lay an aircraft on to take you to Leeds airport, there you will find a Rent-a Car at your disposal for four days. On the morning of the fourth day you will convey your two Sergeants to the airport where you will collect air tickets for the three of you. Transport will pick you up at Heathrow and convey you to the Savoy Hotel where rooms are booked for the three of you and I will take care of the bill. Next morning you all will report here to the Embassy. When our interview is finished the Sergeants will be given an itinerary for the next few days, of course you will be their chaperone during that time. On its completion they will return by air to Leeds where RAF transport will be waiting to return them to their unit to await further orders from me. In the meantime a signal would have been sent to the Station Commander at RAF March requesting the two Sergeants be released for at least four days and Colonel Barrett will pick them up by personal transport, the dates of course will be included in the signal. I want to know if any obstacles of any kind are put in your way and by whom."

"I think they have learned their lesson about that, sir. By the way sir, I will be staying with friends for the first two nights so I don't need the Savoy until I return with the two Sergeants.

"Excellent Colonel, I think we have got everything sewn up, so the next time we meet will be on the day of the interviews." He held out his hand saying as he shook Bill's, "thank you Colonel and in the modern idiom I think you and I are on the same wave length."

"We certainly are sir and thank you for everything."

As he turned to leave, the door appeared to open by magic and a member of staff appeared to show him out.

"Jackson was waiting in the car and as Bill climbed in he asked "Well?"

"You have got a lodger for a couple of days old friend."

"Bloody brilliant, I phoned Joyce to tell her you were back in town and her reply was, 'bring him home with you'. How did the interview go and before you tell me…it went in your favour, right?"

"Right, but wait till we get home then I can fill you both in of our experiences in Aljibia but my priority is to phone Tommy."

"You can phone her as often as you like Bill."

Jackson pushed Bill forward when they entered the house; he opened the connecting door to the lounge slightly and saw Joyce was reading a newspaper. Without looking up she asked. "Have you brought him home?"

Bill answered. "No but *I* brought *him* home."

She screamed and jumped up from the chair and came to him with arms outstretched so she could hug and kiss him.

"Oh you lovely man it is so wonderful to see you, how is Tommy?"

"She was fine when I left but Jackson said I can phone her from here so you will be able to ask her yourself because she will definitely want to speak to you both."

"Can I make you a brew and something to eat?"

"No thanks I will eat when you do but I would like a shower to freshen up please and a beer afterwards."

"He is staying with us for a couple of days love so we will be able to get all the gen from the horse's mouth."

"Oh that is wonderful, the bed is made up but give me a minute to put you some towels out. Get him a beer Clarry while he is waiting and get yourself one to be sociable."

He looked at Bill and with a wink said. "I am right glad you came."

"There is no call for you to be facetious Jackson." was the call from the stairs.

After freshening up Bill asked if he could use the phone.

"Of course you can it is at the foot of the stairs,"

He got through to Tommy quite quickly, on the first ring she picked up the receiver. "Hello Barretts"

"Hi flower, were you waiting by the phone for me ringing?"

"No not really, I was just passing by."

"You are telling Porky Pies and setting a bad example to the staff."

"Where are you phoning from?"

"The Jackson's house, I am staying here for two days then I have been given leave to go to March for three days to see our family and bring the two Sergeants back to London for interviews although it is a foregone conclusion that they are coming to Aljibia." He quickly ran through the day's happenings then asked what kind of a day she had. Do you want a word with Joyce and Jackson?"

"Oh yes please that would be lovely."

"Joyce! your presence is required" Bill shouted.

Joyce could not get to the phone quick enough.

"Hello Tommy love this is some bonus being able to speak to you."

"Would you like another beer Bill? They will be chatting for some time yet so we might as well relax with a drink."

Bill commenced telling him their experiences starting with the flight to Aljibia, their accommodation and what a couple of pearls they had got with Thomas the Chef and his wife Leila who think the world of us both but thinks Tommy walks on water. He was well into his experience with the spying episode when Joyce called.

"Clarry, your lady friend wants a word."

Jackson got up grinning and hurried to the phone. "Hello Tommy good to be able to speak to you I believe you have settled down nicely, how is your Arabic coming along, have you learnt the swear words yet?" and so it went on for some time until Bill was called for.

"I will ring you tomorrow about 6 o'clock your time love will that be alright?"

"Mashy," he heard her laugh. "Salaam love."

"Salaam, love." she replied.

"She is really enjoying it out there Bill," said Joyce "and that beautiful Villa I would love to see it."

"Maybe you will Joyce at some stage, we would love to have you both staying with us we have plenty of room, four bedrooms to be exact. Tommy is teaching Thomas the Chef some good old English recipes and already he has proved himself with them. You know how she acted with me and Jackson prior to us going off, well she does that with me and they both curl up with laughter. 'Oh Mrs Barrett,' Leila said one day when Tommy was pretending to give me some stick, "you do make us laugh and please will you stay with us for ever'? Tommy then had to go and comfort her because she had become quite emotional."

"Ah, that was nice, wasn't it Clarry? I'll go now and start making the dinner, you are not a finicky eater are you Bill?"

"Not me Joyce, I like my food, put it in front of me and I will eat it."

After dinner they sat and listened to Bill's tale of life in Aljibia and his role in the reshaping the Recruit's Training.

The following morning he rang Barbara his PA and asked her to bring Major Khaleel to the phone because he did not know his number. "Hello Colonel how are you and how is it in London?"

"Eric this is important to me and I want you to be brief. I have been successful in getting the two Sergeants that I wanted and they are both single people. What will their accommodation be and where? I think they are to be promoted to Warrant Officer Status."

"The two separate accommodations are situated in the domestic area and single service men and women have a personal self-contained apartment in the buildings each has its own restaurant. The alternative is a self contained apartment outside the perimeter of the station but they would then have to support themselves. If for instance they move into the domestic site and decide they want to support themselves they can move into the apartments outside the station."

"Eric, the restaurants…'

"I know what you are going to ask Bill and the answer is yes, they do have a European menu as well so there should be no problem. If you want any more gen here is my number."

"Thanks Eric I wanted to answer the questions they are bound to ask and I am trying to cover everything. Put Barbara back on please. Hello Barbara everything here is going well, I have got what I asked for and more besides."

"I was hoping you would succeed sir and before you ask there are no messages for you either.

"Thank you Miss Battle, Bye for now."

"What are you doing with yourself today Bill?" asked Jackson.

"I don't really know for I am at a bit of a loose end and I don't fancy roaming the streets. I think I'll go and have a shufti in Harrods and see what I can pick up for Tommy. Where is the best place to go to buy an old fashioned Home Recipe Book Joyce? I want one for Thomas our Chef."

"There is a Bookshop close to Harrods that deals in old books but I can't remember its name."

"I know where it is, I'll run you there Bill and if you let me know when you want to come back I will pick you up."

"Thanks, I will stay out for lunch Joyce that is if I feel like any after that good breakfast. Right then, I'm ready when you are Jackson." They grabbed their coats and made their way to the Bookshop.

"Harrods is about a hundred yards that way, you can't miss it. What time do you want me to come for you will 3 o'clock here be alright?"

"That should be fine, I have to phone Tommy at 4 o'clock remember, they are two hours ahead of our time."

He entered the store and began to search for the cookery section. A female assistant asked if she could help. When he told her what he was looking for she led him to the section he wanted. She then showed him the selection of books that matched what he was looking for. He flipped through quite a number before picking one out and taking it to a table where he spent some time browsing through it until he was sure it was the one he wanted. He took it to the sale counter to where the same assistant was waiting.

"You have good taste sir; your wife will love it."

"Actually it is for a foreign gentleman friend who is a Chef in his own country and is interested in Old English Recipes."

"Then if he serves some of these recipes to his clientele his maitre d' will be kept busy."

"Thank you that sounds interesting, would you please cut the price tag out it is to be a present."

"Then he is a very lucky man sir, would you like it gift wrapped, sir?"

"Thank you that would be nice." With it wrapped very nicely and placed in a strong carrier bag he made his way to Harrods. He wandered around trying to think what Tommy had drooled over the last they were here. Finally he decided on bottles of 'Smellies' for Tommy, Leila and Barbara. He asked if he could have them gift wrapped individually. *That takes care of that he said to himself, a good job well done.*

At 3 o'clock Jackson arrived. "Had a successful day Bill?"

"I have, I think I will be in Tommy's good books when I get back."

"Sit yourselves down and I will make you a brew," said Joyce. "Did you get any lunch Bill?"

"No I was too busy doing my shopping and that took too much of my time up. By the way Joyce, can I leave my shopping here until I am ready to go home?"

"Of course you can, that is no problem. Are you taking Bill to the club tonight Clarry?"

"I don't want to go Jackson, I have a couple of phone calls I want to make and what time have you been ordered to pick me up in the morning?" he said with a grin.

"You have to catch the flight at 8 o'clock so you will have to be up early and Joyce will send you off with a good breakfast."

"If I leave my uniform here will you bring it with you when you come to pick me up at Heathrow because I will need it the following morning to sit in with the Emir for the interviews? I would like to make two phone calls if I may, one to book a room at our local pub in the March village and one to Tommy."

"That is no problem Bill you are more than welcome."

"Thanks I will ring the pub first then I can tell Tommy where I am staying." He rang the number to hear Ann's voice say. "The March Hare Public House can I help you?" He did not reply but began to whistle the Blue-Belles' signature tune. He heard her scream "Bill Barrett it is you isn't it?"

"Hello Ann, yes and I am here in London on official business."

"Is there any chance you can come up to see us Bill? Oh please say yes."

"If you can put me up at the pub for three nights commencing tomorrow. Yes."

She screamed in delight. "Is Tommy with you?"

"I'm afraid not but I will be phoning her after I have finished speaking to you."

"Then I cannot offer you the bridal suite she said with a laugh, but you will have the best room we have got. Oh Bill you have no idea what pleasure it has given me to hear your voice. When will you be arriving?"

"I will be on a private aircraft ETD 8 o'clock from Heathrow and there will be a Rent a Car waiting for me at Leeds Airport so I reckon it should be about 11 o'clock when I see you."

"Tim will be sorry he missed you, he is out on an errand just now. I have to leave you Bill I am the only one on duty and I think the natives are getting restless, somebody is banging on the bar, I'll give them banging on my bar when I see who it is give our love to Tommy, bye Bill"

He rang Tommy who answered with "Hello Barretts."

"Hi flower, Tommy wanted to know everything he had been doing and she was chuffed when he told her he had been speaking with Ann Wilson. She sends their love to you and I will phone you from there tomorrow night about 6 o'clock. Do you want a word with Joyce?"

"Yes please."

"Joyce, you are wanted on the phone."

"Hello Tommy."

"Has he been behaving himself Joyce?" and so it went on for some time.

"I think we should have a beer Bill? We could sup a bucketful by the time they hang up."

CHAPTER 14

Before Bill left the Jacksons he put a cheque in a sealed envelope and placed it under his pillow. He gave Joyce a kiss and a hug thanking her for everything. "Don't forget to keep a visit to us fresh in your mind, you can stay just as long as you want and you are more than welcome. Keep reminding Jackson."

"Thanks Bill I will do that, but we will see you in a few day's time before you have to go back to Alibaba."

"Aljibia Joyce."

"Well you know what I mean and it sounds something like that."

At Heathrow Bill and Jackson shook hands. "See you when you get back Bill, have a safe flight."

It was just after 11 o'clock when he pulled into the March Hare car park. Tim and Ann watched him pull in from a window then came out to welcome him. Ann ran to him and smothered him with kisses. Tim grabbed hold of him in a bear hug and almost shook his arm out of its socket. "Come on in," he said grabbing hold of his suitcase while Ann grabbed him around the waist and walked him to the door. Once inside Tim said. "I will take your case upstairs while Ann makes us all a brew."

Soon they were sat down chatting away; Bill was doing most of the talking because he was being bombarded with questions.

"I have asked our little family to come here tonight said Ann because I have something important to tell them. I rang Roy and asked him to tell the others and impressed on him that it was essential that they all came. He rang back to confirm they would all be coming and to expect them about 8 o'clock. You know what Roy is like he was fishing to know what it was all about to get one up on the others of course."

"I need to make a phone call before then Ann if I may to Tommy and no doubt she will want a word with you."

"I will make us a spot of lunch now before we have to open the doors, so you have time to go and unpack."

After lunch Bill decided to call Tommy earlier which gave Ann a chance to have a good chat with her before opening time. When she came off the phone she remarked. "Tommy is certainly enjoying life out there she was really bubbling with excitement telling me about her life style you landed on your feet alright taking that job on Bill and you deserved it."

As time got nearer to the family coming, Ann told Bill he would have to keep out of sight until she gave the word. "I want to give them the biggest surprise of their lives tonight."

When they finally arrived they greeted Ann as always then Roy as was his way being spokesman for the group asked. "What is this important meeting about Ann is there something wrong?"

Tim's voice came from the other bar. "Ann, have you got a minute?"

"Excuse me I will tell you in a minute in the meantime I'll get our temp' to serve you, hang on a minute." She vanished to an adjacent room and the group heard her giving orders to someone. "Now remember these people are very special friends of ours and I want you to serve them with some dignity because they are very special people. Are you listening to what I am saying?"

The group looked at each other and Roy said. "It sounds like somebody has been rattling her cage."

"Now get in there and do the job I am paying you to do."

The group looked to see who it was that had been getting a lashing from Ann when in walked Bill. For a second or two they could not believe their eyes then it was pandemonium, as he came from behind the bar they rushed forward to greet him with hand shakes, hugs and kisses. Viv and Barbara were shedding tears of joy to see him. Ann and Tim were stood behind the bar laughing and enjoying the welcome Bill was getting from the 'Family'.

"You set us up good and proper," accused Roy, but it was well worth it, it is the best surprise we have had for a long time. Crack-open the champagne Tim and let us drink to something worth celebrating."

"Where is Tommy?" was the first thing the girls asked "and what are you doing here?"

"Well if you will all settle down and give me chance to recover from those kisses and hugs I will let you into a little secret."

Ann who was watching the reactions of the group turned to Tim smiling and said. "It is like old times again Tim." Then with a half sob she choked "and we have missed him and Tommy."

"I am here to poach some more of Group Captain Hopwood's staff again."

"You don't need to poach me I will come willingly," said an excited Viv, but only if my Derwent is included."

"Then that lets you out," replied Bill, unfortunately my authority does not run to a storeman. But who knows what could happen because being modest and I mean that in its true sense I have got quite a lot of clout out there and I just happen to be on very friendly terms with his Excellency the Emir."

That remark brought calls of "Whooo! We are in exalted company. Have you chosen anyone yet?" asked Viv not wanting to give the game away that she knew.

"I have and I will be taking them back with me to London in a couple of days for an interview with the Emir who has asked me to sit in with him at the interview. They will only be away a few days, everything has been arranged in conjunction with the MoD and the same rules apply that were the downfall of Pilling and Wings."

"Names Bill," demanded Viv, "I hope my girls are on your poaching list?"

"Let me tell you of our experiences on leaving you at Leeds Airport but first can we have a top-up please Roy because you are in for a long, long session there is so much to tell." He began his tale and well over an hour later he concluded it except he did not disclose the names of the two he had chosen for secondment. Questions flew thick and fast until finally Viv asked for the names of the two lucky people.

"Sergeant Alfred Deacon and Sergeant (w) Dot Dean."

Viv came over and kissed him. "Thank you for that Bill, I am really pleased for Dot she deserves it. So too does Alfred he is one of the best senior NCOs we have, Joe Franks is going to miss him. They have certainly kept it to themselves they must have been bursting to tell someone."

"This bit of information I should really leave it to them to tell you but they will when they return from the interview. They will join my staff as Warrant Officers. I will leave it to them to tell you of the other perks they will be receiving."

"And they will owe it all to you," responded Roy. "We know how you work Bill Barrett you will have convinced the Emir in your recommendations to make it worth their while accepting even though we know that a secondment is a compulsory posting."

"WAF Sergeant Anisa is coming to RAF March for a three months Sergeants training course and she is a very nice person Viv. She was pushed into Drill Instructing even though she was not qualified but you will not find a more eager person to learn. She had nobody to ask for help only me and it is a credit to her what she has achieved in a short space of time. She has applied numerous times for a course but still does not give up applying even though there is no-one who can teach her."

"So your unenviable job is to build a Recruit Training Establishment from scratch. A challenge like that is right up your street Bill but your huge advantage is you have not to go cap in hand hoping someone has a friendly ear. I wish I could come and help you Bill I would love that, get a post for Derwent and we would join you in a flash."

"I can only try Viv; the staff would love to have you there by my side because they went absolutely ecstatic when I showed the BlueBelles films it was like being back in London listening to the crowd's reaction to the final verdict…unbelievable."

"Have you any further news about Sam Barnes?" asked Roy.

"Only that he was arrested at Heathrow trying to flee the country. It has got very political now; the Emir wants him to be tried in Aljibia because he was under contract when he perpetrated the country's security. MI5 want him tried here because he is a UK citizen, so it is stalemate at the moment."

"Are you coming up to the camp to see your other friends Bill?" asked Barbara.

"I would love to but I do not know if I would be welcome, the only alternative is to ask them here."

"If that is so we will keep coming here while you are still leaning on the bar," said Derwent.

"Do me a favour Viv and tell Jackie I will call on her tomorrow evening."

"Telephone call for Colonel Barrett," shouted Ann.

Bill hurried to the phone and had a little chat with Tommy, after a short while he shouted to Barbara to come to the phone. That chat turned out to be a conversation until Derwent was called for, of course Bill had then to go and say his Goodnight."

As the family were leaving and saying their Good nights, Viv said. "You can bet Joe Franks will be down to see you tomorrow night Bill."

Just before closing time after lunch the following day Alfred Deacon and Dot Dean walked into the March Hare. When Ann saw them she held a finger to her lips and beckoned them to follow her. She poked her head round the door and saw Bill reading the paper. When he looked up and saw her she asked if he would like a drink. "I would love a brew please."

"Well hutch-up and make room for these two fans of yours."

He sprang to his feet when he saw who was there as Dot threw her arms round him and gave him a great big kiss with tears of joy on seeing him running down her cheeks. "Oh I am sorry sir I should never have done that."

"If you had not I would have thought I was losing my sex-appeal. Come here Alfred and let me shake your hand the pair of you are a sight for sore eyes"

Ann brought a brew for each of them. "I will leave you undisturbed." She put her arms round the pair's shoulders saying. "You are a very lucky couple not only for getting the chance of a lifetime but having the best mentor you could possibly have."

"Carry on sir."

"Thank you Ma'am."

"Obviously you have been briefed about me escorting you to London. I will pick you up at the guard room at 8am, and then we make our way to Leeds Airport and then on to Heathrow where an Embassy car with chauffeur will be there to meet us and take us to a Hotel where rooms have been reserved for the three of us with all expenses paid. The following morning our chauffeur will collect us and take us to the Embassy for your interview. I will be sitting in with his Excellency the Emir during the interview to clear up anything which he may not be too sure about. He does speak perfect English and so do his subjects, it is their compulsory second language. I can assure you that you will feel at ease in his presence just be yourselves he will appreciate that. Now how long do you think it will take you to become available? You will need to sort out your private and personal affairs, I know you are eager to get out there, will one month be sufficient? Anyway you can think about that. At the interview you will be issued with an itinerary which takes you through the stages until you end up in Aljibia. After the interview I take over as your chaperone while you are in London and depending on time we will go and get you fitted out with your uniforms and everything that goes with it. If not we will have to do that the following morning. There are some perks which I am holding back from telling you until you have been fitted out with all your gear. Now if you have any questions at this point feel free to put me on the spot."

"There is one thing we would like to get off our chests which we have not had the chance to tell you yet and it is. Thank you for thinking of us by giving us this great opportunity. It is hard to put into words how grateful we are but we are sure you will know how we feel."

"You have done the spade work yourselves by making the choice easy to prevent me going to Plan B."

"What if we are not selected, sir?" Asked Alfred.

"Then it will mean I have lost my powers of persuasion. Seriously the interview is just a formality where you two are concerned the Emir has only to give it his seal of approval."

"What is the accommodation like asked Dot?"

"The information I got from Major Khaleel the Commandant's PA is good. You are in separate buildings obviously which are situated on the domestic site and you have a self-contained apartment. It boasts a restaurant with a European menu so your meals are laid on and you do not pay for those. I have not seen inside the buildings but in a few minutes I will phone my PA and ask her if she can elaborate on them. The alternative is an apartment outside the perimeters of the Station but in those you have to fend for yourselves. If you choose the domestic accommodation and you find you do not like it you can then transfer to the outside apartment but I will find out all I can about them to hopefully get you settled. Now bear with me and we will see what gen we can get from Barbara."

"Hello Barbara, yes it is me Colonel Barrett, I am fine and yourself, bored? I will soon change that on my return. Look I have my two protégés here with me and they are eager to know about their accommodation on the Domestic site, can you help in any way by skimming through what you know about it please? I have told them the little bit I got from Major Khaleel and we all are keeping our fingers crossed for your help."

"Let me speak to the lady sir it would be better if we women conversed then we will not get our wires crossed."

"Hello Miss Battle I am Dorothy Dean, I am hoping you will face me in the right direction regarding the accommodation."

"Hello Dorothy, please call me Barbara. I will get straight to the point; my advice to you is take the apartment on the Domestic site. They are beautiful rooms consisting of a separate double bedroom with all the fittings we dream of. A bathroom with bath and a separate walk-in shower room. The shelves are topped up daily with scents, soaps, body lotions all of the finest quality. You will have a daily housekeeper who will be hand picked to take care of you. A first class restaurant is situated between the two accommodation buildings and is accessible via a communicating corridor which runs from each of the two buildings. Among its menus is a European one so you have a good choice of foods to sample as you so wish. Along the communication corridor there are various coffee lounges, Television and reading rooms. Both of the accommodations house people of different nationalities and are of different ranks. The icing on the cake is, it is run on democratic lines and therefore ranks are not used, everyone is on an equal footing. You will find they are a friendly lot and you will have no difficulty making friends. With hand on heart Dorothy I strongly recommend you and your associate to accept the accommodation."

"Thank you so much Barbara, it sounds lovely, my friends will not believe me when I tell them."

"Tell them you are not telling Porkie Pies, that is one of the English phrases the Colonel is teaching our Arab friends."

Dot laughed. "If he ever tells you about him having a gut feeling about anything you can be sure it will be reliable, it has never been known to let him down. All I want now is to get out there as quickly as I can and to meet you."

"Hello Barbara you have certainly made one young woman very happy, the delight on her face told us everything. Does that apply to Alfred Deacon what you told Dot?"

"Everything sir except the womanly things of course."

"Of course! Well thank you Barbara you have been a great help to all of us. Have you anything to tell I may be interested in?"

"Sorry, nothing at all, Mashy."

"Mashy, Barbara."

"What did you mean when you said Mashy, sir, is that the nickname you gave her?"

"Mashy is mine and Tommy's favourite Arabic word, it means Ok or fine. You have some explaining to do to Alfred now Dot and he is eager to get to know it all. I suggest you go in the lounge and have a right good talk. I have to go and pay my respects to Mary Brown. Mashy?"

They both replied "Mashy sir"

"Good you are getting the hang of it."

Ex-Warrant Officer Mary Brown nee Butcher gave Bill a wondrous welcome as old and trusted friends do. They sat and chatted for a full two hours as Bill told her of the experiences him and Tommy had had since leaving the UK and the reason he was here. She laughed, "You will be getting a right reputation for your poaching activities. I would not be at all surprised if Group Captain Hopwood hasn't christened you Poacher Barrett for what you keep doing to his staff." He told her about the Sam Barnes episode. "I am not at all surprised Bill I think he lost his marbles at that meeting or else he played a waiting game to do as much damage to the RAF as possible, I have no sympathy for that man."

"Well I must love you and leave you old girl…"

"You may be a high ranking officer Bill Barrett but…"

"Less of the old," they said in unison with a laugh and an embrace. "Tell Tommy to keep the letters flowing we do look forward to them. Thank her for the photos, as you can see they are in a pride of place." After a hug and a kiss with a little emotion showing from Mary she waved him off.

On returning to the March Hare he immediately reported to Tommy on his day's activities up to the present time. "I wish you could have seen the excitement and delight on the faces of our two protégés when Miss Battle described the living accommodation they would be moving into. Dot took all the details to save Barbara having to repeat them to Alfred. Mary sends her love along with Sam's because he was at work. They are thrilled to bits with your letters. *'Please tell Tommy to keep them flowing, we look so forward to receiving them because they are so descriptive and she puts so much in them we feel like we are getting to know the place* and our photos are in a prime position, she is so proud of them. Viv told me last night that she is sure that Joe Franks will be calling tonight it would not surprise me if he has one or two of the others in tow. Have you any exciting news love?"

"Fred took me and Ella into town this morning I had to go because Thomas gave me a shopping list. Of course I treated myself to one or two odds and sods, why are you laughing? You do realise that now I have to set the standard of dress as becomes *The Colonel's Wife*, you see my darling being famous has its price."

"When I see the Emir again in three days time I will ask him if you can have an extension built on to your walk-in wardrobe. Mashy?"

"No it is not Mashy! It is La. (No) and I have told you before Bill Barrett, stop being facetious."

"Then I will get Fred to make out a report each time he takes you shopping."

"No chance Colonel Chinstrap, Fred knows where his bread is buttered."

"Do you mean to tell me he sits at my table and scoffs my rations, I will soon put paid to that when I get a new chauffeur."

"Then you will need a new Chef, a new housekeeper and a new wife. I am hanging up now leaving you to think about it. Mashy darling? I love you!"

"I do too!!" He quickly rang off before she had time to retaliate.

Over dinner Ann and Tim still kept firing questions at him. "I had a word with Dot and Andrew as they were leaving while you were at Mary's. Dot could not resist telling me about their accommodation, it sounds like a five star hotel Bill no wonder they want to catch the next flight out to make sure it is not a dream."

"They do things in a big way to make their service people happy. Take my office for example. I have a huge desk full of all the latest technology equipment and I do not know how to use half of it. It is self contained, I have a wash room, a bath room and a walk-in shower and the shelves are overflowing with par fumes, after shaves, soaps, you name it and I will have it on my shelves and the brands are of world wide renown. I cannot attempt to describe the building where our major offices are and the restaurant where we have our lunches but I must get a photo of it to send you, it is a different world."

"Come on you two help me wash up then we can all go and watch the news bulletin with a brew, for I think we are in for a busy time tonight." Five minutes after sitting down with the brew both Bill and Tim were fast asleep. *Ah well as the saying goes 'if you can't beat em'...join em' she said to herself as she looked fondly at the two sleeping beauties.*

As predicted that evening was a very busy one when most of the Sergeant and Corporal Drill Instructors converged on the March Hare to pay homage to their Number One Drill Instructor because each and everyone of them had just cause to thank him for what he had done for them., None more so than Warrant Officer Joe Franks who Bill had groomed in such a way that even Joe was not aware of it until he got his promotion to WO. The group filed in quietly and sat waiting for Bill to appear. Ann and Tim were stood in silence behind the bar after Joe had put a finger to his lips.

Bill called to Ann as he was walkng from the back room. "It is quiet Ann has nobody turned up ye.e.e'

He was cut off by Joe shouting. "Officer Present!" everyone jumped to their feet in respect followed by a thunderous round of applause. Bill stood, stared and then it hit him. "Excuse me a minute," he said almost choking on the words. They knew he had had gone to compose himself. Tim pretended to do something to cover his emotions whilst Ann and the rest of the ladies present did a mopping up job on their eyes. When Bill returned fully composed he looked around and asked. "Who gave you the order to sit down? Warrant Officer Franks report to my office next week on the double."

"Yes please sir, thank you sir and can I bring this lot with me?"

"You can and with my blessings." This announcement nearly brought the house down with cheering. When they had settled down he announced. "The first drinks are on me but I beg of you please do not buy me any, I know you would like to see me under the table Brahms and Liszt but I am sorry that is not on, but do enjoy yourselves. You all want to know of my travels and experiences since I left you all but I cannot go round every table to repeat it over and over again. So what I suggest is we have an hour of questions and answers then settle down to try and formulate plans on how to get you on my staff. Who knows what may be round the corner. Remember we are the same old friends and I will appreciate if you will treat me as such, until you get on my staff of course then you will toe the line." This brought loud laughter from everyone. "Okay Joe fire away."

"We have all noticed you have reverted to your poaching ways and oddly enough it is from the same officer. Have you a grudge against him or is there a method in your madness?"

"I have nothing but respect for Group Captain Hopwood, Joe, he is a fine man and a damned good officer, he was the only one who believed in me when we had that bit of nasty business with Pilling and Wings. They suffered for it but he didn't, he is a man I will always trust and I suggest you all do the same. About my mad methods, I was thrust into the deep end because any semblance to a Recruit Training School was enough to want me to throw in the towel. So I rolled up my sleeves and got stuck into the job I was contracted to do." He then told them what he had planned and what he was doing to make it into a Training School the country and RAF March would be proud of. That is why I have poached two of the best Instructors from you. It will not be an easy task for them but as you know letting me down is not a part of yours and their characters." Here he was interrupted by a burst of applause. "As soon as Alfred and Dot join me they will have a week to acclimatise then the two Arabic Sergeants will come here for three months training and I hope you will treat them with respect. They are far from being anywhere near to your standards and yes they speak perfect English it is their country's compulsory second language. To complete your question Joe I know that one of you will ask 'why did you choose Alfred and Dot from the rest of us who perhaps have got more service in'. I want you to think about this very carefully. Alan Fell, Bob Dixon, Peter Wilcox and Ron York. What differentiates them from Alfred Deacon? I'll tell you, they are married men with families. If they went through that huge upheaval for a two year secondment they would be surplus to requirements when they returned here then what would happen to them. I cannot accept the wives staying in quarters while their menfolk swan off into the sun. So what would happen when the wanderers returned and what would happen to the families if they were posted elsewhere because of surplus to requirements? The only ray of hope I could offer is if I can build that Training Establishment up to a similar size as you have here then I could expand my staff. I am not giving you a load of flannel you know me better than that but

I am determined to make a success of this job for my employer, myself and hopefully for my friends. I have not left you out Dot. Dot is the senior Sergeant after Flight Sergeant Margaret Roper so there were no problems there.

I think I have covered everything or you would have been bombarding me with your questions. I would now like a private word with Joe and Viv, if you would please."

Ann gave them permission to go into the back room for privacy. Once they were alone Bill and Joe shook hands very warmly and Viv got her kiss. "The reason I wanted to talk to you both as friends is to ask how are your SNCOs reacting to my choice of Alfred and Dot? I know of Viv's reaction but what about your's Joe?"

"If all of them were single I would have no hesitation in choosing Alfred Deacon, he is the best all round SNCO we have and there is a very bright future ahead for that lad. Of course I am going to miss him who in their right mind would not. With him and Dot Dean you have got the foundation to build your little Empire, Bill," he said making Bill and Viv laugh. "As for the rest, I don't think Bob Dixon was too pleased he has that self opinionated attitude and I think his wife has been getting quite a bit of earache from him but it will not get him anywhere Bill, not in my books. As for the rest they are genuinely pleased for Alfred."

"Thanks Joe you have opened my eyes there and if everything goes according to my plans I would hope to get back to you for any more character assessments. What have you got to tell me Viv?"

"As you already know Bill, my Sergeants are all relatively new to the rank. Margaret Roper is the only one left with some seniority. Surprisingly for Margaret she took the news of Dot's posting quite badly and began to vent her feelings on the Corporals. Alan Fell tipped me off that she appeared under some kind of stress so I asked her to my office and made her tell me about her attitude. Of course there were tears because she had not been picked for the secondment being the most senior etc.etc.I had, had enough of her weeping and wailing so I told her get up off her arse and on to her feet and stand to attention. Now you listen to me madam and listen well. Dot is going on a two year secondment…she interrupted me to say 'but she is getting promoted as well'. Yes and when she returns she will return as a Sergeant. To put it bluntly you are as jealous as they come because someone else has got the posting which you think should have been rightfully yours. Flight Sergeant Roper I just wish the people who put you in the position you hold now could see the pathetic figure standing before me. I have to report this to Squadron Leader Macfarlane because it is too serious an offence from someone of your rank. Now get out of here."

"Bloody 'L' Viv I am glad we are on the same side, phew that was some going over no wonder she did not turn up tonight," exploded Joe.

"She has certainly surprised me if it was a case of losing out on a promotion I could understand it but a posting I have never come across anything like that before. She certainly needs a sharp rap over the knuckles and Mac' is the one to do it and if she does not pull herself together she will find herself in a heap of trouble."

Who would you replace her with Viv if she asked for her discharge? Obviously they are all too junior so you would have to put her in the office as a Sergeant along with Alan Fell. Joe and I will write her name on a piece of paper then you tell us your choice. 'Your choice Viv. 'Marion James.' Turn yours over Joe. 'Marion James.' 'My choice' said Bill turning his paper over 'just happens to be Marion James'. There you are Viv' if push comes to shove you have your decision. How are you getting on with Wings' replacement Joe?"

"He is alright he knows nowt' that is why he does not bother us, he leaves it all to us. I go to him if there is something I want to see the Wingco about, protocol and all that rubbish Bill."

"What's he like then? I have never heard him mentioned."

"Nobody does unless they can't help it he is a big bladder of lard with too much of his own importance and a right 'yes man'. Charles Chaplain is his name he can't help his name I know but it is obvious what the rank and file call him."

"Shall we rejoin the others unless there is anything else you want to tell me?"

As soon as they sat down with their immediate friends a drink was placed on the table for them from Roy. "I have a message for you Bill from Helen Fraser. Actually it is from the Commanding Officer. 'Colonel Barrett I would appreciate it if you can find the time to come and have a friendly chat and a brew with me tomorrow morning at 10:00hrs.'

"Thanks Roy I am really looking forward to that it will complete a great time I have had with my friends. Tell Helen thank you it will be a pleasure that I will look forward to."

"Ladies and Gentlemen." Ann had to shout loud to make her voice heard. Time please, the towels are on the pumps and you have five minutes to drink up and clear these premises but before you do don't you think it would be appropriate if we sang together Auld Lang Syne?"

CHAPTER 15

At 09:00hrs Bill pulled up to the gates of RAF March. He approached the sentry and said. "I have an appointment with the Station Commander."

"Your name sir?"

"Colonel Barrett."

"You will have to leave your car outside the gates sir but if you will step through this gate…he got no further.

"Open those Bloody Gates or I will string you up on them."

Good old George, Bill said to himself with a big grin. He drove through and jumped out of the car as quickly as he could and walked hurriedly to meet Station Warrant Officer George Miller a long and dear friend. George saluted him. Bill grabbed his hand and gave it a good shaking. "Cut out the bullshit it is me Bill, sod what anybody who is watching is thinking. Is Tom Bridges in the guard room?"

George yelled for Flight Sergeant Bridges who had been looking through the guardroom window "To come out on the double. He came out with his face wreathed in smiles and saluted. Bill grabbed his hand and shook it. "It is good to see you again Tom."

"And it is good to see you sir."

He quietly whispered, "Its Bill don't you recognise me under this glorious sun tan."

"And here is me thinking that you have been overdoing it with the sun tan bottle." George said causing them all to laugh.

"What is with the reception committee George?"

"Well I heard there was some kind of a celebrity due in I thought I might get a good laugh or summat' if I was here. If I had known it was you I could have had another hour in bed."

"Now am I going to park my car inside or outside the gates?"

"Aw! Come on you are still giving me earache with your moanings. You can park it In the Sergeants Mess car park; it is not exactly a Rolls Royce is it?"

When it was parked up they slipped into George's Office for a quick brew and to be welcomed by Ian Roberts who ordered three brews on the double. They had very little time for Bill to give them much information before it was time to report to Helen. I will see you later George."

"You had better because Betty is making us a good dinner."

"That has got my taste buds going already old friend," he laughed as he made his way out through the door with 'less of the old' ringing in his ears.

At Helen Fraser's Office he knocked and walked in to see a Wing Commander talking to Helen, her face lit up when she saw Bill.

"Who the hell are you?" the Wingco asked "and don't you wait for permission to come in when you knock?"

Helen saw that look in Bill's eyes and said. "This is Colonel Barrett and he is here by request of the Station Commander."

"Ah the jumped up Colonel from the Banana Republic."

Bill kept himself under control but Helen fearing it would not last for long hastily buzzed the CO to tell him Colonel Barrett had arrived.

"Bring him in Helen" She got up from her seat and the Wingco followed her leaving Bill to go in last. Bill tapped him on the shoulder and said. "Junior officers give way to Senior Officers, so get behind me Chaplain and try to remember *your* place and manners."

"Colonel Barrett sir said a happy smiling Helen" as Bill gave her a wink as he brushed past her.

"Colonel Barrett, how nice to see you and thank you for coming." He shook Bill's hand warmly. Can I interest you in a brew?"

"I would love one please and I must confess I have really been looking forward to an invite from you because after that last piece of unpleasantness I thought I may have been barred from the station."

"And so you should," snorted the Wingco'.

That remark was noted but nothing was said.

"You and I know each other better than that Bill. I hope you don't mind me being familiar for when all is said and done we are of equal rank, so I am John to you."

"That John is a step in the right direction thank you."

In the background the Wingco was making sickly noises. Are you still there Chaplain I ordered tea ages ago? Go and get it. You have met my second in command Wing Commander Chaplain."

Bill just raised his eyes heavenwards.

The CO smiled and said to himself, *'good man you have spotted him'.*

Bill looked at the CO and was sure he saw a cry for help. He nodded and each had an uncanny feeling the message had got across. When the WIngco returned with the tea he gave one to the CO with "Your tea sir." He placed his own at a table then brought Bill's over and as he plonked it down the tea over spilled into the saucer. Without a word he turned to walk away but unfortunately fell over Bill's foot which he just happened not to see. Consequently he fell with a crash to the floor. The CO stifling a laugh asked. "Are you alright Charles?"

"I think so sir but with no thanks to that stupid oaf. You should get back to the Banana Republic which is only fit for rubbish like you."

"Stop right there Chaplain you will apologise to Colonel Barrett at once and that is an order."

"Apologise, sorry sir I could not do that it would be below my dignity."

"You do not know the meaning of the word dignity but you give me no alternative but to place you under house arrest. Have you anything to add Colonel?"

"Yes sir, my report of this incident and the one in your secretary's office will be forwarded to the MoD via the Aljibian Embassy."

"You heard that Chaplain, the first thing you will do is return to your office and clear out your desk, you will not be using your office any longer."

In the meantime Helen had been listening in on the inter-com which had accidentally not been switched off and knowing there would be fireworks after the incident in her office had kept Barbara Page the Wingco's PA informed of what was happening.

"He is coming to clear his desk and is under house arrest Barbara, see you later."

"Well after that little shemozzle Bill I think we need a brew, I never got to touch mine."

"And mine just missed me John."

"Helen will you come and clear these cups away and make a brew for two, no make it three, one for yourself."

When she came to clear the cups she remarked. "You haven't drunk your first cup sir."

"I know that was very remiss of us we forgot all about it didn't we Bill?"

"Indeed. for there is and never has been a dull moment in this office John."

Helen looked at Bill on hearing first names being bandied about. While she was waiting for the water to boil she rang Barbara. "Can I speak Barbara?"

"Yes, it is safe, what have you got for me?"

"It has got to first names now Barbara, I could not believe it when I was called in to clear the cups. It was Bill this and John that just like two old pals and they were laughing away I think it was because they got rid of Charlie Chaplin, the CO could not stand him. Got to go I am the brewing-up lady at the moment."

"Thanks Bill for helping me get rid of that idiot I could not stand him and I could find no excuse for getting rid of him."

"Then your Fairy Godfather came on the scene and waved his magic wand." There was a loud burst of laughter from them both just as Helen walked in with the brew.

"And here is our Fairy Godmother, laughed John."

"Have I done something wrong sir?" She asked.

"On the contrary Helen we were having a joke and you appeared at the punch line. We meant no offence I can assure you. Thank you for the tea."

"As I was saying about Chaplain, how he got to the rank of Wingco' beggars belief, I have never met such an obnoxious snidey character in my entire service career."

"He certainly had it in for me as soon as I walked through Helen's door; he came at me like a Rottweiler. I don't think he has any idea of the mess he is in. What makes people turn into raving loonies I just do not know?"

"Anyway Bill that is over and done with now, what I want from you is your plan of action in Aljibia. From the little I have heard you would like to turn it into an RAF March Number 2."

"I would not go as far as that because there can only be one RAF March for me. I will put you into the picture of me taking over the training completely, what I found and my thoughts and the action I have started. I have given it the operational name of 'Operation New Broom'. John listened intently nodding his head in agreement at times. It ended with John holding out his hand saying I will support you any way I can Bill, I only wish I could come out there and work with you."

"Give me a minute, I think I may have something stirring up here," Bill said pointing to his head. You John are responsible for sending out Instructional staff to help build up a proper Recruit Training Establishment in Aljibia, and it is your duty to check on the progress being made and then report back to your senior staff (Brass Hats) to tell them if is a viable concern for the benefit of the two countries. You could of course supplement your inspections with a bit of leave. That is a rough idea of what I mean.

When we sort it out between us and get the Emir's blessing MoD should follow the line of the Emir's suggestions. That would be the ground work done and if the Emir is footing the bill I am sure the MoD will not put up any objections. Of course it would be quite some time before we could offer this plan, but I will do some checking up on my return and keep you posted of any progress."

"You amaze me Bill and have done so since I first met you how you can pull ideas of that standard out of thin air. Didn't the ex-Air Officer Commanding (AOC) christen you Merlin the Magician? I am sorry but I have to push you off now because I have another meeting in half an hour, come on I will walk you to your car."

"Could I just call and see one or two friends on my way?"

"Of course, you go ahead and take all the time you want with them, I will nip off to my meeting." They shook hands and wished each other well.

Bill's first stop was to see Helen Fraser. He knocked on her door peeped round it asking. "Are you free?"

She jumped up from her chair and came to him with outstretched arms, kissed him on the cheek and hugged him. "Oh we have missed you Bill and it is so good to see you and on behalf of everyone in Station Headquarters I want to thank you for getting rid of that awful man."

"He got rid of himself Helen I just gave him his head and let him dig himself deeper in the hole."

"You know when I came in to clear the debris I could not believe my ears when I heard you calling each other by your first names. At that moment I felt so very, very proud of you."

"I am sorry I have to leave you so soon dear Helen but I will be in touch with your boss from now on. How about organising a work's trip to come and see us in Aljibia?"

"She laughed. "You are still a silly beggar." They kissed and said their farewells with a little tear drop running down her cheek." He noticed she had his framed photo in his uniform on her desk along with the AOC's.

His next stop was the orderly Room to see Sergeant Chris' Graham who Tommy had a soft spot for. As he walked in the room he bellowed. "Stand by Your Beds" the startled faces turned to delight when they saw who it was. He made his way straight to Chris' with his hand outstretched. "How are you Chris?" he asked as they shook hands, "and how is your lovely fiancée, is she not here? Then send for her and tell her an old flame has called to see her." the rest of the staff giggled on hearing this.

Two minutes later a flustered Marion rushed in the room and gave a scream of delight when she saw Bill. He gave her a hug and a kiss to a round of applause from the staff. The noise disturbed Roy who flung back the connecting hatch door and demanded what was going on. When he saw who was causing the commotion he said very politely. "When you have finished molesting the staff Colonel Barrett would you please step into my office?"

Bill had a short chat with Chris' and Marion who thanked him and Tommy for the lovely congratulations card for their engagement. "When you name the day you can stay with us in our Villa, we have four bedrooms, give us plenty of warning for I will need to sort out the travel arrangements. I must be off now to see his nibs." He said his farewells to them both with a hand shake and a kiss. "Take care of each other Tommy and I do."

Roy welcomed him with a warm handshake and the offer of a brew with a chocolate biscuit.

"You are pushing the boat out aren't you; have you come up on the pools?"

"Two teas with Chocky Bickies Chris," Roy yelled through the hatch. "I hear from good authority you are on more than just friendly terms with our Commandant."

"Hello, has your beloved been ear wigging under your instructions."

"Not at all, Barbara gets fair warning of anything that concerns our little family personally. The girls are really chuffed and so are a lot of other people, especially those in the higher echelon, he was a bad egg Bill." He picked up the ringing phone. "Yes he is here George do you want a word?" He handed it to Bill. "George Miller."

"Yes George what can I do for you?"

"You can get off your backside and get down here to my office, have you forgotten you are dining with me and Betty?"

"Sorry sir I am on my way now." Roy and Bill shook hands warmly and gave each other a hug as best friends do. "We'll be in touch Roy; by the way did I tell you the latest on Sam Barnes?"

"No you didn't." "He was arrested at Heathrow trying to flee the country, now there is a political argument between the two countries as to who should put him on trial. Ta ra old friend."

He received a great welcome from Betty Miller and they spent a couple of hours listening to what Bill had to say about his role In Aljibia and the way of life there. I have one more call to make then I must get back to the pub to ring Tommy. They said their fond farewells and promised they would still keep in touch. Will I see you in the morning George because I have to pick up Dot and young Alfred? I will give Tommy your love when I phone her."

"I will be there to see you safely off the premises Colonel," George said with a grin. "Who would have thought I would one day have to salute you. But the bonus is I can proudly say that I can still call my best mate a Colonel, by his Christian name?"

From there Bill nipped back into SHQ and gave Warrant Officer Jock Webster a surprise when he walked into his office. Jock jumped to his feet and before he could say anything Bill grabbed his hand and asked. "How are you Jock it is good to see you again?"

Jock was still speechless until he suddenly blurted out. "I am fine and it is good to see you sir."

"Hang on there Jock, we are on our own in here and it is still Bill to you. I could not leave without coming to see an old friend."

Jock then found his composure. "Aye we go back a good way Bill. I heard you were coming to see the CO and wrongly thought you would not want to know me now with your rise in rank and status."

"Real friends do not do tricks like that Jock. I particularly wanted to see you to tell you about Sam Barnes."

"I heard some silly story about him spying"

"Not a silly story Jock it is true." He then told him the whole story and the part he took in him being found out. Jock was dumbfounded, "It is so hard to believe Bill yet how he turned out I could imagine him doing something daft but not spying. I shudder to think that at one time I was under his influence and I have you to thank for getting me out of it."

"That is what friends are for Jock."

"Aye and they don't come any better than you Bill. put it there old friend," he said as they shook hands.

"Well I'm afraid I have to leave you but you will be able to get any news of Tommy and me through Roy or Viv.

"Thanks for thinking of me and it has been a real pleasure to see you again, please give our love to Tommy."

CHAPTER 16

At 07:45 Bill pulled up at the gates to RAF March after saying his farewells and thanks to Tim and Ann Wilson of the March Hare pub. The sentry did not ask for his identity because George Miller was standing at his elbow. As Bill drove through the gates George saluted as Bill called through the wound down window, "Good Morning to you Mr Miller." He pulled up to the guard room and saw Alfred and Dot were inside waiting for him. "Ready when you are," he called to them.

"Come on you two," George called to two of the guards, "give a hand with the luggage." At the car door George grabbed Bill's hand. "Take care of yourselves it has been great meeting up with you again and tell Tommy to keep her letters coming Betty loves them, she pores over them like reading a book. Have a safe journey back to Tommy, Bill" he said as he saluted and waved them off.

"You know sir I am sure the SWO showed a little emotion seeing you off."

Bill coughed. "It is because we are such close friends Dot and I am not ashamed to say that it cuts both ways."

After Bill had returned the Rent-a-car at Leeds airport they went to collect their tickets. "We are travelling business class." said an amazed Dot looking at her ticket."

"That is your first perk of the day," Bill said with a smile, come on let us go and check in." After this had been done he asked them if they would like some breakfast or wait to have it on board, or do you want a brew? we have plenty of time."

They decided on a breakfast on the flight.

When they went through Departures Bill suggested. "If you two want a stroll round the shops just carry on, don't buy a newspaper they are supplied on the plane along with magazines. We will meet at the Departure gate when we are told to board."

The flight to Heathrow was uneventful and the breakfast was enjoyed by all three, Dot and Andrew enjoyed every minute of the flight. After collecting their luggage from the carousel they made their way to the Arrivals Hall and spotted Jackson almost immediately. After Jackson had loaded their luggage on to one trolley he said. "Follow me I will get you out of here quickly." In a matter of minutes the luggage was stowed away in the car. "Now, welcome back Bill it is good to see you."

"And you." Replied Bill as they shook hands. "Jackson I would like you to meet my two protégés. Sergeant Dot Dean and Sergeant Alfred Deacon, you will be seeing quite a bit of them in the next few days." They all shook hands. "Jackson is the Embassy chauffeur for all VIPs and we have become great friends."

"I have brought your suit of armour sir, Joyce stayed up all night polishing it."

Bill explained that Joyce was Jackson's wife and they would be meeting her during their stay.

"By the way Bill you have got three single rooms obviously," he said with a wicked grin. "Dot has the room between Alfred and yourself. Sign yourselves in as Miss and Mr no service ranks. And here we are folk," he said as he drew up to the Savoy Hotel.

Bill spoke to Dot and Alfred. "This is your perk number two," as the pair of them stared in wonder. As they got out of the car attendants came rushing down to take their luggage.

"Are you doing anything this evening Bill fancy an hour at the club?"

"Sorry Jackson I have to gen these two up then write a bad conduct report out for the Emir."

"Has someone been naughty then?"

"He certainly has and it is costing him dearly too. I'll tell you about it later."

"I have to tell you that you have to answer to Joyce about a letter left beneath your pillow after you left us."

Alfred burst out laughing.

"It is not what you are thinking," said a partially embarrassed Bill especially when Dot and Jackson joined in the laughter. Bill saw the funny side, "What are you lot like?"

"Are you coming in with us to see if there is a letter of instructions waiting for me?"

"There is a letter; I left it at the desk on my way to meet you at the airport."

"Then why did you not hand it to me personally?"

"Orders are orders as you should well know, I don't want to end up on one of your bad behaviour reports Colonel Sir."

"Alright you can then sod off and we will see you in the morning and you can tell Joyce that what that letter contained in that big white envelope was for the phone calls I made and don't be late tomorrow."

"No sir."

After waving him off they made their way to reception where he was instantly recognised. He was given his key and an envelope, Dot and James received theirs. "Your luggage has been taken to your rooms' sir."

"Come on let us go and sit over there and have a shufti at the letter. All it says is we are to be picked up at 10:30 and will be seen by the Emir at 11 o'clock. Right let us go to our rooms and relax, they agreed on lunch at 1o'clock?"

Bill waited outside his door until Dot entered her room. When he heard a muffled scream of delight he smiled and said to himself, *'she is chuffed'*.

At lunch Dot could not stop talking about her room and all that it contained even to a ticket to a West End show. "And the hotel, it is out of this world, what is yours like Alfred?"

"I suppose pretty much the same as yours from the detailed description you gave of it yes, it is very nice," giving Bill a wink, and I have got a ticket for a show as well, have you Bill? I cannot imagine them missing you out."

"Oh yes I have one. Would you like to go to one tonight, you both can go and I will have an hour or so with Jackson? He can pick us all up, drop you both off at the show and we will carry on to the club. Jackson knows what time the shows end then we can come and pick you up and arrive at the hotel together. Decide which show you want to see then I can phone Jackson with the arrangements."

After lunch Bill got in touch with Jackson who was delighted when told about the arrangements. "That means hopefully we can have a good natter, hold on a minute Bill."

"Hello love how are you, Clarry has just told me you are going to the club this evening but I insist only if I am invited too."

"You are more than welcome flower, you know what they say, 'there is no Punch without Judy."

"You lovely man, I'll put you back to Clarry."

"Righto' Bill I will pick you up at 7:30."

"Bill rang the rooms of Dot and Alfred and told them the pick-up time. I suggest we go to dinner at 5:30. OK?" He then settled himself down to write his report for the Emir. Alfred and Dot spent their time taking photos of their rooms and posing for each other while they took more to prove to their friends they had actually stayed at the Savoy Hotel.

Bill received a call from reception telling him their car had arrived. He rounded his little group up and they were greeted by Jackson and Joyce. Introductions were in order and Bill could hear from the passenger seat in front the chatter that was going on with Joyce, Dot and Alfred. *That is a good sign he thought.*

"Here we are at your entertainment for the night," said Jackson. "I hope you enjoy it, I have not seen it yet but the reviews are good. See you at the end of the show."

They booked in at the RAFA Club, Bill booking himself in being an honorary member. Jackson got the drinks in and both he and Joyce listened intently to Bill telling of his meeting up with his old friends and the great welcomes he received. Jackson was more interested in the antics of Wingco' Chaplain and banged the table in delight when Bill told him how he had handled him."

"So what will happen to him now asked Jackson?"

"The MoD will take that very seriously being a slur on the Emir and his country and my feeling is he will be both court-martialled and slung out with ignominy or a dishonourable discharge with ignominy and either way with a loss of rank and service pension."

"And it serves him damned well right too," said an indignant Joyce.

"If we have a quick interview tomorrow can we take them to the tailors to get fixed up Jackson?"

"That is no problem I am yours for the day."

"And will you please chaperone Dot in the tailors Joyce?"

"It will be my pleasure Bill, I think she is a right nice girl, you certainly know how to pick em' "

"And train em' Joyce. By the way here is my theatre ticket Joyce I won't use it"

During their chat various members greeted Bill with "Good Evening Colonel it is nice to see you again." Then the Club President was informed that Bill was in the club. He dropped everything and came over to shake Bill by the hand and to welcome him to the club. "Is this another flying visit Colonel?"

"In a sense yes, I only arrived this afternoon but you know what the persuasive powers of Jackson are like how could I refuse his plea to come and pay my respects?"

"Indeed, Jackson is one of our most valued members and I can see a bright future for him in the club. Any way I will let you get on with your exchange of news. It is nice to see you too Mrs Jackson. Bye for now."

"Little creep," snorted Joyce. "I never did like him."

They had a good ten minutes to wait for Alfred and Dot to emerge from the Show and as they climbed in the car they were immediately asked if they had enjoyed it.

"It was wonderful wasn't it Alfred? We enjoyed every minute of it and guess what? We were in the best seats, what a wonderful night! You know Joyce since I was chosen for this assignment I have been hopping from cloud nine and upwards. I shall remember this for the rest of my life."

"You are not saying much Alfred queried Joyce."

"I have not had the chance to get a word in have I? But I agree with everything Dot has said and we have a lot to thank Bill for and this is just the beginning."

"Yes I agree with you Alfred, we all have something to thank that lovely man for."

At the hotel they waved Jackson and Joyce off with cries of 'see you tomorrow'.

"If you can get over your excitement of this evening I suggest you make yourselves a nice hot drink and get between the sheets because you are going to have a more exciting day tomorrow."

After a good breakfast Bill changed into his uniform and waited until reception informed him his transport had arrived. He knocked on both doors to alert Alfred and Dot "

"My words sir you really look the part you are very smart indeed."

"Good morning sir," said an admiring Alfred it is certainly a smart outfit. Will we be wearing a similar one, without the braid and decorations of course?"

"You will and if you behave yourselves and do what you are told you may even qualify for braid and decorations." He said with a smile.

"We have both got cameras will you let Jackson take our photos with you please?" asked Dot.

"Of course, would like them taken in front of the hotel?"

"Oh yes please, that would be wonderful."

Jackson was waiting for them in the foyer and his face lit up with pride to see Bill in uniform. "Good morning sir" he said as he escorted them out through the doors.

"Would you mind taking Dot's and Alfred's photos with me with these two cameras old friend? They would like us posed with the full view of the hotel in the background with the name showing."

Alfred and Dot stood each side of Bill and were ordered by Jackson to "Come on give me a nice smile and look like you are enjoying it" which brought the result he wanted. "At the end of the day give me the films and I will have them developed and printed for you by tomorrow."

It was only a few minutes drive to the Embassy and as they got out of the car Jackson said. "Good Luck" to Alfred and Dot, I will be here waiting."

They went to the reception desk and Bill reported, "Colonel Barrett and party for interview with his Excellency the Emir."

"Ah good morning Colonel Barrett so we meet again and it is good to see you, how do you like life in Aljibia?"

"Very much thank you and I agree with you the people are exceptionally friendly."

With a smile he asked them to follow him. He took them to a lounge waiting room and asked if they would like refreshments. They each asked for a soft drink.

"Well what do you think of the Aljibian Embassy?" asked Bill.

"Very nice indeed they both agreed."

"You see them on films but they are nothing like this, this is really something," said Alfred.

When the official ushered in an attendant with the drinks he said to Bill. "His Excellency will be calling for you very shortly Colonel."

Alfred and Dot looked at Bill who told them he would be going in because he was sitting in at the interview and the Emir would want a quick word first. By the way Dot do you know how to curtsey? Anyway when you step through the door as a mark of respect give him a little one but don't fall over doing it or we will all get the giggles. You Alfred give a small bow and try not to topple over." He hoped that would help ease any nervousness.

"Colonel, his Excellency will see you now."

Bill entered and saluted. "Good morning Colonel Barrett come and sit by me. Now tell me of your little trip to RAF March and being reunited with your friends."

"I received a wonderful reception from them sir and collected a few tears of joy in the bargain but some sad ones on leaving."

"Yes, friendship is a wonderful thing Colonel."

"I had an interview with the new Station Commander Group Captain Hopwood. He is a good man sir and promises to support us all the way. When I described our project he wistfully said. 'I just wish I was there working with you. Unfortunately I have had to write out a bad report about his second in command Wing Commander Charles Chaplain."

"Let me see it please." After reading it he was furious. "That man's career ends as soon as I report this to your MoD. How does a pompous arrogant ass reach the heights of that rank without being found out his mentality and he having control over everyone of lesser rank than himself?"

"The Station Commander immediately placed him under house arrest sir and made him clear his desk saying 'you will not be using that office any longer'. The Station Commander is now waiting for the repercussions from you and MoD sir." "That was very good and wise of him I will send him a letter of thanks. You did well too, Colonel and why do officers at RAF March throw themselves on their own swords when you are around?"

"It must be the affect I have on them sir. A very good friend of mine repeatedly tells me. 'I would hate to upset you Barrett because it would be the kiss of death."

The Emir roared with laughter. "I promise not to upset you Colonel," he said still laughing. "Now before I send for the interviewees I have some serious news for you which at the moment is still at the need to know stage. That man Barnes was found dead in his cell yesterday morning apparently from heart failure."

"He would never have lasted a long prison sentence sir. He hated my guts sir for a reason no-one ever found out. I did not like the man for his bad attitude to me but I am glad he did not suffer. What will happen now to your prisoner sir?"

"Have no fear Colonel he will get a fair trial, unfortunately for treason he will lose his life. Colonel any wrong must be punished and this man put every living person in my countrys' life at risk, there is no pardon for that."

"Sir, may I make a plea of clemency on his behalf?"

"Colonel, I was expecting you to ask for that and you are a good man it was very noble of you and it will be noted but the answer is an emphatic No."

"And the two English men you are still holding in prison sir what is likely to become of their fate?

"They will probably get a token sentence of six months and they will serve the full term. They were very naïve Colonel and were used as couriers with no idea they were doing wrong. Nevertheless they cannot go unpunished."

"I think you are being very generous with them sir."

The door opened and the official entered. "Bring in the interviewees," said the Emir.

Alfred and Dot entered. Alfred gave a low bow and Dot did a nice curtsey.

"Good morning to you both" said the Emir. Will you please introduce yourselves? Then take a seat."

"Good morning your Excellency," they both replied.

The Emir looked at Bill and smiled.

"My name is Alfred Deacon and I am a qualified Sergeant Drill Instructor at Royal Air Force March."

"Peter bin Aziz!"

Alfred looked in a state of shock. "Yes sir I knew Peter I was responsible for his training and character building."

"Come here young man let me shake your hand for doing a great job on my son."

Alfred was gob smacked. I never knew that sir he never disclosed his real identity with anyone. Can I say this sir he gave me the cushiest six weeks of training recruits that I have ever had. If the rest of my flight wanted to know anything appertaining to drill or airmen's responsibilities I was surplus to requirements, the airmen went straight to Peter. After he qualified I kept looking in every new batch of recruits for another Peter. He will make a fine officer sir and will be well respected I respected him even when he was just an ordinary airman. They broke the mould when they made him sir."

"Thank you for that, I can tell you he spoke very favourable of you. He is doing exceptionally well at RAF Cranwell I am happy to say. No doubt when he comes on leave and I tell him you are here he will make his way to come and see you."

He looked at Dot.

"I am Dorothy Dean and a qualified Sergeant Drill Instructor at Royal Air Force March. Unfortunately for me I cannot produce a Royal Princess to add to my records sir but I do have many grateful female recruits who send me a Christmas card every year and some even remember my birthday. Other than that sir I do my job to the best of my ability, I think it is a really worth while job especially when you see young faces enjoying what is being taught to them."

"Thank you both for your honesty and I want to thank Colonel Barrett for bringing to my world two young intelligent and honest people who I know are trust-worthy. You will not go unrewarded because for starters your new ranks will be Lieutenant. As you know we base our ranks on the army style. Your accommodation is second to none and you will be issued with a courtesy car each. I am supplementing your meagre RAF pittance with a bank account in the Aljibian bank of course, that has nothing to do with the RAF. From here you will be taken to have your photographs taken for your Identity cards, then you will visit our clinic to have your injections, you can be assured that you will receive no ill effects. Lastly, can you wind up your personal arrangements and be ready to leave for Aljibia in three weeks time?"

"Yes sir," they said with great big smiles."

"Before you leave you will receive an envelope of instructions whilst you are here and you will receive all necessary documents through the post for your passage to Aljibia." He shook their hands and welcomed them to his service.

"Thank you very much sir."

They left following the official "Well sir you have made two young people very happy indeed and I thank you for it."

"It is me who should be thanking you Colonel for those two young ones you must be proud of your products.

"I certainly am sir and there are more to follow if needed."

"I almost burst out laughing at the young woman I thought she put over her points in a typical English humorous manner. "So until we meet again Colonel I wish you the best of luck with your project and please give my regards to your wife Tommy," he said with a smile.

They shook hands and Bill saluted then walked through that opened door which mysteriously opens to let in the official to show him out.

"Please wait in here for your protégés Colonel."

Half hour later Alfred and Dot were ushered into the room clutching their envelopes of instructions. Dot rushed to him and flung her arms round him in an embrace thanking him for what he done for them. Alfred followed her with a warm handshake beaming all over his face and thanking him for changing his life round.

"What I suggest," said Bill is to have a quick look at your information and read what it says about your visit to the tailors. I want to know if you both will be using the same one."

They compared notes and read that they were using the same tailors because they make uniforms for both sexes. "That is all I wanted to know. Come on."

"Right Jackson we will go and pick up Joyce she said she would chaperone Dot at the tailors."

It did not take long to pick up Joyce she was already waiting for them. Another few minutes run and they were at the tailors being greeted by the master tailor.

"Colonel Barrett how nice to see you again I was notified we would have two new customers to fit with uniforms and accessories. My tailoress will see to the young lady and I will see to the young gentlemen. Dot and Joyce followed the tailoress, while Alfred and Bill followed the tailor and Jackson stayed in the car.

A good hour or so elapsed before the measuring was completed. The tailor made notes of their ranks unfortunately there were no decorations to be added. You will both go next door to be fitted out with your footwear and I want to see you at 11 o' clock tomorrow morning for your final fitting."

Next door they were gob smacked to see the amount of footwear they had to try for size. On completion they had to sign a form for the shoes. "This footwear will be sent to the Embassy along with your uniforms etc."

Bill explained that their uniforms and footwear would arrive at their accommodation about one hour after they arrived themselves. "So you see you have nothing to worry about. Remember this though, the luggage you bring with you from RAF March Jackson will take it from you and take it to the Embassy because you are allowed to carry one piece of hand luggage only. I now suggest Jackson and Joyce we go to that super restaurant you took Tommy and I to, you know the one which does home cooking."

"That would be lovely Bill," said Joyce that would just make our day. You two will enjoy it for it is mine and Clarry's favourite eating place, the food is really good."

"It is my treat," said Bill. "We are celebrating my two new lieutenants."

After a lovely meal, enjoyed by all, Joyce suggested, "Why don't we all go home and I will make us all a nice cup of tea and Bill can phone Tommy, which he has not been able to do for a day or so."

While Bill was on the phone, Dot in particular, still bubbling with excitement, began telling Joyce and Jackson about the interview.

"Oh he is such a lovely man Joyce; he put us at ease as soon as we met him. We had to introduce ourselves but when Alfred spoke his piece I felt at a disadvantage because, unknown to Alfred, he had the Emir's son in his flight for recruit training. They had a good old chinwag and even the Emir did not know that Alfred was his son's instructor. The name Deacon rang a bell, he just said to Alfred 'Peter bin Aziz' and that started them off. Of course what could I say. I did make him smile though when I apologised for not having a Royal Princess I could talk about."

Alfred gave his version of being as surprised as the Emir about training his son Peter, who never once disclosed his real identity.

"Hello pet, yes it is me, your dearly beloved. Of course I am sorry for not phoning you earlier but I could not do that from the hotel you never know who could be listening in on their switchboard and I did not want to downgrade yours and my status Lady Barrett after all Jackson's good work in getting us that status. I think I told you that the Emir asked after you after he greeted me when I first arrived and as we left him this morning he asked me to give you his regards. Yes everything went well at the interview and the Emir upgraded them both in rank to Lieutenants. They are over the moon we have just been to get them tailored for their uniforms. Had lunch with Joyce and Jackson who took us to that lovely restaurant where they took us and I can still hear Dot telling them about the interview, she is absolutely bubbling with excitement. Of course you can have a word with her…Dot, Tommy wants a word."

"Hello Dot, congratulations on your promotion that has made my day, including Alfred's of course. You will obviously have met the Emir he is lovely isn't he?"

Dot then took over and tried to get everything that happened in one sentence "and guess what Tommy, Alfred and I will be in Aljibia with you in three week' time, isn't that wonderful?"

"Can I now have a word with Alfred please Dot?"

"Alfred," she shouted nearly bursting Tommy's eardrums. "Tommy wants a word with you."

"Hello Tommy, how nice to be able to speak with you although we will be speaking without a phone in three weeks time."

"Yes Dot told me and a million other things I could not take in but I want to congratulate you on your promotion."

"Thanks Tommy and we owe it all, every bit of it to your Bill. You hear of people having heroes, well he is certainly mine and Dot's, for what he has done for us that is something we will never ever forget."

"That is very sweet of you Alfred and I am looking forward to seeing you in three week's time. Will you ask Joyce to the phone please?"

"Hello Tommy how are you my love?"

"Nice to hear you Joyce I understand you might be suffering from a bit of earache," she said with a laugh.

"Bless her, she is so full of excitement I can understand why for what has happened to her today but she is a lovely girl. Clarry and I are doing quite well and we look forward so much to your letters because you make them so interesting. It is a pity you could not have come over with Bill we would have had a nice reunion. Yes Bill said I have to keep badgering Clarry for us to come and stay with you it sounds wonderful out there. Would you like a word with him? Right Tommy we will keep in touch. Clarry! Tommy wants you and you can tell her I will do her a swap!"

"Hi Tommy, how are you doing love? We were sorry Bill was not allowed to bring you with him but there is always another time and we hope soon. Yes Tommy, I am getting the message. No doubt I will be getting more earache after our company has left. Yes, I am kept busy with Embassy work and the taxi business is really doing well can't grumble. Are you still enjoying life out there? What a daft question to ask, of course you are. Anyway, I will love you and leave you and put you back to sir. Bye love."

"When do you expect to be back love, Leila and Thomas ask every day, they are missing you? Ella has been popping round on occasions to keep me company and taking me for a drive in the city. Of course it involves a little shopping but it is mostly food I have to get in for Thomas. I am getting myself a nice golden sun tan with having plenty of time on my hands. I was asking Ella the other day what has happened to those dinner parties she told us about? She had no idea I think they might have gone out of fashion which really does not bother me. Anyway, I will let you get back to Joyce and Jackson and your two new subordinates. Bye love. Mashy?"

"Mashy, Bye love."

"Well shall we now leave these lovely people in peace?" asked Bill. "And don't forget Jackson, we have to be at the tailors at 11am tomorrow."

"Very good sir and where do you want dropping off now?"

"The hotel for me please. What about you two?" They both chose the hotel. "Thank you for today Joyce, we will probably see you tomorrow because on the following day we all will be saying our farewells to you – these two to RAF March and me to sunny Aljibia."

"Don't forget your parcels you left with me," Joyce reminded him.

"Thank you for reminding me Joyce. I had completely forgotten them with all the excitement we have been through today. Yes, I will take them with me now."

After thanking Jackson and waving him off Bill said. "Study your information packet and if I can help in any way just give me a shout. I am going to do some planning for your arrival. Come in for a minute while we have a little chat…

In the first week after you arrive you will be off duty to become acclimatized to your new surroundings and the temperature. I will get my chauffeur to give you driving lessons during that week – about the local rules of the road and all that goes with it – for when you want to drive yourselves into the city and round about. Another perk is, you can fill up your fuel tank on the station for free, plus car servicing. You will find the city is very modern and you can purchase anything there, so minimise what you bring with you. We will be in touch with Viv in the Mess, so if you are in any doubts as to what you really need and think you will not be able to buy here, make a list and we will talk to you. It is extremely clean and you will see no beggars and you can be assured you will feel safe here. We also have an Ex-Pats Club which is very nice and the people are friendly mostly Europeans. It is run on democratic lines you leave your rank and status outside the door when you walk in. It boasts that you can buy a drink there from practically everywhere in the world. I have not tried them all, so I cannot verify that claim, we will take you there to become enrolled members. In your accommodations you have a housekeeper, now I do not know if it will be a personal one or one you will share. Bear with me a minute I will ring Tommy to ask Leila about your housekeepers. He did manage to get through to Tommy.

"Hello Barretts."

"Hi flower, it is only me. Dot and Alfred will be living in the Station's accommodation. Will you ask Leila if they will have a personal house keeper or if they will share one? Yes I will hang on."

"Hello love, Leila says they will have a personal one each but for the man he will have a personal male housekeeper."

"That figures. Where will they live?"

"In separate accommodation buildings each housekeeper is connected by phone to the person they look after. Is there anything else love?"

"No that is fine for now love, thank Leila. Salaam."

"Well you lucky people you will each have a personal Housekeeper to look after you. They all live in accommodation buildings for separate sexes of course and you are also linked by phone."

"Oh, that is brilliant, Bill it is like going into another world," said Andrew.

"What more lovely surprises are we going to get? Oh I am looking forward to it Bill I wish we were going tomorrow," said a very excited Dot.

"Why all this extravagance Bill I mean the cost of us three for instance must be enormous." Alfred asked.

"For a start it is an oil rich country that is why our two countries are so friendly and work together for each others benefits. Then the Emir, he is a very compassionate ruler and only wants the best for his people consequently he uses the country's riches to make a better place and life for his people, that is why the unemployment is practically zero. Take for instance your personal housekeepers, where in this world would you find a one to one situation similar to yours, *if* you could find one? We need to count our blessings for our good fortunes. The reason you are joining us early is because two weeks after you arrive the present batch of recruits pass-out and you will be there for their last week, then you take over from the two Sergeants who then come on a three month course to RAF March. You then set your stall out in readiness for the new recruits. Your first tip, although they speak perfect English it is natural they will converse in Arabic and you must order them to speak English in your presence at all times. If there is anything else you want to know just ask me, off you go, study your information and put your thinking caps on and waken me about 6pm for dinner or if you are thinking of going out waken me before then."

The following morning Reception rang Bill to tell him his transport had arrived. He promptly knocked on the doors of Alfred and Dot to tell them to get their skates on Jackson was here waiting for us. They both emerged smiling.

Joyce was sat in the car waiting and greeted them asking if they had a good night. "I'd like to bet it took you quite a while to drop off to sleep thinking of this morning's trip to the tailors."

They both laughed. "You would have won your bet Joyce," replied Dot.

"And you would have lost your bet with me," added Alfred.

In the car Jackson handed each of them their photos. "There is no charge they are our little gift to celebrate your promotions. I had one or two extra copies printed of us all. Joyce and I hope you will send us one of all three of you together in your uniforms."

At the tailors they each went for their fittings accompanied by Bill and Joyce. It went well because no alterations were needed for either of them. They signed the paper work then the tailor told them that everything would be sent to the Embassy.

He wished them both well and success in their new venture.

Bill told them the reason everything that went to the Embassy would be specially stored in diplomatic containers. "Now where do you want to go from here asked Bill of Dot and Alfred? Remember, tomorrow will be your last day."

"Can I suggest that you go to Harrods, I pick you up at 3 o'clock, take Bill and Joyce back home then take Alfred and Dot on a Jackson's Tour of London then we all have dinner at home and you can make plans for tomorrow there?"

"Clarry, it is a very rare occasion when you come up with a bright idea and I could kiss you for it but I have not time now I am off to Harrods."

"Then bring something special back for dinner from Harrods, you know an army marches on its stomach and we have three hungry Army/Air/Force mouths to fill."

"There you go and spoil yourself, if the RAFA Club president heard you he would kick that foot of yours off the rungs of the promotion ladder."

"Arthur would not do that to his favourite club member Joyce would he?" asked Bill.

"Oh yes he would." She shouted.

"Oh no he wouldn't" the rest retaliated with loud laughter.

"Come on," Jackson grinned, "your taxi is waiting."

During the latter part of the tour Jackson received a call on his car phone to report to the Embassy. "Here we go; we cannot finish the tour although we were coming to the end of it. If I have a pick up I will drop you off at home first." When he reported to reception he had to sign for four envelopes, three to be delivered to the Savoy Hotel and one for himself. He laughed when he saw who they were addressed to. In the car he showed Alfred and Dot the envelopes. I am sorry but I must deliver them to the reception, it is ironic but I am afraid I must stick to the rules. At a guess they will hold your Air tickets. At the hotel he handed them in to reception.

"You both can pick yours up now but Bill will have to pick his up personally." He opened his envelope which contained his instructions for taking them to the airport, all three persons having to be there at 8am to check in. He then read his instructions to them.

"We will pick ours up when we go back to the hotel later along with Bill" they said.

Back home Bill was told about the envelopes. "Then we can concentrate on tomorrow's itinerary."

"You men get yourselves a beer while Dot and I slave away in the kitchen over a hot stove," Joyce said with a dramatic sigh.

"Alright love," replied Jackson, "we will keep out of your way and let you get on with it," as he gave Bill and Alfred a wink.

"You have been doing that for years. Men! They turn you into a dogsbody Dot, so be warned."

"Are you ready for another one lads?" He called loud enough to get a banging of pans from the kitchen.

After the meal Joyce was congratulated on her cooking by her three guests. "Didn't I tell you on our way home in the car that you would be in for a treat when you taste my Joyce's cooking?"

"Jackson you are telling your Porkies again."

"Would I do that in front of our guests?"

"Yes, and you have just done so."

When everything was cleared away and they were having coffee Joyce asked. "Have you decided on tomorrow's programme?"

"I think I would like to see the big stores while I have the chance Joyce" said Dot.

"Well I will take you round them if you would like me to," she answered. "What about you Alfred?"

"I would like to go in the Tower of London then to the Palace to see the changing of the guard please."

"That is fair enough, no problem" assured Jackson. "What about you Bill?"

I think I will just stroll round some of the old shops, I find them very interesting and I can find my own way back to the hotel, Jackson."

"Have you any thoughts on this evening Bill?"

"I suggest we all have a nice quiet evening at the RAFA club?" said Joyce.

Everyone agreed. "Then I will pick you up at 8pm. She is a good woman," Jackson said in an undertone to Alfred.

"You are at it again Jackson, you had better behave yourself tonight or I will report you to Arthur."

"You would not do that to your beloved would you light of my eyes?"

"YES!"

At the hotel they picked up their respective letters from reception. Bill's was straight forward. Check in at Heathrow at 8am on the private aircraft to Aljibia. Alfred and Dot were also to check in at Heathrow at 8am and were flying Business Class to Leeds where RAF transport would take them to RAF March.

They had a very enjoyable evening at the RAFA Club where they were introduced to the Club's President, Arthur. Jackson took them to see the photograph of the BlueBelles in its pride of place. "Bill donated that to the club plus a video which has made this the most popular club in the area so much so there is a waiting list for membership. The members here think the world of Bill and made him an Honorary Member."

When he dropped them off at the hotel he reminded Bill to have his luggage ready for me to take to the Embassy. "I can drop it off there before we set off on our tours."

"The following day was enjoyed by Alfred and Dot but it passed all too quickly for them. "I will pick you up at 7:30 in the morning. Joyce insists she is coming to see you all off because she says it may be quite some time before we see you again but I will be picking you up in three weeks' time then sending you off the next day."

After thanking and waving Jackson and Joyce off, Bill announced, "I am going to freshen up then going to dinner after which I will relax with a drink watching Television."

"Well let us know when you are getting ready and we will come down with you."

"Good, I will be ready in one hour."

During dinner Bill told them about Tommy being disappointed with the hotel because with the hotel having such a high class reputation she had not seen one celebrity during our stay.

"Now you mention it Bill neither have I, have you Alfred? Well you must not or you would have mentioned it."

"It might not be the celebrity season," laughed Alfred.

"Are we all ready?" Asked Bill.

"Yes, and I am going to take a leaf out of your book Bill, a drink and Tele'

"Me too and why not," added Dot.

CHAPTER 17

On the morning of departure everybody was up bright and early to have a good breakfast to see them on their way. Bang on time Jackson arrived to find the three of them waiting in the lounge for him. An attendant carried their luggage to the waiting car and helped to load it which got him a good tip from Bill.

"Good morning Joyce," they all greeted her. "How are you after getting up in the middle of the night to see us on our way?"

"It is worth it to see you off although I am not happy about it. I would like you all to phone us you have arrived safely, we can expect your message tonight Bill."

On arrival at Heathrow Jackson got a trolley for Alfred's and Dot's luggage.

"We are not coming onto the terminal said Joyce." So they said their farewells there and then.

"Will you ring Tommy, Joyce to tell her I am on my way please?"

"Thank you Jackson and Joyce for your friendship and hospitality, we have loved being with you," said Dot.

"Be off with you or you will miss your planes said an emotional Joyce."

Joyce and Jackson waved them all the way until they went out of sight into the terminal building.

Once inside Bill said. "Now it is our turn to say farewell but only for a short time."

"They shook hands and a kiss from Dot. I know it is sounding monotonous Bill but we both want to thank you for everything you have done for us we promise that we will be the best subordinates you will ever be likely to have."

"Do you see that Arabic gentleman over there? Well you will report to him when you come here for your VIP flight and that is where I am heading now. Tell Viv we will be in touch with her and give my regards to all our friends and thank them for the great welcome they gave me. Bye for now and roll on three weeks time."

Alfred and Dot boarded their aircraft and felt quite important sitting in the Business Class. "I could get used to this kind of travel," said Alfred. "Bill told me about the private plane to Aljibia all the seating is double seats and recliners. You also get a choice of menus with the meals; I am looking forward to that."

"Hmm! it sounds very nice," replied Dot but I am not complaining about this flight. If all goes according to plan we should reach RAF March by about 11 o'clock and I think that is about the time Bill will be taking off."

They did indeed arrive at RAF March a few minutes after 11 o'clock and the first person to welcome them back was Jackie. After a quick summary of telling her how they had enjoyed their trip to London they made their way to their various rooms. A few minutes later Dot opened her door to see a smiling Jackie with a mug of tea for her.

"I thought you would welcome a brew Dot, I am now going to take one to Alfred."

He was very appreciative of it and thanked her.

After unpacking their cases they went individually to lunch, Alfred was welcomed back by the Chef then went to sit with his mates. When Dot came in Chef also welcomed her back, she obviously went to sit with her friends. They both got waves from the Warrant Officers sat at the top tables. Dot was busy trying to eat her lunch while trying not to get over excited telling them of her experience. Flight Sergeant Margaret Roper after collecting her lunch from the food servery took her meal to another table then approached the table where all the excitement was coming from.

"Report for duty tomorrow morning!" There was no reply from anyone. She raised her voice and shouted, "I said report for duty tomorrow morning are you bloody deaf or summat' Dean?"

"I am sorry Flight I did not hear you," replied Dot.

"I am not surprised with all this chattering you are like a load of bloody monkeys and I am Flight Sergeant to you and don't you forget it." With that she went back to her table and as she sat down the other diners at the table took their meals and walked away to another table.

Viv who had witnessed this scenario from the top table got up and confronted Roper. "You are a despicable creature, report to my office the first thing after lunch!"

Roper burst into tears and ran out of the dining room.

Viv then went over to Dot. "Welcome back Dot I am simply dying to hear how you went on at the interview can we have a chat about it this evening in the Quiet Room please?" By the way if you want your meal replacing because it must be cold by now and that goes for the rest of you I will have a word with Chef."

"Thank you Ma'am they each replied we could not face anything now after that tirade."

Margaret Roper was stood waiting outside Viv's office when Viv returned.

"Give me a minute or two Margaret and I will get back to you." She then rang Sqd.Ldr. Macfarlane's (Mac) Office and spoke to Sergeant Marion Macken, Mac's PA.

"Is the Squadron Leader in Marion this is WO Anderson speaking?"

"She has just walked in Ma'am, I will connect you."

"Squadron Leader Macfarlane speaking."

"Ma'am this is WO Anderson I want to report to you about Flight Sergeant Roper who has just had another outburst more serious than the last one" She explained what had happened then added. "I honestly believe Ma'am she needs medical attention."

"I will ring the Sick Quarters Warrant and have a word with the M.O. I will ring you back."

Viv called Roper in and told her to sit down. "Margaret I am not happy about your outbursts which I find are totally against your nature and I do think you need to seek some medical advice. I have informed our O.C who is now contacting the M.O. for an appointment for you."

"Thank you Viv I think you are right because I can offer no explanation why I am acting in such an obnoxious manner."

The phone rang. "This will be the O.C."

"Warrant, tell Roper to make up her small pack for an overnight stay then take her to Sick Quarters?"

"Very good Ma'am will do. You have to take what you need for an overnight stay Margaret then I will walk you to Sick Quarters. If there is anything else you need let me know and I will see to it." When they reported to S.S.Quarters Viv told her, "Co-operate with them Margaret and you will be back soon, I want you back."

That evening in the Quiet Room Dot was surprised to see so many faces waiting for her, even Alfred was there.

Roy jumped up immediately to ask her if she would like a drink.

"Come and sit down Dot," invited Viv. "When word got around all your friends turned up to hear yours and Alfred's experiences in London. Before you start I must tell you that I took Margaret Roper to Sick Quarters with the blessings of the Squadron Leader, Margaret herself said she realises that is where she should be. Now between you and Alfred how about telling us something to cheer us up and to be proper envious of you both? Alfred has told us you have some photos to show that you did stay at the Savoy Hotel; can we see those at the end please?

They commenced with travelling Business Class to London, meeting Jackson who chauffeured them during all of their stay. Everyone was spellbound when they described their audience with the Emir and what he had given them. "We are now waiting to see our accommodation. It sounds beautiful and having our personal housekeeper is quite something. I should think we will not want to come back here after experiencing that kind of lifestyle, which is all due to Bill." Showing a little emotion she said, "I now say a little prayer every night for Bill Barrett before I go to sleep."

"Right then, let us see those photos; we want to see you posing at the Savoy."

CHAPTER 18

After leaving Alfred and Dot, Bill introduced himself to the young man who took him to the VIP check-in then to the VIP lounge.

"Please make use of all the facilities sir."

Bill thanked him then went and got himself a newspaper, seated himself and ordered tea from the attendant who approached him. Looking at the schedule monitor he saw the flight was an hour earlier than last time. Looking round the lounge at other travellers he wondered how many of the six males he saw would be travelling with him. He carried on drinking his tea and reading the day's news until an announcement told them to make their way to the aircraft. He let the six go before him so that he could chose a seat not too near them; he wanted to be alone with his thoughts.

Soon after take-off the stewardess came round with menus for breakfast. He ordered the Full English Breakfast, thinking 'it is a long time to lunch and it will help me to settle down'. After the breakfast tray had been removed by the stewardess he got a newspaper from a rack and began reading until he felt drowsy. He slept until he was wakened for lunch, after which he took a portfolio from his bag and began to make plans leading up to Alfred and Dot joining him. Soon the Captain was announcing their arrival at Dubai to disembark passengers and, due to a quick turn round no-one else was allowed off the aircraft.

'So I miss the chance to stretch my legs at Dubai again.... ah well, I will manage it one of these days,' Bill said to himself. He returned to his planning and thought *'I hope there is a WAF Officer waiting for me to be interviewed'*.

He was brought out of his reverie by the Captain announcing they would be arriving at Aljibia Airport in fifteen minutes. He looked at his watch which read 5:45. *'Bang on time,'* he muttered. As he disembarked he thanked the stewardess, then made his way to immigration, showing his Passport and I.D card. At Customs he was waved through and went to meet Fred, who was waving madly to him with a big smile on his face.

"You are a sight for sore eyes Fred," he said, as he acknowledged the salute by shaking Fred's hand.

"Welcome home Colonel. There is going to be some rejoicing when you walk through your door, they have all missed you and have been looking forward to today, especially Mrs B when your friends phoned her to tell her you were on your way."

"And how has it been with you Fred? Has she kept you busy with shopping trips and did you do as I asked by keeping her away from clothes shops?"

"Sir, I ask you what chance had I against two determined women?"

"You see what I mean Fred… It is tough at the top!"

"How did your trip go sir?"

"It could not have been better. The Emir granted me everything I asked for and more besides and my protégés will be arriving here in three weeks time." I spent a little time with my friends, who gave me great welcome and I paved the way for Sergeant Saleem and Sergeant (WAF) Anisa for when they go for their three months training course."

"Here we are sir, home."

"Will you come in for a drink and a bite to eat Fred?"

"No thank you sir, I have already eaten, and besides, I do not want to be in the way of your homecoming celebrations. Are you back on duty tomorrow sir?"

"Yes Fred I am, so it will be the usual time for pick-up. Salaam Fred and Shukran."

"Salaam Colonel."

Tommy was waiting in the doorway to greet her husband. They embraced and kissed. "Welcome home love, I have missed you. Come on in, Thomas and Leila are waiting to greet you they have been looking forward to this moment ever since I told them you were on your way."

Entering the Villa he saw a smiling Thomas and Leila, who came to him with outstretched hands to welcome him back.

"What a nice welcome from you both, thank you, it is really good to see you."

"Now what do you want to do? Freshen up and have a beer, or the other way round?"

"I will freshen up first."

"Thomas has held dinner back, when can it be ready Thomas?"

"In one hour Ma'am. That will give sir time to relax a little to enjoy his beer."

"While I am sorting myself out will you phone Jackson and Viv to let them know I am home safe and sound?"

Tommy did not need asking twice. She was on the phone before Bill had left the room. Jackson and Joyce both had a word with her and sent their love. It was not so simple as that when she rang Viv, because she got a blow by blow account of Margaret Roper's outburst and the result of it.

When Bill appeared she got his beer, saying, "I have some surprising news for you from Viv…" She then told him the story.

"I am not at all surprised. I could see it coming." He told Tommy of the first outburst Roper had made about Dot. "You wait and see, she will be medically discharged and then Viv will be without a Flight Sergeant. But Viv, Joe Franks and I had a pow-wow with this in mind and we agreed that Marion James would take over Roper's role. Now she will have to ask for one of her corporals to be promoted to sergeant to fill in the gap Marion will leave."

Tommy went into the kitchen and asked Thomas. "How long will it be to dinner?"

"You can come in now Ma'am."

On entering the kitchen Bill remarked, "You have made my taste buds tingle Thomas, it smells like I am about to have a treat."

When Leila served him, he gave a big smile. "It is Lancashire Hot Pot." After polishing it off and savouring every mouthful he announced. "Leila. Your husband is not just a good Chef, he is a brilliant Chef, and you should be very proud of him. It was a wonderful meal to come home to after a long journey, Thomas."

"Thank you sir," said a very happy Thomas. "But I was under supervision."

"All you need to know are the ingredients Thomas, and you do not need supervising. But thank you for making us a delicious meal. He has made one for himself and Leila and we will get their verdict tomorrow. And if we do not get the thumbs-up sign from you, young man, you will be relegated to doing the housework while Leila and I take over and spend more time in the city."

"Oh Mrs Barrett, you do keep making us laugh," smiled Leila.

"Coffee time now, then as soon as you finish tidying up Leila, off you go and thank you both for taking good care of us."

They had just sat down to coffee when the door bell rang. "That will be my luggage; I will go and let the man in."

"Your luggage sir. Will you sign that you have got everything and it is in good order please?"

Bill duly signed and relieved the man of the single case.

"Do you want another coffee, love? I think that one will be cold by now."

"Have Thomas and Leila gone home yet?"

"It is no problem, I can make you one."

"No, it is not for that reason that I ask, I have something in here for them and I don't want them to see it yet."

"I will go and check." She toddled off to the kitchen and Bill heard her ask. "Haven't you finished yet? Here let me give you a hand you will get me a bad name for being a slave driver."

They laughed. "We would never do anything like that, Mrs Barrett."

After ten minutes everything was spick and span. "Now get yourselves off home and enjoy your Lancashire Hotpot, which I am sure you will. TisbaH ala-kheir. (Goodnight)

"Goodnight Ma'am," they responded, smiling.

"They have just gone now."

When she sat down he handed her a gift parcel. Her eyes lit up. For me?" She unwrapped the gift wrapping and saw that famous name…Harrods. "Oh what is it?" she asked getting all excited.

"Open it and see."

She tentatively and slowly lifted the lid to see nestling in velvet a bottle of perfume. She gasped when she saw the name on the label. Ralph Lauren…'Love' she flung her arms round him, "Thank you, thank you it is beautiful. I saw it when we went in Harrods and straight away I placed it at the top of my wish list but it is very expensive."

"You are worth it love. This one here I have bought for Barbara Battle, you cannot see it because it is also gift wrapped, it is a perfume called …'Princess'. "

"I saw that one as well."

"This is for Leila, I forget what that is called but it is a 'Smellie'. Now this one is for Thomas, we will have to open it because I want us both to sign it."

Tommy very carefully opened it and gave a gasp when she saw what it was. "Oh Bill, what a wonderful present for him he will love it."

"I was wracking my brains on the aircraft coming home for something suitable to write in it. And I have come up with…'To Thomas from a Grateful Colonel and Mrs Barrett', then we both sign it and date it. What do you think of that?"

"That will do fine. I think I had better do the printing mine is neater than yours." She went for her pen from the bureau and carefully printed the wording. "Are you using my pen or yours to sign it?"

"I will use yours because it is a good speller."

"Daft beggar."

Tommy then rewrapped it carefully. "There you are sir; you would never have known it had been opened. Shall we give them their presents after breakfast?"

"We can do if you like so long as Thomas has time to cook my dinner in between reading the book."

"Have no fear Leila will make sure he does that. I suggest we now have a bit of supper then bed time, you are up early in the morning don't forget."

"Leila won't let us oversleep."

At 6am the following morning Leila entered their bedroom with their early morning tea "Good morning Leila, thank you. Leila is here with your tea Noddy so rise and shine."

"Ugh, is it that time already? Morning Leila."

"Good morning sir," your usual breakfast?"

"Yes please."

"And you Ma'am?"

"Yes please but I will have mine after sir has gone otherwise it might put me off my food."

Leila left the room laughing as she went.

"Good morning Thomas how are you today? Bill said when he entered the kitchen."

"I am fine sir your breakfast will be ready by the time you sit down."

"I will have a coffee please Leila it will do me until I can sit down and enjoy my breakfast."

Bill finished then thanked Thomas then went off to get himself ready for Fred calling.

"Tommy, I am ready now."

Thomas and Leila will you come into the lounge for a minute please we have something to say to you. When they were all assembled Tommy spoke. "We want to thank you both for taking such good care of us, helping us to settle in quickly and becoming our friends. In appreciation we wish to show our gratitude by giving you both a little gift" She gave Leila her gift and Bill gave Thomas his gift.

Thomas gave an embarrassing cough and thanked them both while Leila was so overcome she was speechless but threw her arms round Tommy and hugged her until her speech came back. "Oh thank you so much we have never experienced anything like this before but we do love you both."

"I am sorry to break up the party but Fred is here and I must leave for another hard day at the office," Bill said grinning. "I will see you all later," he kissed Tommy. "See you later love."

They all went to the door to wave him and Fred off.

"Fred saluted. "Good morning sir you have had a good send off this morning is that a sign of thank goodness he has gone now we can relax?"

"On the contrary Fred I had to fight them off trying to keep me. You know this popularity is getting a bore now I would like to get back to normal. Hey watch your driving," as Fred swerved due to an uncontrolled splutter. Do you like football Fred?"

"Yes sir I watch the English teams playing on Television when I can."

"Have you got a favourite team?"

"Yes sir Arsenal, I have watched them as often as I could from being a young boy, many of my work friends support them too." He pulled up at the entrance gates and Bill returned the salute he always got from the guards. "I forgot to ask you sir, were you successful with your mission in London?"

"I was indeed Fred the Emir rubber stamped everything I asked for plus more besides." I have no plans for wanting you again Fred until it is pick-up time for home but who knows. See you later."

He silently opened his office door, sat at his desk, pressed the intercom and a voice came over, "You are back, you cannot fool me Colonel Barrett." He entered Barbara's office with a big smile on his face.

"Ah, your mission was successful you are wearing a big smile. Welcome back sir."

"Thank you Barbara, shall we have a brew then you can come into my office then I can tell you all about it unless of course you are too busy?"

She laughed, "I am still waiting for that to happen sir. Anyway I will be with you in a jiffy."

When she brought in the brew she also brought in a chocolate biscuit.

"Aha! A Chocky Bicky is this to celebrate the return of the Prodigal Son?" He then told her about his interviews with the Emir and the reactions of Alfred and Dot from their interviews with him, Dot by the way is dying to meet you. He told her about being reunited with all his friends and the great welcomes he got from everyone except of course from the Wing Commander and his outbursts."

Barbara was utterly disgusted with the behaviour of such a senior Officer and was delighted with his punishment. "The man was not fit to be in charge of people."

"Now the good thing is, Alfred and Dot will be joining us in three weeks time and aren't they just looking forward to coming, given a chance they would have come back with me. Now what news have you got for me?"

"More entries in the diary sir and one or two diners in the restaurant have asked where you were, other than that…nothing. Now you are back things might hot up."

"Well to compensate for your misery being left here all alone here is a small gift."

"Well thank you sir, I will open it after I have washed the pots."

A few minutes later he heard a scream of delight. She came scurrying through to thank him again. "It is very kind of you and it is deeply appreciated, thank you very much sir it is lovely."

He gave her time to settle down then asked her to contact the Major if he was free to see him.

"You can go right away sir and it sounds like another fan is looking forward to seeing you."

"Come in" was the answer to his knock on the door." Eric jumped up from his chair and came forward with outstretched hand. "It is good to have you back Bill; I have kept looking at the calendar wondering if each day would the next one I would see you back. Come, sit down and tell me about your visit to the UK."

Bill told him as much as he wanted to tell him, my two protégés will be joining us in three weeks time as Lieutenants. The Emir was so impressed with them he upgraded their rank. Now what I am about to tell you is confidential and on a need to know basis I do not know if you have been informed but Sam Barnes…Eric interrupted.

"Yes Bill we have been told and I appreciate you taking me into your confidence, that in my book is a true sign of friendship, thank you."

"What about the WAF officer I asked for Eric I need to interview more than one to choose the one I want? I want one here before the new intake of WAF recruits arrive.

"I will have a word with the Commandant Bill."

"Thanks Eric I am now going to see if there are any improvements in the standard of the present recruits since I last saw them."

"Barbara, if I am wanted I will be with the recruits or Captain Khatib. Yes I have got my bleeper."

As he approached the airmen Sergeant Saleem must have been tipped off that the Colonel was approaching because he immediately swivelled on his heels and saluted Bill. Bill returned the salute and told Saleem to put the recruits through their paces. After a few minutes Bill told him to call them to a halt and stand them at ease.

"I am not happy with the non-progress you have failed to administer while I have been absent. I would like to place you in the ranks and drill you with the rest of the recruits but that would be an insult to your rank as a supposedly Drill Instructor. If it was left to me I would strip you of your rank and kick you off the Station and what becomes of you after that I would not care less. Now get back to your flight and try to instruct."

A very chastened Sergeant saluted and tried to march back to the flight with dignity.

From there Bill went to see how Sergeant Anisa was shaping. She saw Bill approach and immediately halted her flight, turned and saluted Bill. "Good morning Sergeant Anisa how are your girls coming along with their drill?"

"Very well sir, after seeing your film they have taken more interest in it and I do believe they are enjoying it. They are even trying to sing the Blue-Belles signature song."

"That is pleasing to know and I see they are taking more interest in their appearance too. I have also got some good news for you. When these girls pass out you will be going on a three months Drill Instructors course to the UK."

She had to stifle a little scream of delight. "Thank you sir I will do my very best for you."

"I suggest you start to put your personal arrangements in order ready for the move. Incidentally I have told the Warrant Officer who will be in charge of your training of your capabilities and I can assure you that you will be in good hands. Carry on Sergeant."

He hurried back to the Major's Office determined that Saleem would not go on that course to the UK. He knocked on Eric's door and was told to enter.

"You are looking very stern Bill; I sense you are not happy about something."

"Too bloody true Eric. I have just been to see how Sergeant Saleem was getting on with his flight. He has not made one iota of improvement to their drill while I have been away. He is lazy, incompetent, and has not a clue what to do. Eric I want him as far away from here as is possible to put it bluntly I want him off the premises because he is detrimental to my training programme and I would like an interview with the Commandant please."

"Stay here Bill I will go and see him right now."

Ten minutes later he returned. I have told the Commandant the reason you would like to see him and he sounded very sympathetic, you can go in immediately.

Come on I will take you in and good luck Bill."

"Colonel Barrett sir," Eric announced. Bill saluted.

"Come and sit down and tell me all about this Saleem problem."

Bill told him all the reasons he wanted Saleem removed from his staff. I encouraged him and pointed out to him the right way of training recruits. Those airmen have not learned a thing since I have been away. If you could see the results from the teachings of the instructors on the men and women you would without any shadow of doubt say the women were trained by a qualified instructor and the men by a novice it is so bad sir."

"I can sympathise with you Colonel you apparently have a bad egg on your staff. I will get rid of him but how are you going to replace him for we have no qualified Instructors in reserve in fact we have no reserve."

"With respect sir, I would like to suggest to you that my two subordinates are posted to us as quickly as possible. As you know they were due here in three weeks time but this is an emergency sir. I will get them to train the present recruits up to their passing out. I am hoping you can delay the next intake of recruits for three weeks which will give my subordinates time and grace to acclimatise them to the environment, then to make plans ready to receive the new intakes. I will personally take charge of training the men until I can hand them over to my subordinates. RAF March will have to be notified of the change that Sergeant Anisa will be the only student sent from here for the course."

"Colonel that is well thought out and I can find no objections to it. I would like you now to send Saleem to Major Khaleel's Office."

"Thank you sir," he saluted and left He went into Eric's office and gave him the thumbs up sign. "I have to send Saleem to you to receive a wave of good bye."

"Well done Bill you are certainly sorting that lot out. "

"I have given it the name of 'Operation New Broom' Eric.

"Very appropriate Bill I will tell that to the Commandant he will like it."

Once again Sergeant Saleem was warned of Bill's approach. He turned on his heels and gave Bill a salute which Bill returned. "Sergeant Saleem go and report to Major Khaleel's Office immediately."

"Yes sir." he saluted and marched off.

Bill faced the airmen. "That is the last you will see of Sergeant Saleem from now on I will be instructing you and if I do not get a one hundred percent effort from you I will run you so ragged you will think that any free time you may get will seem like a holiday. I am now going to dismiss you and tomorrow morning at 9 o'clock we will commence with a Barrack Room Inspection, following that there will be a Personal Inspection. I will give you a little advice though…Play the game with ME and I will play the game with YOU. Mashy?"

"Mashy, sir," they yelled.

"Parade… Atten…Shun. Dis…Miss."

He smiled to himself as he marched off. An airman's free time is sacred to him they will respond there is no fear of that.

Back once more in his office he buzzed Barbara. "Are you ready for lunch Miss Battle?"

"I am sir."

On the way there she asked have you had a busy morning sir."

"Indeed I have and will you insert into your diary 'Operation New Broom' please?"

"Oh dear that suggests some-one in your military jargon has got the 'chop' am I right sir?"

"Have you been speaking to the Commandant?"

"No sir Major Khaleel. He came bursting into your office full of excitement and he just blurted out to me that Sergeant Saleem had got his marching orders."

"I will tell you over lunch," he said as a waiter escorted them to their regular table.

After giving him their orders he told her the reason he had taken action against Saleem. "I will be in my office very little in the next few days for I am taking over instructing the airmen. I have asked for the arrival of my subordinates to be brought forward as quickly as possible to fill the gap before the new intakes arrive."

"What about their acclimatisation do you call that fair pushing them into the deep end straight away?"

"Barbara you are forgetting something, I trained them they will not query my decisions or judgement they will know there is a purpose behind this and they will give me one hundred percent back up. I have asked for the new intakes to be put back for three weeks after the present intakes pass out. Then Alfred and Dot can relax and become acclimatised and make plans for when they commence training the new intakes."

"I am sorry sir I should stick to my secretarial work but I feel I am part of this dramatic reforming of the Recruit Training Centre."

"And so you are Miss Battle and so you are."

Later in the day Eric entered Bill's office with his face wreathed in smiles. "Congratulations Colonel you have won the day again for us. The requests you made have been accepted and your two subordinates have been notified and will arrive here Thursday."

"That is great news Eric, the Emir does not let grass grow under his feet but gets on with the job. I will now go and have a word with Captain Khatib."

I will be with Captain Khatib, Barbara if I am wanted."

Approaching his office he acknowledged the smiles of Khatib's team with a slight wave of the hand. "Good day to you Captain Khatib, shall we sit down I want to put you in the picture of what is happening concerning my training staff. It will probably be no surprise to you when I tell you I have got rid of Saleem for his total incompetence. I am trying to get the services of a female officer to be in charge of all my female staff which will include your two Lieutenants. You will then be in total charge of the airmen which include your two Lieutenants that goes without saying. I want you to prepare an office for the arrival of the Female Officer who will be of the same rank as yourself. That leaves us with one vacant office which I want for my two Lieutenant subordinates whose services I have acquired as Qualified Drill Instructors to teach our recruits. As such they will have the authority to check on those wall charts which you and your Lieutenants have so brilliantly displayed, I commend you all on that. I must tell you that my two subordinates are highly qualified in the use of those wall charts they were taught that in their training. Instil in your four staff it is not a take over of their domains but I will insist on full co-operation from every-one on my staff with myself and each other. They will obey my rules or I will get rid of them it is as simple as that. A word about my subordinates Captain Their aim will be to turn out well disciplined recruits plus character building and they are at the top of their profession to do that. Their own characters are impeccable and likeable as you will find out. By the way I have had their postings brought forward because of the Saleem incident; I will introduce them to you on Monday. Is there anything you wish to ask Captain?"

"No sir you have made it very clear and I can assure you they will be made welcome to my staff," he said with a smile. "I will brief my staff on what you have told me sir."

"One other thing Captain, whatever you want to make those offices comfortable and your other three use my secret weapon and you know where to find me if you have any problems."

"Thank you sir I will do that," he said with a smile.

As Bill left he gave the four officers a friendly wave then returned to his own office.

"Will you join me in a nice cool soft drink Miss Battle?"

"That would be nice sir, thank you."

CHAPTER 19

On arriving home he was greeted with a kiss from Tommy. "Get yourself freshened up love and I will have a cool beer waiting for you."

When he returned he asked what kind of a day she had.

"Very nice it became very excitable after you left when Thomas and Leila opened their gifts. They were absolutely thrilled to bits especially Thomas his eyes nearly popped out of his head when he saw what it was, they will be thanking you later. What has your day been like were they glad to see you back and did Barbara like her little gift?"

"She was thrilled to bits but I have got more exciting news for you. Alfred and Dot will arrive here on Thursday."

"Why what has happened? But it is not giving them much time to do whatever they had to do."

"Calm down now it is only an emergency," he teased with.

"What emergency? What has gone wrong? You do not leave that chair until you tell me what is going on."

"He laughed, "I was only teasing you love." He told her the whole tale. "You see it really is an emergency but not of the kind you were thinking of. I have made plans which will concern us all. You and I will go and meet them at the airport and we will take them a meal in baskets which Thomas and Leila will make up, oh yes, we will put one of our cards in the baskets then they can get in touch to speak with us. We will see them to the door and let them have their independence, what do you think about that?"

"That is good thinking, shall I ask Thomas to make up sandwiches for us as well because we will be quite late getting back and it will not be fair for them to be hanging about waiting for us to turn up then having to tidy up after dinner?"

"Yes, that is what we will do. Friday you could take them to town to get their money sorted out at the bank then give them a quick shufti round the shops. They then could either stay here for dinner or go to their own restaurant. Now I will phone Viv to ask about their reactions then you can have a word with her afterwards. Mashy?"

"Mashy."

"Then you read me the numbers."

"RAF March Sergeants Mess can I help you?"

"I would like to speak to Warrant Officer Anderson please."

"Who is speaking please?"

"Colonel Barrett."

He heard a scream. "It is me sir, Marion Macken, oh you have caused a panic here, I will get Viv she will tell you all about it."

After a little wait Viv came to the phone. "What are you doing to our staff Colonel Barrett?"

"It is an emergency Viv, I have got rid of the male instructor and I am taking over until Alfred arrives." He then told her the whole saga.

"You should see the pair of them here they are leaping about like two year olds, I have never seen excitement like it and believe it or not it is contagious with our staff we are all so pleased for them."

"Will you tell them Tommy and I will be at the airport to meet and greet them? I will be in touch with you before then Viv thanks and my regards to the family. Now Tommy is almost snatching the phone out of my hand to speak to you. Bye love."

"Hi Viv, isn't it wonderful news we are so looking forward to them coming." Their chat went on for long enough.

When she came off the phone she said "We had better go to dinner or Thomas will be saying 'your dinner is in the oven'. We are coming Leila, sorry about that Thomas but it was a very important call we had to make."

"It is no problem Mrs Barrett please be seated Leila is ready to serve you. Before we start we would like to thank you sir for the wonderful gifts it is very kind of you.

The recipe book is now my second priceless possession."

"What is your first one Thomas, if I may ask?"

"My wife Leila, Ma'am."

"That is very nice Thomas and I agree with you."

When the table had been cleared, Bill and Tommy were discussing if its size was suitable for four persons. "I think it is big enough Bill, besides it is so homely in here, having it in the dining room would make it too formal."

Leila was listening to the debate with a puzzled look.

"This little chat we are been having will concern you both Leila. The Colonel has two Lieutenants, who incidentally are friends of ours assigned to his staff and they arrive here on Thursday. They are being accommodated on the Domestic Site; remember we asked you about it Leila. Will you please make up two baskets of food for them on Thursday; sandwiches will do fine. The reason for this is their restaurant will not be open at the time they arrive therefore we think they will feel more at ease having sandwiches. I am sorry I did not mention that they are a male and a female. On Friday I will take them into town to do their banking then have a shufti round the shops and we shall invite them here to dinner. We were looking to see if the table was adequate for four diners."

"Oh yes Ma'am it will easily seat four."

"Thank you Leila. We would like a cosy meal not a formal one. I do not know what you think Thomas, but I am thinking on the line of a nice Arabian meal. You have a good idea of what our tastes are like so I am sure if you judge the meal on that it should be Mashy. Do you agree with that Thomas?"

"I will serve you a meal you will enjoy Ma'am."

"My memory is playing tricks with me at the moment with having so much to tell you. On Thursday we shall meet them at the airport and take the sandwiches with us, but we do not know how long we will be. Therefore we have decided that we would like you to make us sandwiches for dinner, then as soon as we return you both can go home."

"But madam…"

Tommy interrupted her. "Leila, I have an idea what you are about to say but thank you, please accept our decision. Now can we have coffee please? Then you can go home."

As they sat drinking their coffee Bill jumped with a start. "I must phone Jackson. Tommy, will you call out the numbers, you will hear what I have to say. Hello Joyce it is Bill Barrett. If Jackson is there I would like a word with him."

"Hang on a minute Bill, while I wake him up."

"Hello sir, your batman speaking."

"Then stand to attention when you are speaking to me. I would like you to do me a favour Jackson. Can you get me an Arsenal football shirt, a large size please? I want it for my chauffeur. With no number on the back but the word Arsenal – and put it on my bill please."

"No problem Bill and I will give it to Alfred Wednesday evening, then he can put it in his luggage."

"It is obvious you know their arrival date has been brought forward; it was at my request." He then told him why.

"You certainly have been busy since you went back. Can you find a job for an ex- Station Warrant Officer? I would be in my element there… SIR!"

"If only Jackson! What a team we would make. Tommy is here and she would like a word with yourself and Joyce, so get yourself a beer while you are waiting for her to come off the phone," he rounded off with a laugh.

"Hello Jackson, yes fine but at present with this lark going on it is hectic…" After a few minutes chat he told her to "tell Bill the ETD on Thursday is 10 o' clock." He then handed her over to Joyce.

A few minutes later Bill was oblivious to anything… he was fast asleep.

"Good morning sir," said Fred as he saluted. Are you ready for another day at the office?"

"My days are *always* busy. I do not have the time to go swanning around the countryside in the boss's limo'."

"It must be tough at the top sir, but you have broad shoulders and you can take it in your stride."

"Fred, I have a job for you on Thursday, it is voluntary of course… but you will take me and Mrs Barrett to the airport to pick up my two subordinates and then transport them to their accommodation on the Domestic Site, is that clear?"

"Yes sir," he answered smartly.

"Thanks Fred, I knew I had only to … ask!"

"I heard you had got rid of Saleem. That man was a waste of space and he was anything but popular with the rest of us. You did us a favour there sir, but now he has gone you have no instructor."

"I will be standing in until my subordinates arrive."

"Then you will be throwing them in the deep end sir, on arrival, with them getting no chance to acclimatise themselves."

"Yes! That is correct. I am a hard task master and when I shout *JUMP* everyone jumps."

"With the exception of…"

"What do you mean 'with the exception of?'"

"Mrs B. sir."

"That is all I needed to start my day… thank you very much!" As he got out of the car he snarled. "Don't call me… I'll call you."

Fred sped away, laughing his head off.

"Good morning Barbara, any messages for me?"

"Not a thing sir."

"I will be spending most of today with the male recruits and I will see you at lunch time and yes, I have my bleeper. If the Major comes, wanting to see me, tell him I do not want to be called back here unless it is very important. I have a very busy morning ahead of me. Ta-ra."

He made his way to the airmen's accommodation and the airman on the lookout for him coming shouted "Officer Present," as Bill stepped through the doorway to see all the airmen stood to attention outside their individual rooms with the doors opened.

"Stand… at… Ease," he called, commencing his inspection with the first room. "Your windows… get them cleaned." He found many faults but the biggest one was dirty windows. In the ablutions he found them very unclean. "Lock your room doors and fall in outside and MOVE YOURSELVES." They scampered out and formed up in threes. He then ordered them 'Tallest on the right shortest on the left in two ranks SIZE!" They wandered about like headless chickens looking at the heights of each other to see who was the tallest. "STAND STILL" he yelled. "Have you been taught how to size?"

"No sir," was the reply.

"Very well we will learn how to carry it out this morning. In the meantime I shall inspect you." He inspected each airman minutely and pointed out his faults. He then addressed them by saying. I am very disappointed in your turnout you are far from reaching the standards I previously set you. Your rooms and your personal appearance are a mess. The main fault I found in your rooms was your windows. I do not know if they were dirty or shaded to keep out the sun's rays. They will sparkle for tomorrow's inspection won't they?"

"YES SIR!" they shouted in unison.

"We will now learn the art of Sizing. Step by step he took them through the routine and to Bill's amazement they picked up the routine very quickly. "Very good, we will now take a break for fifteen minutes, break ranks and move into the shade where we can have a little informal chat. I assume you know that Sergeant Saleem is no longer with us."

"Then who will instruct us in drill sir?"

"On Monday you will have a brand new Drill Instructor taking over, his name is Lieutenant Deacon. I have just returned from the UK and recruited his services along with Lieutenant Dean who will take over the training of the airwomen. The two new instructors are very highly qualified as Drill Instructors, how I know this is because I trained them myself. You are very fortunate because Lieutenant Deacon trained the Emir's son, you can then proudly say that you have been trained by the Instructor who trained the son of the Emir." There were loud murmurs of approval from the airmen. I will give you a little tip, if you do exactly what your instructor tells you, you will have made a friend. Now I am going to try a little experiment with you. We will do a little marching to show me what you know if anything. I will then teach you what you should know and when I am satisfied that you have solved the problem of how to identify your left from your right I will march you past the airwomen's flight and show them what they have to do to try and beat you in the contest. Are you with me?"

"Yes sir," they shouted with enthusiasm.

After some marching and learning the basic manoeuvres Bill positioned himself at the head of the flight and marched the airmen round to where the airwomen were going through their routine. As they approached the airwomen Sergeant (waf) Anisa called her flight to attention and saluted. Bill acknowledged the salute by ordering his flight of airmen to Eyes Left. After the order Eyes Front Bill ordered an About Turn and the flight retraced their steps. Bill marched behind them and as he drew level with Anisa he gave her a wink which was noticed by the girls who began to giggle. When the airmen had retraced their steps from where they had started Bill brought them to a halt. "You did very well so much so when I dismiss you, you can stand down for the day but remember I will inspect you and your accommodation tomorrow. Dis…Miss."

From there he paid Captain Khatib a visit.

"Good morning Captain what progress have you made with the two offices?"

"Come I will show you sir. You see sir we have given them a good cleaning and they are furnished similar to ours."

"Good man, I did not expect them to be any different. What was the reaction of your staff when you told them of the additions to your staff?"

"I was pleasantly surprised sir at their reactions they are genuinely looking forward to them arriving."

"You did not expect that?"

"No sir, knowing how my people react to new people especially to foreigners who they think are encroaching on let us say their 'patch' but I told them what you told me about your subordinates' sir and they were quite impressed."

"I thank you for that Captain because I was concerned about the reception they might face and being relatively young they lack the world wide experience of old campaigners like you and me." That complement brought a pleasing smile from the Captain. As Bill left he gave the thumbs-up sign to the four smiling faces looking through their office windows.

"I have not had any calls on my bleeper Barbara; do you think it needs a new battery?"

"The reason for that sir may be due to the fact that we are being ignored," she laughed.

"Well I will have to see if I cannot change that by letting them know we are here and a force to be reckoned with…will you back me up please?"

"You are incorrigible Colonel Barrett I think you need some lunch."

"Good gracious how time flies when you are having fun. I am ready when you are Miss Battle. Before we go will you ask the Major if I can see him for a minute?"

"He says yes he is free sir."

"Good morning Eric this is the first time I have seen you today, you are not hiding from me are you?"

"Of course not but you appear to be in a cheerful mood what is the reason for that If I dare to ask?"

"A question I would like to ask Eric. Captain Khatib, I would like him promoted to Major. He is doing sterling work and looking to the future he is going to be a real asset to us. He is sensible, reliable and dependable on the whole he is the kind of senior officer I am looking for to help build up my training programme."

"I will inform the Commandant of your request Bill and we will take it from there."

"If he approves Eric I would like the promotion to take place before my subordinates arrive on Thursday."

He returned to collect Barbara for lunch.

"You have had a very busy morning Colonel I can tell from your joyful manner, has it given you fulfilment?"

"Partly yes and partly hopefully. This morning I gave the airmen some drill training and I got more from them in two hours than that useless Saleem did in as many weeks. What condition were all the previous recruits in who went through his hands? It does not bear thinking about it must have been a right shambles. I have also put in a request for Captain Khatib to be promoted to Major he is interested in what I am trying to do and he has been very supportive, given his promotion he will make a good right hand man."

"Well you are certainly making big changes to this place in such a short time but you are getting the backing from the top to do so."

"It is what I am being paid to do and I am honour bound to return the confidence they have in me."

"How is your wife settling down here in Aljibia sir?"

"Tommy? She loves it. Speaking of Tommy she is hearing so much from me about here in our environment she would like a tour. Do you think it is possible?"

"Why don't you ask the Major, sir? He is very close to the Commandant."

"Hmm, I might do just that when we get a bit more settled."

It was well into the afternoon; Bill was making plans for when Alfred and Dot took over the Drill Instructing when he was interrupted by a knock on the door. "Come in" he called.

Eric entered. "Are you free to receive a visitor sir?"

"You are in aren't you Major what can I do for you?"

"It is not me Colonel it is this gentleman" and to Bill's delight in walked Major Khatib with a smile from ear to ear. He saluted Bill who promptly jumped to his feet with hand outstretched to shake his hand and give him a manly hug. Congratulations Major Khatib you have deserved this promotion."

"I want to thank you Colonel for getting this honour bestowed on me I will never forget your kindness."

"You have earned that promotion Major and I feel proud and privileged to have you on my team and I know four officers who are in for a big surprise too, go and give them that surprise Major."

"May Allah Bless you Colonel," he said, then saluted.

Bill went into Barbara's Office and said. I do not believe it. Do you know who has just walked into my office? Major Khatib."

"It does not surprise me one iota Colonel, you put forward a good request and it was accepted because the Commandant saw the sense in it. Congratulations sir, you have made him a very happy man and now he will be your friend for life."

"Do you know something Barbara? I am going to really enjoy my dinner this evening"

"Why, are you having something good sir?"

"It is good every evening Barbara, I have not had one dinner since I have been here that I have not enjoyed. Thomas is a really good Chef. When he cooks Arabic food I do not know what the heck I am eating but so long as I keep enjoying it I couldn't care less. Talking about food reminds me, isn't it time we were making tracks for home? Call Fred if you will please."

Fred saluted as Bill approached. As they set off Fred said, "I hear you have been making someone happy sir, that is better than kicking them up the backside off the station."

"They both earned their rewards Fred. News travels fast; it is only an hour ago that I knew for definite myself."

"I must congratulate you sir on your judgement; you can certainly spot the good from the bad."

"Bloody creep! I wonder what the end result would have been if I had sat on the panel for choosing my own chauffeur? Watch your driving!" as Fred reacted to Bill's inference. "Who taught you to drive, a woman instructor? Or have you been taking too much notice of your backseat driver telling you what to do?"

"If you are referring to Mrs Barrett, sir? She will be none too pleased when I report your attitude."

"Threats, that is all I get! And me giving her glowing reports of your driving skills."

"Can you give me one good report you have made sir?"

"Well, not off hand. I have too much to think about for trivialities."

"I rest my case sir."

"Sod off Fred! I am going to get more earache as soon as I step through that door."

"As you English say sir... 'we all have a cross to bear' Adios Colonel."

"Hey-up a minute, that is not English for goodbye!"

"It is not Arabic either sir. Salaam."

"Salaam Fred, see you in the morning." He watched Fred drive off, laughing as he gave Bill a wave. 'Whoever chose Fred to be our chauffeur did us a great favour.'

Tommy greeted him with "Hello love" and a kiss. "After you have showered and changed you can tell me what sort of a day you have had."

He skipped through his news then asked her what she had been up to.

"I had a quiet one, wrote letters to Nessie and Jackie then had an hour beside the pool this afternoon."

"Dinner is ready" called Leila.

"Salaam Thomas and Leila," greeted Bill, "how are my favourite couple today?"

"Fine thank you sir," said Thomas.

"And I am also fine, thank you sir," replied Leila.

Bill and Tommy sat and enjoyed the meal Thomas had made.

"Thank you Thomas, that was excellent. I have what I think is a very good idea Mrs Barrett. Why don't I ask the Emir if we can keep Thomas and Leila here permanently?"

"That is a very good idea Mr Barrett, but maybe Thomas and Leila would not like to stop."

"Oh we would Mrs Barrett, we would, wouldn't we Thomas?"

"Of course we would. They were just teasing us because they enjoyed their dinner so much. It was their way of paying us a compliment," he told Leila, laughing as he did so.

"Don't be upset Leila. It was our roundabout way of saying how much we appreciate you. She then went to Leila and gave her a kiss and a cuddle. Serve us coffee then go home and rest; remember tomorrow you will be making food for two more hungry mouths."

"I want to check with Viv that everything has gone according to plan because Alfred and Dot should be in the Savoy Hotel now. Call me the phone numbers love."

"Sergeants Mess can I help you?"

"Is that you Viv?"

"Hello Bill, I knew you would be ringing about this time so I have been waiting here at reception for your call. Yes, they got off alright with no problems, maybe short of sleep due to the excitement they were going through. Oh Bill, you should have seen Dot, she was on cloud nine. A few of us waved them off. Dot was in tears but they were tears of happiness and they were delighted to know you and Tommy would be meeting them at the airport."

"We will phone you Friday at 6pm your time because we are hoping they will come to dinner. If so, I am sure Dot would love to speak to you. Bye for now Viv, here is Tommy wanting a word."

"Hello Viv, isn't it getting exciting…" She then began to tell Viv the arrangements they were making for the pair of them. During this time Bill was fast asleep in his chair, and seeing this Tommy took full advantage of it. "We are alright for a bit Viv, Bill is away with the fairies fast asleep."

CHAPTER 20

Thursday had arrived and there was great excitement in the Barrett's household and everybody was trying not to show it.

"Do you need any more provisions from town Thomas?" asked Tommy.

"I am just checking Ma'am, I do think a trip into town would not be a bad idea I could do with some fresh vegetables at least."

"Your car or Fred's?"

"Mine for preference please."

"Will we be able to purchase two small baskets for the sandwiches Thomas?"

"I know a basket maker who if he has none he will soon make two for you. Failing that I know of a place that sells containers for the very purpose of people taking their own sandwiches to their places of work. My choice Ma'am would be the containers they would be adequate for what you want."

"That settles it I will take your advice Thomas."

"I am going love, Fred is here and I do not want earache from him by keeping him waiting."

"Coming love." She gave Bill a kiss saying, "See you soon and have a nice day at the office!"

"Do you want Fred today?"

"No, Thomas is taking me in his car because he needs some provisions."

At the door she gave Fred a wave then waved them off as they pulled away.

"Good morning sir it is going to be a long day, are you prepared for it?"

"What do you think I am a senile old dodderer?"

"No comment sir."

"I know there was something I meant to ask you. You told me you lived in the Sergeants accommodation. Is that the same accommodation my subordinate will move into?"

Fred laughed. "No sir far from it, we have our own quarters it would not do for us roughnecks to be seen hobnobbing if that is what you would call it mixing with the elite."

"I could not have put it better myself…I have no further comment," Bill said with a snigger.

"That is one point to you today, sir."

"Naturally, I wonder what it feels like to be an ignoramus Fred?"

"I have no idea sir but I can find out for you."

"Touché, one each Fred, I'll see you later. Auf Wiedersehen."

"Hey up sir that is not Arabic for goodbye."

"And it is not English either," replied Bill doubled up with laughter at Fred's Hey-up.

"Good morning Miss Battle how are you today?"

"Fine thank you and if I was as happy as you look with that great big smile I would be feeling on top of the world."

He told her of the teasing that goes on between him and Fred especially about Fred's 'Hey-up' she cracked out laughing.

"You are teaching Major Khaleel Royal Air Force expressions and now you are teaching Fred Northern Country Twang. What next are you going to get up to, sir?"

"But I curled up laughing the way he said it, it was hilarious."

"I am sorry I cannot stop Barbara but duty calls I have an accommodation inspection to carry out and also some what used to be scruffy individuals. Yes I have my bleeper with me. I will see you at lunch time. Ta ra."

On entering the airmen's accommodation he told them to stand at ease. He was satisfied with the cleanliness of each room but there was still room for improvement in the ablutions. "Fall in outside," he ordered. When they were lined up for inspection he was surprised to find very little wrong with their personal appearance. "I am impressed with your effort, now you have reached that stage I want you to keep it up, the more you try the more I will be satisfied. There is just one little drawback with your efforts, your ablutions need to be brought up to the same standard as yourself and your rooms. Today will be the last day I will be instructing you because Lieutenant Deacon will take over on Monday. A word of warning, you will find him just as keen as I am with your overall cleanliness. I suggest we now brush up on your drill and see what else you can learn. He took them through what he had already taught them then gave them grounding on the rest of the basic movements for two hours then finally brought them to a halt. I am pleased with your efforts with the new movements you have learned you are not perfect by any means but at least you will know now what your instructor means when he gives you the orders. I wish you good luck with your progress but do not let yourselves down. You are now dismissed for the rest of the day, Fall Out and have a good weekend."

He went to have a word with Sergeant Anisa who brought her girls to attention and saluted Bill. He returned her salute and asked how things were with the girls and their drill.

"Quite good sir they have improved since you had a word with them."

"I would like a word with them after I have put you in the picture of what I have planned for you. Stand them down for a few minutes while we talk." When this was done they walked into the shade. "Sergeant after the girls Pass-Out you are going to England for three months to be trained as a fully qualified Sergeant Drill Instructor."

Her face broke into a huge smile. "Thank you sir."

You will be travelling there alone because as you know Saleem has been discharged for incompetence. To replace him I have been to the UK and acquired the services of a Lieutenant Deacon and Lieutenant Dean she will replace you. They are both highly qualified and you will like your replacement she is very nice and you will learn a lot from her before you leave she will tell you all about RAF March and the people you will train with, ask her questions and she will answer them. Now between now and when you leave us get all your personal arrangements sorted out and if you want any free time to do so just ask your Lieutenant. What are your thoughts on that Sergeant?"

"It sounds wonderful and I cannot thank you enough for giving me this chance sir. Allah has at last answered my prayers."

"When I have told the girls you can stand them down until Monday morning. Come, I will have a word with them while they are relaxing. As he approached the girls they stood to attention. "Relax I just want a short talk with you. When you Pass-Out from here Sergeant Anisa will be leaving us for three months to attend a three months course in the UK. I am asking you to give her a send off she will remember by putting on a real good show on your final parade. On Monday you will have Lieutenant Dean in charge of you. I have just returned from the UK after obtaining her services. She is a highly qualified Drill Instructor and I can assure you that you will like her she is a very nice person, that is all I wanted to say. Carry on Sergeant."

From there he went to see Major Khatib. As he walked towards his office the four Officers came to the windows of their offices to applaud him. He returned their gesture with a nod and a wave. Good morning Major it is good to see your promotion is popular with your staff."

"When I walked in yesterday afternoon they had to take a second look to believe what they were seeing the first time, then they descended on me and smothered me with congratulations, it was wonderful sir."

"I have come to tell you I have stood the recruits down until Monday morning. After their passing out parade I am sending Sergeant Anisa to the UK for a three months course to qualify as a Sergeant Instructor."

"That is very generous of you sir and she fully deserves it."

"Well I will leave you to it Major and I will see you on Monday morning with our new subordinates." They shook hands, the Major clasping Bill's with both hands in appreciation.

"Have we time for a cool drink before we go to lunch Barbara?"

"We have sir we have half an hour to spare." As she went to the fridge to get them she asked. "Have you had a successful morning sir?"

"I think so, after giving the airmen a couple of hours drill to which they are now responding to very well, I stood all the recruits down until Monday."

"That is nice for them I'm sure they will appreciate that. Is Tommy going with you to meet Dot and Alfred at the airport?"

"Oh yes I think she is as excited as Dot. She is even getting our Chef to make sandwiches for them to eat in their apartments. They would not want to come to our place for dinner they will be too excited looking over their new accommodation. They can then eat when they feel like it. Tommy is taking them into town tomorrow to see the bank manager then going for a quick shufti round the main stores and shops then coming to our place for dinner and to phone their friends to let them know they are safe and well."

"You are certainly taking good care of them sir."

"They are worth it Barbara you will see why when you get to know them. I am feeling a bit peckish now shall we wander over to your Luncheon Box as you call it?"

Once again there was a ripple of applause with smiles and a nodding of heads when they entered the restaurant. Bill returned the compliments with a slight raising of his right arm, smiles and nods.

"It looks like I have got some more Brownie Points from our friendly diners Barbara."

"The way you are turning this place upside down sir we can expect a standing ovation very soon."

"Miss Battle you are making me feel embarrassed."

"Que sera sera. I have just had a thought sir, on Monday shall we bring Alfred and Dot here for lunch and if we cannot get a table for four you take Alfred and I will take Dot."

"Yes that sounds fine then in future they can pick their own table without feeling self conscious, good thinking Barbara."

Back in his office Bill was concentrating on his plans of action when a sudden thought came into his head. "Barbara I will be with Major Khatib if I am wanted."

He entered the Major's office and after the greetings he said "Major you know that with a promotion comes more responsibilities. First and foremost I welcome you as my second in command and now will you tell me your first name?"

"I have chosen George sir."

"Thank you that is how I will address you when we are alone and I will reciprocate by asking you to call me Bill and here is my hand on us becoming a good team George."

"Thank you Bill it is an honour and a privilege to serve with you."

"Now, down to business, what can you tell me about the Bedding Store and who is in charge of running it?"

"Lieutenant Yaseen. His two subordinates are Sergeant Abbas and Sergeant (WAF) Hikmat.

Yaseen has an oversize ego with a couldn't care attitude. Abbas is lazy but Hikmat is industrious and she gets little or no support from the other two"

"That situation is right up my street George shall we go and sort out our Mr Yaseen and Mr Abbass?"

"I am going to love this Bill."

They entered a building and were met by an unventilated smell coming from the stored bedding. They made their way to Yaseen's office and walked straight in.

A startled Yaseen sprang up from his chair and shouted at them in Arabic. George immediately told him to speak in English.

When he realised he was confronted by two senior Officers he apologised. "I am so sorry sir for my outburst," he said speaking to Bill. "What can I do for you sir?"

"You will get yourself properly dressed for a start then you will order your people to open all the windows it smells like a brothel in here but first lead us to where your people are working and shall we do it quietly? We do not want to wake them up do we Yaseen?"

Yaseen took them through a maze of aisles to a small rest room. Peering through the window they saw half a dozen male bodies stretched out on makeshift beds fast asleep.

Bill whispered to George, "Shout fire in Arabic with some urgency then stand back."

George grinned and did what he was asked. The result was pandemonium with everyone trying to get through the door first. When they saw who was standing there watching them they calmed down and stood to attention.

Bill addressed them. Get yourselves properly dressed, open some windows then go and stand outside the office until we return. Now Yaseen take us to where the WAFs are working."

He took them towards the far end of the building where the air smelt cleaner, they came across the Sergeant who with a clipboard in her hands was directing her charges in what looked like a check count on the bedding. When she saw them she immediately saluted. Bill asked for her clip board then made his mark at her last entry. He gave it to Yaseen and told him to carry on with the check.

He took the Sergeant out of earshot then introduced himself and George. "Tell me Sergeant in your own words what goes on here and speak freely. What I mean is who works and who shirks?"

"Lieutenant Yasser sir stays in his office all day when he is here. If I go to him with a problem he waves me away and tells me to sort it out myself."

"Why then do you not ask the advice of Sergeant Abbas?"

"He would not know what to do and he spends his time in the men's rest room. The men are sent to find something to do but they do not know what to look for so they just sit around doing nothing."

"Then who runs this place Sergeant?"

"I do sir with my girls otherwise it would be a complete shambles. We are the ones who make sure the dirty sheets are sent to the laundry."

"How often are the sheets changed and who issues clean ones and who collects and distributes them?"

"Each accommodation building's housekeepers are responsible for that sir they are changed three times a week except the recruits they are changed weekly."

"I want the recruits to have theirs changed to three times a week along with the rest."

Bill looked at George with a frown. "How many girls are you in charge of Sergeant ?"

"Six sir."

"If you were in total charge here what number of staff would you need to run it efficiently?

"Twenty sir. Six men and a Sergeant plus twelve women and a Sergeant."

"Good, thank you Sergeant shall we return to see how your stand-in has managed?"

He took the clipboard from Yaseen and saw there was nothing entered under his mark. When he was asked why Yaseen replied, "I did not know what to do sir."

"Sergeant Hikmat, leave any instructions with your girls then report to me at the office. Yaseen follow us."

At the office he approached the six men. "Abbas if you have any personal possessions collect them up then go and wait outside my office, he then beckoned Yaseen into the office. Collect your personal possessions then go and wait outside Major Khaleen's office and make it snappy!" He went to the five men and told them. "I am giving you one chance to show that you can carry out your duties how they should be carried out. You have been under the influence of Sergeant Abbas now I want you to shake that influence off. Sergeant Hikmat will be in total charge here until further notice and you will obey her orders to the letter otherwise you will be through those gates without your feet touching the ground, Mashy?"

"Mashy.sir." they replied.

"Now wait there for her orders". When Sergeant Hikmat arrived Bill said. "Sergeant I am putting you in complete charge here until I get it confirmed. Can you manage it?"

"Yes sir, you will not regret it."

"These men are now waiting your orders and this man pointing to Yaseen clearing his desk is on his way out. We will wait a few minutes to make sure he leaves quietly. If you get any problems Sergeant contact Major Khatib. Come on Major let us go and make our report. Yaseen was standing outside Eric's office when they knocked and entered.

"What is going on Colonel?"

"It is alright Eric you are among friends George is now my second in command?"

"Welcome to the clan George," said Eric," shaking George by the hand.

"That little toe-rag waiting outside is a waster who neglects his responsibilities and puts them on the shoulders of Sergeant (WAF) Hikmat. He has a Sergeant Abbas who is tarred with the same brush who spends his time sleeping in the airmen's rest room and orders his men to do the same. I want them both out Eric, they are a liability to us. How those girls have been coping I do not know. That Bedding Store is a big business to run and seven girls cannot live with that kind of pressure for long. Here is what I am requesting. Sergeant Hikmat to be promoted to Lieutenant, one male Sergeant and six airmen, one WAF Sergeant and twelve airwomen. At present we have five airmen and six airwomen. The reason for doubling up on the airwomen is because they are responsible for receiving dirty linen having it laundered and issuing clean linen. The airmen will be employed on doing the heavy work. When you consider the amount of sheets alone that are handled from all the accommodations three times a week is a very big task for the airwomen. George and I have great confidence in Sergeant Hikmat filling that post and running it as it should be run."

"To me Bill your request is a good one and I cannot see the Commandant turning it down but I will go and put it to him. When I take Yaseen in to see the Commandant will you please bring Abbas here?"

After fifteen minutes Eric returned to take in Yasser and give Bill and George the thumb-up sign. Will you go and bring Abbas please George." asked Bill."

"It was a little time before Eric emerged with Yaseen. "Major Khatib will you please escort this person to his accommodation to collect his personal belongings then further escort him off the station?" Eric then marched Abbas in to see the Commandant. It took just a few minutes. When Eric came out with him he said, "I have nobody to escort him off the station."

"Don't worry, I will take him over and get one of George's officers to do the honours. I will not be long then I will come back to you."

"Lieutenant Habib, do me a favour. Major Khatib is now my second in command and we are short of an officer for an escort duty to take ex-Sergeant Abbas to his accommodation to collect his personal belongings and then escort off the station, services no longer required."

Habib grinned. "It will be a pleasure sir."

"Good man."

Back at the Major's office Eric shook Bill's hand. "Well done Bill. The Commandant is quite chuffed with you weeding out all the undesirables. I think he may want to see you to offer his thanks. At the moment he is interviewing someone.

That someone knocked on Eric's door and was told to come in. In walked Lieutenant Hikmat with her new badges of rank attached to her epaulets and wearing a lovely smile.

"Thank you so very, very much Colonel. Never in my wildest dreams did I ever think I would rise to this rank."

Bill shook her hand warmly. "Congratulations Lieutenant Hikmat. You have more than earned it after what you have been through."

"I would like to offer my congratulations too, Lieutenant Hikmat, and you will be getting your extra staff pretty soon."

"Thank you so much Major. Everyone is being so kind."

"I will see you tomorrow Lieutenant, to give you a bit of advice in running your department."

"I will look forward and welcome that sir." She then saluted and left.

"We have got a good girl there, Eric. I had better return to my office and report to Miss Battle."

❖ ❖ ❖

"I am back Miss Battle," he said, poking his head round the connecting door.

"You have got that look on your face which I recognise as one of self satisfaction. I know what it is; 'Operation New Broom' has been sweeping more rubbish out."

"Right first time Miss Battle. Major Khatib is now my second in command. Lieutenant Yaseen and Sergeant Abbas of the bedding store have been given the boot. Sergeant (WAF) Hikmat has been promoted to Lieutenant and replaced Yaseen and with more female staff."

"That does sound good. He was not a popular person. He was a friend of Cartwright."

"Would you please ring for Fred, I am ready for home now?"

"And so you should be sir, we are running late."

As he settled into his seat Fred remarked, "I heard on the grapevine you have had another busy day sir."

"Fred, come clean, have you planted a bug on my person? You appear to know what I have done before I do."

Fred laughed. "You will be surprised, sir, at how fast news travels on the grapevine."

"Not any more Fred, what is your call sign, 'F-for Foxy? Now to business, what time are you picking us up?"

"Five thirty sir, the aircraft's ETA is 6pm so we have plenty of time to meet it."

"You know the schedule don't you Fred?"

"Off by heart sir."

"Alright smart arse, don't you go putting me in a bad mood to meet Mrs Barrett or she will go ape."

"Only if I tell her you have been swearing at me … Sir."

"You had better watch your step m'lad or there will be a Flash message on your grapevine… Tally Ho' F-for Freddy is being 'hounded'!"

Once again Fred drove off having a good laugh.

Tommy greeted him with a kiss saying, "It won't be long dear, it is getting to the exciting stage now."

"I thought that stage began when I told you Alfred and Dot were coming in the first place."

"You know what I mean. The real excitement. Oh go and get yourself ready and I will see if Leila can find you a beer."

Bill smiled as he walked away, thinking *that is all I need, a follow-on after Fred.* When he returned and before he could sit down Tommy grabbed his arm and pulled him into the kitchen.

"Come and see the containers we bought for the sandwiches."

"Salaam Thomas… Leila how are you?"

"Don't you think Thomas did well finding them for us? They are ideal aren't they?"

Bill looked across at Thomas and Leila… "Yes dear, they are just the thing you wanted."

"And you should see the selection Thomas has put in them. He has done similar ones for us for later. oh, they do look good."

"If you tell me any more about them I will start eating mine now."

"Oh No you won't!"

"Oh yes I... I am not getting any back-up. Alight dear, if you say so."

Everyone started to laugh at him then. "By the way, have you put our address card in the boxes?"

"No, I will hand them one each and don't look at me like that I will not forget, the only thing I am likely to forget is you so stick closely to me then I won't lose you."

Thomas and Leila were in stitches listening to Tommy putting on her mother-act for Bill.

"Here comes Fred, right on time."

"Good evening Mrs Barrett, you are looking very smart this evening, is that a new outfit you are wearing?"

"Yes Fred, it is nice when it is noticed and thank you for your compliment."

"Bloody creep, not another word out of you. I have had nothing but earache since I stepped foot in that house and I blame you for it."

"Stop blaming Fred for your bad mood."

Bill looked across at a smiling Fred and gave him a wink.

"It looks like the aircraft has not landed yet," observed Fred, "but as soon as it does we can go to reception."

Five minutes later it pulled into its off-loading slot and the three of them went to meet Alfred and Dot. Very soon Tommy gave a scream and began to wave. "There they are, they have seen me."

"Who could miss," Bill said to Fred.

Dot made a run towards Tommy and they hugged and kissed each other with tears of joy flowing from the pair of them. Alfred and Bill shook hands warmly then they switched over and all got hugs and kisses while a smiling Fred looked on. He picked up and carried their hand luggage to the car where Bill introduced him as, "Fred, my personal chauffeur and our friend. These, Fred, are Lieutenants Deacon and Dean, who you have heard so much about." They all shook hands.

Bill and Fred said nothing but listened to the excited chatter from the rear seats.

"Will you take the three of them to the city tomorrow morning Fred? Mrs Barrett wants to take them to the bank to get their money sorted out with the bank manager then a shufti round the shops. You will probably be sent home until the afternoon to stop you becoming bored."

"What time sir."

Bill called to the rear, "Have you decided on going to the city tomorrow?"

They listened to Tommy explaining about the bank.

"Yes please, we are going," answered Tommy. "10 o'clock alright with you Fred?"

"Mashy Mrs Barrett, I will pick up your two friends at 9:45 is that alright?"

"Mashy Fred," said Dot, giving a giggle.

"Here we are folks. Ladies first. Here is your entrance and where I will pick you up. Go to reception and introduce yourself to the female Duty

Officer at reception and she will hand you over to your housekeeper who will take you to your apartment. Your luggage should arrive in about an hour Ma'am."

Bill butted in. "Have you given them our calling cards Tommy?"

"She answered with a scream, "Oh no, I completely forgot. Here you are. Our phone number is on them. Give us a call later on to tell us what you think."

"Thank you Fred, Salaam" said Dot. "Salaam Ma'am,"

"Here we go, round to the other end of the building for you sir, the same thing applies, check in with the duty officer and your housekeeper will take over. Your luggage should arrive in about an hour sir."

"Thank you Fred, I will see you in the morning and thank you for the sandwiches. Tommy I am sure to enjoy them.

"Good night sir, thanks a lot."

"Give us a call later Alfred," said Tommy. "Thank you Fred you have been a great help to us and we do appreciate it, don't we Bill?"

"Well yes, and it is times like these when I think I could begin to like you Fred."

"Don't be so horrible; what would we do without Fred?"

"Get a new chauffeur, of course," he said with a laugh.

"Take no notice of him Fred, that is his mean streak showing."

"You English have a saying about sticks and stones, does that apply Mrs Barrett?

"It certainly does, well said Fred."

"Here we are folks, home sweet home."

"Thank you very much Fred, salaam," said Tommy.

"Thanks Fred," said Bill, putting out his hand to shake Fred's. "Salaam."

"10 o'clock Mrs Barrett."

"Hey-up Fred, 7:30 for me first!"

"Sorry sir, I completely forgot about you." He drove off as usual, having a good laugh.

Thomas and Leila were waiting for them returning. "Were your friends happy to see you Ma'am?" Asked Leila.

"They were indeed. Now look, you two get off home and thank you for everything you have done for us today. Goodnight and salaam."

"Salaam Ma'am … sir."

"Shukran and salaam," responded Bill After enjoying their sandwiches they relaxed watching Television waiting for phone calls from Alfred and Dot. They were thinking about retiring when Dot rang.

Tommy grabbed the phone and was soon into a long conversation with her. "Yes we will see you in the morning Dot, Night Night. She is over the moon Bill and thrilled to bits with her apartment. Her housekeeper is a middle aged lady called Sarah and is very nice, she has just left so Dot is going to eat her sandwiches then go to bed. She will be full of it tomorrow telling us more about her luxury apartment. Here comes Andrew," she said picking up the ringing phone. "Hello Andrew what do you think of your luxury apartment? We have just had Dot on the phone and she loves it. Yes alright see you tomorrow. He is impressed Bill and his housekeeper seems alright his name is Simon and he is very informative."

"Do you want a coffee to go to bed with? Tommy asked.

"Go on then and a biscuit."

CHAPTER 21

"Good morning sir, have your subordinates settled in?"

"Good morning Fred. We received a call from them last evening and Dot is thrilled to bits. You can bet we will get plenty of earache tonight. They are coming for dinner. Alfred seems to have taken it in his stride like us macho types. He tells us his housekeeper is called Simon."

"Oh I know Simon sir, he is a nice guy."

"He is not limp wristed is he Fred?"

"I don't know what you mean sir?"

"You know, one of these guys who stands with one hand on his hip and the other up in a curve singing 'I'm a Little Teapot'. Eh-up FRED!" Bill shouted. "Watch your driving will you? You will wrap us round one of those bollards one of these days."

"You make me do it sir with those daft English phrases you keep saying."

"I see I am wasting my time trying to educate you. Take it steady and keep your eyes on the road. If you are concentrating we will talk business. Will you please run Alfred and Dot back to their accommodation tonight. I have no idea what time but can I or Mrs Barrett call you? if you have something on it is quite alright. Then, when it is convenient, will you teach them some road sense for when they start using their own cars?"

"Of course I will, in both instances sir, they won't distract me by using some of your English phrases will they sir?"

"Now that is something I cannot promise, Fred, although seeing as you are a close friend of mine I will speak to them. There you go again, you wobbled. Thank goodness we have arrived here safely. Have a nice day Fred."

Fred sped away as fast as he dared, laughing of course.

"Good morning Miss Battle, are there any messages?"

"Good morning to you sir. Yes, we have one from Major Khaleel; he would like to see you at your convenience."

"Thank you Barbara. I will hop round and hear what he has to say."

"Good morning Bill, sit yourself down please. The trials of the spy and the two Englishmen have been held. The spy's sentence was a foregone conclusion. He pleaded guilty to all charges. Cartwright and Smith also pleaded guilty to acting as couriers. The court ruled that they were very naïve and were the victims of the deceased Samuel Barnes, therefore the court looked upon them with leniency and sentenced them to six months imprisonment, the full sentence to be served here in Aljibia. The time they have already served will be taken into account."

"Well that is over and done with Eric."

"Not entirely Bill. The press are making it Front Page News. You and I are to meet them at 2 o'clock this afternoon. Bill, it is no good you shaking your head, it is a command from his Excellency the Emir."

"Eric, I am not one who seeks publicity but there is no way I will let his Excellency down. It looks like you and I are going to hit the headlines old friend. How are we getting there?"

"Official transport Bill, we will leave here at 1:30 and see what happens."

"Barbara, I am going to see the airmen and Major Khatib, then I have a surprise which I will tell you over lunch."

The airmen stood chatting in a bunch outside their accommodation but formed quickly into three ranks when Bill appeared. "Sorry chaps to keep you waiting, but I had an important meeting to attend, so I am going to stand you down until Monday because I shall be tied up for the rest of the day. I suggest you spend your time cleaning your accommodation and your kit. Lieutenant Deacon arrived last evening so put on a good show for him. Good Luck." He then carried on to see Major Khatib, giving his staff a wave as he made his way to his office.

"Good morning George, my plans for today have gone to pot, Eric and I have a very important meeting in the city this afternoon. What I would like you to do is go to the Bedding Store and advise Lieutenant Hikmat on the use of wall charts similar to the ones you have just done, but instead of names to use all bedding movements you know the drill…quantities 'In' and 'Out' days for changing etc. She will need similar items to what you used so measure up then take her with you to put in a demand for the items. You know what to do if any objections are put in your way."

"Your secret weapon Bill."

"Good man. I will see you on Monday, by the way our subordinates arrived last evening."

He returned to his office and asked Barbara to make a brew. "Bring yours in my office and I will tell you the surprise now." When she had settled down he told why Major Khaleel had wanted to see him."

"You both are going to be spread all over the front pages of the daily papers and when that happens you will get that standing ovation in the lunch box we joked about. It is going to be very interesting reading especially by the ones who know you. Can I give you a word of warning sir?"

"Of course you can Barbara."

"Beware of your new friends crawling out of the woodwork because you are certain to get some."

"It is inevitable Barbara I agree that is human nature at its worst, at its best they scurry back into the woodwork." Shall we go to the Lunch Box then I can practice my bows and you your curtsies?"

"Silly beggar," she replied, "but no walking on the red carpet yet."

When they returned to their offices Bill asked Barbara. "Do we have a miniature tape recorder I could place in my tunic pocket to use undetected?"

"I think I can fix you up with one of our latest gadgets sir." She showed it him then fixed it up telling him what he had to do to switch it on and off. "It is so sensitive it will record very clearly through the fabric of your tunic."

"Thanks Barbara I want it for a back-up in case the interview goes pear shaped, I have my gut feeling again."

"It won't let you down sir and neither will your gut feeling from the account I have heard of it. Good luck sir."

"Are you ready Colonel?" asked Eric when he entered Bill's office.

"I certainly am Major let us go and meet the press."

"A smart limousine was waiting for them with a uniformed chauffeur who saluted and opened the doors for them. Bill as senior officer returned the salute and as he was climbing in the car he asked the chauffeur. "Are you a friend of Fred my chauffeur?"

"Yes sir he replied with a smile."

"Good, I will have something to tease him about when he picks me up later."

"All of us in the Motor Pool have heard about your teasing sir."

"What is your name?"

"William sir but everybody calls me Bill."

"That is a good name Bill, honour it."

They pulled up at a huge building which housed the Press offices and the news- paper printing rooms. At reception they were met by an official who took them up in a lift to the chief editor's office. "Thank you for coming gentlemen I am the chief editor of this newspaper and I am known as the Chief."

Bill could not resist asking. "Who by sir all your Indians?"

The chief looked perplexed until Bill explained the joke then he burst out laughing. "I like that Colonel." He then pressed a buzzer and a smart young man entered. This is one of our stenographers who will take down in detail the part you played in uncovering those spies."

"Excuse me sir but we can only tell you so much, you see we are duty bound by Aljibia's Official Secrets Act."

"Ignore that in this case Colonel our National Press is exempt from that."

"With respect sir, no Press in this world has any rights to override the law of the land to expose its country's security."

"Colonel, you are being obstructive and I do not like it. You will do as the Emir orders," he thundered banging his desk with his fist.

"Are they his Excellency's orders or are they yours sir and is his Excellency aware that you are telling me to betray his National Security? I do not like your attitude Chief and I am not one of your bloody Indians. I shall leave here and a signal will be sent to his Excellency in London containing my report with Major Khaleel here as my witness. Good day…Chief!" Bill and Eric got up and walked out leaving a fuming chief.

Outside the building Bill stopped and took in a lungful of fresh air. "I did not want that Eric but I am damned if I was going to bow down to that little arsehole."

"Bill, I thought you handled him like an expert I was so proud listening to you upholding the security of my country."

In the car Bill switched off the recorder then told the chauffeur. "Take us back to sanity Bill and move it."

"Do you want me to put my clog down sir?"

"Hey-up Eric he is learning." They all joined in laughing. "Eric, how do we go about sending a signal to London?"

"Leave it with me Bill I will first report to the Commandant for his approval but I will keep you informed."

He gave Eric the recorder. "Then ask him to listen to this Eric."

"Why you crafty old so and so," said Eric with admiration. When they got out of the car Bill had a word with the chauffeur. "Thanks Bill for a comfortable ride and you can tell Foxy-Fred we had no wobbles on this journey. I hope to ride with you again sometime, Ta ra." He laughed as he returned the salute.

"My words that was a quick interview with the press sir." greeted Barbara.

"Make me a brew and I will tell you all about it."

"You have that look on your face I guess you have been upsetting someone."

"I most certainly have and I think it is going to turn out to be quite serious." He told her who he had locked horns with.

"I see what you mean sir, he is quite an influential man but it seems he has become too full of his own importance by thinking he is above the law that is taking it too far. You must have had a premonition to take a recorder which was fortunate for you and your gut feeling did not let you down. The reply from London is going to be very interesting."

"After a most disappointing day Barbara I am ready for home. Shall we shut up shop and will you call Fred please?"

"It is time we were leaving anyway sir perhaps Fred will cheer you up on the way home."

Fred saluted as he held open the passenger door. "I am sorry sir this car is the best I could get because the Limo' is being thoroughly cleaned."

"It will have to do Fred although it was a treat to be driven in a luxury car with a superb driver who never made one single wobble I could not fault Bill's driving one bit. it was like floating on air."

"Your press conference was short and sweet I understand sir."

"It was short but not sweet it was just the opposite Fred very bitter indeed. As we English would say…there's trouble in mill."

"Will you please translate that sir I like the sound of it whatever it means?"

"If for instance there is a dispute in a workplace which is going to be difficult to resolve and someone asks what is going on, the reply would be, there is trouble in the mill, and you substitute mill for the workplace or whatever it alludes to."

"So you have some trouble on your hands sir."

"I am afraid so Fred."

"If you want a back-up I will get my friends to come and stand by you."

"Thank you Fred that is good to know. How did today go with Mrs Barrett and co'?"

"They stood me down until 4 o'clock. Your two subordinates are very nice we got on famously together but isn't the one you call Dot excitable, she loves everything."

"Here we go Fred into the lion's den so wish me luck. By the way has Mrs Barrett said anything about a shopping trip tomorrow?"

"Not as yet sir but I am expecting a call."

Stay there a minute I want to check on something, no it is not about shopping this is personal I will not be a tick."

"What is a tick sir?

"A few seconds of time, were you never educated?"

He rushed in the house and asked Alfred "have you got a parcel for me from Jackson?"

"Yes sir here it is."

Bill grabbed it and ran outside. He handed it to Fred saying. "Here you are Fred you deserve this. Salaam."

"Shukran and Salaam Colonel."

When he returned into the house he greeted everyone then told them I must go and freshen up. When he returned there was a beer waiting, Alfred lifted his beer and they toasted each other with 'Cheers'. "So you like your luxury apartments do you?"

"They are out of this world," answered Dot" she and Alfred gave their accounts.

"We have got two satisfied customers Tommy. Tell me how did you like your first meal in the restaurant?"

"First class Bill anything you wanted was there on the menu, the English breakfast was what I chose it was better than at the Savoy it was excellent, if the rest of the food is as good that will suit me."

"I really enjoyed mine too, I did not have as much to eat as Alfred but it was beautifully cooked. The décor is fantastic when you go in you immediately feel at ease especially with the service, I could stay here for ever."

"And what do you think of our Villa I would think Tommy has given you a tour.

"Oh this is really something you have everything you need and more besides."

"Have you made any plans for tomorrow Tommy?"

"No not unless these two want our services."

"We were thinking of taking it easy by the pool."

"The reason I asked is because Fred said he would be available in the morning to give you some local rules of the road lessons then you can use your cars as you want for getting from 'A' to 'B'."

"Yes please they both answered that would be great. We have had a look at our cars the keys were in the information envelope we got and they are little beauties."

"Do we want Fred tomorrow Tommy?"

"I wouldn't mind having a browse round then having lunch in that in-store restaurant we ate in when we first arrived."

"I will ring him now. Fred, tomorrow morning are you free to give your road safety lessons? You are, that's great. Mrs Barrett and I would like to go into town in the morning and here is what I suggest. Pick up the Formula One Team in one of their Lotus models at 10 o'clock then pick us up and drop us off in town, carry on with your driving lessons then pick us up at 4 o'clock in the usual place. Mashy Fred?"

"Mashy sir", salaam."

"Leila announced dinner was ready."

"Salaam Thomas…Leila," greeted Bill.

They both returned the greeting.

"Leila served each one saying, "We hope you enjoy your meal."

"We asked Thomas to cook something special with him knowing our tastes. We do not know what he has cooked so let us tuck in then we can give him our verdict afterwards."

"How did you get on with Mr Haddad at the bank?"

"He was lovely he could not do enough for us. 'Give my regards to Colonel Barrett' he said as he personally ushered us out."

"What did you think of your nice little account?"

"Very pleasing indeed when we got over the initial shock."

"Now we have all finished what is your verdict Dot?" asked Tommy.

"I have not a clue what it was but if all Arabic food tastes like that I am converted. Thank you very much Thomas."

"Dot has said it all for me, congratulations Thomas I think you may have changed my eating habits," enthused Alfred.

"Thomas you have not let me down yet but that meal was fit for the Emir himself. Thank you." was Bill's verdict.

"After all that Thomas I think you have proved that you are well up the list along with the professionals," applauded Tommy.

Thomas looked embarrassed when everyone joined in to applaud him. "Thank you very much you are so kind. I cannot tell you the recipe because it is a professional secret but this I will tell you, it is one of our Emir's favourite dishes and it has been my pleasure to have served it to you my very special friends."

Over coffee Dot rang Viv and gave her a blow by blow account of the events since they arrived and Tommy finished the call with a lengthy chat taking advantage of Bill and Alfred who were asleep after watching Television for a few minutes. When they woke up Alfred and Dot decided it was time to leave so Fred was called who whisked them away to their own apartments. The weekend went well for all parties; Fred was satisfied with his two driving pupils. Bill and Tommy had Sunday to themselves lazing by the pool and Thomas and Leila had the day off.

"Good morning sir greeted Fred saluting Bill, "are you ready for what today is going to throw at you?"

"I am ready for any eventuality Fred and I have accepted the driving wobbles as par of the course."

"I have not had the chance to thank you for my present sir until now. I am really grateful to you. Bill even offered to exchange the Limo' for it, that shirt is worth its weight in gold and it fits me perfectly."

"Were the driving lessons a success?"

"No problems in that department sir they are ready to use the public roads. Here is a bit of information from the grapevine for you sir; we have a VIP in town a very big VIP if you follow my drift sir."

"Thanks for that Fred I have been half expecting it and I will be standing by."

As Fred let Bill out of the car he saluted and wished Bill luck.

"Good morning Barbara have we any messages?" he called as he sat at his desk.

"No messages sir," she called back but I have two applicants who are asking for an interview to apply for a Drill Instructor's Post."

"Bring them in Miss Battle."

"Lieutenants Deacon and Dean Sir."

They both marched in and saluted smartly.

"Well you do look smart in your uniforms how do you feel in them?"

"You had no trouble finding my office I presume, when I first arrived a young officer had to direct me. Well now you are here we have to get cracking because I think I will be called to a very important meeting, maybe this morning or this afternoon. Miss Battle I will be at the training area for some time and yes I have my bleeper with me. Before we leave I will show you my round my self-contained office. When they saw what his office contained they could not believe it.

"You want for nothing sir," said Dot.

"Look at all those gadgets," said an amazed Alfred, "it is almost like an aircraft's flight deck."

"I don't know what half of them are for Alfred it is all new to me."

"When I can find the time sir I will come and run through them with you."

"Come I will take and introduce you to Major Khaleel he is PA to the Commandant we work very close together and became very friendly. Here is his office. He knocked and walked in, Major Khaleel I would like to introduce my subordinates Lieutenant Alfred Deacon and Lieutenant Dorothy Dean."

They both saluted and Eric came forward to shake them by the hand and welcome them. "We have all been looking forward to you joining us here in

Aljibia, your expertise has preceded you and we hope you can help us turn this Training Centre into one which will be the envy of our neighbouring states."

They saluted then withdrew and waited outside for Bill.

"Eric got all excited, "Bill the Emir is in town he must have come to sort out that idiot Chief. You had better prepare yourself to be called in to see him sometime today"

"Thanks Eric for the pre-warning, I would like us to be there when the Emir goes for the jugular. See you later." He then rejoined Alfred and Dot. "Come on we will go and be introduced to my second in command Major Khatib and his staff."

Major Khatib, I want to introduce the two new members to our staff. Lieutenants Deacon and (w) Dean." They saluted and were welcomed by the Major with a firm handshake. "The Major is your immediate boss" Bill informed them "and I will ask him if he will take and introduce you to the rest of his staff." While the Major was doing that Bill inspected their office and was satisfied everything was in order.

"This is your joint office," the Major told them, "If there is anything we have missed that you need or could be added let me know I am sure we can supply it."

"Come on then," said Bill and I will introduce you to your responsibilities, the recruits."

They both saluted the Major and thanked him.

"What did you think about the rest of the staff?"

"They were very friendly, I hope it was not top show because the Major was there," spoke Alfred.

"I think once you have settled in and have got to know each other more you will feel better.

"What about you Dot what were your thoughts?"

"They seem a couple of nice girls I don't think I will have any problems there."

"I will tell you both something, those wall charts have only been up a matter of a few days on my instigation of course. They know you have been trained in using them so you can tell them a thing or two about how to use them, discreetly of course because you don't want them to think you are a couple of 'Know it Alls' do you? There are your girls Dot, Sergeant Anisa has done quite a good job with them to say she is not qualified. They have seen us, now they are being stood at ease ready to salute us. As they approached Anisa brought them to attention then saluted Bill. "The parade is ready for your inspection Sir," she said proudly. "Stand them easy Sergeant Anisa. I would like to introduce you to your officer i/c recruit training Lieutenant Dean. Anisa immediately saluted Dot who returned the compliment and shook her hand warmly saying. "I have been looking forward to meeting you Sergeant Anisa after the glowing reports I have had from the Colonel and in the next few days while we are together before you fly off to the UK I hope we can get to know and respect each other."

"Lieutenant, don't forget at midday report to my office for lunch, which goes for you as well Alfred. Carry on" Bill returned her salute then marched off with Alfred in tow. "I was quite impressed with that little introductory chat she had with Anisa, you could see in her eyes that Dot had found her number one fan."

"When we round this building you will see your young charges standing in a group wondering where the hell we have got to then as soon as they spot us there will be a mad scramble to form up on parade. See there they go. As Bill and Alfred got closer one of the boys called the flight to Attention. Bill saluted them then ordered them to stand at ease then to stand easy. "Good morning or is it afternoon? I have lost all sense of time but that does not alter the fact that I am late on parade, for that I apologise. I could place the blame on your new Instructor because it has been necessary to introduce him to practically everybody on this station. You gentlemen of the world know that when you are introduced to someone it is impolite to just shake hands then clear off saying I will see you later, mate." The boys loved Bill making them laugh. "You know why I am here it is to introduce you to your new Drill Instructor Lieutenant Deacon." The boys interrupted with applause for Alfred. "To save his blushes I am not going to repeat what I have already told you about him. Thank you for the few days we had together I enjoyed them. They are all yours Lieutenant, Carry On."

Alfred called the flight to attention then saluted Bill. The boys saluted Bill with applause. They certainly like you sir."

"Aye, they are not bad lads Alfred, see you at lunch time."

As Bill marched off whistling the BlueBelles signature tune the boys clapped their hands to the beat of the tune until he was out of earshot.

CHAPTER 22

Meanwhile at the Press Office Building there was pandemonium when it was known they were to receive an imminent visit from the Emir. While the rest of the staff were running about like B.A.flies the 'Chief' was debating with himself whether to play safe by changing his underwear because he knew that he was the reason for the visit. Everybody got stuck in to tidy up every room in the building; it was like a Bull Night on an RAF camp. Eventually the 'Chief' and other departmental heads lined up waiting and hoping for a benevolent smile or a nod from the head of state. A spotter whose duty was to warn of the Emir's arrival came rushing in to tell them he was here. That started off clothing adjustments, clearing nasal passages and wiping sweaty palms on handkerchiefs.

In stormed the Emir stern of face with his robes flowing behind him followed by his aide-de-camp he pointed a finger at the Chief and flicked it inwards to mean take me to a private room ignoring everyone else as he followed the panic stricken Chief.

He went and sat at a small table his aide standing behind him.

He looked at the Chief who was mopping his sweaty brow. "I want an explanation of the incident concerning yourself, Colonel Barrett and Major Khaleel."

"Excellency it was a misunderstanding which the Colonel had not seen clearly and immediately took umbrage."

"And what was the misunderstanding?"

"I said my stenographer would take down in detail the parts you both played to catch those villains, the Colonel jumped up and said I will tell you what you need to know and nothing else. I confess I lost my temper with the arrogant man and reminded him that you required him to give me the information I needed and if he was not prepared to do that he could get out of my office and I would report his conduct to you. They both then left my office Excellency."

"I did NOT receive a report from you."

"Well you see sir what happened was…he got no further, the Aide gave the Emir the recording Bill had made he then placed it on the table. "Listen to this you lying imbecile he then switched it on and watched the Chief's face go different shades of grey as he listened to the recording. "Look me in the eyes and tell me that is not a true fact of what happened."

The Chief broke down in tears. "Forgive me your Excellency I must have been out of my mind."

"You are a lying piece of camel dung who tried to besmirch the character of a gentleman who cares more for the National Security of our country than you ever did or ever will, you are not fit to lick his boots. You thought you were untouchable and full of your own self importance you played on that as Chief Editor of our National newspaper and it has taken a man whose integrity is beyond question to find you out as he did with that other traitor. As from this moment you no longer hold the position of Chief Editor as a matter of fact you hold no position whatsoever." He motioned to his Aide who brought in the Sub-Editor. The Emir addressed him. "Tell me truthfully do you think you can hold down the position of Chief Editor of this newspaper?"

"Yes your Excellency I can."

"Then with immediate effect you are the new Chief Editor and use your position wisely. How long do you think it will take this cretin to hand it over to you?"

"Approximately three days sir."

"Very good, as soon as it is completed kick him off the premises."

"You will hand over your passport to the security police until I decide what to do with you, also hand over to the new Chief Editor in a civilised manner or there will be a prison sentence facing you. Do you understand?"

"Yes, Excellency."

"Now get out of my sight."

CHAPTER 23

"I am back Miss Battle, no messages?"
"No sir everything is very quiet."
"Have we time for a brew before lunch?"
"I will not be a minute sir."
"Come and sit down while we drink it. What do you think of Alfred and Dot now you have met them?"
"Alfred is a very nice and polite young man and very clever too. Dorothy is a sweet person I like her and I can see in her a young lady who is full of determination."
"When I introduced her to Sergeant Anisa and the girls she had them eating out of her hands. Alfred fared just as well with the airmen, he spoke to them on their level and they appreciated it. They are all near to leaving us and I can visualise the new intakes becoming the best that has ever passed out here but to be fair all the other intakes have not received a good training. These new ones will set a precedent others will have to follow and improve on and those two young people can do just that. By the way I have told them both to report here at midday for lunch."
"So now the pressure is off you sir."
"Not quite Barbara there is that matter about the 'Chief' to be resolved and the Emir is here now to sort it out. Fred will probably be able to give me a blow by blow account of what happened, I will just get the verdict."
"How does Fred get to know the ins and outs of what goes on here?"
"I do not know except he tells me he gets it from the grapevine and believe me Barbara that grapevine is red hot. Ah, here come the workers," as he called "Come in" to the knock on the door. How is your first day at work going?"
"Smashing," replied Alfred me and the troops are on the same wave length they have done everything I have asked of them."
"They are in competition against the girls at the end of the course?"
"Yes sir, they told me and they want me to help them to win."
"My girls are pretty good too and they would like to win the competition to give Sergeant Anisa a good send off when she leaves."
"That is good to hear from you both and it sounds like you have a fight on your hands. Are you ready Miss Battle?"
"Ready when you are sir."
On entering the restaurant Bill asked the waiter if there was another table for two close to the one where I usually sit.
"Of course sir, please come with me." He led Alfred and Dot to a table adjacent to where Bill and Barbara usually sit and where they could converse with each other easily.
"That is fine thank you."
"I noticed you were well received by the other patrons sir."
"Watch this space," Barbara told Alfred, "you will see them give him a standing ovation quite soon."

Alfred and Dot laughed not knowing that there might be something in what Barbara said.

When they had ordered their meals Barbara asked. "How do you like the Luncheon Box? That is my name for it."

"It is lovely," replied Dot, "Our accommodation restaurant is very nice but this is grand."

"In future you have no need to come to my office at lunch time just make your way here any time you like, we come here every day so we will meet up."

After the meal they all went into one of the lounges for coffee where Barbara Dot and Alfred chatted getting to know each other while Bill sat and listened to them.

During the middle of the afternoon Eric came bursting in Bill's office. "Come Bill you and I have been summoned to the Commandants' office."

"I am off to the commandant's office Barbara."

They both entered on command to see the Emir along with the Commandant, they immediately saluted.

"So we meet again Colonel and it is good to see you again Major," greeted the Emir. I have sent for you both to personally thank you for the excellent piece of work culminating in the capture of a nest of spies in our midst. Not only that but the way you handled that Chief Editor Affair, he has been removed from that position and replaced by the Sub-Editor. I have also confiscated his passport until such time when I can decide on his punishment. I am very impressed with both of you gentlemen for the manner in which you work together as a team what you both have done for Aljibia deserves rewarding. For you Major Khaleel I am promoting you to be on par with your friend and 'Brother in Arms' to Colonel and I want to be the first to congratulate and thank you."

The Commandant offered his congratulations then Bill shook his hand and congratulated him.

"Your reward will come at a later date Colonel Barrett."

"You have given me my reward Excellency by promoting my friend."

"A very noble gesture Colonel but you will not wriggle out of it so easy," he said with a smile. "Honour your friend Colonel Khaleel in the way he honours you. Take this Colonel you may need to use it again sometime" as he handed him the mini-recorder. "The recording has been erased of course."

They both saluted but Bill was stopped at the door by the Emir. "Colonel Barrett please give my regards to your wife Tommy." Bill smiled at him, "she will cherish that Excellency, thank you."

Eric was waiting for Bill in his office. He embraced him and showing a little emotion thanked him. "I owe it all to you Bill," then grabbing his hand he said. "Allah has been merciful to me by sending you to be my friend."

When Bill told Barbara about the interview and Eric's promotion she replied.

"You are an amazing man Colonel Barrett you are collecting life long friends as easy as pie all done by your respect and kindness for people and I count myself among them."

"Thank you Barbara," he said as he kissed her on the cheek, "I knew we were compatible the instant I walked into your office on my first day here"

She cleared her throat. "So the 'Chief' has got his comeuppance, he must be a very worried man."

"Ring for Fred please Barbara I am dying to know what he has picked up on the grapevine. You might say it has been quite a strange day I know Tommy will be delighted when I give her the Emir's message. See you tomorrow, Ta ra."

Fred saluted and waited until Bill had climbed in the car. "So another Indian Chief bites the dust sir, I heard from the grapevine the Emir had smoked the pipe of peace at the meeting of the Big Four."

"And who are they Fred?"

"The Emir, the Commandant, yourself and Colonel Khaleel."

"Have you planted a bug in the Commandant's office by any chance Foxy?"

"Indeed we haven't sir and not even a mole."

"How can I join your secret society?"

"That is not possible sir foreigners are not permitted to join the Loyal Grapeviners."

Bill could not stop laughing. "Is there anything else I would like to know about my movements of the day?"

"The sub-Editor has got the Chief's post and the 'Lying piece of Camel Dung' as the Emir called him is now in the process of handing over the reins."

Bill smiled and shook his head in amazement at the information he got from Fred. As he got out of the car at the Villa and returned Fred's salute he asked. "Is there any chance of knowing what tomorrow holds for me?"

"I will tell you on the way home tomorrow, Salaam Sir," as he drew away laughing.

Tommy greeted him with a kiss, "Go and get changed love then we will chat."

When he returned he took a swig of his beer. "Bai gum but I was ready for that. Have you had an interesting day pet?

"Ella came round and asked me to go into town with her to keep her company. She wanted to go to the bank then we had a shufti round the shops, I did not buy anything for myself just a few bits that Thomas wanted. Ella asked why we had not been to the club for a week or two. I told her we had been so busy especially; last week and I told her why. We must see about getting Andrew and Dot made members. Do you fancy doing it this coming Saturday love?"

"I will ask them tomorrow if I remember, anyway why not phone them you will frighten Dot to death wondering who is phoning her."

"Dinner is ready madam," Leila informed them.

"Salaam Thomas…Leila," greeted Bill as he entered the kitchen.

"Have you had a good day at the office sir," asked Thomas.

"More of an interesting one. I had a good chat with the Emir, oh by the way Tommy as I was leaving the Commandant's office he called me back and said. 'Colonel, please give my regards to your wife Tommy.'

Tommy was thrilled to bits. She told Thomas and Leila, "each time the Colonel is in conversation with the Emir he always sends his regards to me, he is such a lovely man."

"You have met the Emir?" asked Leila looking wide eyed.

"Yes Leila I met him in London prior to coming here. We will have our coffee in the lounge please. I see Thomas has almost cleared up so go home put your feet up and relax; we will do the same after I have made some phone calls. Noddy here will switch the Television on and in two minutes he will be fast asleep won't you dear?"

"If you say so dear." He replied giving Leila a wink making her laugh.

When they had drunk their coffees they commenced by phoning Viv.

"Sergeants Mess," said the voice.

"Is that you Viv?" Bill asked.

"Hello Bill you were lucky I was just passing reception when the phone rang, how are you?"

"I will be putting Tommy on in a minute but can you get someone to ask Roy to stand by I have some very interesting news for him?" he heard her speaking to someone.

"OK Bill I have sent someone."

Tommy took over the phone. "Hello Viv, yes we are fine I thought I would bring you up to date with Dot. Well…" fifteen minutes later…

"Roy is here Tommy I think we had better let him talk to Bill because he is showing signs of impatience. Give Dot my love I will spread the word amongst the girls, Bye.e.e."

"Hi Bill, don't these women twitter on….ouch, that was Viv giving me a dig in the ribs. How are you old friend and what is this special bit of news you have for me?"

When Bill told him about Sam Barnes he exclaimed. "Bloody Nora that was a shock Bill, yes I agree he would not have survived long in prison but what happened to the two English bods?"

"They were given a lenient sentence of six months to be served here in Aljibia because it was thought they were naïve and did not realise they were couriers. The main man was executed. They do not pussy-foot out here Roy they believe that anyone who does wrong must be punished. Yes Roy I fully agree with you. Yes I am winning the battle here it is taking shape but I have a way to go yet. Anyway I must leave you now I will be in touch old friend. My regards to everyone by the way let Jock know about Sam, Cheers mate."

CHAPTER 24

"Good morning sir," greeted Fred as he saluted Bill.

Bill returned the greeting with a salute. "What is my programme for today Fred anything I should know?"

"Sorry sir the grapevine is not on air yet." When Bill got out of the car Fred gave him an envelope. "Will you please give these car security stick-on labels to your subordinates they are to be displayed prominently to show the car is registered on the station."

"Mashy Fred."

"Good morning Miss Battle, no messages?" He asked as he entered his office.

"No messages sir."

"I will be with the Colonel then for a little while Barbara I have more planning to do for the recruits' accommodation. Mashy?"

"Mashy sir," she said with a smile.

"Come in Bill you are looking as if you mean business."

"I certainly am Eric and here is what I am proposing. Prior to the new intakes I want the recruits' accommodation emptying and thoroughly fumigated and all bedding to be replaced. Now here is the crunch. I want a room set aside for a living in housekeeper / security person. A telephone installed and the room furnished to a very good standard. In the corridor fire extinguishers placed in strategic positions and a fire alarm button installed. Do and Do Not Fire instructions placed in prominent positions. One more thing Eric, I am still waiting for a General Duties (WAF) Captain to take charge of all WAF personnel. I think that is enough to be going on with for the moment. I will get the bedding store and the Hygiene Department organised. One other thing Eric are our bleepers on a two way system?"

"No Bill why?"

"Because the holder of a bleeper is at a disadvantage when he/she is out in the field and can only receive, not send in an emergency."

"I see your reasoning Bill I will point that out to the Commandant. If a two way bleeper is not available then perhaps we can obtain a similar device to do what you want. Leave it with me Bill I will keep you informed, I like what you are doing."

"Good morning Lieutenant I have finally managed to get round to seeing you, how are you doing as boss lady?"

"Lieutenant Hikmat smiled, "I am doing alright sir it is hard going at present but I am getting there. I have got my full compliment of staff I asked for thanks to you and they all seemed satisfied with their lot, even the men are doing as they are asked quite a change from the life of idleness they had been used to. I am now working out how to set my wall charts out."

"If you would like a little help I can get Major Khatib to send one of his female officers to help."

"I would appreciate that sir because the quicker I can get it functioning the quicker I can turn my attention to supervising."

"The reason I have come to see you is"…he told her of his plans for the recruits' accommodation.

"That will be no problem sir I will get the airmen to check everything thoroughly ready for the changes."

"Good, you are in full control of the situation I will now go and organise your helper."

Major Khatib complied by sending (WAF) Lieutenant Basma. Bill then put George in the picture by telling him of the plans for the recruits' accommodation he had put forward for the Commandant's approval. "If you can spare a bit of your time come with me to have a word with the Hygienist. They went to the health centre and asked the receptionist, "Who is in charge of the Hygiene Section?"

"Captain Alam sir and the Hygiene section is a little way to your right from our entrance it is sign posted sir."

"Bill thanked her. Ah, there it is George we should have seen that sign it is big enough. The entrance was through a double door which led to an office. They saw through the glass door a male wearing a white coat. Bill knocked and entered. "Good morning we are looking for Captain Alam."

"I am he and who are you?"

"I am Colonel Barrett and this is my second in command Major Khatib."

Alam pretended to look busy by rustling some papers on his desk. What can I do for you?" he said indifferently not looking up.

Bill looked at George and said. "This is going to make my day." He leaned over the desk and snarled. "You can get up on your bloody feet and pay some respect to Senior Officers."

Alam leaped to his feet like a startled rabbit. "Er…er…er. "Stop it right there!" Bill bellowed. "Now sit down. We want some co-operation from you and I am giving you an option. You either co-operate willingly which I hope you will do so sensibly or if you do not your feet will not touch the ground as you exit the station travelling at a great rate of knots through the entrance gates but in your case the exit gates as we wave you bye, bye. Do you understand what I am trying to tell you?"

"Yes sir."

"Then tell me your answer."

"I will co-operate with you sir."

"Good man, I thought immediately I saw you that you looked like a man we could rely on." George had to turn away to try and control his 'coughing'.

"Now Captain Alam here is what I want your men to do. He explained in detail what he wanted "and you will co-operate with Lieutenant Hikmat who is in charge of the Bedding Store. That is an easy assignment don't you think Captain?"

"Yes sir we will have no problem carrying it out."

"Excellent I wish all people were as co-operative as you Captain. He shook his hand saying, "If there is anything we can do for you don't hesitate to contact either of us."

"Thank you sir."

When they got outside George doubled up laughing. "I just do not know how you get away with scraping someone from the soles of your shoes then having them eating out of your hand, you are an amazing man Colonel Barrett."

"It only comes with experience George. I will have a look at the recruits then return to my office to see if Eric has any news for me, I will let you know if he has."

Dot and Anisa were facing the girls when Dot said. "The Colonel is approaching Sergeant "

"How could you know Ma'am you are facing front."

"Take a look at the girls' faces Sergeant they are smiling, do you know of anyone else who can make them smile like that." Stand them at ease then when I say 'go' bring them to attention do an about turn and salute him…Go."

Bill returned Anisa's salute. That was clever how did you know I was approaching when you had your back to me?"

Anisa smiled at Dot, "we women have ways and means sir."

"Are you trying to make me believe you have eyes at the back of your heads? Nothing surprises me." He drew Dot on one side. "How are you getting on with them Dot any problems and have you checked their accommodation?"

"No sir on the contrary they are putting their hearts and souls into it and their living quarters are satisfactory. This short spell of training these girls is a good experience for when I get the new intake and can start training them from scratch; I am looking forward to that sir. Can you tell me why the recruits are only taught drill? What about classroom work and physical training?"

"Thanks Dot for bringing that to my attention I have been so busy sorting out drill training that I have completely overlooked the other essentials to their training. I will go and check on that right away, well done Dot you will get a brownie point for that."

"Entering Eric's office he asked, "do we have a gymnasium on site?"

"Yes Bill."

"What about PT instructors male and female?"

"Yes we have those as well Bill."

"Then why have the recruits been neglected by not giving them PT exercises?"

"That I do not know Bill."

"Then when the new intakes arrive PT will be on their curriculum. Who is in charge of Physical Training Eric I will have a word with him. Then we come to the reason why recruits are not attending Educational Classes, can you enlighten me on that?"

"It is thought that with the quality of education they have already received at the various colleges it is not necessary to extend it."

"Have your people never heard of further education Eric? it is imperative at this stage of their service life they continue to learn and also to be taught about life in the service. Do the authorities not realise that these young people are the future of Aljibia? I will have a word with Miss Battle, being an ex teacher here in Aljibia she may be able to guide me in the right direction."

"Captain Rashid is the man in charge of PE Bill."

"Thanks Eric, has the Commandant studied my proposals for security in the recruits' accommodation yet? And I am still waiting for a (WAF) Captain."

"If he has he has said nothing, be a little patient Bill remember you have already turned this place upside down."

Back in his own office he called Barbara. "I have a problem." He told her about the education for the recruits. "You are the only person I can think of who will understand the problem and I am hoping you can help me. From what you say there are no buildings that can be converted into classrooms, I wonder if there are any qualified teachers in the service, get Eric on the phone I will ask him."

"Eric, Bill here. Are there any qualified teachers in the service? There are but not here. Is there a training school for them when they enlist in the service? There is good well that is a start. Do you know off hand if there are any buildings on our site that could be converted to classrooms? OK Eric I will wait until you find out thanks a lot."

"You heard that Barbara there is a tiny glimmer of hope. I cannot come to terms with how and why this training school has been run right down into the ground but it will not beat me. Come on let us go to lunch I may feel better after it."

They acknowledged the smiles and nods as they were escorted to their table and had to smile to see Alfred and Dot joining in the greetings along with the other patrons.

"It is nice to see you two are picking up the local courtesies." They ordered their meals and chatted a little. "I am going to see Captain Rashid this afternoon Barbara he is in charge of Physical Training do you know of him?"

"I only know he is one for the ladies, he tries to capture them by flexing his muscles."

Bill turned a few heads when he laughed aloud. Excuse my outburst Barbara but I never thought I would cross swords with a Muscle Mechanic out here. The crossed swords I intended to be a pun because that is the PT instructors' badge of office. Alfred, tell Barbara what the badge of office is for Muscle Mechanics."

"It is a badge showing crossed swords Barbara."

"I do not dispute that sir," she retorted, "the only things I query are the RAF sayings you are teaching the locals words and sayings which even I do not know."

"Don't worry Barbara you will soon learn them then you can add those to your language qualifications."

It was Barbara's turn to swivel heads with her laugh. "Silly beggar!"

Bill entered the building containing the gymnasium and made his way to the office only to find it was empty. He wandered along a corridor in the direction of where he could hear sounds of vices shouting excitedly. He looked through the porthole windows in the swing doors to see a group of four men and four women playing basketball. Looking the other way he saw a lone figure lying on his back pushing a bar containing weights up and down. *I'll bet that is my man Muscles he said to himself.* He pushed his way in only to hear shouts in Arabic addressed to him from the basket ball group. One giant of a man came bounding over mouthing Arabic.

"Speak English Bill snarled."

When the man saw Bill's rank his mouth opened but nothing came out of it.

"Where is Captain Rashid?

The man just gaped and pointed down to the man lying on his back.

"Now get back to your netball."

"It is basket ball sir."

"Where I come from our women who play it call it netball."

He wandered over to where the figure was doing his exercises oblivious of what was going on around him. Bill half bent down and shouted. "Captain Rashid."

"Who are you and what are you doing in here you are out of bounds?" he carried on with his weight lifting ignoring Bill. When the bar with weight was at his chest Bill placed his hand on it imprisoning Rashid who struggled to free himself.

"If you stop struggling Rashid I will tell you who I am and if you understand what I am saying blink your eyes three times because you will find it difficult to nod your head. "Gasping for air and wanting to be released he did as he was told. Bill then helped him to put the bar with weights back in its place of safety. He then handed Rashid a bottle of water which was standing by the exercise machine. Have you recovered sufficiently enough to understand what I am saying? Either speak or nod your head, I would prefer you to speak because it is more courteous to do so."

"Yes I am alright now but you will suffer for this outrage."

"Captain Rashid my name is Colonel Barrett and I am your Commanding Officer.

Go and take a shower to freshen yourself up then we will retire to your office for a nice cool drink and a friendly chat. When you are ready give me a call I will be having a chat to your staff. Mashy?"

"Mashy sir." he said with a sickly smile.

"Off you go then." Bill wandered over to where the group had stopped playing basket ball and was standing around having been watching the proceedings with their boss. "Hello I am your Commanding Officer and I would like a little informal chat with you. I take it you all hold the rank of Sergeant and it is no good telling me your names because as soon as I walk through that door I will have forgotten them." It got a laugh from them. *Bill thought hey-up they are relaxing now.* "Do you spend much time putting your victims through the mill?"

One of the women replied. "We do not have many people come in for exercise sir and when they do it is mainly in an evening."

"Then how do you spend your time it must be very boring for you not able to carry out your trade as you would wish?"

"It really is sir."

"Tell me when did you stop having recruits come to you for PT?"

"We have never had them sir we only wish we did. Can you do anything about it sir?"

"That is why I have come to see your boss to draw up a curriculum ready for the new intake of recruits and to put you back in business." The smiles on their faces said everything. "I do not know what your relationships are with Captain Rashid but if you can come up with any good suggestions get him to listen to you and if he won't, come and tell them to me. Mashy?"

"Mashy sir," they answered in unison each wearing a big smile.

"I have got to leave you now because I think I am being paged."

Taking a good slurp of his drink he remarked. "That is what I call a good refreshing drink thank you Captain. The reason I am here is because I want you to formulate a curriculum for taking recruits of both sexes on Physical Training. Your staff tells me you have never had recruits to do PT which is through no fault of your own so I am changing that. As from when the new intakes arrive that is when you and your staff will find yourselves back in business. I see from the look on your face that you are in full agreement with me, is that so Captain?"

"Allah must have sent you to us sir because we were in the depths of despair with having absolutely nothing to do and nobody will listen to us."

"I have been listening to your staff and their feelings coincide with yours. I have told them of my plans and they are eager to contribute so I ask you please listen to them when they approach you with suggestions. I cannot promise they all will be good ones but if you use a little tact you can ease any disappointments. We have not a lot of time to spare before the new recruits arrive so I would appreciate it if you gave our planning priority. Captain Rashid, welcome to my team," Bill said shaking him by the hand, "and thank you for the drink."

"Thank you sir," replied a beaming Captain.

"I have sorted the Physical Training out Eric, Rashid is drawing me up a schedule and he is co-operating fully. My fingers are crossed regarding the Education etc."

"What is the etc Bill?"

"A (WAF) Captain."

"Oh! Yes I am sorry about that Bill but I am a little concerned about the Commandant he has not been like his normal self ever since the Emir was here, there is something troubling him Bill I can sense that. I cannot go into his office and ask him have you got a problem sir, can I?"

"Keep your eye on him Eric and if he does not appear to improve we shall have to do something about it. I will be in my office if you need me."

"Have we time for a brew Miss Battle?"

"I will be with you in two minutes sir."

"Did you have any luck with Captain Rashid sir," she asked.

"He was like a little pussy cat once I flexed my muscles, now he is behind me one hundred percent and so are his staff. Physical Training is just another department which has been neglected I do not understand whoever has been responsible for the run down of all these departments how they have got away with it for so long and my gut feeling is back again Barbara and I do not like it one little bit.."

"Then please be careful sir confide in no-one, you know that saying…softly, softly, catchee monkey."

"Thank you Barbara I will bear that in mind. Isn't it time you were ringing Fred I have had enough for today."

"Are you ready for home sir?" asked Fred saluting.

"Yes Fred I certainly am."

"You look a little grim faced sir has someone upset you?"

"Not me personally Fred but to the environment which is worrying me."

"I wish I could be of assistance to you sir."

"I wish you could too Fred but thanks."

For the rest of the journey there was silence. Fred saw that Bill was deep in thought and feeling concerned for Bill he did not interrupt him until they had arrived at the Villa.

"We are home sir."

"Ah good, how long have you served on this station Fred?"

"A few years sir."

"Have you got any idea why the recruits never received any education lessons and no Physical Training when those are paramount to their training? There are no signs that there ever were any classrooms and there are five Physical Training Staff wasting their time doing nothing because they have no-one to teach. What has gone on Fred? That is something I do not understand?"

"I will have a word with some of my friends who have been here longer than me to see if they can throw any light on the subject."

"Thank you Fred you are a good friend and one I can trust. See you tomorrow. Oh one more thing, what is the relationship between the Emir and the Commandant and are they the best of friends?"

"They are cousins sir and I believe there was some friction between them when the Emir was changing his political cabinet and the Commandant was left out in the cold. Thank you very much Fred you have shown me a light at the end of the tunnel. One more thing I must ask you Fred, please do not divulge our conversation to anyone else that must be top secret between you and I. Mashy? Salaam Fred."

"You can rely on me sir. Salaam."

That evening after dinner Bill told Tommy, "It is imperative that I write a very important report tonight so I will be using your writing bureau and please do not disturb me or I am liable to lose my train of thought. I am sorry love but it is extremely important. It was midnight when he was satisfied with the report. He turned to Tommy who had been sat reading knowing she gave Bill comfort by just being there and said. "I have finished love can we have supper?"

"She went to him, kissed him on the forehead saying. "I am not going to ask you what it is all about because you will tell me when you are good and ready unless it is marked 'Most Secret'. I will go and make supper now."

CHAPTER 25

"Good morning Fred," he said returning the salute. I am sorry I was morbid yesterday but a good night's sleep works wonders. Is there any news from the grapevine to cheer me up this morning?"

"I am afraid not sir the only news I have for you is anything but cheerful."

"Why what has happened?"

"The Commandant and his wife were found dead in their bed by their housekeeper this morning. I do not know any details sir."

"That is a tragedy I don't know what to say. Thinking back to yesterday I was speaking to Colonel Khaleel who told me that the Commandant had not been his normal self since the visit of the Emir. Maybe we will get the circumstances Fred and maybe we will not. Speaking prematurely I hope Colonel Khaleel gets the Commandants Post."

"And there again sir you could be in line for it."

"No way Fred that is entirely out of the question it would not be ethical for a foreigner to be given that position. I will see you later; I would like to bet that your grapevine will be running red hot today. Salaam Fred."

"Salaam sir."

"Good morning Miss Battle, yes I have heard the tragic news from Fred."

"I agree sir but doesn't that fit in with your summary of the recent events?"

"You realise I cannot answer your question Barbara until my findings have been proven."

"Yes I do understand sir but I think…."

"Hold it right there Barbara for the time being. Now what has been going on here has the Colonel been round wanting to see me?"

"No sir I expect he will be very busy just now and will want to see you when he can find the time."

"Get me Major Khatib please Barbara. Hello George, Bill here, will you inform your staff that it is business as normal we want to take their minds off this sad business that is if they have heard about it. I will be here in situ if I am wanted."

After lunch Bill received a phone call from Eric to say the Emir wants a word with him.

"The Emir wants a word with me Barbara I'll see you in a bit." He took the report he had written the night before with him saying to himself, *I think I am going to need this already.*

On entering Eric's office they both shook hands without saying a word. "Come on Bill I will take you in. He knocked on the door and announced, "Colonel Barrett sir," then he withdrew much to Bill's surprise. Bill saluted the Emir.

"Sit yourself down Colonel you and I have a little sorting out to do. First I must tell you that I am not in mourning for what has happened because that man brought dishonour on my family and Ajibia. You are nodding your head in agreement Colonel why and what do you know?"

"Sir, what I am about to tell you is just coincidental but it refers to the present situation. "I put in requests several times for improvements to the training school and I was getting no answers which concerned me so I asked Colonel Kheleel if he could explain the reason. He told me that the Commandant was not his normal self and had been in that state ever since your last visit here sir. Yesterday I tried putting two and two together sir and I did not like what my gut feeling was telling me. Last night I burned the midnight oil until everything clicked into place. I made out this report and here it is for you to read sir."

The Emir took the report with a look that said, am I hearing correctly what this man is telling me. He read the report then he re-read it. "And you had no outside help with this report Colonel?" he asked.

"The only information I was given sir was your rejection of the Commandant by not including him in your cabinet. I knew straight away that was the key I wanted."

"Yes you are right Colonel he funded and gave the ranks to Barnes, Cartwright and Smith, he was the number one in that spy nest and he knew that his demise was imminent. Tell me what would you have done with your report and findings if this incident had not arisen?"

"I had no option sir, loyalty and conscience mean the same thing to me I would have asked for a private audience with you."

"The Emir rose to his feet, held out his hand. "Colonel Barrett one of the best decisions I have ever made was to take you into my service and I am proud to call you my friend.

"Thank you sir that is the greatest honour I have had in my whole life and I dedicate my service to you."

"Now to business Colonel, give me your honest opinion of Colonel Khaleel's capabilities."

"I presume you are considering him to be your new Commandant. The first thing that came into my head when I heard the news was I hope Eric gets the post. You could not get a better man to fill that post sir and I will do my best to help make him a Commandant we can be proud of but if he vetoes my requests you had better look for another replacement sir." The Emir thought it was funny and they both had a good laugh together.

"We will meet again soon Colonel and please give Tommy my best wishes and tell her we will be meeting soon."

"I think I had better give her your message after dinner sir because she will be too excited to give me any."

"You and your sense of English humour Colonel it never fails to give me a laugh.

Send Colonel Khaleel in please.

Bill saluted.

"Come on Eric the Emir wants a word, I will take you in. He knocked on the door and announced, "Colonel Khaleel sir." He closed the door on a burst of laughter.

When he returned to his office he told Barbara to stand by for a whirlwind. A few minutes later the office door burst open and a voice shouted, "Stand by Your Beds Commandant Present!"

Bill jumped to his feet and was immediately enveloped in a bear hug. Eric with his eyes filled with emotion kissed Bill on the cheek but could only manage to half sob his thanks.

"Would you honour us sir by taking tea with us?"

"I would love to Colonel and we will have less of the sir except on ceremonial occasions if you don't mind."

"Here are your teas gentlemen."

"Aren't you going to join us Miss Battle asked Eric?"

"No thank you sir I will leave you boys to have a nice little chat," she said with a smile.

"I presume you have taken over command from immediate effect Eric and have you changed your rank?"

"Yes I am now in command and my title is Brigadier. There is one thing lacking though I am without a P.A."

"Brigadier or not you can take your beady eyes off my P.A. Where do you propose getting one from? Just a minute, Miss Battle can you come in here please? The Brigadier has no P.A. Can anyone of your friends fill the bill and who would be interested in the post and could start immediately?"

"I know of two who would welcome a change of employment and one of them I would definitely recommend she is multi lingual and Arabic is her forte, she too is an honours graduate of Oxford University and at present she is working as a temporary lecturer. If you will give me permission to leave now I can start by genning her up, pardon the RAF phrasing sir but it is catching. If she is agreeable I could bring her to see you tomorrow morning to talk terms."

"Excellent off you go and do not take no for an answer."

"What a stroke of luck Bill if she accepts."

"Barbara will do her best to win her over and you had better take your nameplate down and get your new one put up this afternoon to make an impression for her arrival."

"I had better get on with that straight away, thanks Bill."

"And use your rank if they say they cannot do it now, don't ask them...tell them and show you mean business after all you are the boss...Sir."

Eric left laughing.

Bill rang Fred telling him to pick him up. Fred saluted and asked. "Has the new boss commandeered your P.A. Sir?"

"It sounds like the grapeviners have been very busy today Foxy Fred. What other gems of information have you for me?"

"I think congratulations are in order after you solved that problem that puzzled you yesterday."

"Only with your help Fred you gave me the key to the answer that I could not find."

"So what is the outcome sir?"

"As you know our new Commandant is now a Brigadier without a P.A. so my P.A. is trying to fix him up with one and hopefully my requests will now get authorised. My priority right now is to get a (WAF) Captain to take charge of all our (WAFs)."

"Tell your boss to ask for (WAF) Captain Fahima, sir they do not come any better than her." "Well thank you Fred that has certainly earned you a brownie point."

"The grapeviners thought that how you handled Muscles Rashid was hilarious. Here we are home again once more sir and I hope you enjoy your dinner better and do not burn the midnight oil it only spoils your beauty sleep. Salaam sir."

"I cannot fathom you out Foxy Fred, not yet though but I will. Salaam my friend."

CHAPTER 26

After freshening up Bill sat enjoying his cool beer. "What kind of a day has it been love?" Tommy asked.

"A very good one, he then proceeded to tell her about the day's happenings. The Emir sent you another message as well. 'Give Tommy my best wishes and tell her we will be meeting soon'. I don't know what he meant by that love."

"But I do, this arrived by post this morning." She handed him an invitation card to attend an award presentation ceremony to be held in the Royal Palace on Monday at 11 o'clock. Servicemen and women to wear uniform, civilians smart casual dress. You are going to get that reward later he told you remember? And I am going to buy a new outfit for the occasion and that means I will need Fred tomorrow morning at 10 o'clock sharp. I have already asked Ella to come with me and she jumped at the chance to do so. I will ask Leila to check your dress uniform and titivate it up it will probably need it. Oh Bill isn't it exciting, we will get to see inside the palace and there are sure to be some dignitaries and important people there, I wonder if we will be fed cucumber sandwiches similar to our Queen's garden parties."

"I very much doubt it love. I hope Eric has got an invitation I cannot see him being left out because the Emir calls us 'Brothers in Arms'. Answer the phone love."

Tommy lifted up the receiver and spoke. "Hello Barretts! Yes, oh how nice to speak to you Barbara, we must meet up I am dying to meet you, yes he is here one moment please. It is Miss Battle for you Bill."

"Hello Barbara is there something wrong? Oh that is good. Yes, yes, excellent he will be chuffed in the morning. Do you know if he is married? The reason I ask is Tommy and I received an invitation through the post today to attend an award presentation ceremony on Monday and I am hoping Eric will also have got one."

"No, he is not married sir."

"Thanks Barbara you can fill me in with all the gory details tomorrow, Mashy?"

"Mashy sir,"

"She has talked her friend into coming for an interview in the morning."

"Dinner is ready Ma'am," announced Leila.

"Salaam Thomas…Leila how are you both and how has the slave driver been treating you today?"

"She told me to tell you that if you asked I had to say very well indeed sir."

"Well I have just asked you and what is your answer?"

"Not bad sir."

Of course that caused everyone to burst out laughing.

"I don't believe it," said Bill, trying to keep a straight face. "It must be the air in Aljibia. It is turning everyone into comedians."

"Good morning Fred," he returned Fred's salute. "Who is going to be a busy little 'B' taking Mrs Barrett shopping for a new outfit…?"

"To wear at a presentation ceremony on Monday at the invitation of his Excellency," interrupted Fred. You are not taking us are you?"

"I am sir. I would not miss it for the world."

"Blast, so we will miss out on the Limo. Eh-up Fred, here comes trouble."

"Would you like to take me into town this morning Fred?" asked Tommy.

"I was just about to say to the Colonel I have not taken you for a ride for some time Mrs Barrett, will 10 o'clock be alright?"

"I will take you for a bloody ride if you don't get this heap of junk moving."

"That will be fine Fred, thank you we will be picking up Mrs Jackson as well."

"That is no problem Mrs Barrett."

"You will have more than a problem if you don't get moving," snarled Bill under his breath.

"And you will have a problem if you don't show more respect to *my* chauffeur. Ignore him Fred, he is in his usual happy mood this morning."

"Are we ready sir?" Asked a grinning Fred. "See you later Mrs Barrett."

"Are we picking anybody else up on Monday Fred?"

"No sir, just you and Mrs Barrett."

"Now tell me Mastermind of Aljibia, do you know anybody of any consequence who is also on the invitation list and any who I should be wary of."

"The British Consul and his wife, Mr and Mrs Waters sir; he is full of his own importance and she talks down to people, especially if they are in the lower echelon of the local society. Typical Lord and Lady of the Manor. They are not liked by any of the Brits or anyone else sir. I suggest you and Mrs Barrett go straight in, firing from the hip."

Bill laughed. "If she upsets my wife she will go straight for the jugular."

"I would love to be there to see it sir. Can't you take me in with you as your interpreter or personal bodyguard?"

"I wish I could Fred but won't you get a blow by blow account of it on the grapevine?"

"Good thinking sir. I will have a word with the boys to put me on the no interruptions channel."

"Have a nice day Fred."

Before going to his own office he nipped round to see if Eric's nameplate had been changed on his door. *'Good lad,'* he said to himself, *'he has had it fixed.'*

"Good morning Miss Battle, any messages?"

"No sir and the Brigadier is busy interviewing his potential P.A."

"Thanks for the phone call. Tommy was chuffed having a quick word with you – and what was your friend's reaction when you put the question to her?"

"She was interested and said 'It sounds as if it could be interesting and if you like your job it should be worth me going for an interview.'"

"A word about Monday sir, can I speak freely to you?

"Of course you can Barbara and I hope you always will."

"Beware of people with their noses in the air, they stand out a mile, especially the British Consul and his wife, John and Sophie Waters. Be on your guard against them. Tell Tommy especially about Soapy, the wife."

"Thank you Barbara, I will warn her. She is off to town this morning to buy a new outfit. Incidentally, now you have warned me about the Consul, I am considering taking that recorder with me for a safeguard. Do we go through a security search?"

"No, I think it will be safe for you to take it."

It was well into the morning before Eric, wearing a great big smile, came to introduce his new P.A. to Bill. "Colonel Barrett, I would like you to meet Miss Rosemarie MacDonald, my P.A."

Bill rose from his chair and offered his hand to a tall, attractive, fair haired woman, who looked a little younger than Barbara. "I am very pleased to meet you Miss MacDonald and to welcome you to our happy little team. Can I offer you and you sir a brew or a nice cool drink?" They both declined.

"It is almost time for lunch sir," reminded Barbara.

"I tell you what Barbara, take Miss MacDonald to lunch and show her the ropes, I will follow on when I have had a word with the Brigadier. Sit at our table. I will find a spot when I come, Mashy?"

"Mashy sir," she replied, with her usual smile.

When they left Bill asked, "Your place or mine Eric?"

"Mine, because I want to get used to sitting in the boss's chair. They went into Eric's new office laughing.

"Have you got an invitation from the Emir for Monday?"

"I certainly have Bill. Remember what the Emir called us? 'Brothers in Arms'. I could not see him inviting one of us without the other, especially to a grand occasion like that."

"How are you getting there Fred? My chauffeur is taking Tommy and me."

"I think Bill is taking me in the Limo," he said ,grinning.

"Now that is what I call downright favouritism," said a supposedly indignant Bill.

"It is tough at the top Bill!"

"Have you met The British Consul Eric?"

"No, why do you ask?"

"I have been advised from two different sources that both he and his wife are nasty pieces of work and they live in a self styled superior world to us mere mortals so try to avoid them. Tommy and I have experience of dealing with those kinds of idiots. We have served with them. When does your P.A. start?"

"Tomorrow."

"Then you had better get her name-plate on her office door. I am going to lunch now, are you coming?"

"No thanks Bill."

"Then can you get (WAF) Captain Fahima to report to me for an interview this afternoon at 2 o'clock? She is a *must* to be in charge of the WAFs, so I have been told."

"Where are you getting all this first-hand information Bill?"

"It is not ethical to disclose one's informant sir."

"Not even if one pulls rank Colonel?" he said with a grin.

"I have a friend who outranks you Sir!"

"I thought you said you were going to lunch! Was it 2 o'clock you said you wanted Fahima?"

Bill left, whistling Colonel Bogey, leaving Eric laughing his head off.

After lunch he told Barbara he was interviewing Captain Fahima and he would like her to sit in while he was doing so.

When the Captain arrived he introduced himself and Barbara. "I hope you have no objections to Miss Battle sitting in with us Captain because rules demand I have a female witness when conducting an interview with another female."

"I have no objections sir."

"Excellent! Please be seated, I asked you to come here Captain Fahima because I need a woman... he was interrupted by both women starting to giggle. He continued ... to take charge of the WAFs who are on my staff but primarily the WAF recruits. That faux pas I just made was a deliberate ploy on my part to test if you had a sense of humour. Thank goodness you have. What I want from you is the ability to talk to the young girls on their level yet being firm but understanding. I want a motherly figure to look after their welfare. I have had it on good authority that you are the person to fit the post. Would you like to go away and think about it or would you like a private chat with Miss Battle?"

"I accept sir and I would like to thank you for giving me the opportunity to do what I have always longed to do – to work with young people."

"What is your present post Captain? I'm sorry I should rephrase that to what was your last post?"

"I worked in Administration sir."

"Well that will serve you well in your present post. Tell me, will this change affect your accommodation and when can you come to me?"

"Not a bit sir, my accommodation is here on the domestic site and I would like a day to clear my desk sir."

Bill stood up and held out his hand. "Welcome to my team Captain Fahima."

She saluted and left.

"Is that your team complete now sir?" asked Barbara.

"It is in a sense, yes. I only need classrooms and teachers. then we should be up and running. Physical Education is more or less organised."

"I had a word with Eric about Monday. Apparently he is travelling alone. I told him to beware of the Consul and his wife. I also asked if he was coming to lunch but he declined... strange. What does your friend think of the P.A.s post?"

"Rosemarie? She thinks it will be interesting and, as you would say... she is chuffed."

"Rosemarie is a nice name. I have only ever heard it once and that was in a film. Yes, I remember, Janette MacDonald and Nelson Eddy sang it."

"Her parents loved that duo and named their daughter after the song, which fits in nicely with her surname – but never shorten it to Rose when addressing her, she likes her full title."

"Thanks, I will remember that. It would be a pity to shorten it. I hope Eric has not dropped a clanger. Anyway, Miss Battle, it is time we were not here."

Fred saluted him with a big smile.

"Alright, get in that driving seat and stop looking so smug. My P.A. came up with the same advice I got from you this morning about the Consul, quite a coincidence don't you think Foxy? Does she happen to be one of your grapeviners by any chance?"

"Not a chance sir, it is male members only."

"OK Mr Brain of Aljibia, tell me why our new Brigadier is travelling alone in that beautiful Limo."

"Because of his rank sir. You would not expect him to share that beautiful Limo with the riffraff would you?"

"Alight, alright, point taken. Now, was this morning's shopping expedition a success?"

"My lips are sealed sir, under threats."

"Fair enough Fred, I know what you are up against. Have you got any news from the grapevine?"

"I am afraid not sir, you are quite up to date."

"See you in the morning Fred, Mashy?"

"Mashy Colonel."

"Hello love," greeted Tommy, giving him a kiss. "Have you had a good day?"

"Yes, you can say that and a very interesting one it turned out to be, especially the info I have for you, but I will tell you that later." When he had freshened himself up and had a drink of his beer he asked about her shopping spree.

"It went like a dream. I could not go wrong. I was actually spoilt for choice. I will show you my outfit later."

"I want it to be very special, for the reason I will tell you later."

"Dinner is served Ma'am," announced Leila.

Bill gave Thomas and Leila his usual greeting when he entered the kitchen. "I will not ask if we are having something good, Thomas, because you always come up with something special."

Over coffee Bill told Tommy about the Consul and his wife Sophie. "Barbara calls her 'Soapy'."

"That does not worry me, love. I can play the game rough or smooth. It is odd that Fred and Barbara warned you about the same subject, so they must have a reputation of sorts, but don't worry love, we will play it as it comes. I am going to do a bit of phoning around now. Is there anyone you would like a word with?"

"Wait until Monday evening. You may have something interesting to tell them."

"Good idea, I think I will do just that."

CHAPTER 27

"Good morning sir," greeted a smiling Fred.

"And a Good morning to you Fred, what have you got to be so cheerful about this morning?"

"Last night I was speaking to my fellow grapeviners and telling them the problem you have to find classrooms for the recruits and I have been nominated to take you to a building which they think will be ideal. It will need some renovating but they are confident it is what you are looking for."

"That is excellent news, just what I needed to make my day a good one. First I will report to the office and clock in."

"What does that mean sir?"

"In the UK quite a lot of factories and workplaces the employees need to prove they have reported for work and are given a card for each day of the working week. They have to insert their card into a machine which stamps on the card the exact time they booked in and they go through the same procedure when they finish work for that particular day. A clerk adds up the total of hours shown on the cards and that is what they get paid for. The service does not work to that rule because we are paid for the full twenty four hours."

"So why are you reporting now?"

"I don't have to, but it is courtesy for me to let my P.A. know that I am around. I will go and tell her where I am going then I will be back, Mashy?"

"Mashy sir."

"I am going exploring with Fred, Miss Battle, and I will take my bleeper just in case."

"Come on Fred, take me to Eldorado."

Eldorado proved to be a single storey building adjacent to the Gymnasium. Fred had keys for the building which he had to sign for from Security. "If you intend keeping the keys sir, you must sign for them on your way home but keep them locked away in your safe. Once the building has been completed the keys are to be returned to Security, then they take over its security. Here we are sir, you will find there are a number of small rooms and well equipped with toilet facilities. Administration used this until they moved into a better equipped building. I think this has only been closed about one year."

They gave the building a good inspection and Bill was delighted with what he found.

"You and your fellow grapeviners have done me proud Fred, please tell them how grateful I am. Now run me back and I will go and report to the Brigadier."

Back in his office he told Barbara about the find "Will you ring the Brigadier's P.A. for an interview with him please?"

"You can go right away sir."

"Hello Miss MacDonald, are you settling in?"

"Yes thank you sir, come I will announce you. Colonel Barrett sir," she said on opening the door.

"Hello Bill, what is your problem?"

"No problem Eric, I have just been shown a building which is perfect for classrooms. Would you like to come and see it for yourself?" It is only a short stride away and the sooner you approve the sooner it can be converted."

"That is good news Bill. Miss MacDonald, get me Major Hassan please. Hello Major this is the Commandant speaking... I want you to meet me at the building adjacent to the Gymnasium ... yes the old Admin' building ... I am on my way now. I have my bleeper with me Miss MacDonald."

The Major was waiting and saluted Eric, who introduced him to Bill. "You will know of Colonel Barrett won't you Major?"

I certainly do know of him sir. I admire what you are doing for this training site, Colonel, and you can count on my support sir."

"Thank you Major, it is good to know I am getting a good backing voluntarily. I usually I have to flex my muscles a little to get co-operation. I want to congratulate you for the professional way your men go about doing the task you have set them. You run a damned good department. Right then, let us get down to business. I was looking for a building to turn into classrooms for the new recruits and I find this one would be admirable for that purpose. The recruits have never had any education lessons to help them in the various trades they have chosen, people tend to forget that the youngsters of today are Aljibia's future and my job here is to give them the best basic training and to build up their confidence and character. Please can you convert this building into our own mini-college for the sake of Aljibia's future generation?"

"Colonel, how can I refuse such a request? I have children and I would not like them to miss out on any education. Colonel Barrett, you are a good man to our people and I hope you are never forgotten for what you are doing for our youngsters and Aljibia. Here is my hand on it." They shook hands warmly. Give me the keys and I will get my men here to draw up some plans for the conversion."

"Marleesh (never mind) the expense Major, we want it comfortable for the youngsters, Mashy?"

"Mashy," replied the Major as he and Eric burst out laughing at Bill's Arabic.

"Now Eric, while we are out in the field I think you should show yourself to your troops, they will appreciate it and it will help your popularity tremendously because everybody appreciates a leader who shows an interest in them."

They spent the rest of the morning visiting the departments and sites which came under Eric's jurisdiction and received a good welcome at each; being visited by their Commanding Officer was something they had never experienced before.

"Thanks Bill for that. It was as much a good experience for me as it was for them. Remind me that I must make a regular habit of having a wander round."

"Try and fix a day or date when you feel like doing it and I will accompany you. tell your P.A. to make a note in your diary or engagement book whatever."

Back in his office Bill found a note on his desk. 'Gone to lunch with Rosemarie. BB' *'Looks like I am to be a lone diner now,'* he said to himself. On entering the restaurant he asked for a table for one, ordered his meal and gazed around him, catching the eye of Alfred, who gave him a wave. So did Dot when she was told Bill had entered. Barbara got the message and she turned and waved. *Looks like Rosemarie has not got to the waving stage yet.* Alfred and Dot stopped at his table on the way out and asked if he was having coffee in the lounge. "Yes. I will see you in there I want to talk to you both." Barbara and Rosemarie were chatting at the table when he left. He ordered a coffee then sat with Alfred and Dot.

"That was very nice the C.O. coming to see us and I'll bet that was your suggestion," said Alfred.

"We have got a building to be converted into classrooms, it is situated adjacent to the Gymnasium and Major Hassan has got his men drawing up plans now. It was the old Admin building and it is in very good nick. The next surprise is your new O.C.WAF joins us tomorrow you will like her Dot, she is of the motherly type and reminds me very much of Mary Butcher. She is from the Admin' section and you will never guess who recommended her to me… our friend Fred. You know he is a clever man and worth listening to. Also, on Monday Tommy our C.O. and I have been invited by the Emir to an award presentation ceremony at the Palace."

"Wow, that is some invitation," said Alfred. "You are going to get a gong for that spy incident, what else could it be?"

"Can you smuggle us two in?" asked Dot.

"So there you are, up to date with the news. Oh yes, the C.O. has got himself a P.A. – Miss Rosemarie MacDonald, with many qualifications. She was a foreign language Lecturer. Have you both settled down in your accommodation?"

"Oh yes," said Dot. "It really is comfortable and my housekeeper is lovely. I am ringing Viv tonight; is there anything you want me to tell her?"

"Yes, tell her Tommy will ring her Monday evening, she will want to tell her about our day at the Palace."

"How are you getting on with your housekeeper Alfred?"

"He is good and will make somebody a good husband. He really looks after me. I'll tell you something else, the dinners are great in our restaurant aren't they Dot?"

"Indeed they are. We keep trying different foreign dishes; the ones we do not like are taken away and the menu is brought back for us to choose something else. Why are you sitting by yourself?"

"It is because of the new P.A. Barbara and she are friends and she is trying to help her settle in. I am alright on my own."

"We can get a table for three if you like, then you can sit with us. We are not particular who we sit with, are we Alfred?"

"Of course not, we will sit with anybody." They both laughed.

"Cheeky young beggars, get back to work. I will come with you, I want to see the Major."

"Hello George, I have come to tell you that Captain (WAF) Fahima will be joining you tomorrow as O.C.WAFs I will bring her along to introduce her. Also I have just left the C.O., who sanctioned a building to be converted into classrooms for the recruits. Major Hassan has already got his men drawing plans up for its conversion. You will know the building; it is the old Administration building."

"Yes I know it but I thought some other section was using it for whatever. That is really good news Bill, we are getting there and soon it will be a site to be proud of."

"Hopefully we should be up and running in time for the new intakes. Incidentally George, you will be in full charge on Monday. The CO and I have a date with the Emir."

On his way back to his office he called to see Rosemarie. "Miss MacDonald, will you ask the C.O. if he can spare me a couple of minutes please?"

She called him on the intercom. "Sir, Colonel Barrett is here asking if you can spare him a couple of minutes."

"Send him in please."

"You can go in sir."

Bill knocked and entered. "It will only take a minute Eric. When we go to see the Emir on Monday it means the Training Wing will be without someone in charge and the only substitute we have is Major Khatib."

"We never thought of that Bill, but the Major is a reliable and trustworthy person. Yes, he can stand in for me. I will tell my P.A. to contact him if necessary. Thanks for reminding me Bill."

"I will tell my P.A. the same Eric. Ta-ra.

Miss Battle, Major Khatib will be the stand in substitute for the C.O. on Monday, refer to him if any problems arise."

"Very good sir."

"We have got a building to convert into classrooms at last. Major Hassan has his men drawing up plans ready for its conversion all we need now are teachers."

"Well done sir, that is great news. You are certainly making things happen."

"With your experience, how many teachers do you think I should apply for Barbara?"

"I think five: one in overall charge and two of each sex. I would prefer a female to be in charge."

"Excellent, I will ask the C.O. to get on with that tomorrow. Get me Captain Rashid please. Hello Captain Rashid, Colonel Barrett here, I am in need of that curriculum you promised me, right now. Have you finished it yet? Good man, then send someone over with it *gildi* (quickly) Mashy?"

Barbara was killing herself laughing at Bill's Arabic.

"I do not know why you are laughing, Miss Battle, because on Monday or even tomorrow I would like you to make start on a rough curriculum entailing days and times for recruits attending Physical Training, Drill and Education Classes in that order. It need only be a rough guide but it will be something the Drill Instructors, the P.E. Staff and the Teachers can use for a guide. I suggest they all meet somewhere quiet to sort out an agenda which will be agreeable to all."

"Now that is what I would call a very sound policy sir."

"Come in," he shouted in response to a knock on the door. The P.E. (WAF) Sergeant he had chatted to in the Gymnasium entered with the curriculum. "Thank you," he said, taking the envelope from her. "Did you all have a say in formulating this?"

"Yes sir, and the Captain appreciated some of our suggestions."

"Tell me, is the Gymnasium in tip-top condition for holding P.E. training? I am talking about equipment, showers, toilets, changing rooms. Everything must be on top line, tell the Captain he is to get his inventory out and check every single item of equipment; anything not in first class condition will have to be replaced. I want a list of any defective items and I will get them replaced. Will you convey that message to your Captain and if he has any queries to contact me. Thank you Sergeant, we are going to make a good team."

Both he and Barbara studied the curriculum and agreed it was well worked out.

"Barbara, about the Education Centre and Offices for the staff, should we have a single office for the Head and one office for the other four or one office for the two men and similar for the two women?"

"I suggest sir that to have harmony I would go for just the three offices"

"Right get me Major Hassan please. Hello Major, Colonel Barrett speaking, yes I am fine thank you and your good self? You are busy with your thinking caps on, you know what they say Major…it is tough at the top. Why I am ringing you is, we have come to a decision, who is we? My P.A. who is a qualified teacher in her own rights and an Honours graduate from Oxford University with a list of qualifications the length of your arm. Oh yes she is clever but I shall not tell her that or she will take over my job yes, thank you for your support. As I was saying, the decision we made is this. We need five teachers, two male and three female, one of the females will be the Head of the school, we would like one office for the Head, one office for the two males and one office for the two females. Does that spoil your plans Major It doesn't? What a star you are, my P.A. is giving you silent applause. Thank you Major for all you are doing for us." You heard most of that Barbara, he is a good man I cannot wait to see his end product it will be a show piece I reckon. Well Miss Battle it is getting time for us to shut up shop, thank you for your help today it has been invaluable and we are getting much closer to our objective. Please give Fred a ring."

"Had a good day sir?" asked Fred as he saluted.

"A very satisfying one Fred that Admin' Building is perfect for classrooms. Major Hassan has already got his team working on it; all we want now are teachers."

"You should have no trouble getting those sir, there are a few in the reserve pool and the reason for that is they do not seem to last long when they are posted out, their excuse is no-one is interested in further education."

"They won't last long here either if they do not do their job right or they will be returned to the pool after being kicked out through those gates. Is there anything new from the grapevine Foxy?"

"Not today sir although it could be buzzing on Monday." Is Mrs Barrett getting excited sir?"

"You know what women are like on ceremonials, it gives them a chance to buy a new outfit then the excitement is showing it off providing someone has not a similar outfit."

"What happens if that occurs sir?"

"I suppose they toss a coin to see who leaves the room."

"What happens if the coin lands on its edge?" asked Fred.

"Then they both leave the room," Bill said with a grin. Salaam Fred."

"Salaam sir."

Tommy greeted him with a kiss. "Hello love have you had a good day?"

"Yes it was very good and it will be even better when I have had a drink of a nice cool beer." When he had showered and changed his clothes and had a good slurp of his beer he asked. "And what sort of a day have you had."

"Ella popped round and we chatted by the pool, she asked if we were going to the club on Saturday, I told her we were taking Alfred and Dot to sign-in as new members. She then asked if she and John could join us I told her of course they could it would have been very discourteous if I had said no wouldn't it?"

"Yes it would and it will be quite a little while before we can go again when the news breaks."

"Oh yes that is when we go into hiding isn't it? I had forgotten about that."

"Dinner is ready Ma'am," announced Leila.

"Salaam Thomas …Leila, said Bill giving his usual greeting when he walked into the kitchen. Both Thomas and Leila laughed as they responded with alekum salaam (peace be with you).

"Why did they laugh when I greeted them?" he asked Tommy.

"Only because you said Goodbye to them." that gave everyone a laugh.

"But I always say that."

"And they always laugh," replied Tommy.

"Do you want Fred today love?"

"No I don't think so but I will be going to town tomorrow."

"Yes and so will I to take some snaps for developing, I am taking the camera with me this morning to take snaps of Alfred, Dot and me all together in uniform to send to the family and friends. I will get extra films while we are there we will need plenty for Monday. Here comes Fred so I must be off," they kissed and he went to meet Fred.

"Good morning Colonel," was the cheery greeting from Fred as he respectfully saluted.

"And a good morning to you Fred you sound very cheerful today."

"I am always cheerful when I come to pick you up sir it is a privilege to do so."

"Bloody creep, what are you wanting a rise in your pay packet? pick me up in a Limo' every day and I will see you get one until then wind your neck in."

"What would Mrs Barrett say if she knew you keep swearing at me?"

"She would say, '*if that Fred does not treat you with more respect just tell me and I will do a Cartwright on him*'! Watch where you are going you are doing another wobbler," Bill shouted. "I'll be glad when I can get out of this old banger."

"Here you are sir," said a smiling Fred, "safe and sound once more, Salaam sir."

"Salaam Fred."

As he entered his office he called, "Good morning to you Miss Battle," as he walked to her office, how are…Ah! Captain Fahima and a good morning to you too. Give me a couple of minutes to catch my breath then we will do our rounds. Would you like a drink of tea before we set off or a cool drink?"

"No thank you sir."

"I'll get my bleeper and we will go. Any messages Miss Battle?"

"No sir."

"Come on then Captain let us go and give your girls a treat." He took her first to meet Dot and her girls. Lieutenant Dean I want you to meet your O.C.Captain Fahima. They saluted each other and shook hands exchanging pleasantries. Bill then took her to meet Major Khatib. She saluted him and he shook her hand. "I will now leave you in the Major's good hands, he will introduce you to all our WAFs and of course your own private office. Incidentally Captain, Major Khatib is my second in command of the Training School."

Captain Fahima thanked him.

Bill's next stop was to collect Alfred and Dot and take them to a quiet spot which would give a good background for his intended photographs where he had arranged for Fred to meet them to take the three of them as a group. Dot had left Sergeant Anisa in charge while Alfred had stood his flight down until he returned. Fred was waiting when they arrived at the rendezvous. "Sorry Fred," said Bill, "I got held up."

"Now when you are ready and not pulling funny faces I will begin." As they smiled over the funny he made he clicked the shutter immediately. "I will take one a little more serious this time, Mashy? Of course that comment made them laugh all the more. "Third time lucky as you English say," and it was. "While I have hold of your camera I may as well carry on." When it was all over he asked Bill when he was taking it to be developed.

"Tomorrow Fred."

"Would you like me to run into town with it now sir it will be ready for you in the morning and when you all go to town you can choose what extra ones you want for your friends."

"That is very kind of you Fred, thank you but before you leave us I would like Alfred to take one of you and me."

Alfred took hold of the camera, looking at the pair of them he told them, "Come on you can do better than that; try to look like friends and not enemies. Come on shake hands that is better you can always wash them afterwards." As he said that they grinned and Alfred clicked.

"That should be a good one," said a watching Dot.

"Before you go will you be coming with Fred, Tommy and I tomorrow in his old banger or will you be using your up to date top of the range model?"

"Do you think we should follow them Dot just in case they have a break down?" asked Alfred.

"No I think we will risk it after all there are two of us and Fred would appreciate two extra pairs of hands to help him push."

"I am going I do not mind you insulting me but not my pride and joy my lovely car.

"Salaam."

"Salaam Fred," they laughingly responded.

"Before you two rejoin your flights I want you to remind me at lunch to tell you about the project I have lined up for you, it should test both of your organising capabilities .Mashy?"

"Mashy sir," they responded as they saluted and marched off.

"How are you getting on with that curriculum Miss Battle?"

"I have not finished it if that is what you are referring to having had it only an hour or so. With your help I suppose we could have it finished in a few minutes sir."

"Touché Miss Battle touché!"

"If you are interested sir your seat at the luncheon table will become vacant as from today."

Bill's face lit up. "Why have you and your friend had words?"

"She is not my friend and never was she is just an acquaintance who I am now regretting having recommended her for that P.A post but she did have the best qualifications. She doesn't like the post and she bitches about almost everything. With a little pressure she will walk out through the door and I give her at the most one month. I told her yesterday at lunch to find another table because I wanted to eat and enjoy my food without her moaning all the time."

"So you won't be speaking now."

"What a relief."

"I wonder how Eric is coping with her perhaps he would unknowingly want a little help from his friend. That sounds good I think I could write a song about that."

"You are too late sir the Beatles have beaten you to it."

"Have they really?"

"You sir are incorrigible, you are just winding me up."

"Now would I do that to my favourite secretary?"

"YES! And how many secretaries have you? Come on it is lunch time let us go and stop that tummy rumbling."

"You sound just like my wife."

They were escorted to their table by a waiter receiving the usual nods and smiles from the other diners and big grins from Alfred and Dot.

"Nice to see you back in your usual seat sir" smiled Dot.

They ordered their meal and gazed around the restaurant. "I can't see any sign of Rosie" said Bill, "maybe she has brought her own?"

"Most likely taken the huff, never mind her I don't want to spoil my meal even thinking of her."

"I am going to have a word with Alfred and Dot about the curriculum you are working on and I want them to do the same with drill. I know we will be talking shop perhaps you will not want to stay and listen."

"I don't mind perhaps I can give them some pointers and when I return to my office I will run them each a copy of the one we have from the Gym."

They went into the lounge after their meal and joined Alfred and Dot for coffee.

"I want to tell you about that task I want you both to do." He unfolded the plan and concluded with; Miss Battle will run you a copy of the one she is working on at present. One of you can come back with us to pick one up or both of you can come."

"You had better go Dot because Sergeant Anisa can take care of your girls" said Alfred.

When they returned to the office Barbara showed Dot the start she had made on the curriculum then made her two copies of the Gym' copy.

Eric came into Bill's office. "You will never believe it Bill but that bitch of a P.A. has taken to her heels. She left a note saying...*This P.A. job would drive me mental as from now I am no longer in your employ.* "She signed it of course."

"Eric, you do not know how lucky you are to be rid of her." He repeated what Barbara had warned him about and her forecast of the length of time she would stay.

Why not go and have a chat with the Officer in charge of the Admin' Office and ask if she has one of her staff who is capable of filling the position? You will have to promote her according to the status she will hold."

"That is a good idea Bill I will go now.

As soon as Eric left Bill went to tell Barbara the good news. "That is absolutely wonderful sir and to think that at lunchtime we were wishing she would walk out and she did without any pressure from us. So what are his plans now sir?"

"I have advised him to see if he can get any joy from Admin' and he has now gone to see if they can help."

"With hindsight I think that is the best thing he could do, as the Commanding Officer he should have a local P.A."

Later in the afternoon Eric came to see Bill. He entered with a big smile on his face.

"Success Bill, I interviewed quite a youngish woman in the presence of the Major in charge of course and she is very much qualified with office procedure. The Major has allowed her to come to me on Tuesday because as you already know I will not be here on Monday."

"What is her rank Eric and are you going to promote her?"

"She is a Lieutenant and I have told her that on Tuesday I want to see her enter my office as a Captain and in your parlance Bill, she was quite chuffed."

Bill shook Eric's hand saying, "let us hope you have got a winner this time, sir!"

CHAPTER 28

Alfred and Dot arrived at the Villa in Alfred's car. "We came in the car because we want to do quite a bit of shopping and will stay in town for our lunch. In the meantime may we will leave our car here?"

"Its alright with us but I don't know why you had to come in your car in the first place that was a bit daft, come in it tonight fair enough because we are taking you to get signed in at the club."

"Come to think of it Bill it was a stupid thing to do."

"Young Officers I've…"Don't you dare say it Bill Barrett or you will get grounded." snapped Tommy. "Here comes Fred now and don't say a word, do you hear me or am I talking to myself?"

"I do not know who is worse you or Barbara Battle."

"It is good to know somebody keeps you in check when you are away from home."

"Good morning everyone" greeted Fred.

In return he got three Good mornings Fred and one grunt.

"Is everyone in and accounted for sir?"

Grunt, accompanied by roars of laughter came from the rear.

At the parking area Tommy took charge. "Will 4 o'clock be convenient for you Fred?"

"Anytime you say Mrs Barrett it is Mashy with me."

"Take your finger away from your throat William and act your age or are you already doing so? Now Dot what do you plan doing?"

"I want to shop for a sun hat, and perhaps a smart swim suit. Cotton dresses, sandals and Flip Flops."

"What about you Alfred?"

"Snazzy shirts, shorts, trousers, sandals, Flip Flops and Gucci sun glasses."

"Oh yes, thanks for reminding me Alfred I could do with a super pair of sunglasses too."

"Right William, you take Alfred and I will take Dot and we will meet at the restaurant in that super store, will 1 o'clock be alright?"

The shopping went really well, Alfred got a good range of snazzy shirts. "Are you going to wear those for a bet?" Bill asked. Alfred just grinned. When Alfred saw an optician's window full of top of the range sun glasses he zoomed in on it and was inside the shop in a flash. Bill sat watching Alfred trying pair after pair. "You do realize we have an appointment with fear at the restaurant, you can come back here after lunch until it is time to meet Fred you should have tried every pair in stock by then."

"Bill, you are out of date a guy has to look smooth now-a-days to pull the birds."

"With some you have tried on would be enough to frighten them away, are you thinking of buying those? What did you say they cost? 'HOW MUCH'?! You've got more money than sense."

Only my sandals and flip flops to get now, have you to get anything Bill?"

"No not at present, shall we make our way to meet the girls then?"

"How have you got on Alfred, got everything you wanted?" Tommy asked. "We have been waiting about half an hour for you."

"We would have been here an hour ago but for 'The Sun Glass(es) Kid' here. Wait until I tell you how much he paid for them Tommy."

"Bill he is a young man and he has to make an impression…Bill cut in and told her the price. Stifling a scream Tommy blurted out, 'HOW MUCH'?!

"I have them insured Tommy."

"Did you buy a pair Dot? Alfred asked.

"I did but I got mine from Woolworths."

"There are no Woolworths here," offered Bill.

"Well I thought the Arabic sign over the door meant Woolworths" she replied giving Tommy a wink."

"If you bought a sun hat Dot get it on quick the sun is affecting you."

Laughing, they all went into the restaurant and enjoyed a very nice lunch.

Their next stop was the photographers where they spent quite a time choosing frames for the ones to be put on personal display.

Fred was waiting when they arrived at the car park. "Hey look there at Mr Gucci you look so handsome and suave like a million dollars."

"Thanks Fred it is good to meet someone who knows class when they see it."

"Come on get in the car quick Tommy has a migraine coming on haven't you love?"

"NO!"

"Well I have, now step on it Fred."

"Don't you mean 'Clog It' sir?"

On arrival at the Villa Fred helped to carry the parcels in. We will not need you now until Monday Fred that should give you time to get this heap of junk roadworthy, and do not go and leave the starting handle behind."

"What is a starting handle sir?"

"It is the one to get you going if I shove…'

"Don't you dare William Barrett! Salaam Fred."

"Salaam Mrs Barrett."

"Are you two staying for dinner or not?" asked Tommy.

"No we will eat at our place thank you. What time do you want us tonight?"

"Be here for 8 o'clock, John and Ella are coming with us too. Mashy?"

"Mashy."

"What time would you like dinner Ma'am?" asked Leila "We will have it as fast as you can make it Leila then you can have an early night.

Isn't it yours and Thomas' day off tomorrow?"

"Yes Ma'am."

"That is good and on Monday you will have an easy day with us away for the day, I do not know what time we will get back but we will try not to be too late. Will you bring a beer in for sir before he falls asleep please?"

CHAPTER 29

Monday morning and all was peaceful and quiet in the Barratt household the stage had not yet been reached of "Have you got? Where is my? And don't forget, last by no means least was that old chestnut…Do I look alright are you sure?" All went well until breakfast time." I don't think I can eat that,"

"Well you are going to be very hungry by the end of the day and cucumber sandwiches will not fill you."

"How do you know we will be having cucumber sandwiches we could be having Curry and Chips for all you know."

"This is Aljibia love not India."

"Well Mr Clever Clogs for your information they do make curries here don't they Thomas?"

"Yes Ma'am"

"Well come and eat your breakfast it will make you glow and perhaps make you the Belle of the Ball "Some hopes Soapy will try to put a stop to that you'll see but she won't get away with it."

"Atta girl that's fighting talk now eat your breakfast."

"It's cold."

"THOMAS, another breakfast for tiger please" Bill said giving him a wink.

While all this banter was going on Thomas and Leila were having a good laugh.

"Keep your eyes on the Television today" Bill told Thomas and Leila you may get a nice surprise especially if the cameras focus on tiger here."

"We will not have any time to watch Television sir we will be too busy."

"If you get your work done by lunch time you have my permission to watch Television, start to check from 11 o'clock onwards, yet again it may be on only with the News Bulletin."

"Thank you sir."

"Now we must get ourselves ready? We have to be there before 11 o' clock.

Leila gave a shout, "Fred is here."

Bill and Tommy appeared dressed in their finery. Leila put her hand to her mouth in awe. She ran into the kitchen and brought Thomas out to see them. "You both look absolutely wonderful," he was speaking for Leila who could only nod her head because of her emotion.

Now the check began…"Have you got the invitation" "Yes" Have you got the camera?" "Yes" How do I look?" "Well you heard what Thomas said, and now we will wait for Fred's verdict."

"Good morning sir and who is this lovely vision on your arm, Mrs Barrett you look absolutely radiant."

"I knew what the little creep would say, now are you satisfied?"

As they approached the car the heads of Alfred and Dot bobbed up in view waving Invitation Cards. "Why you crafty young devils you kept that a secret didn't you," said an astonished Tommy.

"It was hard work trying not to give the game away."

"Come on Fred let us get this show on the road our party is now complete and that includes you. Just a pity you could not find the time to clean whatever it is we are travelling in."

"Stop it William, stop picking on MY favourite chauffeur or you will find yourself walking the rest of the way."

"Shukran Mrs Barrett that is most kind of you."

"Where did you learn to creep like that from your Nannie?"

"No sir from a male English tutor." That retort brought a round of applause from the rear and a call of 'Good Old Fred' from Alfred."

"Do they show Fred's cartoons at the Stations' Cinema then Alfred?"

"Yes sir with English sub titles."

"Do you get the same response?"

"I am not sure if they do it is not shown in the sub titles."

"How can you expect to get audience response on the screen? You are getting as corny as this plonker driving this heap of junk."

"We are now on the driveway approaching the Royal Palace folk isn't it a marvellous sight?" He gently drew up behind a small queue of vehicles waiting to discharge their passengers. "There will be ushers inside to direct you where you are supposed to be. When you are leaving I will be notified and I will pick you up here. Now go and enjoy our Aljibian hospitality." The car doors were opened for them and were then ushered up two flights of steps. On entering they produced their invitation cards, Bill was ushered to a different room which when he saw Eric he realised it was a private room for the award winners. Eric came to meet him and they shook hands. "What is the procedure now Eric?"

"The highest award winner irrespective of rank or status will be called in first then the rest follow in pecking order down the line to the lowest award."

"Tommy was hoping she would see our presentation."

"Have no fear Bill she will, families will see it from a special viewing area then when you withdraw to a reunion room they meet you there. After that we will probably be interviewed by a Television presenter then a photo call by the Press. Following that there will be a communal gathering where refreshments are served. The ceremony is shown to the rest of the people on short circuit Television so that they do not miss out on knowing who has been awarded with what. I do believe the Emir will later mingle with his guests."

When a bell rang Eric explained, "That means the ceremony is about to begin and carry your hat under your left arm Bill."

"Colonel William Barrett" a member of the Palace staff called. Bill stepped forward with Eric's voice whispering in his ear, "Good luck my friend." He was directed to where the Emir was stood on a raised dais. Bill bowed saying "Your Excellency."

Another member of the Palace staff began to read from a scroll. "Colonel William Barrett was the chief instigator in the tracking down and bringing to justice a nest of agents who had infiltrated our security system therefore becoming a threat to our country and National Security. Our country's appreciation is shown by awarding him its highest honour, The Gold Aljibian Star. Furthermore for his strong dedication to the training of our young people who are joining our Air Force he is awarded the Legion of Honour with clasp."

The Emir placed a Blue Ribbon around Bill's neck with a large Gold engraved Medallion with a Gold Star on a Green background in the centre encircled with Diamonds. The Emir shook his hand. "If anyone deserves this award Colonel it is you and for your personal record you are the first foreign person to receive it. He then pinned the Legion of Honour medal to Bill's tunic saying "Thank you for what you have already done and the progress you are still doing to help my people, you are Flying the Flag not only for Aljibia but for Britain"

"Thank you sir you have made me feel very humble but very proud and I am deeply honoured to serve you."

Meanwhile watching the proceedings on screen Tommy and Dot were both in tears watching Bill receiving his awards. Even Alfred had developed a husky voice and a cough. "I will see you later I have to go to the reunion room now to give my hero a hug and a kiss. You can give him one later Dot."

Bill was waiting for her. "Did you see it love?"

"Come here you big lump" she choked as she threw her arms around his neck and kissed him. "I am so proud of you."

A civilian approached them and introduced himself as the presenter for National Television. Congratulations Colonel on your awards but will you spare a few minutes for us to have a little chat on the network?"

"Can my wife be present please?"

"Most certainly I am sure the women of our country will love to hear a few words from you Mrs Barrett, will you step this way please?"

Tommy held Bill's hand and gave it a squeeze as they followed the presenter. A make-up girl approached and applied the make-up necessary for getting the best results from facing the cameras. They were then ushered outside and directed to a spot where they would be in focus for the cameras. The presenter told them, "Keep calm we will converse as if we were holding an ordinary conversation."

"Colonel Barrett tell me briefly how and why you came here to Aljibia to become a member of our Air Force?"

"His Excellency the Emir was looking for a reputable training establishment to give his son basic training before proceeding to Royal Air Force Cranwell to finish off his training to become an Officer. Fortunately my RAF Station was chosen because his Excellency was impressed by our training methods and our results. His son was assigned to us and I was in charge of his training. His son proved to be an excellent trainee actually one of the best recruits we have ever had. If his Excellency is watching this interview that statement is perfectly true sir, I am not grovelling for another medal. From then on things moved at lightning speed, I received a letter from his Excellency asking me to join his team here in Aljibia and within three months I resigned from the RAF and wound up here, it was the best move I ever made.

"Can you tell us anything about your part in the arrest of those agents?"

"First I must stress that Major Khaleel who is now Brigadier Khaleel and my Commanding Officer played as much a part as myself in that activity, we bonded together and formed a team which is as strong now as it was then and it is my privilege to serve under him."

"Thank you Colonel. Now Mrs Barrett what does it feel like to be the wife of a Hero."

"He has always been my hero ever since we met while serving together on the same RAF Station. But calling him a hero now would only make him feel embarrassed. Life together as a married couple could not be better we laugh and joke but are very protective to each other. My husband lives by a saying...'Give respect and you will get respect' which has been proved over and over again. Living here in Aljibia I think it is wonderful we find the people are so nice and friendly. We have been fortunate in obtaining a local married couple as a Chef and a housekeeper and we regard them as family that is the value we put on their friendship. Coming here to Aljibia as my husband said is the best thing that as ever happened to us and we are so grateful to his Excellency for giving us this opportunity."

"Thank you Colonel and Mrs Barrett and may you enjoy a long and happy stay with us."

All the Television staff gave them a spontaneous round of applause.

When they returned to the reunion room they met Eric who was also waiting to be interviewed on television. They immediately hugged and congratulated each other on their awards Eric also was sporting the Gold Star. "Tommy, this is Eric my Commanding Officer."

"At last I have the pleasure of meeting you Eric after hearing so much about you, congratulations on your award you certainly deserve it. I am sorry we have kept you waiting." At that moment the TV interviewer called, we are now ready for you Brigadier Khaleel."

"I will see you both later, lovely meeting you Mrs Barrett."

Bill and Tommy then went into the general assembly room where everyone was talking and taking in refreshments. As they entered they were met by applause which Bill acknowledged by mouthing 'Thank you' as they made their way towards where Dot was waving wildly.

"Am I allowed to hug and kiss you here?"

"I will be very displeased if you don't, come here" he said reaching to take her in an embrace, Alfred wrung his hand warmly with his congratulations.

"Come on Bill I am dying for a cup of tea" gasped Tommy.

As they were served Bill heard a voice say "Congratulations Barrett." Bill swivelled round to face a stranger. "Allow me to introduce myself, my name is John Waters and I am the British Consul here in Aljibia. "I am glad I have met you Waters" Bill replied in the same vein.

"Perhaps you did not hear me with you being surrounded by all this euphoria, I am the British Consul."

"I heard you alright and my title is Colonel which you either did not know or overlooked. I am glad I have met you which gives me the opportunity to ask why have the two Englishmen who are languishing in prison for their misdeeds not been visited by a member of your Consulate staff? That surely is one of your duties to assist your countrymen in time of need."

"Are you trying to teach me my job?"

"Well it is obvious someone needs to."

"Why you…'

"I advise you Mr Consul to stop digging a hole for yourself."

"I do not expect you to realise you are wearing an Eighth Army Clasp among your decorations under false pretentions…I *am going to love this, Bill said to himself.*

"Really" replied Bill in mock surprise and how do you come to that conclusion were you in the Eighth army?"

"Of course not I was in the Royal Air Force."

"Damned fine show old boy congratulations, where were you stationed?"

"In Egypt, I was a supplier to the Desert Air Force. Where were you stationed?"

"Up in the desert, I was a Tank Commander with the Eighth Army that is why I am wearing the clasp."

"Oh dear it appears I have made a boob."

"You have and a bloody big one, you have put one foot in your mouth try not to put the other one in, Old Boy!"

Their two wives who had not been formally introduced glared at each other without saying a word, until the Consul's wife broke the silence. "Your husband was out of order speaking to the Consul in that manner."

"Are you a relation of his?" asked Tommy with tongue in cheek.

"I am Sophie Waters the Consul's wife and you are?"

"Tommy Barrett I am the Colonel's wife."

"Sophie smirked, what kind of name is that to give to a woman?"

"My maiden name was Atkins and in the service anyone with that name was nicknamed Tommy after the First World War Tommy Atkins and I wear my nickname with pride Soapy…oops! Sorry Sophie and people with the name of Waters were invariably nicknamed Muddy."

Sophie then did a faked wobble and surreptitiously tipped her cup of tea over the front of Tommy's dress. "I am so sorry I keep wobbling over in these wretched shoes they make me so unsteady."

"Do not worry it was an accident I have worn it once it will now go in the rubbish bin I can afford to buy another new one. I would advise you though to get rid of those shoes before you do have an accident."

"Thank you I will do." She turned her back on Tommy when she heard someone say 'The Emir is coming this way', then as she stepped forward with a self satisfied smile it was immediately wiped from her face when Tommy slyly tapped her heel which sent her crashing to the ground. Tommy immediately bent down to help her up asking "Have you hurt yourself dear?"

Sophie snarled "Take your bloody hands off me you bitch you tripped me." The Consul helped her up glaring at Tommy who immediately retaliated with, "You just heard her admit her shoes made her wobble and unsteady on her feet so why are you glaring like that at me Mr Consul?"

"They were interrupted by the Emir. "Mr Waters I want an explanation in writing and an apology from you both concerning the foul language your wife uttered in mine and my guests presence" He beckoned to a steward telling him to assist the Consul and his wife to our medical room. When they had left he said "It is nice to see you once more Tommy, welcome to my humble Palace. Tommy curtsied and replied "I have been waiting for this moment for a long time your Excellency."

"Did you enjoy the ceremony?"

"It was lovely sir but very emotional which will live with me for ever."

"I saw a re-run of your Television debut and I was most impressed with you both. I had to chuckle when you pointed out to me personally you were not grovelling for a further award Colonel, my staff also joined in the laughter. It was also typical of you but very commendable that you refused to take all the credit for yourself over that nasty incident. You Tommy will have two very happy people to greet you on your arrival home."

"That is what I want to thank you most sincerely for sir those two lovely people and of course our lovely Villa."

"For the two nicest people ever to come to Aljibia you deserve the best. Ah, I see you have your two assistants here with you Colonel. He shook their hands asking if they had settled down and if they too were as fond of Aljibia as the Barretts?"

"It is a wonderful place and we feel really at home with your people sir" replied Dot.

"And I agree with what she said entirely sir and it is a pleasure to be working with the Colonel again sir."

"You would not happen to be grovelling would you young man like your boss?"

Everyone around who was listening to the conversation burst into applause and loud laughter. I am expecting my son Peter shortly I will tell him you are here he will come and see you."

The Emir left them to circulate among the other guests. Alfred and Dot were thrilled to bits with the Emir's interest in them.

"It appears the Waters are in for a rough time" said Bill then whispered "Nice one."

Tommy just squeezed his arm in acknowledgement.

Various dignitaries and people of consequence congratulated Bill on his awards.

They saw Eric in deep conversation so they did not encroach on him. After the Emir had retired the guests slowly began to drift away. As Bill, Tommy, Alfred and Dot made their way outside to their car The Press photographers descended on them like flies to take their photographs. Bill thanked them then they were ushered to their car. Fred apologised for not being able to salute them by not being allowed to step outside the car while waiting for its passengers. Once aboard they were waved off to be replaced in the queue by another car.

"How did you all enjoy your day?"

"It was wonderful Fred the Emir came and spoke to us all he was ever so kind."

"He was not very kind to the Consul and his wife was he?"

"You know about that Fred?"

"It is only what I get from the grapevine Ma'am. I do know a lot of our people will be toasting your health for the way you both rubbed their noses in the dirt. You English say 'watch this space' when something imminent will happen soon, which could be in the form of a new Consul."

"If anything comes from the grapevine" Bill explained to the others "you can bet it will either be true or it will happen."

"The full coverage of today's event will be broadcast on TV tonight at 6 o'clock and tomorrow's newspaper editions will also feature today's story. I will get few editions for you to send to your friends?"

"Thank you Fred" they all chorused.

"Are you two staying for dinner" asked Tommy.

"No thank you we decided to leave you to wind down and take it easy besides we will be glad to get out of uniform and into something comfortable, .Mashy?"

"Mashy"

Thomas and Leila were waiting to greet them. Thomas came forward with hand outstretched. "Congratulations sir we did not know you were getting such a high award we are very proud to serve you. "Thank you Thomas and we are very grateful to have you and Leila to take good care of us."

Leila came and shook his hand, "When we heard of your award we both cried with joy."

Bill showed them the Star of Aljibia they were absolutely delighted he had done so. "It is so beautiful" Leila said while Thomas was lost for words.

"At 6 o 'clock there is a full coverage on the Television so if you can make us an early dinner you can go home and watch it" Tommy told them.

They did not need telling twice they scampered off to the kitchen. Bill and Tommy went to freshen up, Bill for a shower and Tommy for a soak in a highly fragranced bath. Bill was ready first, he went in the kitchen to get a beer out of the fridge, Leila gave him a glass then he went into the lounge sank into his arm chair had a long drink from his glass and sighed with contentment as he settled down *murmuring to himself, this is the life.* Tommy joined him a littler later.

"I feel much better after that soak love. As I was lying there I thought after the TV programme we had better take the phone off the hook just in case."

"Good idea."

"I will be phoning Viv afterwards I can't wait to tell her what a wonderful day it has been for us both."

"Dinner is ready Ma'am" announced Leila.

During the meal Tommy told Thomas and Leila. "After the TV programme we are going to take our phone off the hook you can understand why. Unless there is an emergency we are incommunicado Mashy?"

"Mashy Mrs Barrett" they replied laughing.

Over coffee Bill and Tommy recapped on the day's happenings. "The Waters turned out to be every bit as nasty as was predicted, not a nice couple were they,"

Bill said "and when Soapy tripped I thought you are over doing Soapy old girl by prostrating yourself at the Emir's feet."

It took Tommy quite few minutes to recover from laughing at that remark. When she did she said "I am glad the Emir was there to witness it, I wonder if she will be featured in tomorrow's newspapers?"

"Here we go" said Bill "The Barretts' of Aljibia."

The programme gave a good coverage of the awards ceremony, the interviews and reception. "It was a good job I held my handbag low in front of me or that tea stain would have shown" said a relieved Tommy as she took the phone off its hook. "Our friends must have been impressed to see the Emir laughing and joking with us. I would love for us to have a recording of that Bill do you think you can get one for us?"

"I will ask Fred where we can get one."

"What are you going to do now while I ring Viv?"

"Oh just watch TV for a bit."

"Till you fall asleep you mean, go on settle down I will shake you when it is time for supper."

CHAPTER 30

When Bill and Tommy went for breakfast Thomas and Leila greeted them with huge smiles. Leila took Tommy in her arms gave her a kiss and thanked her. "Oh Mrs Barrett you were wonderful and we cried when you spoke about Thomas and me, you will make us famous. When we saw you and the Emir laughing it made us laugh."

"Have you got today's newspaper Thomas?" asked Bill.

"It had not come before we came here sir it must be a late delivery, shall I go to see if it has come?"

"No, Fred is bringing me one when he arrives I can wait for him."

When Fred arrived he brought with him a small bundle of newspapers as promised.

"Come on in Fred while I have a quick shufti."

"It is a good write-up sir the Press has certainly done you proud."

The headlines read. BRITON HEADS TWO MAN TEAM TO UNCOVER SPY NEST.

Colonel William Barrett along with Major Khaleel now Brigadier Khaleel exposed the nefarious activities of agents who had penetrated our National Security. With careful planning they brought the perpetrators to justice. For their diligence in preserving our country's defence and security they were both honoured with our country's highest award The Aljibian Gold Star. Colonel Barrett became the first foreign recipient to receive this award. Furthermore he was also awarded the Legion of Honour with Clasp in recognition of the services he is carrying out for our Air Force and the young people who are joining it. The awards were presented by his Excellency the Emir of Aljibia.

It followed with a brief summary of Bill's achievements in training both men and women of the Royal Air Force.

"Well that is a good write-up and so are the photographs."

"I must say Mrs Barrett" said Fred you are very photogenic the pictures of you are excellent."

"With that finger down throat remark I think you and I Fred had better get going before I ask for bucket to be sick in."

"Salaam Mrs Barrett" said a grinning Fred.

"Salaam Fred" said Tommy who joined him in grinning "and thank you."

"Did you give Alfred and Dot a newspaper Fred?"

"I did sir."

"Good man. Do you know where I can get some recordings of yesterday's event?"

"You tell me how many you want sir and I can get them within two days."

"That is great thanks Fred. Now let me see, I would like eight please, do you want the money up front?"

"I will tell you the cost when I have ordered them."

"Wait till I tell your number one fan this evening she will be ecstatic."

"Is there anything new from the grapevine Fred?"

"They were impressed with the awards sir and send you their congratulations."

"Did you watch the programme on Television last night?"

"Yes and I thought it was very good, you and Mrs Barrett each made a very nice little speech just the kind our people like, you both must have made a lot of friends."

"Here we are sir back to the grind once more. Salaam sir" he said as he saluted.

"Salaam Fred and thank you."

"Good morning Miss Battle any messages?"

"Not yet sir but I am expecting the postman to arrive any time now with sacks of fan mail. Congratulations sir I watched the program last evening and I thought you and Tommy were superb you both came across so humble and considerate which will have earned you a myriad of friends. Did you get involved with the Consul and his wife by any chance?"

Bill laughed, "Look can we have a brew and I will tell you all about it?"

"Here you are sir now for the gen as you put it I think I am going to enjoy this."

"It was funny how it worked out, the Consul and I squared up to each other then it was the turn of Tommy and Soapy. Anyway this is how it started." He began by telling Barbara word for word about the exchanges that passed between them.

"She enjoyed the changes between Bill and the Consul but roared with laughter at the outcome between Tommy and Soapy. She clapped her hands in glee saying "well done Tommy that was priceless I do wish I could have been there to witness Soapy biting the dust. Please tell Tommy she has made my day I know I will burst out in laughter every time I think about that."

"The end of the story is Fred thinks that was their swan song and they will be replaced pretty soon. By the way have you seen today's newspaper?"

"I am afraid not why are you featured in it?"

"He went and got one from his brief case, "Here you are with my compliments" he said giving her the paper. Have you seen Eric's P.A. yet? I would go round and have a word with him but he will be too busy showing her the lay-out, instead I will have a stroll and see how things are at the sharp end I will take my bleeper with me."

His first stop was to see how Alfred's flight was progressing. Alfred saluted him and said, "The flight is ready for your inspection sir."

"Stand them at ease I want a word with them. You know that you Pass-Out from your training on Friday and enter the world of the Air Force for real. You will go from here to learn the trade of your choice and I wish you the best of luck in that respect and I want you to carry what you have learned from us at basic training for the rest of your service career stick to its principles and you will benefit by them. There is just one more thing you can do for me and Lieutenant Deacon when you parade for the last time here, make it a good one we can be proud to say, we trained you. Your families and friends are most welcome to attend the parade so give them something to be proud of also. He asked Alfred if he thought they would put on a good show."

"Watch this space sir."

"Tell me straight Alfred, will it be worth me trying to get the Emir to take the salute?"

"Yes sir it will and to save any embarrassment it is not going to be a contest between us and them."

"That sounds very interesting I will now go and have a word with the girls." Alfred brought his flight to attention and saluted Bill.

As Bill rounded the building hiding the girls' flight he heard a shout of 'Scramble' then saw a flurry of bodies forming up in three ranks to await his arrival. Sergeant Anisa called them to attention while Dot saluted Bill. "Stand them Easy Sergeant" he ordered "I want a little chat. Good morning ladies, on Friday you will be on parade for the last time here." He then repeated what he had told the airmen. It will be Sergeant Anisa's last parade with you and I am sure you will want to make it something for her to remember with pride and not fear." He drew Dot on one side. "Reading between the lines I think we are all going to be pleasantly surprised on Friday with that in mind I shall try my utmost to get the Emir to take the salute. Don't mention it yet until I confirm it."

"Wouldn't that be wonderful if he did sir, thank you."

"What did you think of this morning's newspaper?"

"Brilliant, the Press did you proud. tell Tommy I am sending one to Viv."

"Will do" he said returning Dot's salute.

"Oh by the way have you made any progress with that curriculum?"

"No sir."

"Then I suggest you both get your fingers out and get cracking on it I would like it yesterday Mashy?"

"Mashy Sir."

He then carried on to see Major Khatib his second in command. As he walked along the corridor to the Major's office he received a round of applause from all the officers, he returned the compliments with a salute and mouthing "Thank You." George greeted him with "Congratulations Bill" and a warm hand shake. We were all glued to the Television and when your awards were announced you must have heard the cheering from here every body was delighted for you."

"Thank you George I am being overwhelmed with good wishes everyone is being so kind. You will soon be very busy in here when the new batches of recruits arrive. Have you received the documentations for the new intakes yet?"

"Not yet we haven't but we have received a signal that everything is in hand and we should be receiving them very soon."

"Good, I will go and thank the staff then go and see Lieutenant Hikmat." He went to each of the staff and shook their hands. "Thank you for your good wishes and also for being a credit to the Training Team." He went in to have a word with Captain Fahima. He shook her hand and asked "Are you settling in Captain and have you got everything you need for your office?"

"Yes sir Major Khatib is taking care of me very well."

"What about the rest of your WAF brood have they accepted you as their O.C?"

"Everyone is being very co-operative and yes sir we are very friendly and they are very nice people a pleasure to work with."

He knocked on Lieutenant Hikmat's office door and entered. She immediately jumped to her feet. "I am sorry if I startled you but please sit down. This is just a courtesy call to see how you are getting on. I see you have been busy getting your wall charts bang up to date."

"It was with the great help I received from Lieutenant Basma sir she was wonderful but there is still much more to do before I am satisfied."

"Have you had any bad reactions from your staff since you took over the helm in here?"

"It is just the opposite sir they are really helpful and their co-operation is beyond question, even the airmen are now happy in their work."

"It appears you are a good influence for them. You know of course after Friday you are going to be extra busy with the change over of the new intakes."

"Oh yes sir I am aware of that and everything is now under control."

"Well done, what about your staff do you need any more bodies?"

"I should not think so but if I do I will notify Major Khatib."

"What more can I say except you are running this place like clockwork and I am very much impressed. Thank you Lieutenant Hikmat I will leave you to it."

Returning to his office he called "I am back Miss Battle."

"The C.O. would like a word when you are free sir."

"I am on my way. "Hello I am Colonel Barrett" he said to Eric's P.A. "I am to believe the C.O. wants to see me."

"Colonel Barrett is here sir" she said over the inter-com.

"Send him in please" was the reply.

"This way sir" she said ushering him to the connecting door. "Colonel Barrett sir" she announced.

"Come in Bill and take a seat, I am sorry we could not get together after the ceremony but I got tied up with well wishers. "I heard your interview on Television and I would like to thank you for the boost you gave me it has lifted my status with some very important people of our community."

"Eric, please remember we worked as a team it was the best chance I had to get you officially recognised for the good man you are. Tommy and I saw you engrossed in conversation and we did not want to interrupt you, so as soon as the Emir withdrew we quietly slipped away only to be confronted by the Press who fair enough wanted a few words with photographs. Have you seen today's headlines they gave us a good write-up."

"Yes I did and to their credit they did not make it into a fairy story. I did hear you and the Consul locked horns and that you came out top."

Bill laughed, "He was pathetic but the highlight was, as soon as he withdrew defeated Tommy and Soapy commenced their no quarter given fight until the Emir came in as referee and judged the Barretts to be the winners."

"I wish I could have been there to witness it Bill that would have been the icing on the cake for me. I have it from good authority the Consul is to be replaced; they were never a well liked couple your incident looks like it was all that was needed for the final push. Now, is there anything I can do for you Bill?"

"I am glad you asked me Eric, there are two things and one is very special. The other is I want five school teachers, two men, two women and a Headmistress for when our new school is finished, Major Hassan has promised me it will be ready for when the new intakes arrive. I suggest we get the Headmistress first then she can choose the other four because she will be qualified to do so. The main request is I would very much like the Emir to come and take the salute at the March-Past on Friday. The reason I ask is my two assistants are training the two flights to give a mini-type BlueBelle display which I am sure the Emir would like to see. It will not only justify our training ability but it will show that his youngsters can respond and carry out a drill that has never before been produced in Aljibia. Personally Eric I think he will be very proud of them."

"Putting it like that Bill how can I refuse, as you English would say it will put another feather in my cap."

"How do you like your new P.A. Eric does she fit the bill?"

"Indeed she does and is very efficient too I think I have struck gold there Bill."

"Well I had better go and take Miss Battle to lunch besides I am feeling a bit peckish. Thanks again for everything Eric I appreciate what you are doing not only for me but the Training School."

"We are still a team Bill and if I say so a damned good one."

"If you are you ready for lunch Miss Battle let us get off to the Luncheon Box."

On the way there Barbara was telling how much she enjoyed the write-up in the newspaper. How are you going to cope with being a celebrity?"

"In the same way you will be coping with all my fan mail."

"Well, are you ready for the red carpet treatment sir?"

"I don't think I will bother with lunch here I will get Fred to run me home Thomas will rustle up something quick, would you care to join me?"

"You are not going to chicken out of it so easy Colonel Barrett I do not think you would disappoint your fans and spoil their lunch would you?"

"Mine is spoilt already."

"So am I going to be deprived of being escorted into lunch by Aljibia's number one celebrity?"

"Go on then if you put it like that I always was a soft touch. Are you going to take my arm and flash a beaming smile to everyone?"

"No way I would get mobbed; your fans will think I am frog marching you in."

"Come on then I will put on a brave face just for you."

As they entered and were being escorted to their table by a waiter they received a standing ovation even Alfred and Dot joined in. At his table before sitting down he turned to the patrons bowed and said "Thank you very much you are so kind."

"You see, that did not hurt I do not know why you made all that fuss, you men!"

"Has he been giving you a hard time Barbara?" Dot asked.

"Do you know I had to force him to enter here, he wanted to go home for his lunch he acted like a right prima donna."

Of course they all had to laugh at that.

"I'll wipe the smiles from your two faces, where is that curriculum I asked for, are you trying to sabotage all my good work?"

"We are very sorry about that Sir but I can only suggest that you carry your complaint to our friend the Emir" said Alfred.

"Look here young man you are going to have to do better than that I am not yet ready to be made redundant. Are you ready for coffee Barbara?" As they were leaving to go into the lounge for coffee patrons wanted to shake his hand as he was passing their tables offering their congratulations and a well done Colonel. As he sat down in the lounge he said "Thank goodness that is over and done with."

"I would not be too sure of that sir. These people do not lose their gratitude overnight."

"Alfred handed Barbara a large envelope. "Apparently Barbara you have been waiting for this since yesterday."

When she opened it she smiled, looked at Bill, "I have got my Drill curriculum sir."

"I should think so too you have waited long enough for it you need to check it thoroughly you know how slapdash young officers can be nowadays. You two had better put on a good show on Friday because you will probably be having the Emir taking the salute."

"Dot gave a scream, "Oh you lovely man if you we were not in uniform I would kiss you."

"Bill looked at Alfred…and don't you even think of it."

"I will see you back at the office Barbara I am off to see Major Hassan."

The Major saw Bill approaching through the glass windows in his office door and waved him in. "Good to see you sir" he said rising from his chair and holding out his hand in greeting and telling Bill to sit himself down.

"It is nice to see you too Major" he said giving the Major's hand a warm shake. They passed a few pleasantries the main topic of course being the award ceremony For which the Major congratulated Bill. "Now let us get down to business I am sure that is why you have come to see me sir."

"First thing first" said Bill "you and I are at an age and rank where we can dispense with protocol when we are alone and I think it would be more friendly to address each other by our first name and to start it off I am Bill and here is my hand in friendship."

"Thank you Bill I am Harry and I feel honoured to call you a friend and here is my hand to seal our friendship."

"So, as you were saying Harry I have come to see you about some business. On Friday the recruits have their Passing-Out Parade ceremony and I have asked the Emir through the Brigadier if he will honour us and take the salute. I have reason to believe he has accepted the invitation but I want a saluting base for him and that is where you and your merry men come in. Can you produce one in the short time we have left?"

Harry laughed. "You English have some quaint sayings which come straight to the point and I will quote you one right now which I think is very appropriate…If you fell in a dung heap Colonel Barrett you would come out smelling of Roses."

"Bill burst out laughing "I don't believe it Harry, you are going to tell me you already have one, right?"

"Right Bill, I have had one for as long as I can remember but I have never seen it used. It will take a little while to dust the cobwebs off it but I am sure it is still in good condition. Come on I will take you to see it."

As they walked through the workshop Bill got applause from the airmen carrying out their tasks to which he responded with a smile and a wave. In a storeroom they found the Dais and indeed it had been strongly built. "See, it only needs a good clean how about that for service is there anything else you need?"

"Yes, I would like it covered in a red carpet." He looked at Harry and saw the twinkle in his eyes. "You have got that as well haven't you?"

"I can still smell Roses Bill and when it is complete my men will deliver it to the site and place it just where you want it."

"You know Harry I never stop being amazed at your people's efficiency it beats anything I have come across."

"That is the advantage we have over your people Bill we work together not against each other to earn what you English call…Brownie Points."

"Well said Harry."

"Do you want to take a look at the school Bill?"

"I would like to Harry but I would rather wait to see the end product in that perspective I can compare the before and after scenario. Anyway I must get back, thanks for everything you are doing for us Harry."

"All quiet Miss Battle?"

"Yes sir, no messages and no phone calls."

"Would you like to take a break and make a brew and hear what I have to tell you?"

"Most certainly that sounds like it could be interesting, I will be with you in a couple of minutes."

"Bring it in my office it is more comfortable."

"Here you are sir now make my day with something exciting."

"Tommy received a telephone call from the editor of the National Newspaper, he would like to feature us in a magazine and would we call in to see him to discus it."

"And what are your reactions?"

"If it will be what the public would be interested in I will be all for it thinking in my way I would be repaying in part the kindness they are showing to Tommy and me, if there is money involved I would veto it immediately. All I would ask for would be a few free copies to distribute to my close friends."

"You would be subjected to a great deal of upheaval while they take all the photographs they will need both at home and with permission here on the station. You are now a very important person here in Aljibia sir and you will need to come to terms with it whether you like it or not. You will no doubt be snapped by ordinary people in the street but you will have the consolation of knowing that you will not be followed around by the type of inconsiderate photographers that are rife in Europe. If you think that you and Tommy can cope with the upheaval then I say go ahead I am sure that apart from the people here liking it your family and friends will love it. Please put me down for a copy."

"I am glad I told you about it Barbara I am looking at it from a different point of view now, thank you and we will both sign your copy. We are going to see the editor Saturday morning I have not the time this week. Give Fred a ring please then I will be off home."

Fred saluted. "Has it been a good day for you sir?"

"It certainly has Fred very satisfying."

"Yes, he is a good man is Major Hassan very obliging he will help anyone even I cannot remember when that Dais was last used."

"Do you think the red carpet will be in good condition when it comes out of its wrapping?" Bill said with tongue in cheek.

"Oh without a doubt sir you will have no problems in that respect."

"What about the Emir is he definitely coming to take the salute?"

Wild horses would not drag him away from that sir he is quite excited about it. Don't tell Alfred but his son is coming with him."

"Very nice."

"You don't sound surprised sir."

"Fred, I have given up being surprised at all the things you tell me and I have also stopped wondering where you get all the gen from…does that surprise you?"

Fred just chuckled. "I have your CDs sir and I must say they are very good, Mrs B will be really chuffed with them and somehow they seem to bring the sparkle out in her if you don't mind me saying sir, you make a really handsome couple."

"Fred! You are getting all emotional."

"It has been known sir that I have made the odd sniff or two on the odd occasion."

"Well do not wipe your nose on your uniform sleeve it will make it shiny."

"Thank you for that tip sir I will write it down in my book of The Englishman's Do's and Don'ts."

"Here we are sir and here are your CDs, shall I carry them in for you sir?"

"Go on then I have my brief case to carry, besides Mrs Barrett I expect will like a word with you."

Tommy met him with a kiss. "Hello Fred how nice to see you again, what have you got there in the parcel am I allowed to know?"

"Fred looked at Bill who nodded his head. They are CDs of the award ceremony."

"She screamed with delight, oh how wonderful."

"Inside the box are the wrappings in the form of cardboard cartons for sending them overseas and Customs labels. If you are posting them off tomorrow I will come with you to the Post Office to help you through the system in case of any snags."

"Shall we wrap them this evening Bill then they can be on their way?"

"Yes if you like and thank you for the offer Fred to guide Mrs Barrett like you said in case there is something she will not be able to understand."

"Will 10 o'clock be alright for you Mrs Barrett?"

"That will be fine thank you Fred."

"Salaam sir…Mrs Barrett"

"Salaam Fred" they both responded.

"Aren't we lucky to have Fred" Tommy enthused, "what would we do without him?"

"I am off to freshen up" stated Bill "you can unpack the box if you want."

When he returned his beer was waiting for him and the box had been unpacked.

"Fred thought of everything, all we have to do is box and address them and fill in the customs forms except the one for us, Alfred and Dot, Thomas and Leila that leaves us with six. Who are we posting the others to Bill?"

"Nessie, Roy, Viv, Ann and Tim, Jackson, and George Miller. I need two more one for Barbara and one for Mary." Have you anyone else you would like to send to?"

"Apart from Jackie but I do not know if she has a CD player. I will ask when I phone her which reminds me I will do that tonight are you phoning Roy?"

"I might as well he will want to know from the horse's mouth after getting the gen from Viv."

"Dinner is ready Ma'am" announced Leila."

"Good evening Chef" greeted Bill on entering the kitchen "have you had a hard day slaving over a hot stove?"

"You don't know the half of it sir I am sure I am losing weight each day."

"You want to eat some of that good food you put in front of us you will soon put it back on again."

"What has been your programme today love?"

"Answering that damned phone it has been ringing all day. English people I have never heard of inviting me to coffee mornings and us to dinners, would I like to address different clubs etc etc. Leila eased the strain by answering to tell them I was not available. It was no joke I can tell you."

"Do you fancy coming to the Passing-Out Parade on Friday I think Alfred and Dot are going to put a good show on for the Emir."

"Will the Emir be there?" Tommy got all excited asking. "In that case I most certainly will be going. I would have gone anyway to support Alfred and Dot. Will I be staying for lunch?"

"Of course."

"Leila I will be out for lunch on Friday I am going to watch a parade on the base."

Bill had to explain to Thomas and Leila what the parade was about.

Over coffee Bill asked "Are we phoning first or what?"

"We will wait until 8 o'clock remember we are two hours ahead of them and it will be a good time to get hold of them."

"You do the writing of the addresses because you are a neater writer than me" Bill said "I will do the wrapping up."

Everything went smoothly and at 8 o'clock Tommy was speaking to Viv., half an hour later it was Bill's turn to put Roy in the picture of the recent events.

"Had Roy any news for you love?

"Not really he said the C.O. asked him if he had heard from me and how was I getting on with the Training School. He is going to see him tomorrow to tell him of my Awards."

"Viv said everyone she told was thrilled to bits and send their congratulations. She told me that Dot had phoned her but Dot was so excited it was difficult to make sense from a lot of what she was saying. Oh I must phone Jackie to ask if she has a CD player. Read the numbers to me Bill. Hello Mum how are you? Half an hour later Tommy managed to ask about the CD player. You have, good we will be posting one to you tomorrow, no, you must wait and see what it is about but you will be pleased with what you see. Yes I will when he wakes up yes we love you too Mum.

All is well love she has one. She said everything is back to normal in the Mess they are all happy with my old friend."

CHAPTER 31

"Good morning sir" said Fred saluting.

"Good morning to you Fred, what is the news from the grapevine?"

"The Head teacher will be reporting today for an interview."

"Have you got any gen on her?"

"She is highly qualified and well respected by the ones who really know her, the ones who dislike her do so because they cannot accept her code of conduct and being a stickler for the rules"

"That is good to know Fred, thanks I think we will get on well together. By the way you and I never did find the time to discuss my meeting with the National Newspaper Editor did we?"

"We will talk about that on the way home sir we have not the time now, your P.A. will be waiting to tell you about Captain Basira…your Head teacher. Salaam sir."

"Salaam Fred."

"Good morning Miss Battle what time do we expect Captain Basira? He called through the open connecting door.

"If you will please step in here sir you will find out."

On entering Barbara's office he came face to face with a very striking and good looking officer smart and well groomed and about Barbara's age he thought. "He approached her with outstretched hand saying "Captain Basira I am so pleased to meet you. She saluted and shook Bill's hand. "Thank you sir I am delighted to meet you, I have learned quite a bit about your service record especially after seeing the Television programme and I would like to offer you my congratulations on your awards. What draws me to this interview sir is your flair and knack of getting the best out of young people but not only them but also people of all ages. Those are the qualities I respect and admire sir that is why I want to become a member of your Training Staff."

"Captain Basira, I too know a little, only a little of your record as a teacher. You keep to a code of conduct and do not suffer fools gladly. You are highly qualified and stick to the rules that does not please many of your subordinates. Therefore I really think that to make you go through an unnecessary interview would be an insult to your intelligence. So Captain Basira it is my pleasure to welcome you to my Staff. I would now like you to officially meet my P.A. Miss Barbara Battle, you two have something in common, Miss Battle is an Honours Graduate from Oxford University. Look, shall we go in my office and I can put you in the picture of my plans.

Miss Battle and I usually have a drink of tea about this time would you care to join us?"

"I would love to sir thank you."

"We drink from mugs Captain you can have a cup if you wish," explained Barbara.

"Oh a mug will do me fine thank you I enjoy a good mug of tea myself."

Barbara sat in with them while Bill explained his plans to the Captain. "When will you be available to join us Captain?" Bill asked.

"I would like to come on Monday sir because I will need to order lots of items to make it a functional school plus choosing the right type of teachers I want."

"Have you got any in mind asked Bill?"

"Oh yes the four I want have worked with me before and I have always found them conscientious in dealing with pupils. I will be very disappointed if I cannot have them because I can use their experience."

"Excellent then I will hand that responsibility to you. if you will give us their names we can then summon them for interviews, that will be your department then when you are satisfied we arrange accommodation which will be on the domestic site and you can be assured Captain the accommodation is first class. What about you will you want our accommodation if so would you like to see it?"

"Yes please."

"Miss Battle would you ring Major Khatib and ask him if I could have the loan of Lieutenant Fidda to show Captain Basira the WAF accommodation she has just been appointed Headmistress of our school and will be posted in on Monday. Make sure you pick the accommodation that suites your requirements Captain then report back here and we will take you to lunch if you so wish."

"Thank you sir it is most kind of you."

"Ah! Here comes your chaperon Captain, this is Lieutenant Fidda who is in charge of all the WAF accommodation, Fidda saluted and pleasantries were exchanged. You are in good hands Captain the Lieutenant will take excellent care of you and will make sure the apartment you choose is to your standard. Thank you Lieutenant Fidda."

"Well Barbara, give me your honest opinion."

"I think she will fit the bill perfectly sir and she is genuinely enthusiastic over the project."

"Will you do me a favour, will you take her to lunch and have a woman to woman talk with her please I am sure it will help her to know she has made the right decision."

"Of course it is a long time since that I have held a conversation with a well educated and knowledgeable woman I am looking forward to that."

"What about Eric's P.A"

"Never met her sir, at present I have not had cause to."

"You will be attending the parade tomorrow won't you to see what progress Alfred and Dot have made with the recruits. "I think they are going to put on a show which will surprise everybody even I do not know their routine. I am bringing Tommy to see it and I am wondering if you would keep her company because I will be tied up with the Emir and officials."

"Oh that would be nice it will give Tommy and me the chance to get to know each other."

When the Captain returned she was full of praise for the accommodation. "My apartment was not hard to choose because there was so very little difference in the ones I saw and the Lieutenant assured me that all the apartments were of a similar standard."

"Well I expect we are all ready for lunch, I have asked Miss Battle to accompany you then you can both chatter with women's talk because you must have something in common even if it is about teaching."

The three walked together to lunch Bill told her that the restaurant had been christened Barbara's Luncheon Box. The Captain was overwhelmed when she entered and saw the décor and furnishings. "Good gracious this is what I call luxury dining. A waiter ushered the two ladies to Barbara's usual table after Bill had signalled wanted a different one. As usual he was acknowledged by the other diners while Alfred and Dot looked perplexed to see Bill sitting alone. Bill gave them a wave of assurance.

"After Barbara and the Captain had chosen their order Barbara introduced Alfred and Dot saying these are Lieutenants Deacon and Dean they are drill instructors to the recruits and this is Captain Basira our new Headmistress to the school."

Over coffee the group sat and chatted getting to know each other a little more. On the way back to the office Bill said. "I will leave showing you work being done on the school until later Captain first I shall have to find you a temporary office to work in, would you mind sharing an office until yours is ready to move in to?"

"No I do not mind sir so long as the person I will be sharing with does not put up any objections."

"I will try to sort something out which will be compatible. On Monday I will show you how the work is progressing on the school. So Captain Basira we will see you on Monday" Bill said shaking her hand.

"Ring Fred please Barbara, tomorrow is going to be a very busy morning so I shall come in a little earlier."

Bill returned Fred's salute, climbed in the car and asked. "What is the latest from the grapevine Foxy?"

"There will be a good turn out to watch the parade tomorrow sir that is all."

"Did you manage the two CDs this morning?"

"Yes sir and they were all posted off except one and we had no hitches at the Post Office only Mrs Barrett got another admirer in the shape of the counter clerk who served her and recognised her from the Television programme. You had better watch out sir or she will be putting you in second place of the celebrity stakes."

"What can you tell me about our meeting with the Newspaper Editor Fred?"

"He is a nice guy and still holds you responsible for his promotion to Chief Editor. He is trying to return the compliment by boosting your image to our people through a new magazine which will feature you, Mrs Barrett and your friends. I think you should go along with it sir who knows one day you might become the Foreign Minister to Aljibia," he then burst out laughing.

Bill could not help but join Fred in laughing. "That does it; you definitely will not get featured in my magazine."

As Bill was getting out of the car he told Fred "I would like you to pick me up fifteen minutes earlier tomorrow because I am going to have a very busy morning."

"I forgot to tell you the snippet of the day sir. The Consul has been given his marching orders and he is being replaced by a new Consul David Giles shortly."

"Thank you Fred Mrs Barrett will be quite chuffed when I tell her."

"I will always remember you telling me about your best friend in the UK saying, to cross you would be like the kiss of death and you have had a few victims here since you have been with us."

"You have no need to worry because you have a guardian angel."

"Who would that be sir?"

"To my utter dismay...Mrs Barrett"

"Then the sun really does shine upon the righteous."

"Salaam and sod off" snarled Bill.

"Salaam sir" replied Fred as he drove off having a good laugh.

"What are you laughing" at asked Tommy as Bill entered the Villa grinning?"

"Fred, he does make me laugh with some of the things he comes out with."

"He is a very intelligent man Bill and I for one am glad we have him." She gave him a kiss and asked what kind of a day he had.

"Very good, we now have the headmistress for the school all we need now are the teachers and the school to be finished. I will go and get freshened up." On his return he said "Fred told me you did very well at the Post Office."

"I did and made a conquest into the bargain, the young man behind the counter. when he realised who I was he could not do enough for me and saying how much he enjoyed the Television programme"

"Fred warned me that you might knock me off my perch as the number one celebrity. He also told me that the Consul has been given his marching orders and being replaced by somebody called David Giles."

"Well I hope he is a nicer person than His Nibs."

"Dinner is ready" announced Leila."

"Good evening Thomas, still slaving away I see, you have two women here at your beck and call and neither of them has thought of mopping your sweaty brow. If I had not had a hard day at the office I would have made the effort to mop it myself."

"It is little touches like that sir that makes life bearable."

"When you two poor lost souls have stopped feeling sorry for yourselves do you think I might have my dinner."

"Do you hear that Thomas where has the compassion towards your fellow man gone?"

"I know where you two will go if my dinner is not on the table in one minute flat!"

Leila was curled up laughing at the banter.

"Here you are madam" said Leila serving Tommy her dinner.

"That is more like it Thomas it even looks good enough to eat!"

Thomas at the cooking stove managed to splutter a "Thank You Ma'am."

"You sound a bit chesty Thomas, have you got a cold?" replied a deadpan face Tommy.

"Is there any chance of me being fed in this establishment?" complained Bill after all I am only the bread winner,"

"Good staff is so hard to find these days dear" soothed Tommy, giving Leila a wink. Do you think we should move into a one bedded apartment on the Base or suffer in luxury where we are now?"

"Bill craftily diverted the attention to Thomas. "This meal is up to your brilliant standard Thomas as per usual, I never complain."

"If you have finished prattling on let us retire to the lounge for coffee and leave poor Thomas in peace."

When they sat down Tommy asked "Are we giving them the CD now?"

"We will give it to them when they are going home."

When Leila brought the coffee Tommy asked her to call when they were going home.

"We have finished Ma'am" Leila called a little later.

"Come here then we have something for you both" she handed Leila the boxed CD. "You can open it when you get home."

"You are very kind to us thank you very much. Good night Sir…madam."

"Goodnight Leila."

"Fred will pick you up at 10 o'clock to bring you to the base, he will take you to Barbara who is going to chaperone you during the Parade, have a shufti round my office while you have the chance and see how I am slumming it. Before and after the Parade you will be introduced to some of my colleagues then when it is all over we will go to lunch then all the training staff will stand down."

CHAPTER 32

"Good morning sir" Fred said as he saluted Bill. "This is the big day when all of Aljibia will be watching the results you have made with their sons and daughters.

"What do you mean about all Aljibia will be watching?"

"Wait till you get to the base and see all the gear the Television people have brought with them and the Press will be there too."

"That is wonderful Fred the country is going to get a damned good show to watch. You'll see, the recruiting figures will increase no end. And you know what that means I may get the go ahead to recruit more training personnel from the U.K."

"Then I wish you the best of luck sir."

"Will it be convenient Fred for you to pick up Mrs Barrett at 10 o'clock and take her to Miss Battle please? She is going to chaperone Mrs Barrett because I will be tied up with the parade."

"It will be my pleasure sir."

"One thing I should warn you about, say nothing about the Television or the Press or you will be waiting for her choosing an entire outfit and that could be very frustrating for you worrying if you will miss the Parade, you know what women are like Fred."

"Thanks for the tip sir. Here we are, look at that lot wires and vans everywhere."

I hope they are not going to take all the space from the spectators. I had better look into that. I'll see you later Fred and thanks."

"Good morning Miss Battle I cannot stop just now the Television people need to be sorted out they are all over the place." He scurried out and made his way to where some of the engineers were working. "Excuse me can you tell me where I can find your man in charge?"

"He is in that big van over there sir."

"Tell me are you all set up yet, what I mean is if I wanted you to move to a different site would it cause you a lot of work?"

"No sir, we have only just arrived and we have not started our work yet."

"Thanks very much don't start anything until you get the all clear. Mashy?"

"Mashy sir" they replied with a grin.

He knocked on the van door which was open and a portly type gentleman turned with a mug of tea in his hand, glared at Bill and demanded to know who he was. Bill introduced himself as the Officer Commanding the training school and that he was also the Parade Commander.

"So what can I do for you Mr Parade Commander? He said with a sneer.

Oh I am going to like this Bill said to himself as he entered the van.

"I would like you to move your van and equipment to another site."

"And why should I do that?"

"Because I am afraid you are parked almost on top of the saluting base."

"Then move the saluting base to another site."

"Not for this parade sir."

"That is your problem I shall not move from this site for you or anyone else and if you do not get out of my van I will personally throw you out."

"Are you threatening me sir?"

"Yes I am, now get out."

"Is that your last word sir?" Bill said knowing he had got this oaf by the short and curlies.

The man approached him and grabbed him by the front of his tunic pushing him backwards out of the van. Bill smiled which irritated the man who lost his temper immediately, he let go of Bill's tunic then went to strike him but Bill was too quick for him, he caught hold of his arm and physically dragged him out of the van causing him to fall face downwards. Bill jumped in the van and told a young man who had been watching to "Phone your Headquarters and tell them you want a replacement for him urgently or the Emir is going to be displeased if he is kept waiting." He then went into the nearest office and said to the startled woman occupant. "This is an emergency quick phone the security. Hello this is Colonel Barrett send two officers to the Television van to place a person under arrest for assault I will be there in person, thank you."

He said to the young lady "I am sorry I startled you but thank you very much for your co-operation." In return he got a lovely smile.

He went back to the van where the man was licking his wounds. "I shall see your Commanding Officer and get you stripped for this" he snarled.

When the security car pulled up the two security men saluted Bill. "You sent for us sir" they asked.

Yes, this is the man. He then spoke to him. I am arresting you for assault on my person." As he was being handcuffed he protested, "I am in charge of this Television crew."

"You still would be if you had moved your equipment when asked, it is a big price to pay for refusing to move it away from the Emir's saluting base. In your own words you would not move it for anybody. It is a tough old world. Take him away."

The engineers who had been watching the scenario thanked Bill. "You have done us and the company a big favour there Colonel thank you, they all came to shake his hand.

"Right then let us not hold the job up, where is the best spot for you and also to place it somewhere inconspicuous? Leave it to us Colonel" they said and in a short space of time they had moved it to a place that Bill agreed to. He then returned to his office and asked Barbara to get Major Hassan for him. Hello Harry, Bill here can you get the saluting base over please, thank you."

"Your tunic is crumpled sir" observed Barbara, take it off and I will run an iron over it and you can tell me what scrapes you have been up to. When he told her what had happened she was horrified. How stupid can anyone get, that is his position with the Television Network finished plus the possibility of a jail sentence."

"He must have been extremely disliked by the people he worked with because they all came to thank me and shake my hand. I imagine the cause of it was being power crazy."

"There you are sir your tunic, it is as good as new once more."

He went to his briefcase and brought out a CD. "Thank you Barbara here is a little present in appreciation for all you do for me."

"Thank you sir, can I open it now?"

"If you want to by all means do so."

After opening it and seeing what it contained she said "Thank you very much sir for a wonderful gift, it will give me a great deal of pleasure I can assure you."

"I have to dash off I have the saluting base to see to then I want a word with Alfred and Dot, I'll see you later."

While he was supervising the men placing the saluting base just where he wanted a car arrived and a young man leaped out of it and into the Television van. *That will be the replacement he said to himself he will be getting all the gen from the chap who was inside the van and witnessed the whole thing.* "Thanks chaps" he said to the Major's staff, you have certainly made a good job of cleaning it up and I like those little steps with the handrail. Tell the Major thanks and I will see him later. By the way are you coming to watch the parade?"

"Yes sir the Major is closing down the Workshop to let us all come."

His next stop was to see Alfred and Dot. He got them together and told them. "I will be the Parade Commander. I will shout for you to March On. I will give for inspection open order march then inform the Emir the Parade is ready for his inspection. I will accompany him as you lead him round the ranks. When the inspection is over I will give close order march then tell you both to carry on. You know your first thing is the official march past. I will return to the saluting base and enjoy seeing you going through your routines. I expect you have told them about the Emir, and apparently according to Fred there is to be a big turn-out for the occasion. Tommy is coming and Barbara and I are taking her to lunch so if we all go together we may get a table for five. Mashy?

"Mashy sir"

"So are you clear on what I have told you, it will all fall into place you are no dum-dums on the parade ground. I forgot to tell you that you are being televised and also reported in the press. He shook their hands Good Luck. I wish Joe Franks and Viv were here to see you but we will see what we can do about them seeing you at home."

"Good morning Mrs Barrett, my words you do look smart sir will be proud of you today."

"Well thank you Fred what a nice complimentary greeting. I expect things are pretty busy on the base."

"Indeed they are Ma'am your husband is running round like a …how can I put it?"

Tommy helped him out with "Are you looking for…B.A. Fly Fred?"

"I am sorry I do not under stand that terminology Ma'am."

"Well Fred if you will pardon my French it is Blue arsed Fly which supersedes the headless chicken."

Fred roared with laughter. When I tell that one to my friends in the motor pool they will er er um."

Tommy comes to the rescue once more… "Wet their knickers Fred?"

"They will now after hearing that one. You know you and the Colonel make a great team and Allah has been good assigning me to you both."

"Then you can thank your Allah from us for doing so."

This is where I drop sir off in a morning. Come with me I am to take you to Miss Battle.

"When Tommy entered the building she was absolutely gob smacked. "It is wonderful Fred and he tells me this is where he is slumming wait until I see him I'll give him slumming."

Fred grinned as he began to stir it for Bill. "This is nothing Mrs Barrett in comparison to the opulence of his office. Here is Miss Battle's office, he knocked then ushered in Tommy. Barbara jumped up from her chair and hugged Tommy. "Oh I am so pleased to meet you at last Tommy I have waited for ages for this moment."

"It was exactly the same for me Barbara Bill has told me so much about how you look after him, now that I have met you I know he is in good hands. He often tells me I do not know who is worse you or Barbara."

"He is a joy to work for, he so caring and considerate."

Fred was still standing there listening to what they were saying before they realised they were not alone. "I thought you had left" said Tommy "instead you have been ear wigging haven't you? Now no telling Sir what you have overheard or you will get your knees slapped, Mashy?"

"Mashy Mrs Barrett" he said laughing as he left.

"That man Barbara is one of the nicest you could ever wish to meet he teases Bill something cruel but Bill loves it they are both birds of a feather."

"Would you like a cup of tea Tommy?"

"Can you make it a mug please?"

Barbara laughed. "I think we all come from the same mould where mugs have preference.

"Mine comes from my service days." Tommy confessed.

"And mine comes from my childhood days. Come bring your brew and I will show you the Master's Office."

When Tommy saw that it was a self-contained office she nearly spluttered into her mug of tea. "It is just unbelievable Barbara that it is used as an office."

"The regime believe in providing its top people with work comfort, that is the best way I can describe it, it is supposed to add impetus to the brain power I think but in a lot of cases it makes them lethargic and not wanting to work. That does not apply to the Colonel he is hardly in here he goes out in the field as he calls it, he is definitely a hands-on man. I think we had better go out there and get into position Tommy."

What a surprise they got too, the area was absolutely crowded with people. Parents, friends, service men and women everyone who could come was there. They made their way towards the saluting base and fortunately someone had told Bill because he came and guided them to two seats next to the saluting base. "I saved these especially for you; the Parade will start in ten minutes time. Would you like a cool drink?"

"No thank you sir "replied Barbara.

"Not for me either "replied Tommy "or I would be dashing to spend a penny in the middle of the ceremony."

"I will have to leave you to go and wait for the arrival of the Emir."

"Good luck love" said Tommy.

"Good luck sir" said Barbara.

Bill saluted them both then left.

Many eyes were focused on the two women who the Colonel had saluted not least the Television camera which was panning the crowd of spectators.

Suddenly there was the buzz from the spectators which denoted the Emir had arrived and was being welcomed by Eric the Station Commander. Heads and cameras focused on the welcome and when the Emir came into view there was applause and loud cheering welcoming him from the spectators. He made his way to the saluting base, followed by Eric and Bill. He had to pass Tommy and Barbara but stopped when he saw Tommy.

"So we meet again Tommy," he said, as he shook her by the hand. "It is good to see you again. Are you here to cheer your countrymen?"

Tommy shook the proffered hand and curtsied. "Yes your Excellency, and also the recruits, who I understand are going to give us a Parade which will last in people's memories. Sir, may I introduce you to my husband's Private Secretary, Miss Barbara Battle?"

The Emir shook her hand and as Barbara curtsied he said, "If you are a friend of the Barretts, you are indeed in good company."

"Thank you your Excellency," said Barbara, who then gave Tommy's hand a thank-you squeeze. Eric shook their hands, wearing a big smile and Bill gave them a wink.

After the Emir had acknowledged the cheers from the spectators and sat down, Bill marched round to the front of the saluting base, saluted, and asked, "Permission to March On Sir?" When permission was granted Bill saluted, did an About Turn, then marched a few paces forward before shouting "MARCH ON!" The two flights appeared, marching side by side, the men headed by Alfred and the girls by Dot and Sergeant Anisa. Entering the Parade area both flights right wheeled. They came to a point where Alfred, Dot and Anisa did a left turn while the two flights carried on forward until they reached a point where they all turned left and formed up behind their leaders, who had been marking time on the spot. They immediately picked up the step and the two flights marched forward until they were halted, centrally facing the saluting base. Bill then gave the order, "for inspection Open Order march, Right Dress," then, "Eyes Front" which they carried out with precision. Bill about turned marched towards the Emir, saluted and announced, "Parade Is Ready for your Inspection Sir."

The Emir was followed by Eric, the Station Commander. Bill introduced Lieutenant Deacon. "Sir, he is responsible for training this flight to the high standard it has reached in a matter of two weeks or so."

The Emir shook Alfred's hand. "My son was hoping to have attended this parade but circumstances prevented it. If your march-on is anything to go by everyone here is in for a pleasant surprise." He continued round the ranks, stopping to ask questions from various airmen. He shook Alfred's hand. "Thank you Lieutenant. From what I gather from your airmen you are a very popular figure with them."

Dot called her flight to attention and saluted the Emir.

"This is Lieutenant Dean Sir," informed Bill,. "and this is Sergeant Anisa. She carried on training these girls when there was no-one who would take over from her. She herself is not trained as an instructor but she did such a good job in bringing the girls to a decent standard of drill, the Lieutenant was in a position of finishing it off then putting the icing on the cake to the standard they have now reached. Sergeant Anisa will go to RAF March for a three month Sergeant Drill Instructors Course."

The Emir Shook both their hands and commented on the co-operation they had with each other which is a credit to you both." He carried on with his inspection, stopping and speaking to many of the girls.

"Are you going to give a BlueBelles display?" he asked one girl. "We will try our best sir. You will not be disappointed," she answered him with a big smile.

When the Emir was back and seated on the rostrum Bill saluted him and asked "Your Permission to Carry on Sir." When the Emir nodded Bill turned to tell the Parade to 'Carry On'. Alfred then ordered the Parade to reform ranks. As the airmen side stepped four paces the airwomen marched forward to make one mixed flight. Sergeant Anisa took charge and put the combined flight through the basic drill movements. Dot then took over and took the flight through a combination of drill movements with the minimum of orders, finishing off with two separate flights facing the rostrum. Alfred, Dot and Anisa then marched to the centre of the parade ground and stood facing the rostrum with Anisa between Alfred and Dot. The two flights turned about to face the three instructors. When Alfred gave a nod the airwomen marched in a clockwise direction forming a circle round the three instructors, keeping their momentum. They were followed by the airmen, who marched in an anti-clockwise direction forming an outer circle. When the airmen and airwomen had circled the instructors three times, the instructors each raised one hand. As they did so the airmen raised one hand and the airwomen raised one hand, holding a white handkerchief. They all then paid their respects to the instructors by shouting in unison "Shukran…Salaam! Shukran…Salaam! Shukran…Salaam!"

When the instructors lowered their arms the airmen and airwomen reformed flights. The three instructors marched to the rostrum and faced outwards. At a nod from Alfred the two flights stepped off and, as they approached the rostrum, the airmen waved their hands while the airwomen waved their handkerchiefs to the spectators shouting, "Salaam, Salaam, Salaam". All those watching were on their feet, applauding the young people, many women holding handkerchiefs to their eyes. When they had all passed the rostrum the two flights broke ranks with a job well done.

The Emir called Bill and the three instructors to the rostrum. He shook each one by the hand. "Thank you all. I never thought I would see a display like that from my own people. I am proud of each one of you for training those young people to put on such a magnificent display which made so many people happy and very proud. Come..." he led them to the edge of the rostrum, Bill and Anisa on one side of him with Alfred and Dot on the other, facing the spectators with his arms spread to say, 'these are the ones responsible for that display'. Everyone joined in giving them a rapturous round of applause. The Emir then went to be interviewed by the Television presenter, and the instructors went to congratulate their students for a wonderful display. Gradually it commenced to thin out, students leaving with their families for some leave, others returning to their places of work and the clearing up of the area began. Barbara and Tommy went back to the office to wait for Bill, Dot and Alfred.

Eric and Bill were waiting for the Emir's interview to finish then they could say their goodbyes to him. When the Emir did appear he said to Bill. "Colonel Barrett I have been informed that you were the victim of an assault by the leader of this Television detachment, what is the story?"

Bill told him what had happened and there were plenty of witnesses to corroborate his story.

"I do not dispute what you tell me Colonel, but that man will be punished.

"Sir, the man was obviously under stress with it being such a special occasion, especially with you being the main attraction. When you do punish him, please do not send him to prison, I beg you sir. There are times when we do or say something hastily but regret it as soon as it occurs."

"Colonel Barrett, you never fail to amaze me. For what you have done for me and my people today I will respect your wish."

"Thank you very much sir. I can now continue to enjoy the rest of my day with an easy mind."

The Emir climbed into his car then called to Eric. "Brigadier, you are fortunate to have a good man like Colonel Barrett at your elbow. Take good care of him. When the car was slowly pulling away the Emir rolled down the window. "Colonel Barrett, tell Tommy she was looking very pretty today." Eric and Bill smiled as they saluted him.

Eric held out his hand to Bill. "Thanks Bill; for what you are doing for me indirectly may Allah bless you."

"Remember what the Emir called us Eric... 'Brothers in Arms' and that is what we will remain. I will now pick up the girls and my hero and heroine and proceed to lunch. You know, I am feeling peckish. See you on Monday sir," he said, as he saluted Eric.

On entering his office, the first thing he did was to say to Dot, "Come here... nobody is watching... then gave her a great big hug and a kiss. turning to Alfred he shook his hand and gave him a manly hug.

"What about us two friends of the Emir, don't we get a kiss? Tommy pointed out.

"You are so impatient Tommy Barrett, but I love you. He faced Barbara. "Do I have permission?" She did not reply but flung her arms round him, kissed him and said, "You were wonderful ... you all were."

"Well you two you certainly pulled one out of the bag there. The Emir is absolutely chuffed and the crowd went wild. It was like the finale at the Millenium Dome wasn't it love? And the icing on the cake for you my love is that the Emir said to me on leaving, 'Tell Tommy she was looking very pretty today'. Right then ... are we all ready for lunch?"

At the Luncheon Box Bill asked if it was possible to have a table for five.

The Maitre-d' responded with, "Of course sir, follow me please. Bill pushed Alfred and Dot to the front to receive the applause from the patrons, who rose to their feet to applaud and call 'Bravo'.

At the table they all stayed on their feet, waiting until the applause had stopped. Bill had to hold up his hands, requesting them to stop. "Ladies and gentlemen, on behalf of my colleagues we thank you very much for the honour you have just shown us, you are most kind. Since we arrived here we have been met by nothing but respect and friendship from you. We are dedicated to serve his Excellency the Emir and you his people to the best of our ability and may our bond of our friendship grow ever stronger, thank you."

That little thank you speech brought more applause, to which Bill, Alfred and Dot responded by applauding the patrons.

At last they could order their meals and while they were waiting for it they chatted about the morning's event. Bill said "I am going to get CDs of that; they should be very good. They will make good keepsakes for us all. I will ask Fred to do the honours as he did with the Awards ceremony and I will ask him to get some of tomorrow's newspapers too, so don't go buying any. Incidentally, you two are now on leave until a week on Monday, which was owed to you for being shoved in at the deep end on arrival when you should have been getting acclimatised. You and I, Barbara, will have to report for duty on Monday to keep the flag flying."

"Yes, it is going to be a very busy time for us sir."

"Barbara, you are now a family friend and when we are off duty it is Christian names. Protocol has its own place, Mashy?"

"Mashy Bill," she replied with a smile. "Thank you, and I would like to thank you publicly, Tommy, for introducing me to the Emir; it was a great honour for me."

Tommy patted her hand. "You are now a fully fledged member of the 'I Have Met the Emir' Club. The rest of the party gave a little cheer.

"What do you think of the Luncheon Box Love?" asked Bill.

"It is out of this world, absolutely lovely, and I suppose this is another of the places you come slumming besides your office."

"I was just pulling your leg love."

"I won't pull your leg when we get home, I will tear it off!"

The patrons looked at them every time they heard their laughter and joined in, but only with smiles.

As they made their way to the lounge for coffee, patrons put out their hands to shake hands and say "well done and thank you."

When they had settled down, Bill told Alfred and Dot, "I am commandeering your office for the Headmistress until the school is completed and I suggest you move in with Lieutenant Yassen and Lieutenant Basma respectively, then you can spend your time helping them fill in the wall charts. I am sure they will appreciate your help. If you have any personal stuff in there you can always nip in and move it. The Headmistress arrives on Monday. Mashy?"

"Mashy sir," they both replied, bringing smiles to everyone's face.

"Has Sergeant Anisa got her movement order yet?" asked Bill.

"She leaves a week on Monday," answered Dot, "and I have been telling her all about RAF March, what to expect and how to address different ranks. she is now aware that she will not be living in accommodation as grandiose as she is now. Sergeant (w) James has volunteered to be her chaperone during her stay and I have told her to take warmer clothing."

"You obviously have got all this gen from Viv," queried Bill.

"Oh yes, I keep in touch with her on a regular basis."

"That is good Dot, you are using initiative befitting of your rank. It will be in the early hours when she leaves here. Fred and I will take her to the airport."

"Please can I come along Bill? I would like to see her off and another friendly face may help to loosen any tension."

"We are going to town tomorrow," announced Bill, "anyone want to come along, or are you two going in under your own steam?"

"We will come with you, thank you very much."

"Have you anything planned for the weekend Barbara?" asked Tommy.

"I am spending the weekend with a friend who is a tutor at the university; we spend a lot of time swapping experiences since we last saw each other."

"Are there many English tutors there?" asked Tommy.

"Quite a few they are mainly English Tutors. The rest are a mixture of Foreign Language Tutors."

"Well folk are we ready for going home? You Barbara have your own transport, you two are on Shanks' Pony and we two are reliant on Fred. We will see you two tomorrow at the sane time as usual, Mashy?"

"Mashy" they both responded.

Back at the office Fred was called. "Have a nice weekend Barbara" said Tommy, we have had a very nice day together, thank you."

Fred was waiting for them with a big smile on his face. He saluted then held the door open for Tommy. "Front or back seat sir?" he asked Bill.

"Front please where I can keep an eye on your driving."

"Did you enjoy the parade Mrs Barrett?"

"Very much Fred I think everyone who was there enjoyed it."

"You certainly pulled the rabbit out of the hat today sir in the very short time that you had to train those youngsters."

"They responded very well to good instructors Fred they don't come any better than those two. What was the grapeviners' verdict?"

"Top marks, they were very impressed they are looking forward to you training the new intake from scratch. If you form an all girls display team as you did with the BlueBelles will you name them The Desert Orchids?"

"Oh what a lovely name" Tommy said. "You must keep that in mind Bill."

"I certainly will, tell your friends thank you it is an excellent name."

"Funny we were talking about the kiss of death the other day, another one has bit the dust."

"What is that all about?" asked Tommy.

Before Fred could open his mouth Bill said, one of the Television Crew men had an accident, he fell out of the van."

"Did he hurt himself?"

"Only slightly, his pride suffered the most. Fred will you call and order me twelve CDs of today's Parade please?"

"What about the newspapers sir."

"I will get them from the Boss Editor you know we have an interview with him tomorrow."

"Mashy sir."

CHAPTER 33

"Good morning Thomas…Leila how are you this beautiful morning?" asked Tommy but take no notice of his lordship he is on another planet at the moment."

Bill gave Leila a wink.

When they sat down Thomas and Leila came to stand before them. "What is this all about have you gone on strike or are you handing in your resignations?"

"We would never do that Ma'am replied Leila we just want to thank you for that CD present and to say that you are the most wonderful people we could ever wish to serve and we love you both very much."

"Come here Leila let me give you a big loving hug. Bill shook Thomas by the hand, "It is us who should be thanking you for the way you take care of us, for that we are truly thankful. Having said that I hope we are not to get a burnt offering for breakfast."

Thomas laughed, "There is no chance of that happening sir us HP Club members must stick together."

"When you two have finished consoling each other is there any chance of a breakfast in this establishment or is it to be turned into Brunch?"

"One breakfast coming up madam" as he placed Tommy's favourite breakfast before her.

Tommy gave him a beaming smile "thank you Thomas your breakfasts are always worth waiting for."

"You weren't saying that a minute ago and you never hear me complaining. Come on Thomas get your finger out I'm starving."

Thomas and Leila really love this bantering.

"Come on slow coach, Fred will be here in a minute."

"But I have not finished my breakfast yet."

"Then bring it with you, or ask Leila for a doggy bag!"

"What is the programme for today?" Fred asked after he had parked the car in town.

"We are staying here for lunch so we will not need you until about 4 o'clock." Tommy informed him.

"That applies to us two as well Fred."

"I am doing an errand for Sir can I do anything else for you?"

"No thanks Fred we will see you later." was the reply.

"Where are you eating, at the same place?" asked Dot.

"Yes, so we may see you it depends how long this interview takes."

They went to reception in the newspaper office where Bill spoke to the receptionist. "I am Colonel Barrett and this is my wife Mrs Barrett and we have come to see the Chief Editor."

"Do you have an appointment sir?"

"Well you could call it that it is not a timed one it is more or less an open one for today."

"I will see if he is in sir to confirm what you say."

"Before you do that would you mind checking the engagement book please?"

"I can tell you now sir before looking in the book your name is not in for any kind of interview."

"Please just check if it is?" he said with a charming smile."

With a deep sigh and eyes looking heavenwards she fished the book from a drawer, opened it at the relevant page then gave a gasp of dismay for there at number one on the list read Colonel Barrett and in brackets (priority). She began to splutter an apology...'

Bill looked at her with pity and said, "Don't try, just inform the Chief I am here."

This she did which resulted in him coming down to greet them personally. Colonel and Mrs Barrett how good of you to come I have been waiting days for this moment to thank you" he said shaking their hands, "come let us go to my office."

As they were about to follow him Bill looked at the receptionist and gave her a wink of consolation.

She returned the gesture with a weak smile.

When the three of them were seated the Chief asked if they would like refreshments.

"I would like a cool orange juice please" Bill said.

"Mrs Barrett?"

"A cool grapefruit juice please."

These were brought in by a young woman.

"You may not realise it Colonel but you have become a celebrity with our people and you will appreciate that in my position as a newspaper editor I have to use news to the best advantage to sell papers and in your case I can proudly say I have given you an excellent coverage and the public are asking for more. Today I have whet their appetites by giving them good front page material of yesterday's Parade. Have you read it Colonel?"

"Not yet with coming to see you I was hoping you would give me a few copies to send to our family and friends in the UK who are following my progress here in Aljibia with some interest."

"How many copies would you like?"

Bill asked Tommy, would twelve copies be enough do you think love?"

"Yes I would think so."

"I can always supply you with more if you need any" the Chief suggested. He then contacted someone on his intercom and asked for twelve wrapped copies to be delivered to his office.

"Now as I was saying Colonel, it is obvious you cannot take over the front page every day with your exploits so I thought of printing a magazine covering you and your wife, family and friends and I will tell you what it will entail. First and foremost it will need you to be very patient that is the hardest part of the scenario. "There will be a photographer and a reporter assigned to you who are at the top of their profession and they will keep the sessions down to a minimum. For you Colonel I will get permission for them to come on the base to record you at your work. For you Mrs Barrett they will come into your home to picture you with the Colonel off duty. You will be asked if you have any objections to posing and you are quite entitled to refuse as you can also do with any questions put to you. Before we go to press you will be asked to proof-read the first copy to your satisfaction and give us the go ahead. What do you think or would you like to think it over? If you veto it then I will scrap the idea?"

"What do you think love?" Bill asked "I like the sound of it but it can only succeed if we and the staff can work in absolute harmony."

"Those are my sentiments too" added Bill. "Have you got a name for the Magazine?" he asked the Chief.

"Not yet but I am open to suggestions. So I take it you are agreeable… yes?"

"Yes" they both said and it was sealed with a handshake.

"When can we start?" The Chief asked "I suggest that as soon as you can get permission for your staff to enter the base, confirm the necessary with me on the base then I can get a little time off for you to concentrate on our off duty life."

"That is excellent Colonel thank you for your co-operation you will not regret it, I promise we will do you proud." He then spoke into his intercom and asked for the newspapers. A young man brought them all neatly wrapped. "Here you are Colonel with my compliments. Come I will see you out."

As they walked past reception Bill gave the receptionist a wink and the thumb up sign, she gave him a thumb up sign in return plus a big smile. The chief shook Bill and Tommy by the hand thanking them "we will be in touch with you quite soon."

"On the way to lunch Tommy said "It should be very interesting Bill especially the end product. I am looking forward to seeing that." They went up the escalator to the restaurant and saw Alfred and Dot waiting for them. "Have you had your lunch?" Tommy asked "No, we thought we would have a drink while waiting for you and watch the world go by."

"Come on then" I am feeling peckish let us go and grab a table" said a hungry Bill.

"How did you get on with your interview?" Alfred asked.

"Very well; it was quite informative." Bill then told them what it would entail. "But the snag is, the magazine has not got a name; can you two come up with any bright suggestions? And 'Barrett of Aljibia' is out! Do not focus it on me, think of something general like 'The Sun' although that is out. Hang on a minute … I have just thought of one, how about 'The Sentinel' to start with."

"I like that," said an enthusiastic Tommy, at present I vote it Numero Uno."

After lunch they strolled round the shops until it was time to meet Fred at the car park.

"I see you got your newspaper sir, it makes good reading and with one or two excellent photos. How did your interview go; was it in your favour?"

"The end product will be, Fred, but we cannot find a name for this special magazine; will you ask your grapeviners if they can help out? We have been struggling to find one but 'The Sentinel' is the best we can offer. By the way Fred did you order the CDs?"

"Yes sir; we should get them on Monday. Will you need me tonight sir?"

"No thank you Fred, we are not going to the club yet. We would like all this euphoria to die down before we show our faces there."

"I have had enough with phone calls from friends crawling from out of the woodwork," Tommy stated. I do not want to face them at the club; we would get no peace."

When Fred pulled up at the villa, Tommy asked them to come in while they gave Alfred and Dot their newspapers. How many do you want Alfred?"

"Two please. I will send one to Joe Franks."

"I will have two please Tommy," Dot said. "I will send one to Viv."

"That leaves us with plenty to send around. What are you two doing tonight?"

"I am watching football on TV; it is a good sports programme on Saturdays."

"I will write a letter or two. Are you phoning Viv tonight Tommy?"

"I had that in mind Dot."

"Then I will phone her Sunday or Monday. Right, I am ready for home Fred, come on Alfred, Salaam everybody."

"I will get you a beer, love, then we will see what we have got in the mail. Hello Thomas and Leila, is everything alright?"

"Mrs Whittaker phoned and asked you to phone her back," Leila told her.

"I will just get our drinks and I will do that, thanks Leila."

"I'll bet Ella wants to know if we are going to the club, here goes. Hello Ella sorry to have missed you when we were in town. No, sorry dear, we are giving it a miss for a week or two to let the euphoria die down. Remember when we first met you told me about all the friends we did not know we had? Well they all phoned me. Finally I had to take the phone off the hook, it was so frustrating. We just want to relax in peace and quiet, especially Bill. You can imagine how busy he has been of late. Thank you Ella. I knew you would understand. We will have a lot to talk about when we see you and John again. Give him our best wishes Ella. Bye.

That's that, now let us see what news we have in the letters…"

She looked at Bill and smiled to see him fast asleep with half a glass of beer left so she carried on opening the mail. After an hour or so she woke Bill. "Come on love, it's time you went and got freshened up; it'll be time for dinner soon."

"Here you are dear, read this letter from Viv while I phone her, then let me know if you will want a word with Roy. I can then ask her to send somebody for him."

"Sergeants Mess," someone answered.

"I would like a word with Warrant Officer Anderson; my name is Mrs Barrett. Would you get her for me please?"

"I am not allowed in the WRAF living quarters and I can see nobody about, sorry."

"Then ask one of the staff on reception. Look young man, I am speaking from Aljibia and it is important. Would you mind telling me your name please?"

"No way lady. I do not know who you are."

Bill could tell from the tone of Tommy's voice that whoever was at the other end of the line was giving her a hard time. "Give me the phone," he told Tommy. "Hello whoever you are, my name is Colonel Barrett and I am speaking from Aljibia. I want your name for a start, then you will go and bring Warrant Officer Anderson to the phone via Warrant Officer Shaw. Now your name…"

"Sergeant Smithers sir."

"Very good Sergeant Smithers, we are now getting somewhere. I want you to go personally and bring W.O. Shaw to the phone, now off you go."

"W.O. Shaw speaking."

"Roy it is Bill; is that bloody moron still with you?
"Yes Sir."

"OK Roy, I get the drift, send him out of earshot. He was right really but he had the wrong type of approach. Tommy got really frustrated with him. Put a flea in his ear, that should be sufficient. Now then old friend, Tommy was going to speak to Viv then send someone for you to speak with me. The reason is Tommy has just opened a letter from Viv telling her about the words you had with the AOC on his annual inspection."

"Yes, we had a nice little chat Bill, which held up the inspection for a little while. He is quite concerned you did not pay him a visit when you were here. I told him you had it in your mind that you did not want to risk having the door slammed in your face, knowing how friendly you were with his ex C.O. and what happened in the Cody incident. I told him that you had not lost any of the respect you always had for him and never would. I have to tell you that he is very proud of your achievements and insists you visit him the next time you are in the UK or he will send a task force out there to Aljibia to bring you back here. He said, 'Give him my best wishes, Warrant Officer Shaw; he is doing the Royal Air Force a great service.'"

"Thanks Roy, you are truly a good friend; as a matter of fact, you are my best one. I have no idea when Tommy and I can manage a trip but we will make sure it will be worthwhile. By the way, you cannot have received a parcel I sent you yet and there will be another on its way next week. No, you must wait and see. I will call you sometime next week for your reaction. If you are going to the March Hare tonight, give Ann and Tim a kiss with our best wishes. Can you get Viv to the phone Roy? Tommy is going ape here wanting to get on the phone. Here she is with a kiss for you."

"Hello Roy, I have been earwigging here to the pair of you – and they say that women can natter! I too am looking forward to coming to see you all and to give you a big smackeroo in person instead of over the phone. Here you are Roy 'X' by-ee. Get Viv for me please."

When she came off the phone half hour later she said "Isn't it grand being able to keep in touch with our friends and all your fears about the AOC being anti-Bill Barrett were well unfounded."

"Aye, I am very relieved about that."

CHAPTER 34

On Monday morning Fred arrived at the Villa carrying the CDs of the Passing out Parade that Bill had ordered. "You certainly wasted no time in collecting these Fred," said a surprised Bill.

"I received a phone call early this morning to tell me they were ready and because they were for you they got top priority. You see sir, being a celebrity has its advantages. I collected them early because I thought Mrs Barrett would want to post them this morning.

"That is very considerate of you Fred. I would like to do that, thank you."

"Are they the same price as the last ones Fred?" asked Bill.

"Yes sir."

Bill paid him. "They are worth every penny Fred, and we appreciate what you do for us."

"You are worth your weight in gold Fred," said a beaming Tommy.

"Just a minute, don't you mean 'cold' old girl?"

"As Mary Butcher used to remind you Bill Barrett… less of the OLD if you don't mind."

"I will take four of the CDs and a couple of newspapers with me. See you later love," he said, giving Tommy a kiss. "Come on Fred, lets get this show on the road. Any news of any interest developed over the weekend?"

"That TV guy you had a tussle with is now out of work. The grapeviners are looking forward to seeing if your staff will turn the new intakes into something special for the parade ground."

"Where do the new intakes come from and how do they arrive here?"

"They come from the Central Clothing Depot where they are kitted out and arrive here in coaches usually on a Wednesday morning. It gives them time to settle in ready for a Monday start."

"Good that gives me something to work on now. On the Monday I will give them all a welcome talk in the cinema and show them the BlueBelles film and the one we have just had. So you can tell your friends they will be more than welcome to come and see the films. Now I would like you to do me a favour Fred. Would you mind delivering a CD and a newspaper to Alfred, Dot and Sergeant Anisa please?"

"That is no problem sir I will do it with pleasure."

"Fred, when you say it like that you bring a tear to my eye. Have you come up with a name for that new magazine yet? I have updated mine to which I think will be a winner…The Aljibia Sentinel… and take your bloody finger from the back of your throat before you answer."

"We are here sir this is where you get out to go to work."

"That is just an excuse to avoid answering the question."

"Salaam sir I will see you later."

"Not if I can get Bill to give me a lift in his Limo'. Salaam Fred."

Fred drove away laughing and shaking his head, what is that man like.

"Good morning Miss Battle" he called out from his office "any messages?"

"One from Major Hassan sir he would like you to meet him at the male recruits accommodation and Captain Basira is here."

"Ah! bleeper at the ready Miss Battle and here I come. Good morning Captain" he said returning her salute, "Have you moved into your apartment yet?"

"Yes thank you sir I arrived last evening so I am now settled in."

"Priority one is to take you to your substitute office. I will then report to the Major Miss Battle it sounds like he may have hit a snag." On entering the Admin' building he received applause from the staff there which he acknowledged with a salute and a thank you. He got a similar reception as he was approaching Major Khatibs' office.

"Good morning sir said the Major offering his hand in congratulations. You and your two assistants certainly put on a magnificent show for us which we have never seen the likes of from our youngsters before, you are working miracles with them. Incidentally sir your assistants have not arrived yet."

"It is my fault for not informing you Major, they are on a weeks' stand down, remember when they first arrived I sent them in at the deep end without that week to acclimatise. I promised them they could have that week when the recruits had passed out and I think they have jolly well earned it, don't you?"

"Indeed I do sir I know just how hard they worked."

"Major I would like you to meet the latest member to our team, Captain Basira the Headteacher for our school." They shook hands and exchanged pleasantries. "Captain Basira is using that joint office as a temporary measure until her own office in the school is available. I would like Deacon and Dean to move in on a temporary basis with Yassen and Basma. I have told Deacon and Dean if they have any personal stuff to move it so they could pop in anytime to do so. Very well Captain I will leave you with the Major who will take care of you. I am off to see Major Hassan I fear he may have a problem in the recruits accommodation." Before he left he popped into Captain Fahimas' office. "Good morning Captain I have come to apologise I feel I have been neglecting you of late."

"There is no need to apologise sir I understand you have been extremely busy and from that display you put on I do understand."

"Deacon and Dean are on a weeks stand down, when they arrived from the UK I had to throw them in at the deep end without giving them the week to acclimatise and this coming week they have got it in lieu. Also I have let Captain Basira have the use of their office until such times as her office in the school is ready. This will be a busy time for you at present with the new intake about to descend upon us."

"I have all the necessary details of the intake and that is keeping me busy sir."

"I am only on the end of the phone line if you want me Captain."

"Hello there Harry I got your message I have taken our new Headmistress to meet Major Khatib and place her in a temporary office. I hope you are not going to spoil my day with some big snag."

"I am afraid so Bill you cannot have an apartment for a housekeeper in either of the two accommodation blocks, we would lose too many single rooms to make one. I suggest we utilise two of the single rooms into an office for the use of a housekeeper during the day, at night they stay in their own accommodation."

"I think that is a more sensible solution than mine Harry. How is the school coming along?"

"Fine everything is falling into place as planned."

"Can I bring the Headmistress along to have a shufti at what you are doing? She is making a list of the requirements she wants for the school you may be able to help her in that respect by advising her with suggestions."

"Tell her to bring a note pad with her Bill and I will do my best for her, will after lunch be convenient?"

"Do you fancy a brew Miss Battle?" Bill asked as he entered her office.

"Give me two minutes sir."

When she brought it he told her to sit down then we can have a natter. "We are not seeing Eric as often as we used to, I know he has more responsibilities but he has not called me into his office for days."

"He will be taking his responsibilities very seriously as he should. You will know that saying sir…heavy is the head that wears the crown. How did your interview go with the Newspaper Editor?"

Bill told her all about it and how we are trying to come up with a title for the magazine. "My suggestion is holding first place at present with…The Aljibia Sentinel."

"Oh I like that" Barbara enthused "I must see if I can topple you from the top perch with an effort from me."

"I have something here for you" he said as he opened a drawer in his desk to pull out Saturdays' newspaper and gave it her along with a CD.

"Is this a CD of the parade?" she asked.

When he confirmed it was she thanked him profusely. "I will watch this tonight and if it is as well made as the other one it will be excellent. Have you watched it sir?"

"No, Fred only delivered them this morning but I will do tonight."

Barbara picked up the ringing phone "P.A. to Colonel Barrett speaking, very well I will inform him, thank you."

"That was the CO's P.A. He would like to see you at your earliest convenience sir."

"I wonder what this is for."

He knocked and entered the P.A.s office.

"You are expected Colonel Barrett I will inform him you are here. Colonel Barrett is here sir." she said over the inter-com.

"Send him in please."

Bill knocked and walked in. "Come and sit down Bill and fill me in how things are progressing out there."

"Everything is on schedule Major Hassan is doing a great job with the school, we are waiting for the four teachers to turn up for their interviews, I have given that job to Captain Basira who is more qualified to interview them. There is something else you should know Eric. I have a gut feeling that the Newspaper Chief Editor has received word from above that he has to print a one off magazine I think for propaganda purposes showing me as the main subject. You should be notified anytime now of a photographer and a reporter having permission to do what they have to do in this area. They will be issued with a security identification badge and I will be responsible for their actions while they are on the base which I think should only take half a day. Then they will invade my home to record a family background. I would very much like you Eric to write the foreword in the magazine."

"That sounds very interesting it will be my pleasure to do so Bill. That will be a good thing to show our people what is being done for them. I hope I will receive an autographed copy."

"Now you are Commandant and have mega responsibilities what do you think of it?"

"I think I have slotted into it very well Bill and between you and me I find it very good for my ego," he said with a laugh. "I now have a lot of influential people calling me by my first name."

"What is your P.A. like Eric is she good for you?"

"She is a very reserved lady she does what she has to do but not a person you can hold a conversation or share a confidence with. I cannot fault her work she is excellent in that department but I do wish she would loosen up a little."

"Perhaps she is overawed with your rank Eric it can happen you know but I have no cure for that except give her a bit of time to get used to you and her job."

"Thanks Bill I will bear that in mind."

"Are you ready for lunch Barbara I know I am?"

"I am ready when you are Bill."

On entering the Luncheon Box they were greeted with smiles and nods from the other patrons which Bill courteously replied to. "Ah, I see Alfred and Dot are here can't you keep away from this place for a few days?"

"Well we do have to eat and we wanted to see if you are missing us" smiled Dot sweetly "and we wanted to thank you for the CDs. Are you sending one to Viv she will be thrilled to bits to see how we are upholding the tradition?"

"I am also sending one to Joe it will be interesting to hear his views on your finale if it is not up to his standard Alfred he will recall you for a refresher course."

"I know, that what scares me"

"Have you come up with a name for that magazine? If not I cannot see you being in it. "I expect my update version will sweep the board."

"Which is?" asked Dot.

"The Aljibia Sentinel."

"I like the sound of that" said Alfred, "it will take some beating."

"Captain Basira has taken over your office temporarily have you moved your personal effects out?"

"Not yet there are only bits and bobs to move we can do that in a couple of minutes."

"Well don't leave it too long. Mashy?"

"Mashy" was the reply.

"Can you see Captain Basira anywhere Barbara?"

"Yes she is sat over there dining alone."

"Good I want to see her before she leaves."

"What are you two doing with all this spare time you have got?"

"Lazing by the pool and getting ourselves acclimatised!" Dot retorted.

On leaving to go for coffee Bill approached Captain Basira. "Excuse me interrupting your lunch Captain but after lunch will you come to my office armed with a note book and pen please, Major Hassan will take you on a tour of the school and you may want to exchange ideas."

"Thank you sir I will be there and armed to the teeth."

During the afternoon Bill got a phone call from Eric to tell him the two bods from the newspaper will be arriving on the station at 8-30 tomorrow."

"I will give you a call then to see when you are free to receive them sir."

On the way home Fred said. "You are going to be busy tomorrow sir posing for your magazine."

"Yes, and you had better smarten yourself up because you are going to be featured so until you have sat for a mug shot you are grounded. Mashy?"

"Mashy sir."

"Have you and the grapeviners come up with that magazine title yet?"

"No sir but we are trying our best, any suggestions put forward are vetoed if they are not up to our standard."

"Very commendable and thanks for delivering those CDs Fred, have you heard when Sergeant Anisa is leaving?"

"Thursday morning sir and if everything goes to plan she should arrive at her destination by mid-afternoon."

"Salaam Fred, see you in the morning."

"Salaam sir."

Tommy greeted him with a kiss, I had a phone call from the Chief Editor to say the two men have got their passes for the base and they would be arriving there at 8-30 in the morning."

"That is good it means they have started the ball rolling. Eric has agreed to write the foreword which will start it off very nicely. I should imagine they will start here on Wednesday and we will have Thomas and Leila featured in it. Right then I will go to freshen up." When he returned there was a cool beer waiting for him. "This love is what I call one of life's little luxuries. Have you been up to much today?"

"Not really, keeping my hand in helping Leila around the house and talking cookery with Thomas. I am going to phone Viv later to see if the first lot of CDs have arrived they should have got them by now surely."

"Don't be so impatient dear."

"Well I want to hear their reactions it is important to me."

"Dinner is ready Ma'am" announced Leila.

"Hello Thomas…Leila, are you both well and happy in your work?"

"We are both fine sir" replied Thomas. We watched that Parade again last night, it was very clever how you and your two assistants trained those young people."

"It is just like anything else Thomas, practice, dedication and experience, that is why you are a good Chef."

"Thank you sir, I will remember that for when I have my trainees."

"So you want to start a Chef's training school do you?"

"Oh yes sir that is my ambition."

"Will the State help you with the funding?"

"Indeed they will but I must have a certain amount of capital to qualify for it. But that is a dream sir, Leila and I are contracted to this work but someday perhaps we may see it come true and we are saving hard just in case."

"Oh Thomas" said Tommy I feel like crying for you and I only wish we could help. On the other hand if we could help we would lose you both."

"Mrs Barrett, while you are here we would never leave you" replied Thomas.

After coffee in the lounge Tommy said. I am going to phone Viv now she should be standing by the phone now."

"Sergeants Mess, is that you Tommy?"

"Tommy burst out laughing Viv I just said to Bill as I was about to dial, Viv should be standing by the phone and you knew I would be phoning, it is unbelievable."

"And I know why you are phoning and the answer is yes, we have all got them this morning and if you would like to ring back in two hours time I will tell you our verdict we are showing one soon in the TV room, we have spread the word and we are sure of standing room only, so don't let that husband of yours oversleep. Bye for now Tommy."

"They have all got the first CD and they are giving a show in the TV room and Viv says it is going to be standing room only. We have to ring back about ten for the verdict."

"We are going Ma'am" said Leila."

"OK Leila, thank you and Salaam.

"Goodnight Sir...Ma'am."

"Now the time is going to drag" said an exasperated Tommy "Are you putting the Television on and having a sleep dear?"

"I will turn it on but I cannot guarantee I will fall asleep."

"Yes and pigs might fly." Sure enough two minutes of television and Bill was away with the fairies. So Tommy went wandering around the house in and out of the kitchen checking this and that trying to keep her mind occupied. She finally decided to make some sandwiches for supper which kept her busy for a time. Before she realised it the time had flown and Noddy was still asleep. "She gave him a shake, "Come on sleeping beauty time to ring Viv." She rang the Sergeants Mess and immediately Viv's voice came over "Tommy it was wonderful, every one was absolutely thrilled to bits and we are so very, very proud of Bill and when you were both interviewed we thought you were both very magnanimous in your praise for others, of course that is Bill all over he makes sure everyone shares any glory. There were a few wet cheeks I can tell you and we needed a shoe horn to get everyone in. A big cheer went up when you curtsied to the Emir and he shook your hand and had a laugh with you, you were lovely Tommy. Joe Franks could not get over it and George Miller wasn't gob smacked but he insisted that he knew the kind of stuff Bill was made of 'we go back a long way' he said. Oh here is Roy who wants a word with Bill."

"Hi Roy my old friend how are you?"

"I never thought you would be the cause of me taking out my hanky and I am not ashamed to admit it. Bill, we are so proud of you and nobody more than me." This went on for quite a while until Roy asked "have you time for a word with Barbara and Derwent?"

"Of course it is my pleasure. He had a nice chat with them Barbara called him Mr Wonderful and Roy is talking about showing it on the big screen in the Education Section and throwing the doors wide open for everybody to come and see it. Tommy wants a word with you and Derwent, Barbara." As the phone conversations were going on Mess members were leaving and shouting 'Well done Bill keep the flag flying or Atta girl Tommy'. Eventually they had to call it a day or they would have been talking for hours. "What a night, it must have been riotous in that TV room but they all enjoyed it, when they get the next CD the training staff will go wild with enthusiasm. Shall we calm down with a bit of supper then it will be bedtime?"

CHAPTER 35

"Good morning Miss Battle, no messages, no telephone calls, Right?"

"Right sir."

"You will see very little of me for most of the day as you can well imagine but I will see you for lunch…I hope.

The two newspaper men were escorted to Barbara's office by a security guard who handed them over to Bill. Formalities were exchanged and they outlined their plan of operations. Bill told them of the people who he wanted to be involved and they approved but saying they would take it step by step. "What about starting here then with my Personal Assistant who has been my anchor since day one of my arrival?" They set about their business of taking photographs and writing a brief summary of the team work between the pair of them. Everything was wound up before lunch time and Bill was most pleased with how the whole scenario was organised and carried out expertly with very little fuss by the two men. "Now sir we would like to do the family side of the feature."

"You mean today?"

"Yes if it is convenient to you sir it will not take us long, a couple of hours at the most."

"What about after lunch say 2 o'clock you know where I live, if that is convenient to you?"

"That will be fine sir, we will see you then."

Bill called the security guard who then escorted them from the base. He then rang Tommy.

"Hello Barretts!"

"Hi Flower." He then told her of the arrangements. "I will have my lunch here then I will come straight home love." He then rang Eric the C.O. to tell him that he would be taking the rest of the day off to finish the magazine job.

"Come on Barbara we are now off to lunch then I have to leave for home directly afterwards."

Fred was called to drive him home. "So they are going to finish with you in a day then sir, they are very good I think they are the best duo on the staff so you have got first class treatment. Oh to be a celebrity I could certainly get used to it."

"Stop day dreaming Fred you will never be a celebrity as long as you have got a hole in your ear!"

"I know the proper version to that Colonel, it was my English tutor's favourite saying to us students and I know the version of a BA Fly too."

"You know a lot Fred, can you tell me why any serviceman who serves overseas always learns the swear words first in any foreign language. I expect you are now going to tell me that you are an exception to the rule."

"Sir, you amaze me with your many talents and you have just come up with another one which only a mind reader would know."

"Well add this to my collection, I can tell when you are telling me Porky Pies."

"Then how about this from a mindreading student? Yes sir I will sod off as you were going to politely put it."

"Well done Fred you are learning fast, another crack like that and you will be a bloody half-wit! Now you can sod off…Salaam Fred."

"Salaam sir," Fred replied as he drove away laughing.

"Have you and Fred been having fun with each other again?" Tommy asked as she kissed him.

"He is one of the best and I would not swap him for a gold clock. Are you ready for our visitors? Fred told me they are the best two at their job on the newspaper, they are a couple of grand chaps and are very considerate they listen to your suggestions and talk it over with you. Have you briefed Thomas and Leila?"

"Yes they have gone all nervous, do you think we should invite John and Ella after all they were the first ones to befriend us when we arrived?"

"Why not, get on the phone now and get them over"

Tommy rang Ella straight away and explained why she was ringing. "You will? Oh lovely come straight away because we are expecting them at 2 o'clock. They are delighted to come Bill."

"Right then I had better change out of my uniform and into mufti."

By 2 o'clock everyone was ready to greet the newspaper chappies. Bill and Tommy met and welcomed them to the Barrett's Hideaway then introduced Dr. John and Ella Whittaker followed by Thomas and Leila who are part of our family."

"Our plan then," said the reporter "will be to interview you as couples, while I am doing that my colleague the photographer will look for the places where he thinks will do you justice on the photographs. I will start with you Dr. and Mrs Whittaker so will you others please go somewhere out of earshot."

"Would you like any refreshments before you begin asked Tommy?"

"No thank you we have just returned from lunch."

The four of them then went and sat by the pool. Tommy chatted to Thomas and Leila to help calm their nervousness. Just think, you will be celebrities when your family and friends see your photographs in the magazine." She made them laugh when she warned Bill not to pull any funny faces at the camera.

Soon it was Thomas and Leila's turn for the interview. John and Ella came and sat by the pool. "It is very kind of you to want us in your magazine" said John.

"Why should you not be?" replied Tommy, "You were the first people to befriend us when we arrived and this is the first real chance we have had to repay your kindness."

John and Ella wanted to know all about the Award Ceremony and the Parade. "We read the newspapers which gave you an excellent coverage and saw the Television coverage of both events. I was particularly impressed with what you and your two assistants did with those young people in such a short space of time" said John with admiration.

Thomas and Leila returned with their faces wreathed in smiles. Bill and Tommy then went for their interview. It was quite a long interview and both they and the reporter enjoyed it. "That was the most enjoyable assignment I have ever had in my profession as a newspaper reporter and I would like to thank you because I will get a pat on the back from my Chief'."

"Then you will have earned yourself some Brownie points and you have jolly well earned them."

"My part is finished so I will now hand you all over to my partner the photographer."

The photographic session went very smoothly the photographer had done an excellent job of planning his shots with the minimum of fuss. On completion Tommy asked if they would like some refreshments. They declined saying they wanted to do more work in the office and you will be able to come Saturday morning for your proof reading. They left smiling with the thanks of everyone ringing in their ears. "Now what does everyone want to drink asked Tommy?" Bill and John chose a beer; Tommy and Ella opted for a long cool soft drink. "If you would like to go and sit by the pool I will give Leila a hand with the drinks." When she went into the kitchen she gave Thomas and Leila a kiss saying. "Thank you, you were both wonderful." She helped with the drinks and told them both to help themselves to what drinks they want. Leila followed behind with the drinks and some nibbles which she had put on the tray. Of course the topic of the conversation was the magazine. "The magazine needs a name" said Bill. "At present it has only one suggestion and that is…The Aljibia Sentinel, can either of you two come up with a good one?"

"What do you think of ...The Aljibia Tribune?" asked Ella.

"That has possibilities" responded Bill. I would like one or two more to submit to the Chief Editor on Saturday."

"When are you thinking of paying another visit to the club Bill?" asked John.

"We will give it another two to three weeks John the excitement should have waned by then."

"Not when this magazine comes out it won't the excitement will just carry on then they will be waiting for you to autograph their copies."

"Well let me put it this way John I always have a supply of beer in and if you feel like it you can come here anytime for a quiet drink."

"Thanks Bill I will remember that or Ella will. We have to go now because I am on call tonight. Thank you both for letting us share in your magazine I have always fancied being a pin-up boy."

"Your Rock n' Roll days are long gone, you have not got the hair now for a D.A. cut" laughed Ella.

After they had left Bill asked. "How long will dinner be Thomas?"

"It will be ready in half an hour, sir."

"Then I have time for another beer."

CHAPTER 36

Early on Thursday morning Fred pulled up at the Villa with Sergeant Anisa and Dot to collect Bill who is also seeing Anisa off at the airport to commence a course of Instructor Training at RAF March. "Good morning everyone" greeted Bill as he got into the car. "Drive carefully and remember Fred you have three VIPs relying on you."

"You could not be in any safer hands folk just sit back relax and enjoy the ride. I will carry on driving suffering earache there and back but you will never hear me complain."

"Ignore those two" said Dot to Anisa "they are like this every time they meet, I am surprised Fred has lasted so long it must be a mental strain on him."

"And Mental is the operative word too" retorted Bill. I don't know how I have put up with him for so long it is about time he was turned out to grass."

While this banter was going on Anisa was enjoying every minute of it and her nervousness for the time being had left her.

When they arrived at the airport Fred dropped them off at the terminal while he parked the car.

"You will have no problems travelling Sergeant because you will be met and helped all the way, you should arrive at RAF March about the middle of this afternoon." Bill informed her. "I will ring reception at your destination to tell them you are now on your way. You will check-in at that VIP desk and you are going to enjoy this flight to the UK."

"I have told you as much as I can" said Dot and I am sure you will be alright. I will keep in touch with you by telephone and it will be around 6 o'clock in the evening when I do, someone will come to tell you that you are wanted on the telephone. In fact I will phone you this evening to see if you are alright. Mashy?"

"Mashy Ma'am," she said smiling."

"Dot gave her a kiss and a hug. Off you go now and the Best of Luck to you."

"Bill shook her hand, "Good luck Sergeant I will be informed of your progress and we all hope to see you return as a fully fledged qualified Training Instructor and may your Allah watch over you."

They watched her check-in, then wave as she proceeded to the Departure Lounge.

"What is your programme today?" Bill asked Dot when they had got back in the car.

"I will have a good breakfast and I may go back to bed for an hour then I may have a trip to town. Do you think Tommy would like to come with me Bill?"

"I am sure she will; she really enjoys going there and I don't blame her, for it is a fine city."

"I will go in my car Fred, it will give you a break and me more experience driving. Mashy?"

"Mashy Ma'am."

"I do like that word Mashy. Every time I hear it or even say it, it makes me want to smile, it is lovely," enthused Dot.

"We have to thank Fred for introducing it to us, but I agree it is a catchy little word."

"Here we are sir, home sweet home. I will see you in a little while. Salaam."

"Good morning Miss Battle, anything happened in my absence?"

"The four teachers arrived and Captain Basira took charge of their interviews and will be coming to report to you this morning. She did not say if she had accepted them or not. How did you get on with the photo-shoot at home sir?"

"It went down a treat, I must say the men were very proficient. We can go and see the proofs on Saturday morning and as you might expect Tommy is all excited about it. This morning Dot and I took Sergeant Anisa to the airport. I will keep a check on her progress. Dot is even phoning her this evening to see how she fared on the journey and how she is; she is going to keep in regular touch with her.

"Ah, that is sweet of Dot to be so concerned for her."

There was a knock on the door and Captain Basira entered. She saluted on seeing Bill.

"Good morning Captain," said Bill in return for the salute. I understand you have some information for me which I hope is good news. Come through to my office where we can discuss it. Would you like a brew?"

"Yes please sir."

"Sit yourself down, it will be here in a minute. Have you settled down alright?"

"Very much so sir; everyone has been so kind and co-operative."

"How did you get on with Major Hassan at the school? Did you have any differences at all?"

"I would not call them differences sir, it was more like two minds solving a jigsaw puzzle. He is a very clever man and I am very impressed with his workmanship. I broached on several small things which anyone else would think would be irrelevant but not Major Hassan, he even thanked me for pointing them out. When it is finished that school will be a credit to him and his workforce sir."

Bill thanked Barbara when she brought in the tea.

"Now Captain, I would like to hear your verdict on the interviewees."

"Like I told you previously sir, I wanted the four who came for the interview. You might say it was a foregone conclusion but I did give them a good testing to make doubly sure they were right for the positions and were still as good professionally as when we last worked together."

"And have they accepted the terms?"

"Yes sir."

"Have you seen to their accommodation and was it acceptable?"

"Yes sir, they are very impressed with it."

"And when can they report for duty?"

"I told them to arrive on Monday I will need them to help sort out the classrooms.

"The school is coming along at a great rate, I am in the process of making out lists for furniture, instruction books and the very many things to equip a new school, the lists are endless but we are getting there sir."

"You are doing a fine job Captain and speaking to you has made me realise you have got an enormous task on your hands and you are the only person qualified to see it through. Your lists when they are ready I will see they get priority to make sure the school bell rings on time." Thank you Captain Basira you know where I am when needed and you have my full backing."

"I don't know if you heard any of that Barbara but I was very impressed."

"I did hear most of it sir and my thoughts are that you have got a darned good member of staff in Captain Basira. Changing the subject I watched the parade on CD and I liked it very much and I was quite chuffed to see Tommy and I were featured meeting the Emir, I felt so proud when Tommy introduced me. Your Tommy is quite an extraordinary woman and I have grown to admire her in the short space of time we have met."

"I'll just have a stroll to see how the recruits' accommodation is coming along Barbara; I will be back for lunch." He stopped off at the airmens' quarters and had a word with the airmen from Workshops working on the project. "Good morning how is it going, have you hit any snags yet?"

"Good morning sir, we are getting along fine and touch wood, no snags, come and see the conversion. What Bill saw took him by surprise two rooms had been converted into one office large enough for the housekeeper/security man. "Why, you are almost ready to furnish it, well done you are doing a very good job. Is anyone working on the airwomens's' quarters?"

"Oh yes sir we have a team converting that and they are at a similar stage as we are."

"Good morning I have just come to see how you are getting on with the conversion, have you hit any snags?" Bill asked the men working on the airwomen's accommodation.

"Good morning sir, not really, you must appreciate it is a different set up against the mens' theirs is straight forward."

"I have just come from having a shufti at the mens' and they are doing extremely well it will not be long before they are at the furnishing stage."

"Come and have a shufti at ours sir."

"Oh, that is brilliant who ever takes over the housekeeping/ security here are going to be very comfortable, what a transformation you all have made from two single rooms they are a credit to all four of you." From there he went to see Major Khatib at the Training Offices, he confirmed everything was under control. Bill then carried on to the bedding store where Lieutenant Hikmat proudly showed him her completed wall charts and how they functioned. All bedding will be in place two days before the arrival of the recruits I understand that is when the housekeepers take over sir."

"Thank you very much Lieutenant, at last we have got some organisation in here how it functioned before beats me, thank you for what you are doing." He then carried on to the sanitation section to check that they were all geared up to do their spraying when the workmen had finished. Everything and everyone was under control another week should see the school being furnished. He headed back to his office and asked Barbara if she was ready for lunch.

"I am ready when you are sir."

When they arrived at the Luncheon Box and returned the acknowledgements to the other diners they saw that Alfred was dining alone. "Dot told me she was going into town this morning Alfred and picking up Tommy if she felt like going. No doubt they will be dining out."

"There is Dot's car outside the Villa" observed Fred. It looks like you might be having company for dinner sir."

"Aye, I think you are right Fred. Tell me why I have had no little snippets from the grapeviners for a few days, have they dried up or gone off the air waves?"

"Nothing of much importance is happening at present sir."

"I forgot to tell you Fred that there has been another title put forward for the magazine…The Aljibia Tribune."

"That one sounds good sir, who is going to choose the winner?"

"I shall put them to the Chief to choose on Saturday morning he may even have some suggestions from his staff. Anyway I will let you get away, see you in the morning, Salaam Fred."

"Salaam sir."

Tommy greeted Bill with a kiss. "We have company for dinner, go and get changed and there will be a beer waiting and we have something to tell you."

"Hi Dot, have you had a good day? Alfred looked rather forlorn dining alone.

"He did not want to come into town he wanted to top up his tan."

On his return Bill sat and had a good swig of his beer. "That was good, now what is it you are bursting to tell me?"

"We rang the Sergeants Mess to enquire if Anisa had arrived. Jackie answered and of course she went all emotional when she knew it was me speaking. Anisa arrived safe and sound and was busy unpacking when we rang. Jackie went for her and brought her to the phone then Dot took over from me."

"She was thrilled to bits when she heard me Bill. The flights were very good, Marion James met her at Leeds and everyone is so kind to her. Marion will be her close companion during her stay and she is lovely. She is to meet all our friends this evening and the ones she has met are all are asking about us. She sends her Best wishes to us and thanks us for being so helpful and kind and will look forward to hearing from me again because she is sure she will have lots to tell. Jackie then took over and wanted to speak with Tommy."

"Jackie said that they think Anisa is a lovely girl and the latest CDs arrived today. There was great excitement over wondering what they contained and she thinks there will be a showing tonight. She sends her love to you and thanks us for the CDs."

"And what have the pair of you bought today?"

"One or two things Thomas needed and Dot has bought two nice summer dresses and Leila shopped for some personal items and we all had lunch at the usual place in that super store."

"Dinner is ready Ma'am" called Leila.

"And how are you today Thomas and your lovely wife, I understand you were left alone to slave over a hot stove as usual while they painted the town red."

"Well what would the women do without us men folk" replied Thomas getting a load of abuse for his trouble. "Yet we do not complain." This time he got mock sympathy.

They had a chatty meal which centred on Anisa and wondered how she liked her first English meal. "I don't think her little room will go down at all well after living in the style she did here" said Dot.

"It can only do her good" insisted Bill "good for character building. By the way Dot we have had another suggestion for the magazine title…The Aljibia Tribune. What do you think of that one?"

"I think it will give your effort a good run for its money, as a matter of fact I like it."

"Isn't your bed time" asked a miffed Bill?"

"Stop being petulant Bill Barrett" snapped Tommy it does not become you," which she followed up with…"Oh Yes It Does!" to the amusement of Leila.

"So are you going to phone Viv later to see if they have had a showing?" Bill asked.

"If I do and they have had one Joe Franks would probably have been there and you could have a word with him and get his verdict. Are you staying Dot because I will ring at 8 o'clock and if they are having a showing I will have to ring back later when they have seen it?"

"No thanks I will not bother I will very likely ring her tomorrow."

"You will stay for coffee won't you?"

"Oh, yes please and thank you for a lovely meal Thomas it was excellent."

At 8pm Tommy rang Viv to ask her if there was to be a showing tonight.

"Jackie told us you had got the latest CD and thought you may be showing it."

"Yes we are Tommy and we are quite excited about it especially the training staff and I want to see the results from Dot's and Alfred's instructing."

"Bear in mind Viv they had only two weeks to get them into shape to produce a good result. Do you know if Joe Franks will be there because Bill would like a word with him to hear his verdict? Shall I ring about 8pm your time? If I was you Viv I would take Anisa into the show and sit with her, she will then point out and name the people you may be interested in and you will also get an idea of her potential."

"That is a good idea Tommy I will do that, I also had a call from Ann and Tim they were over the moon with the Award video and were very impressed with you hobnobbing with Royalty but when she mentioned Bill getting his awards she just choked up, well you know how fond she is of Bill, he is her Hero. Must leave you now, folk are coming in for the show I would make a bomb if I charged them an entrance fee."

Tommy turned to report to Bill but he was fast asleep in his arm chair. So she did what she had done the last time there was a video show, she went and made sandwiches ready for supper. Afterwards she sat down and compiled a list of names of friends and family they would be sending copies of the magazine to. When it was time for phoning Viv, Tommy shook Bill awake. "Come on love I am ready for phoning Viv."

Viv was waiting for the phone to ring and snatched the receiver off the cradle immediately. "Hi Tommy the show has just finished and what a lovely display Dot and Alfred put on, we are so proud of them and Anisa was more or less giving us a running commentary especially the handkerchief waving a goodbye and thank you tribute to the instructors then as a thank you to the Emir and spectators, we thought that was a lovely gesture. Alfred and Dot looked very smart in their uniforms and when the Emir presented the four to the spectators at the end we all applauded with them. I left Anisa centre stage answering the many questions and she is enjoying every minute of it. That video was the best thing for her she has now been accepted as one of our training staff and yes, I was impressed when she took over to present the basic drill movements. That was obviously the idea of Alfred and Dot to show her off to her own people. I could go on talking about it all night but here is Joe smiling all over his face waiting to talk to Bill. We who received the CDs are so grateful to you, talk to you soon."

Tommy handed the phone over to Bill. "Hello Joe my old sparring partner thanks for coming to the phone."

"Great to be able to talk to you Bill and thanks for the Video I will treasure it; I am going to show that to all the recruits in future and especially to all the NCOs they can learn a lot from that. Alfred and Dot are doing us proud and keeping the flag flying. If they can turn a show like that out in a couple of weeks what are they going to show us from a full course of instructing? Tell Alfred and Dot I bear them no hard feelings for using my idea of a mixed flight but I was impressed with their up-date of putting them through basic drill as such."

Bill had to tell him about all the preparations and work he has put into making it a proper Training School and how he has the full support of the Emir and his own staff. "It took some weeding out Joe to get the kind of staff I wanted and they are supporting me one hundred percent which is very gratifying. Tell me Joe how is Marion James doing since she took over from Margaret Roper?"

"It was the best thing that could have happened Bill she is a natural, firm but caring just like Mary Butcher was and she is well liked as well. I have to keep an eye on Bob Dixon though he has got a chip on his shoulder and is a bit cocky with the other Senior NCOs I have had to bring him down to earth a time or two. I have an idea he thought he should have had that posting instead of Alfred because he shows no interest whatsoever with any of the news we get from you. Alan Fell although he is a damned good Flight Sergeant doesn't use enough authority on him that is explained because their two families live in each other's pockets but I will do summat about it Bill, just watch this space. Well I must leave you old pal I have done enough rabbiting on but keep the news coming Bill the rest of us are more than interested. Hang on a minute there is a young lady here who would like a word with you."

The voice of Anisa came over the phone. "Hello sir I want to thank you for everything you have done for me."

"Hello Sergeant, what a lovely surprise to hear you. How do you like my friends aren't they wonderful people?"

"They have made me so very welcome and I have made many more friends this evening. They have been asking me so many questions about

Aljibia and you especially; my mind is in a whirl. Before I forget, thank you sir for the two videos you are a very kind and considerate person."

"Thank you for taking the trouble to come to the phone to speak to me, I do appreciate it. I wish you the very best of luck when you commence your course I will get all the news about you from Lieutenant Dean. Take good care of yourself, Mashy"

"Mashy sir" she replied with a little giggle.

"I feel exhausted after all that" said Tommy but isn't it wonderful to be able to talk to them?"

"It certainly is, you feel like you are there with them as if you could stretch your hand out and touch them."

"Are you ready for something to eat love I know I am, all that talking has made me feel hungry."

While they were eating Tommy asked, "Did Joe come up with a good verdict?"

"He certainly did, he was as proud as punch with Alfred and Dot and more so because they used his scheme in that mixed drill sequence. He is having a bit of… I wouldn't say trouble with Bob Dixon but Joe thinks he is rather uptight about Alfred by thinking he should have had the posting here. It looks like a bit of jealousy and he is showing his true colours by overlording the rest of the staff. I think Joe has had enough and is ready to clamp down on him. I am surprised in one sense with Alan Fell for not having a word with him yet not in another because their two families are very close and I cannot give Joe any advice unless he asks me for it. Anisa told me she has been made very welcome and has made many more friends this evening."

"How nice, I do hope she does well and Viv is impressed with her.

CHAPTER 37

"Here is Fred with Alfred and Dot" remarked Tommy. "Are you ready Bill?"

"Of course I am ready, don't be so impatient."

"I am not impatient I am just eager to see those proofs that is all. I want to get there before the shops close."

"It is not a shop! It is a newspaper office, they never close."

"They might do on this occasion knowing our luck Good morning Fred" she said in the same breath as she climbed in the car to see two smiling faces.

"Have no fear Mrs Barrett I will get you there on time" said a smiling Fred.

"Thank you Fred I wish someone would make a note of that."

"Fred, tell 'Bill the Limo' to give me a ring if he wants a cushy job." Bill retorted.

"Shall I wait for you sir?" Fred asked as he parked the car.

"Be here about 4 o'clock please, now go and relax for a few hours." interrupted Tommy, Alfred and Dot we will meet you for lunch at the usual place about 1 o'clock. Mashy everyone?"

A united "Mashy" was the response.

"Come on love" she said to Bill "let us go and make the Chief Editor happy."

When they entered the building Bill saw the same receptionist was on duty.

"Good morning we have an appointment with the Chief."

"Good morning Colonel I will tell him you are here." She said giving him a nice smile.

Within a minute the Chief was shaking their hands and welcoming them. As they went up in the lift he said. "I think you are going to be pleasantly surprised with the proofs." When he ushered them into his office he told them to "sit down please, would you like any refreshments?"

"No thank you said Tommy I am too excited."

The chief smiled, "I hope you are still in that mood when you have seen the proofs Mrs Barrett." He had two folders, he gave them one and he kept the other. We can all go through the reading together without having to pass one folder around." They opened the folders at the front cover which showed a full length image of Bill in full dress uniform showing his decorations. In the background were the two flights of airmen and airwomen. There was a blank space ready for the magazine title and each side of where the title would be was the flag of Aljibia and the Union Jack. The Chief looked at the two faces. Tommy was smiling with pleasure but Bill had a studious look. "You have a problem Colonel?"

"No, not a problem but I would like to suggest an addition."

"Go ahead Colonel it is your prerogative."

"I would like to see Lieutenants Deacon and Dean standing each side of me but positioned in the middle foreground. How does that sound to you?"

The chief studied it for a minute or so, excuse me a moment. He phoned someone and asked them to come to draw him a sketch. A middle aged man entered. The Chief introduced him as our Artist. They shook hands and he said, "I am honoured to meet you at last Colonel and it will be a privilege to help you." The chief told him what Bill had suggested and will you give us a sketch of how it would look on the cover plate. As he was drawing he was talking to Bill about the exact location he wanted the two figures and making suggestions on how to improve them. When he had finished Bill shook his hand saying, "thank you very much you have transformed that front cover all it needs now is a title. I do not know if you have decided on one Chief but I have here two suggestions which I would like you to look at and give your opinion."

"I am impressed with both Colonel who may I ask suggested these?"

"I for one and Doctor Whittaker's wife the other but I will not tell you which and I would like you and your staff to choose, unless your staff have any suggestions in that case you will need to have someone who is neutral to choose. Anyway shall we continue with the reading?"

They turned the outer cover to see an excellent photo of Eric and his foreword.

"I like that Chief it is excellent, he will be so proud of that when he sees it. The rest of the magazine brought nothing but praise from Bill and Tommy. Tommy said "you have done a wonderful job on that magazine Chief and it is a great credit to you and your staff, I think the end product will be beautiful."

"And I can only agree with what she says Chief. Your reporter and photographer were absolutely brilliant with everyone they dealt with; they were so considerate and professional in what they did. Please convey our gratitude to them. Now what is the next step Chief?"

"First we must decide on its title, if you agree I will let my staff choose it then we will go ahead and put it to bed, that is the printer's terminology for putting it to press. Once it is ready for distribution I will let you know then you can come and collect your free copies. I do appreciate you have a lot of very personal family and friends so would you be happy with shall we say…forty copies?"

"Chief. Said Bill "I cannot thank you enough you have been so kind to us."

"And would you be offended if I gave you a kiss for being so kind" asked Tommy.

"Mrs Barrett I would take it as a great honour."

"Tommy then kissed him on the cheek saying, "thank you, you wonderful man."

They then met up with Alfred and Dot who were having a pre-lunch drink while they waited for Bill and Tommy who apologised for being so late.

"That is no problem" said Alfred you cannot do proof reading on that scale in a few minutes."

"What is it like Tommy?" asked a curious but excited Dot.

"Come on we will tell you over lunch because I am starving" replied Bill.

When they all had ordered their meal Alfred and Dot sat there staring at Bill. "Why are you staring at me have I said something wrong?"

"No, that is the trouble" exclaimed Dot, "You have not said anything you are just winding us up."

"Put them out of their misery Bill Barrett and if you won't I will."

"Mashy." You tell the tale love you can tell it better than me."

Their meal arrived at that point so Tommy said, "I will tell you after the meal to stop any accidents when I tell you the good news while you are eating. "So be patient just a wee while then all will be revealed."

Over coffee Tommy told them the tale about the magazine in general. "I am not disclosing the front cover except to say that Bill played a part in its design. Also we submitted those two magazine titles to the Chief Editor without disclosing who had submitted which and the newspaper's staff will vote on which one to choose. I can assure you that everyone who gets a copy will treasure it. I just cannot wait to get my hands on one. Have you two done any shopping of any interest?"

"I bought a couple of snazzy shirts a pair of shorts and trousers" said Alfred.

"I only bought some perfume and a dress," added Dot.

"Did you phone Anisa?" asked Tommy.

"Yes and she is already feeling at home, everyone is being so kind to her and Marion James is looking after her like a big sister. She starts her course on Monday in the ops' room and with home work studying Discipline. She takes a dim view of the size of her accommodation and especially with it not having ensuite facilities which is understandable but she will have to get used to it."

"Knowing that everyone is in the same boat she will put on a brave face and not spoil the thrill of being there on that course." Bill added.

"Are you coming for dinner?" asked Tommy.

"No thanks I want to write a letter or two" replied Dot.

And I am thinking of going to the cinema that is if there is anything on that appeals to me" laughed Alfred.

"What are we going to do dear play Snap? If I had one of those magazines I would be happy to just sit there and read it all night. Do you fancy going to the club for an hour? We will have to face them sometime so we might as well get it over and done with. What do you say?"

"And why not, like you say pet we have to go and face them sometime. Give Ella and John a call when we get home on one condition though, you do not do anything that will get us barred."

"Thank you Alfred and Dot, if you had stayed to dinner we would not have made that decision and both Ella and John will be chuffed providing John is not duty MO."

Fred was waiting for them at the car park. "Hi Fred" greeted Bill, You are a sight for sore eyes."

Fred looked at him in amazement and before he could reply Tommy interrupted with, "don't say it Fred just leave it while he is in a good mood. Mashy?"

"Mashy Mrs Barrett with a capital 'M'. Have you all had a good day and how was the proof reading?"

"Brilliant," spoke up Bill, that magazine is going to be a classic the newspaper will be unable to keep up with the demand."

"What if it prints your title to it, what then sir?"

"That is obvious it will sweep across Europe like a giant Haboob (sandstorm)."

"Well the best of luck sir. Here we are safely home once more. If the magazine is as much a success as you think it will be will you give up your day job and go on a world celebrity tour?"

"Fred, you know my answer to that question don't you?"

"Yes sir and I will sod off now. Salaam."

"Salaam Fred" replied both Bill and Tommy as Fred drove off joining in the laughter with Alfred and Dot.

As soon as they got indoors Tommy rang Ella to ask if she and John would like to go with them to the club tonight. "We have decided to go and get it over with Ella." "Indeed we would Tommy; John is sat here grinning in anticipation. Thank you we . will come at the usual time."

Tommy came to Bill gave him a kiss and said. "Thanks love you have just made two people happy and you can include me as well."

"At 8pm John and Ella arrived, John was full of smiles. "What made you decide to go Bill?"

"I thought how long have I to wait before plucking up the courage to face up to it. Tommy came up with the answer, to go and get it over with."

"Well done Tommy and it is the best thing you could have done Bill."

At the Ex-pats club they received a nice welcome from the chairman who congratulated Bill and had a few minutes chat with him. You are quite a celebrity Bill and we are proud to have you as one of our members. I know how you must be feeling about facing the members after all the headlines etc. but I think you will find our members will respect you. Obviously they will want to congratulate you but you will not find them clambering all over you, they will not embarrass you so do have a nice evening."

They found a table and after ordering drinks they chatted about things in general. Tommy still excited about the magazine told them about the proof reading which of course made Ella quite excited and John looking forward to reading it. Various members in passing congratulated Bill on his awards but none encroached on his privacy.

"You know" said Tommy "I have a feeling that someone has spoken to the members about not badgering Bill because to me it seems so unreal. You could expect some slapping you on the back saying "Can I buy you a drink Bill?" Only these people are behaving in a much more civilised manner which I find very strange."

"You can blame me for that Tommy" confessed John. "The last time I came in here the Chairman and I were in conversation and he suddenly asked me, 'do you know of any reason why Bill and Tommy do not come here, we have not seen them for quite a while.' Of course I had to tell him the reason and he understood, that is why he was so pleased to see you both this evening. I do hope I have not offended you both but I did not tell you because I preferred you to make your own decision."

"Thank you John you have not offended us at all, in fact you have acted like a true friend and for that we are grateful aren't we Tommy?

In reply Tommy rose from her seat came round to John and gave him a kiss. "That is for being a good friend to us John, thank you."

"On their way home Tommy asked if they would like to come in for a bite to eat or if you prefer…a nightcap.

"No thanks Tommy it is nigh on our bed time and we are ready for it."

When they parted Tommy asked, "Do you fancy a bite to eat Bill?"

"Go on then I will have a sandwich and a coffee."

"Sunday proved a restful day for Bill and Tommy, except without Thomas and Leila who were having the day off Tommy had to do the cooking. Tommy wrote one or two letters while Bill lazed by the pool reading the newspaper. When Tommy had finished her writing she had an idea. She took a beer out to Bill to put him in a good mood, "Here you are darling a nice cool beer for you."

Hey-Up, Bill thought to himself, she is after summat'. "Thank you love that is very kind of you."

"Yes it is "she replied "I am a kind person! And I have just been thinking."

"Steady on now love don't go and do yourself a mischief."

"Look, do you want to hear this wonderful idea of mine or not?"

"Now how can I refuse such a request after you going out of your way thinking of my needs by bringing me this beer? Carry on love I am all ears."

"So I have noticed but I did not want to upset you."

"Mashy, come on out with it if I don't agree you will want your beer back."

"Why don't we treat ourselves by going into town for dinner?"

"Now what a coincidence I was about to suggest that myself to save you slaving over a hot stove."

"No way, you never did you lying toad but I am pleased you have agreed it will make a nice change for us. I will ring Fred to see if he is available. Yes please Fred 7 o'clock will be fine, thanks."

CHAPTER 38

Monday morning Fred greeted Bill with a salute and "Good morning sir.

Bill returned the salute. "Good morning to you Fred, any news from the grapevine?"

"The four teachers have arrived. Did you enjoy your dinner in town last evening sir?"

"We did indeed Fred as you know it was the first time we had dinner in town and it was a nice experience. I will see you later Fred, tell your fellow grapeviners I am being starved of up to the minute news."

"Mashy sir."

"Good morning Miss Battle have you had a nice weekend?"

"Yes thank you sir it was quiet though, I just lazed and read a little."

"Tommy and I went for dinner in town last evening at that very nice up-market store; we usually go there for lunch on Saturday with Alfred and Dot because we do not know of any other nice restaurant."

Barbara told him of one or two whose cuisine was excellent. "I will write their names down in order of preference or you will forget. They are a little bit pricey but the food is really good."

"Have we any messages Barbara?"

"No sir but the four teachers have arrived, do you wish to interview them at all sir?"

"No, Captain Basira will have instilled the requirements expected from them I may go and run my eye over them a bit later, In fact I will go right now because that curriculum needs to be sorted out hasn't it? I will get my bleeper Barbara and see you in a little while."

On his way he stopped at the recruits' accommodations to see what progress had been made and he was very surprised to see both offices were being furnished.

He then went to see Major Khatib. "Good morning George how are things?"

"Everything is fine Bill Captain Basira has got her new staff and they have been in deep conversation since they reported in."

"Have they been introduced to you George?"

"No, they came in went into her office and that is where they have been ever since."

"I do not like that George unless she is laying the law down first before introducing them to us. I think I will stay for a little while and see what happens. I see Deacon and Dean appear to be busy or is it top show because I am here?"

"No they have had their heads down and they are all getting along fine with one another which is very nice to see. Would you like a cool drink Bill?"

"George, I would love one."

"He beckoned to one of the girls and it was Dot who came in. "Bring two orange juices for us please Lieutenant." When she returned Bill said. "Good morning Lieutenant are you busy?"

"Yes sir very and it is interesting too."

"Why do you find it so interesting you are already qualified in that kind of work so what is so different?"

"The Arabic names sir they are fascinating."

"But of course forgive my ignorance."

"The teachers are moving out Bill" said George.

Bill jumped to his feet and saw the four of them sauntering to the exit.

"Where are you people going?" Bill shouted after them.

"Back to our accommodation sir" was the reply.

"The hell you are, and on whose orders?"

"Captain Basira's sir."

He pointed at one of the females. "You, go and tell Captain Basira to report to me."

"Who shall I tell her to report to sir?"

"Colonel Barrett and jump to it then you all stay where you are."

He returned to George's office and had just sat down when Captain Basira came hurrying in, saluted and reported "You wanted to see me sir?"

"Yes Captain I want you to explain to me why you did not present your four teachers to your immediate superior Major Khatib when they reported in to you? And what was the reason for dismissing them to their accommodation when you wanted them here today to help you with the school furnishings? Lastly, have you formulated your curriculum, if not why not or if you have why has it not been handed to my PA to make copies for all concerned in coming to an agreement on the times and dates the recruits will adhere to?"

"Not presenting the teachers to Major Khatib was a serious error of judgement sir. The reason I dismissed the teachers was I had no immediate work to occupy them with. I have not even started on the curriculum because I have been too pre-occupied ordering everything that was needed for the school sir."

"On the first count on your own admission you did make an error of judgment but you have just made another one by not apologising to Major Khatib which you will do after I have left. I am puzzled about you not being able to find your teachers something to do. The two drill instructors have nothing to do because they have no recruits to train, yet they have found useful jobs helping Lieutenants Yassen and Basma. Why could you not employ your teachers in ordering items you need and planning how and where the furnishings will go, while you concentrate on your curriculum which I want on my desk in two days time? From now on Captain you will liaise with the Major on everything he should need to know concerning the school. When the school is up and running I will re-appraise it, I will now go and have a word with your staff. He approached the group who were busy chatting. "You do know that the school is not quite ready but it will soon be, that means there is a lot of preparation to be done on your part to make sure that when you get the go ahead you can with some forward planning slot everything into place. Outside of your teaching abilities I do not know if you have any other qualities but there is nothing to be ashamed of in asking for help. Captain Basira has a big job on her hands and it is your duty to support her. She chose you because she thinks you are the best, I chose her because I think she is the best which points to the fact that I have struck gold, don't let her or me down, carry on." As they moved to re-enter the office Bill stopped them. "One moment, have you forgotten or do you think that saluting a senior officer does not apply to you?" They immediately jumped to attention apologised then saluted. "That is much better now don't you forget that. Mashy?"

"Mashy Sir," They all responded with a grin.

As he was making his way back to his office Barbara bleeped him. He put on a spurt and on entering his office he asked, "Is it an emergency Barbara?"

"In a way yes, the British Consul is at security wanting an interview with you sir."

"Tell security to escort him to my office Barbara. I will go and meet him at the entrance to the building."

When the Consul's chauffeur driven car drew up the security guard stepped out and saluted Bill who thanked him and told him. "I will take over now."

When the Consul stepped out he saw a very smart middle aged man who Bill saluted and introduced himself. The Consul came forward with outstretched hand with a big smile and introduced himself as David Giles. "I have wanted to meet you Colonel because all I have been hearing since my arrival are the exploits of Colonel Barrett."

"Come into my office sir where I will put these so called exploits in their proper perspective and we will have a little light refreshment. When he got his guest seated Bill asked him what would you like to drink.

"I would like a tea please, from my experiences in various foreign embassies I found that tea can cool one down in hot weather and warm one in cold."

"I would like to wager sir that you would prefer a mug to a cup."

"You would win your wager Colonel."

"Miss Battle can we have two mugs of tea please?"

When she brought them Bill introduced her. Miss Battle I would like you to meet our new Consul Mr David Giles. Miss Battle is my PA sir and also my right arm. They exchanged pleasantries.

When Barbara had returned to her own office Bill told the Consul, "She is an Honours Graduate in languages from Oxford."

"Well Colonel are you going to put me straight on all these tales I have been hearing about or do I have I to take them with a pinch of salt. I have heard the same tales from a few different people and they do not differ in the telling so I think I can forget the pinch of salt."

Bill told him how he was recruited by the Emir right up to the present day. "There is one thing that I am concerned about sir, the two characters who were imprisoned were never visited by the previous Consul and I think my confrontation with him about his duty as a Consul triggered off his downfall."

"Yes I am aware of the two men Colonel and I can assure you I will be in constant contact with them to see to their well being. Yes, I believe my predecessor was not a very conscientious person but we are not all tarred with the same brush Colonel. You have played down all the stories I have been told and that makes you in my eyes a very humble man Colonel and I am proud to have met you."

"Would you like to meet our Commandant sir followed by a tour of what we are trying to achieve as a Recruit Training Establishment?"

"That would be very nice and I could have a word with your two subordinates at the same time. I will have a quick word with Miss Battle before we go."

When they entered Eric's PA's office Bill told her that he and the British Consul would like a word with the Commandant.

"Sir, Colonel Barrett and the British Consul would like a word."

"Send them in."

They entered Eric's office and Bill saluted him. "I would like to present Mr David Giles our British Consul sir.

They shook hands and Eric asked if they would like refreshments? After a good long chat Bill asked. Have I your permission sir to give the Consul a tour of what we are achieving in building a new Training Establishment?"

"By all means Colonel we are very proud of our achievements Mr Giles."

The Consul was very impressed with what he saw and the plans of improvement. Alfred and Dot were quite chuffed to being introduced to him and the chat they had.

On returning to his car he shook Bill by the hand. "Thank you Colonel I will know in future when I hear your name mentioned linked to all the good you are doing for the Air Force and the young people entering it that a pinch of salt will not be needed. No doubt we will meet up again and rest assured I will visit those two characters in prison because administrating to all the British ex-pats IS my duty."

"It has been a pleasure to meet you sir we can now sleep in our beds in peace."

"But of course Colonel" he said with a laugh." Bill gave him a salute as he was driven off.

CHAPTER 39

"Major Hassan for you sir" called Barbara.

"Good morning Harry what can I do for you?"

"You can meet me at the Airmen's accommodation to see the finished product, then we will proceed to the Airwomen's accommodation and finally we will pick up the Headmistress and inspect the school."

"You mean they have all been completed Harry, what a star you are, I am on my way. Barbara, the accommodations and the school have all been completed and I am on my way to have a shufti at them, isn't that great news?"

"Tell me all about it on your return sir when you have come back down to earth from cloud nine."

Bill was delighted with the two rooms in the recruits' accommodation. "The housekeeper/security people will certainly be comfortable in those rooms Harry."

Harry decided to go on ahead while Bill collected the Headmistress.

When Bill knocked and entered her office everyone jumped up from whatever they were doing to stand to attention. "As you were and relax, I have only come to kidnap your boss. Get your headgear Captain and if you have any of the school plans bring them along with you." As they were leaving Bill looked back to see four puzzled faces following them. "It is nothing really, just that the school is now completed!"

It took about five seconds to sink in then they gave such an almighty cheer that Major Khatib came out of his office to find out what was going on while the rest of the staff were looking in disbelief. "It is alright Major they are just celebrating the news of the school being completed." The staff heard what Bill said and decided to join in also with a cheer.

When Bill and the Captain met up with Harry a smiling Headmistress gave Harry a salute. "Thank you sir for the wonderful news we have just left the staff celebrating."

"Yes. I could hear them from over here our aim is to make people happy. Come, I will show you my staff's handiwork."

Bill and the Headmistress were amazed at the transformation. "You have done a wonderful job for us sir all it needs now are the furnishings and it will look even better."

"Yes Major you have certainly done us proud and it is a great credit to you and your staff, this is a school to be proud of," Bill added. "I like the conference room which I think will be very useful, plus the facilities to show items on film in each classroom, that was well thought out and will be a great asset to learning. I could go on and on talking about its virtues it is unbelievable, I still cannot come to terms with the transformation. You Captain have some hard work and thinking to do now which I am sure you and your staff will take a delight in doing."

"If you want help moving in and helping to set out your furniture Captain just let me know and I will send in my heavy gang," the Major said with a grin. "We are here to give you all the help you need."

"Thank you so much, I am still overwhelmed with the place and cannot thank you enough sir."

"How is the furnishing situation Captain?" Bill asked.

"It is piling up in the stores building just waiting to be moved out. sir."

"Then when can they start to move in Major?" Bill asked.

"They can move in whenever they are ready sir."

"Do you hear that Captain? It is up to you now."

"I will accept your offer sir of the loan of your men, I will split my staff to guide your men where to place the furniture, so long as it is put in its place we can titivate it up later."

Bill returned to his office while Captain Basira went to the Stores to arrange delivery of the furniture and equipment for the school.

"From the look on your face sir you are well satisfied with the school" exclaimed Barbara.

"Satisfied!? That man has worked wonders converting that ex-Admin' building into what I can only say…our pride and joy, when Captain Basira and her staff have finished I will take you to see it. Are you ready for lunch?"

"I am ready when you are sir."

They got the usual smiles and nods from the other diners which they returned in kind as they were escorted to their table. Alfred and Dot were already dining.

"You certainly caused some excitement when you came to whisk the Headmistress away, what is the gen on the school?" Alfred asked.

Bill commenced to satisfy their curiosity but he was interrupted when they were served with their lunch. "I will tell you later over coffee."

During the afternoon Bill was asked to report to the Commandant. On entering Eric's office he saluted. "Sit down Bill I only wanted to inform you that since the Passing-Out Parade the applications for admittance to the Air Force have soared sky high, if you will pardon the pun, especially with the females, our Brass Hats are delighted."

"My news for you sir is…The school is finished, Major Hassan and his staff have done a cracking job, and Captain Basira is busy furnishing it." The two Offices for the security people in the recruits' accommodations are now completed. Everything will be ready for the arrival of the intakes. Incidentally Eric, has your P.A. come out of her shell yet?"

"I'm afraid not Bill she either does not want to loosen up or she cannot so I am just leaving her to do what she is here for and to let her come round in her own time."

"Why don't you have a stroll to see the school it is well worth the visit, if you want an escort just give me a tinkle."

"How about now Bill?"

"Mashy, grab your ball and bat and let us go."

"What do you mean grab your ball and bat?"

"It is the London cockney slang for hat."

Eric laughed. "Your English sayings amuse me."

"Just remember not to use any when you are in an important meeting."

On arrival at the school Captain Basira and her staff were busy putting things in their rightful places.

"Good afternoon Captain Basira," Eric greeted her.

Not wearing a hat she came to attention and returned the greeting.

"The Colonel here persuaded me to come and see for myself the excellent work you and your staff are doing here at the school. Have you time to give me a tour?" After the tour he thanked the Captain exclaiming, "You have a school there Captain to be proud of I am impressed with its construction and also the way you are furnishing it. Thank you for the tour."

"Shall we go and congratulate Major Hassan for the conversion sir?"

"Indeed we will Colonel, he has done a fine job."

On entering the Workshops the Major saw them and came hurrying from his office to salute Eric.

"I want to congratulate you Major on your conversion of that building into a very modern school."

"Would you like to come into my office sir? I have plans and photographs of the old building and you can see for yourself the stages of conversion."

"That will be very interesting, thank you Major."

"Well wasn't that visit to the school worth going to see Eric?"

"It was indeed Bill, and it is something to be proud of."

"Is everything quiet Barbara, no messages, no visitors?"

"Quiet as a church mouse sir and I will be glad to get that curriculum from Captain Basira."

"You have nothing to add to it have you?"

"No, but I want to check it and make copies to get it to the recipients to get together to finalise it."

"She is pretty much tied up at the moment but I will see you get it soon, leave it to me Barbara. Give Fred a ring please it is time we were not here."

"Good afternoon Colonel" said Fred as he saluted.

Bill returned the salute and greeting. "What is new Fred, anything from the grapevine?"

"No sir there is nothing happening worth a mention, have you anything new?"

"I hear that since our Passing-out Parade was shown on television the rate of applications to join the Air Force has gone sky high, more so from the females. I wish I could do something about it."

"Like what sir?"

"The Desert Orchids remember Fred? A permanent female Display Team."

"If only sir."

"Yes Fred, if only."

Tommy greeted Bill with a kiss after waving to Fred as he was returning to the Base.

"I have some news for you love we are to collect the magazines tomorrow morning the Chief rang this afternoon to tell me. Isn't it exciting?"

"Well it is something to look forward to and reading a copy will certainly keep you quiet for a while. I wonder what title has been chosen."

"You will be disappointed if it is not yours won't you?"

"No of course not I have been winding everyone up it would be childish if I thought otherwise. I think we had better start making a list of who we want to send a copy to."

"I have already made a start."

"Then we had better put on our thinking caps and make a complete list. Tomorrow we will go to the Post Office and buy forty envelopes and address labels for the magazines then we can spend the weekend getting the ones for the UK ready for Fred posting them on Monday."

Fred arrived for them on Saturday morning with Alfred and Dot on board.

"Good morning sir and Mrs Barrett are we ready for an exciting day?"

"I do not know about anyone else Fred but I certainly am I cannot wait to get hold of one of the magazines" said a jubilant Tommy.

"And as soon as you get one in your hands you will forget all about shopping" said Bill.

"That is all the shopping we are doing today my dear except for going to the Post Office."

"Can I be of any assistance there Mrs Barrett?" asked Fred.

"We are only going for envelopes and address labels for the magazines thank you Fred."

"Do you want me to wait for you or will you want me at the usual time?"

"I think the usual time Fred, Alfred and Dot will be shopping and we will be staying for lunch."

"And if we are not here on time Fred come looking for us because we may be sat on a bench somewhere reading magazines." Bill said looking skywards with a resigned look. "Come on flower let us get it over with."

When they approached the reception desk in the Newspaper Building the receptionist on seeing them smiled then immediately phoned the Chief Editor. He came hurrying to them beaming from ear to ear with a huge smile. Shaking hands to greet them he said. "I will not say anything about the magazine you will be its judges." He sat them at his desk and asked if they would like refreshments.

"No thank you I for one am too excited my shaking hands could not hold the glass steady."

"How about you Colonel would you care for a drink?"

"No thank you Chief I think my wife's excitement is catching."

"Very well then" he reached into a drawer and pulled out two copies and handed one each to Bill and Tommy face down. "Turn them over please."

When they did they both gave gasps of astonishment. The front cover was far better than they had imagined.

"I can see from your faces that you like it but what do you think of the title is it to your satisfaction Colonel?"

"The Aljibian Magazine" Bill said out loud. "At first I was not too sure but taking a longer look I think it grows on you, after all it is what it states. Yes Chief I think it is the right one and thank you for this front cover it is really something and it makes me feel so proud. I presume your staff chose the title."

"They did indeed Colonel and there was a good deal of rivalry to choose the winner but they all agreed that it was the best one. What are your initial thoughts Mrs Barrett?"

"As soon as I saw it I came over with emotion and could have burst into tears with happiness, I think that cover is a classic and it does full justice to my husband and I am so proud of him. The title, yes I do think it is the right one."

"So shall we carry on looking through the magazine?" asked the Chief.

As Bill and Tommy scrutinised every page the Chief smiled hearing the Ahs' of pleasure at every page they came to. Finally they came to the end. Bill looked at the chief and said. "I have not the words in my vocabulary to say how I feel about what you have done by portraying my wife, me, our family and friends so graciously. What can I say that could override my sincere thanks to you and your staff?" He then rose to his feet and offered his hand to the Chief who shook it warmly.

"Thank you Colonel and I shall never forget what you did for me."

"Tommy came to him and gave him a kiss. "That is my token of appreciation Thank you."

The Chief escorted them down to reception where a young man was waiting with a Valise. "Here are your complimentary copies Colonel I am sure whoever receives a copy from you will always treasure it."

As Bill and Tommy began to make their way to meet Alfred and Dot Tommy suddenly gave a little scream. "We have forgotten to go to the Post Office Bill."

They made a slight detour and purchased what they wanted then met up with Alfred and Dot who were having a drink while they waited for them. "From the looks on their faces here comes two very satisfied people Alfred" observed Dot.

"There will be more people than us with big smiles on their faces when they see these Classic magazines" retorted Tommy, "and you two are in for a real treat."

"Please can we take a shufti at one of them now Tommy?"

"NO! you jolly well can't you must wait until we get home, if you saw one now you would have us all barred from here with your whooping and cheering. We have seen them and we are going to really enjoy our lunch aren't we dear?"

"We most certainly are. It is tough at the top and you two have a long way to go but you will get there one of these days…Maybe! "

"You are mean Bill Barrett" responded Dot. Here is Alfred and me slaving our socks off for you trying to make you God's gift to Aljibia and you won't even let us have a tiny little squint at the magazine. It is enough to make us refuse the gift of one."

"Don't you include me in your ramblings Dot Dean" spoke up Alfred I think it is being sensible to wait a wee bit longer."

"Mashy, then I can cross you off the receiving list can I "?

"Don't you dare Bill Barrett or I won't let you promote me further up the ladder to Captain!"

The four of them could not help themselves but burst out laughing.

"After that tirade Madam Dean you deserve a shufti but promise…no loud reactions in here bottle it up until we get home. Here is one for you also Alfred." Tommy gave them one each faces down. When they turned the magazine face up Dot stared at the front cover then her eyes filled up with tears of happiness. She rose from her seat and came across to Bill, flung her arms around him, kissed him and said. "Bill Barrett you are a wonderful man and I love you, thank you ever so much I will treasure it all my life."

All Bill could respond with was, "you are wetting my face"

Alfred came over to him and gave him a hug. You are the best friend anyone could have Bill, thank you very much. You were right in what you said about it being a classic Tommy the front cover says it all. I cannot imagine how our friends at home will react when they see their copies."

"Come on then have a quick shufti then we will go in for lunch."

Over lunch the subject of the title was brought up and they all agreed it was the best one. "I am not going to do a thing all weekend but sit curled up with a magazine in my lap" said a determined Tommy.

"The hell you are" drawled Bill in his best voice imitation of John Wayne. "While I am signing them you will be writing the address labels if we want to get them in the post on Monday."

"It will cost a bomb for postage sending them to the UK by airmail" said a concerned Alfred.

"Well Alfred we think our friends deserve it, they are always hungry for news from us and we think they are very special friends."

"What part did you take in the designing of the front cover Bill" asked Dot.

"I put you and Andrew on it."

"Thank you Bill that was a wonderful gesture and it makes it even more personal and precious to me."

"Well I had to do something to avert attention from me standing there like Piffy on a Rock bun."

Dot and Alfred just smiled knowing the reason went much deeper than that.

"We may be getting a call from Ella later asking if we are going to the club, if so would you two care to join us" asked Tommy.

"As much as we love your company Tommy" said Dot "I think you need some time with your other friends. Besides I want to spend the evening ogling my pin-up boy."

"And I want to watch the Saturday sport" smiled Alfred.

"Have you two any shopping to do?"

"No, we just came along for the ride because it was a special day and we had to collect a magazine commemorating it thank you."

"You are a cheeky young madam scolded Tommy playfully. Mashy, shall we go and see if Fred is waiting for us?"

"Now that is a fine sight to see, four happy smiling faces.

"Fred, we have had a wonderful day that is why we are all happy and we hope to make you happy too before you leave us, now put your clog down!" Tommy said with a big grin.

"Mashy Ma'am" was the reply.

On arrival at the Villa Tommy invited everyone inside. "Would everyone like a drink? Bill and Alfred want beers. Fred? 'A soft drink please.' Dot? 'A soft drink please.' And a soft one for me, excuse me while I go to get them organised so just make yourselves comfortable and at home."

While Tommy was seeing to the drinks Bill was sat at the bureau signing four copies of the magazine. When Tommy re-appeared she was followed by Thomas and Leila carrying the drinks on a tray. When they all had settled down Bill spoke. "Ladies and gentlemen it is our pleasure to present you with a token of our friendship and esteem, something you all have contributed to namely The Ajibian Magazine." Tommy then gave out the copies. As was expected Leila came over all emotional and Fred giving a big grin came to Bill shook his hand declaring "I shall treasure this sir thank you I cannot wait to show it to the grapeviners."

CHAPTER 40

Monday morning and Fred greeted Bill with the usual salute and "Good morning sir."

"Good morning Fred" responded Bill returning the salute "Today is the beginning of the New Aljibia Recruit Training Establishment."

"I never thought I would see it as organised as it is now sir, you have done a marvellous job for us."

"It all comes with experience Fred, nobody here had that, they could not even run a booze-up in a Brewery but it has turned out alright in the end. Just remember Fred, experience is a wonderful thing, it enables you to recognise a mistake when you make it again! Today I am going to be very busy making sure everything has been carried out to the letter."

"In other words sir you will be running around like a BA Fly!"

"That is it Fred you have hit the nail right on the head."

"You English never fail to amaze me with your funny sayings." Here we are sir, are you going to have a cup of Rosie Lee before you start?"

"Make that a mug Fred. By the way how did the grapeviners like the magazine?"

They were thrilled to bits sir all of them are buying one today they think the front cover is something really special and they agree with all the write ups too."

"Tell them from me 'Thanks' but each time they look at the front cover it should remind them that they are starving me with the lack of grapevine titbits. Salaam Fred."

"Salaam sir, will do."

"Good morning Barbara, have you anything for me this morning?"

"Good morning Bill you sound very chirpy but no there are no messages."

"Today is the start of the week when the new Aljibia Recruit Training Establishment opens its doors to a new wave of recruits. That means this week will be what you might call hectic so you had better have a stock of tranquilisers handy."

"Do you mean to tell me that a man with your experience will stoop to using tranquilisers?"

"Believe it or not Barbara I am just a normal human being. I shall start off by checking that every department has done everything that was required of them. Incidentally have you received the curriculum from the headmistress?"

"No sir."

"Get her on the phone."

"Captain Basira, Colonel Barrett speaking, why have I not received your curriculum? What! It is not quite ready? And when will it be ready?"

"Tomorrow morning sir?"

"I have news for you Captain if it is not on my desk the first thing after lunch you will be explaining your reasons to the Commanding Officer." He then rang off.

"I do not understand that woman Barbara I appreciate she has had a busy time with the school but she has four assistants and she is not capable of even running a bloody raffle, God give me strength. Mashy! I am now off to do my rounds so it will be lunch time I think when you will see me unless you bleep me before then. So just sit back and relax, have you got a book to read to pass the time away?"

"Indeed I have not!" said an indignant Barbara.

"In that case I had better find you something." He went into his office and brought an Aljibian Magazine in its protection cover and gave it to her. "You might as well keep it Barbara I have already read it." Before she opened it he left her with "See you at lunch time."

His first stop was at the Airmen's accommodation where he ran into a hive of activity of the staff from the bedding store taking into each room clean mattresses and bedding. He saw the Sergeant in charge of the staff and asked him if the entire building had been fumigated. "Yes sir it has, Lieutenant Hikmat checked that personally and she will do a double check when we have completed our task."

"Well done you are doing a good job, thank you Sergeant."

The same scenario occurred at the Airwomen's accommodation with the (w) Sergeant

He went on to visit the Gym where Captain Rashid assured him that all equipment that needed renewing had been replaced; all plumbing throughout the building had been rigorously checked. Bill thanked him then presented him with a magazine "With my compliments Captain."

His next stop was at the Bedding Store. I want to thank you Lieutenant Hikmat for the way you have handled the situation here in the bedding Store and your staff, you have made it into a different world. He then presented her with a magazine. "With my compliments Lieutenant."

Leaving there he went to see Major Khatib at the Training Offices. Good morning George. I see Captain Basira and her teaching staff have vacated that office."

"They left on Friday Bill, they just up and went without notifying me."

"That does it George that woman thinks she is a law unto herself she will not fit into our system. Right I am off to see the Commandant but before I go here is something with my compliments and please give these four to your staff with the exception of Deacon and Dean, they already have one. I will let you know the result with Basira."

He then hurried to see Eric. "Will you inform the Commandant that I must see him urgently" he told Eric's PA.

She spoke to Eric on the inter-com and told him Colonel Barrett wanted to see him urgently.

"Send him in at once."

Bill saluted and said "This is serious Eric." he then told him the saga of the Headmistress. She is not complying at all Eric she is doing just what she likes and thumbing her nose at the rest of us. I want her off this station, she may be a good teacher but she will not conform to our methods"

"I see what you mean Bill she is by-passing her seniors to suit her own purposes. Very well we will have her in and see what she has to say for herself." He told his PA to inform Captain (w) Basira to report to my office immediately. You stay here Bill."

Minutes later the PA ushered a flustered Captain in.

"You wanted to see me sir?"

"Get out and come back in showing some respect." She turned to go to the door but Eric stopped her. "You will also show me respect when you are leaving my presence."

She immediately saluted then exited.

Eric then snapped "ENTER" in reply to the knock on the door. Basira entered and gave Eric a salute. "Why did you not do that in the first place?"

"I was flustered sir not knowing why I was commanded to report to you."

"How do you expect your subordinates to act if their senior officer cannot act like one? I have called you here because I have been getting serious complaints from Colonel Barrett. Apparently you want to wrap yourself in a cocoon solely of your teachings and blatantly ignoring anything else even your senior officers. I understand you are a good teacher I applaud that but as an Officer you are rubbish. Therefore I have no place on my station for a person like you who chooses not to conform. You will go from here and you will gather your personal possessions together and leave my station to report to from whence you came. Now Get Out"

She showed not a flicker of emotion as she saluted and left.

"Well Bill how did I do?"

"Great, you certainly deserve a Blue Peter Badge for that." Bill then had to explain what the Blue Peter Badge was about, much to Eric's amusement.

"So now you want me to apply for a new Head teacher."

"I will go and interview the four teachers and choose one as a temporary substitute who will get a fair crack of the whip, if he/she proves their worth they will get the job if not we can apply for a replacement."

"Sounds good to me Bill I will then leave it to you."

"Good then accept this with my compliments. He handed over a magazine still in its cover, saluted then left before Eric opened his gift.

Bill then decided to go to the school and sort out the situation. On entering he found Basira talking to the four teachers. "Have you finished collecting your personal possessions Captain?"

"Yes sir I have."

"Then please leave and clear your accommodation."

When she left he asked the four to follow him to the conference room. When they were all seated he asked. "Do you know anything about the curriculum the Captain was supposed to give me some time ago?"

"Yes sir we all knew about it" replied one of the females.

"And you are?" Asked Bill.
"Sergeant Amina sir."
"Which one of you has been in the teaching profession the longest?"
"Me sir" replied Amina.
"I do not know if the Captain has told you her side of this unfortunate affair but I would like to tell you mine. I chose her because as a teacher she ticked all my boxes with her qualifications. Unfortunately what has let her down she had no time for senior ranks outside her world of education. She was a professional in that world and she was dogmatic in her attitude that she was untouchable to the extent that at every opportunity she would bypass us and our instructions. The Commandant informed her that he could not tolerate such behaviour and ordered her off the station. What I cannot understand is I always thought that good teachers were kind and considerate people but when the Captain received her marching orders she showed not a scrap of emotion. By that my thoughts were this woman has now shown me her true colours. The Commandant wanted to ask for a replacement but I talked him out of that to give one of you four the chance to take over as the School Head. The reason I asked for the most senior of you four is because I believe in giving the most senior one the first crack of the whip. Sergeant Amina are you prepared to take over the responsibility of Head Teacher?"
"Yes sir."
"Have any of you got any objections to Sergeant Amina becoming the school Head?"
"No sir" was the unanimous response. One man said. "She is well fitted to take over and we all respect her."
"That is very gratifying to know because I have no need now to ask you to respect her and give her your full support and I thank you for that. Now I am going to whip your Sergeant away for a short time only to send her back to you as Lieutenant Amina. Thanks again for your understanding and respect. Come on Sarge' we have some shopping to do." They left the three teachers having a good laugh. Bill took her to the clothing store where she was issued with her Lieutenants' Bars. Bill then took her to the Workshops to see Major Hassan. "Major I would like to introduce Lieutenant Amina the new Head teacher of the school. Anisa saluted and a very puzzled looking Major shook her hand and congratulated her.
"Will you change the name plate on the Head's Office door please Major?"
"It will be in place this afternoon Colonel."
"Will you please leave us for a couple of minutes Lieutenant."
"What's gone on Bill?"
Bill told him what had happened.
"Good, I could never have taken to her Bill there was something about her I could not put my finger on I think you have chosen a good replacement in that young woman."

"Thanks for everything George please accept this as a token of our friendship," he said as he gave him a magazine.

Outside he asked. Are you ready Ma'am? Let me take you to school!! You know about the curriculum so will you make it your priority to get it to me as soon as possible please? It is very important we get the schedule ready for the arrival of the new intakes."

"I'm back Miss Battle" he shouted from his office…it's lunch time!"

"I hope you have returned in a better mood than when you left. sir."

"Come on get your skates on then I will guarantee you will enjoy your lunch from what I will tell you."

In the meantime Captain Basira entered the office she had vacated in the Training Offices. George spotted her and went to investigate. What are you doing in here Captain and why have you entered without my permission?"

I do not have to answer to you anymore because I am not a member of your staff any longer. But to satisfy your curiosity I am collecting my personal possessions and getting the hell out of this dump."

"You carry on speaking to me like that and you will leave here having had to answer to a charge of insubordination madam. Now collect your things and Get Out of here."

George's raised voice brought his staff to their office windows to see what was going on.

George saw them and he gave them a wink and a thumb up sign as Basira marched defiantly out. He went straight back into his office and phoned the Security Guard on the main gate. "This is Major Khatib you will shortly have Captain Basira leaving the station as a result of losing her post. I would like you to stop her for a thorough search to make sure she is not absconding with any of our equipment…and take your time with it."

That will teach the bitch he said, as he afforded himself a big grin. He called his staff to him because he knew they would be waiting to see if he would be putting them in the picture of the happening. "I am afraid I have some sad news for you all, Captain Basira has been given the chop." He was interrupted by applause and calls of well done Colonel Barrett. "I have not heard from the Colonel yet but it is a good guess he would be behind her dismissal. Lieutenants Deacon and Dean your office is now available for when you want it, that is all."

Alfred and Dot told the other staff members. "We will be speaking with the Colonel at lunch time we will give you all the gen afterwards."

"So what has been happening this morning to make you so cheerful?" asked Barbara after they had ordered their lunch.

Bill leaned over towards her and in a loud whisper he said. "Have you noticed that Alfred and Dot have paused in their eating?"

She looked towards them and saw two grinning faces. "We would like to know as well Barbara." Dot then leaned towards Barbara and in a loud whisper said. "And we have had a bit of excitement in the Training Offices and the Major was brilliant."

Bill leaned forward to say. "And I would like to know Barbara."

Barbara burst out laughing, "I am the pig in the middle and I know the least of any of you, I think we had better leave it until we have coffee that is settled, now get on with your meals."

Over coffee Bill told his story from his meeting with the Commandant right up to taking the Head Teacher to school. The CO went straight for the jugular and sorted her out" said Bill "she left with a flea in her ear alright."

"I have spoken with Amina and I think she is a very nice woman and she is very intelligent I might add." Dot told them. She continued by telling them of the events that took place in the Training Offices. When the Major saw Basira going into our office he went and asked her what she was doing there without his permission? She back-chatted him which caused him to raise his voice and order her out because of her attitude to him and the training staff in general. He took umbrage and contacted the gate security to search her to make sure she was not leaving with any of our equipment and for them to take their time in doing so."

Bill clapped his hands together and gave a guffaw, "I must go and congratulate him that was priceless" I have asked Amina to get her curriculum to me as quickly as possible we must have the end product finished tomorrow. A meeting will and must be held tomorrow morning to sort out the time and day schedules. You two will represent the drill training, Amina the Education and Rashid the Physical Education. You two will also find slots for teaching discipline. I think I had better chair the meeting and I would like you to attend Barbara, your knowledge will come in very useful. Everyone will be contacted and told the time the meeting will start and it will be held in the conference room in the school. Mashy?"

"Mashy sir" was the reply.

At 3pm Lieutenant Amina entered Barbara's office. "I have brought the curriculum for the Colonel."

"I am the Colonel's PA and I would like to congratulate you on your promotion to Head Teacher and rank I will see if he is in. She pressed the intercom and there was no answer. "That is unusual he always tells me when he is off somewhere I had better take a look in his office. She shouted "are you in the shower sir?"

Suddenly a wet face and head poked round a door. "Were you shouting for me Barbara?"

Barbara laughed. "Lieutenant Amina is here with the curriculum would you like to see her?"

Yes please, make her a brew I will only be a few minutes."

She went back into her office still laughing. "He will only be a few minutes he would like to see you. Would you like a drink while you wait? He told me to make you a brew.

"I would like a cool drink please."

"Sit yourself down you might as well be comfortable while you wait. I believe the school is very nice have you got all the equipment you need?"

"Oh yes everything we have asked for we have got; now we are looking forward to giving our first lessons in a brand new school."

Bill burst in at this point. Amina immediately got to her feet to salute. "Sit down Lieutenant and relax, I am sorry to have kept you waiting but I did want to see you. Now about your curriculum, Miss Battle will check it over and make copies. Tomorrow morning at 9 o' clock yourself, the two drill instructors and the Officer PE instructor, he may bring one of his staff with him will meet in your conference room to make a united curriculum giving times and days you will be teaching or instructing the recruits. I will be in the chair aided by Miss Battle who is a qualified teacher in her own rights. You may if you wish bring along one of your subordinates. I would appreciate you having refreshments in the form of drinks to hand and place settings for individuals please. Mashy?"

"Mashy sir."

"Get me Captain Rashid please Barbara."

"Here he is sir."

"Captain, Colonel Barrett here, please report to the conference room in the school for 9 o'clock tomorrow morning we are going to sort out a times and days schedule for the recruits, you might like to bring along with you that bright (w) Sergeant as support. Mashy?"

"I have just had a quick look at this curriculum and it looks pretty good. I will now print-out all the copies needed." Barbara informed Bill.

"Good, I will be with Major Khatib if I am wanted."

George and he swapped tales and had a good laugh over Basira getting searched. I would have liked to have been in the background to see her reactions" laughed Bill, "I'll bet she was livid "I had it from good authority Bill security almost stripped her car they were so thorough, she got away after a two hour delay."

"I am going to see the CO now he will howl when I tell him the Basira saga."

"I forgot to thank you for the magazine Bill my words but they did you proud."

"And thank you George you were very generous in your contribution as was everyone else."

"Come in Bill I was expecting you and I want to thank you for the magazine, I see I was awarded the place of honour with my foreword."

"I want to thank you for that Eric to me it was the sign of a good and true friend…thank you. I have come to put you in the picture concerning the Basira saga. You know it did not end when she left your office I called in at the school to find her there chatting to the other teachers. I ordered her to leave and clear her accommodation. I then got the three teachers together and chose the replacement Head which is Sergeant Amina. She is the senior and my gut feeling tells me I have chosen well. Of course a promotion to Lieutenant was in order for her position as Head of the school with three subordinates. Afterwards I went to see Major Khatib and what a story he had to tell concerning Basira. Apparently she returned to her temporary office in the Training Offices without notifying George. He immediately went to question her and received a lot of insubordinate back-chat from her. He ordered her out and being determined she was not going to get away with that sort of conduct he rang security at the Station entrance. He told them that Basira had been relieved of her position and had been banned from the station and to search her to make sure she was not carrying any of our equipment and to take their time doing so."

"Well done George laughed Eric what a wonderful send-off she got; she would not have liked that Bill."

"Here is the icing on the cake Eric. They almost stripped her vehicle then after two hours she was allowed to go."

Eric began laughing so much he had to hold his aching sides. I must phone George to give him my congratulations because that is the funniest thing I have heard for a very long time. It goes to prove that you cannot mess senior officers about and hope to get away with it. What is your next step Bill?"

"A conference to sort out the time schedules for the recruits tomorrow morning. I will give them the gen on what action will be taken when the intakes arrive. By the way sir Thursday morning they will come to the cinema where I hope you will welcome the recruits to your station. I will then give them my party piece of what I require from them. I will introduce them to their Drill Instructors, Physical Training Instructors and the Teaching Staff. Following that I will show the main BlueBelle's Film ending with our recent Passing-out Parade. The recruits will then be stood down until Monday morning that is when the 'Battle will Commence'."

"Well done Bill you have got it well organised thank you."

"Any progress with 'Her' next door?"

Eric shook his head, "not a scrap I am leaving her to it."

"Why not have a word with her previous boss she might throw some light on it."

"Bill, so long as she does what she is here for that is all I ask."

"Right then I will be off sir and I will keep you informed of the progress made. There is one other thing sir I would like to take some UK leave starting a couple of days after the cinema show. The staff are quite capable of running the show in my absence they have everything under control."

"How long a leave are you thinking of taking Bill?"

"Four weeks."

"I think you have earned it go by all means with my blessings,"

Thank you sir, he then saluted and returned to his office.

"My words sir but you are cutting it a bit late, any longer and I would be on overtime."

"Sorry Barbara but I had to put the CO in the picture of what went on with the Basira saga then he wanted to know my plans for the intake arrivals. I keep telling you it is tough at the top."

Barbara replied by putting her hand to her mouth to smother an imaginary yawn.

"Don't you go all bolshie on me madam, get on that phone and ring for my chauffeur chop chop."

"Yes sir" she replied throwing up an imaginary salute.

He gave her a nod. "That is more like it."

As soon as Bill got in the car Fred commented. "You have had quite an eventful day sir."

"It has had its moments Fred."

"Khatib's revenge was one hell of a classic move sir, the grapeviners have been talking about it all day. Promoting Amina has saved you from being toppled off the top of the grapeviner's popularity poll, she is a favourite with us."

"I am glad you approve so tell the grapeviners that I thank them for their vote of confidence. Thursday morning I am addressing the new intakes then showing them the main BlueBelle's film. You are all welcome to come and have a shufti but you will not be called in until after I have finished my address. Kick off time will be 10 o'clock Mashy?"

"Mashy sir. The boys have been waiting for this moment and they will be delighted.

"Fred, No football songs and no barracking or it will be Red Cards for the lot of you. Salaam Fred, I will see you in the morning."

"Salaam sir and thanks."

"Have you had a good day love?" asked Tommy giving him a kiss.

"A very satisfactory one pet, have you?"

"Go and freshen up then we can chat, your beer will be waiting."

On his return Tommy told him that she invited Ella to go to town with her, Fred driving of course. When she arrived I presented her with the magazine with your compliments. When she removed it from its sleeve you should have heard her, she gave such a loud scream of delight Leila came in on the run to see what was happening. Oh Bill, if we had given her the moon she could not have been more delighted she threw her arms around me and really hugged me. Of course when she opened it she absolutely drooled over each page and I had to tell her who most of the individuals were and I have to thank you for signing it. We will get it all again when they come for us to go to the club; it will be John's turn then. Fred carried all the magazines to be posted and we did not have a problem. The same young man served me and I got his version of him seeing us on Television. From how I interpreted it I think he had been playing the one-upmanship game with his colleagues that I was a regular customer of his."

"Dinner is ready Ma'am" announced Leila.

"Good evening Thomas...Leila are you both well I hope?"

"We are fine sir" replied Thomas, have you had a hard day at the office?"

"Thomas you may not believe this but my secretary had to keep mopping my brow to stop the perspiration running into my eyes."

Tommy looked at Leila. "If we believed that Leila we would believe anything, don't you agree?"

"Yes Ma'am."

"Well I believe you sir" said Thomas with tongue in cheek.

"Oh you little creep Thomas, birds of a feather flock together don't they Leila?"

"Yes Ma'am" laughed Leila.

CHAPTER 41

"Good morning sir" Fred greeted Bill with a salute.

"And a very good morning to you Fred" Bill replied as he returned the salute.

"This is the last day before your grand opening Colonel are you having a dress rehearsal?"

"What are you on about Fred what do you think it is a bloody pantomime?"

"I refuse to answer that sir in case it incriminates me."

"Didn't I once ask you to ask 'Bill the Limo' if he would swap jobs with you?"

"You did, on many occasions sir, but I did not want to hurt your feelings with his answer."

"Come on Fred, you know I will not take umbrage."

"Very well sir, you asked for it. Bill's reply to my request was… 'What! Drive for *him*?' My religion bans me from drinking alcohol but chauffeuring that man around would drive me to drink."

"That's it. I do not bear grudges but as soon as you drop me off I will have him off this base so quickly his feet will not touch the floor. Watch your driving, you are swerving all over the sodding place!"

"Sorry sir, I was thinking when 'Bill the Limo' gets kicked off the base with my seniority I will get the Limo job."

"Over my dead body you will."

"No comment sir, and here we are at your office or would you like me to drive you over to the motor pool?"

"No don't bother, I will take a stroll over there when I can spare a minute. Salaam Fred."

"Salaam sir," Fred replied as he drove off laughing.

"Good morning Barbara, anything for me this morning?"

"No sir, just my grateful thanks for that brilliant magazine. What a wonderful job the newspaper staff made of it. I did not have the time yesterday to read it properly but last night at home I savoured every page, I loved all the comments from different people and I agreed with every one. You have certainly made your mark here Bill."

"Thank you for your contribution Barbara. I thought it was very nice; Tommy thought it was rather sweet. It was fortunate Basira was not here when the reporters were or I would have had to reject it and have it reprinted."

"That front cover was very well done and thought out Bill it attracts one to the magazine. I would say it will be a best seller."

"If we are ready for the meeting then let' go."

They arrived at the conference room a few minutes early to see everyone else was there. As they entered everyone stood in respect.

"Good morning ladies and gentlemen, please be seated. You know why you are all here. I apologise for calling this meeting at such a late date but recent events prevented me from calling it earlier. I would like to thank Lieutenant Amina and her staff for working very quickly in providing the key piece to our curriculum jigsaw. Miss Battle will hand each of you a copy of your original curriculum plus blank sheets of A4 for your jottings. I suggest PT, Drill then Education in that order. If you agree, hold up your hands … good you all agree. Now comes the hardest part; your job is to agree on time schedules from 8am to 1pm which covers six hours taking into account a break between each class. We will leave you to it and when you all have come to an agreement please contact Miss Battle just in case I am elsewhere, she will bleep me. One word of advice I will take a dim view if there is any anger over disagreements, you are all on the same team so I want harmony, Mashy?"

"Mashy sir" was the unanimous and smiling reply.

"There was nothing else we could do Barbara only let them sort out the times.

If there is a hitch then we shall have to put it right. Come, I will show you round the rest of the school."

After the viewing they decided it was lunchtime. When they entered the Luncheon Box they saw that Alfred and Dot were already there.

"What's the gen then?" asked Bill.

"We have sorted it out," said Alfred, but with it being nigh on lunchtime we decided to leave it until after lunch to let you know."

"Good thinking Alfred … and was everything amicable?"

"Oh yes, we had some fun, you would have enjoyed being there sir," Dot replied. "You spoke about us all being on the same team. Well be assured you have got a team that is already showing signs of becoming a very friendly one. You are a very lucky man, Colonel Barrett, to have us."

"Dot, if I had been there as much as I would have liked from your account I would have been a gooseberry and perhaps you may not have found your friendship quite as quickly. But what a bonus to have a team who are all pulling together in the same direction. My gut feeling tells me that this New Recruit Training Establishment is going to be a huge success."

After coffee they all made their way to the conference room. When all had assembled Bill was given the finished paper to check over. Both he and Barbara scrutinised it very thoroughly. Ladies and gentlemen" he said most solemnly "I have to tell you that after all the hard work in sorting it out to an acceptable conclusion… you have made a damned good job of it congratulations and thank you." They all then applauded themselves. He gave the script to Barbara and asked her to put the finishing touches to it and to make sure you make enough copies. She left the room to do what Bill had asked.

"Now ladies and gentleman I will put you in the picture of what I have planned for the next two days. Tomorrow, Lieutenants Deacon and Dean will make themselves available to receive the intakes whose ETA is approximately 3pm. You know the drill about accommodating and settling them down you have done it often enough. You will not have time to teach them room discipline that can be done Monday morning. Thursday morning you will march your recruits to the station cinema to be seated at 9.45am. The rest of you will also report there at that time with your entire staff. The Commanding officer will welcome the intakes to the station and I will follow him with my expectations of them. You all will make your way on stage, you as team leaders will be introduced, you will then introduce your team individually, I call it familiarization. Any questions so far? None? Good. That concludes that part of the proceedings. There will be a short interval to allow the station personnel who wish to see the film show to enter. The films will consist of the RAF BlueBelles Drill Team and they will be followed by our recent Passing-out Parade which took place on this station. I will give an introductory talk on each. Have you any questions?" Anyway if you are not too sure of anything at the time I will be on hand to help."

"I would like to thank you for your interest, co-operation and most of all for being part of a team I can be proud of."

He received a ripple of applause in reply.

Leaving the conference room he made his way to see Captain Fahima in the Training Offices. He knocked on her door and entered. He told her to remain seated when she began to rise to her feet. He told her about Thursday's programme. I want you to be present for me to introduce you to your young ladies as I am doing with the rest of the training team; Major Khatib is also being roped in for the same reason as yourself. You need not do any talking I will do that I will tell them what your roles are. Are you happy with that Captain?"

"Yes sir but I hope I do not get stage fright."

"There will be no fear of that you will not be on stage long enough to get that."

They both laughed about it. "How are things in here have you any problems at all?"

"No sir everything is fine. Thank you for your lovely magazine I will treasure that."

"And I would like to thank you for your contribution it was most kind of you. I must leave you now to give the Major his instructions for Thursday."

He gave the staff a wave as he made his way to the Major's office. "Hello George have you got your staff under control?"

"They are no problem, it was a good day for us all when you first arrived and turfed us out of that TV room. Just look at the difference in them now they are never idle, we all have a lot to thank you for."

Bill told him about Thursday morning, "

When he returned to his office Barbara had the schedules printed out for him. "Well done Barbara some of these will now be pinned up in the recruits' accommodation. I will distribute some of them tomorrow morning it is too late now, how many have you printed off?"

"Twenty, I think that should be enough for now sir."

"Excellent Barbara, will you ring for Fred please?"

Fred saluted. "Had good day sir and has everything gone according to plan?"

"Everything is tickety-boo Fred it could not be better. I will tell you something else too; this new Training Establishment is going to be a winner.

"Those were the exact words of the grapeviners sir. I told them about us having to wait to be called into the cinema and they promised to be on their best behaviour."

They bought their magazines today and asked if you would sign them."

"Bring them with you in the morning and I will do the honours then."

"I already have them here sir" he said with a smile.

"When we arrive home Fred I will sign them with pleasure. Is there anything they would like me to write?"

"Just the usual 'With Best Wishes', please."

Bill duly signed the ten copies. "If you get any more bring them in and I will sign them. Salaam Fred."

"Salaam Sir."

CHAPTER 42

"Good morning sir" greeted Fred throwing up a smart salute.

"Good morning Fred" Bill replied with a salute "This is the big day sir many interested people are looking forward to. Are you excited?"

"Yes Fred I am. This is the first time I have ever constructed a Training Establishment from scratch but the icing on the cake will be when it is up and running to my satisfaction."

"What can go wrong sir?"

"Nothing that I can think of Fred but we have a saying on occasions like this… 'There is many a slip twixt cup and lip' which means not to take things for granted."

"Before I forget sir the grapeviners thank you for signing their magazines they say it makes them more of a collector's item.

"They are not being mercenary and thinking of flogging them to the highest bidder are they?"

Fred laughed "I would not think so sir they think too much of you to do that."

"I am a very fortunate man to have made so many good friends here in Aljibia. When my Military Service comes to a close Fred I think I will seriously think of making it my permanent home. Got to go now duty calls I will see you later you will let me know what has happed today won't you."

"You can count on me sir." Salaam."

"Salaam Fred."

"Good morning Barbara how are you this lovely morning?"

"Not quite as chirpy as you Bill but I am feeling alright thank you."

"Will you ring Major Khatib and ask him to send either Deacon or Dean over and then ask Rashid to send one of his staff. Then ask Amina to send one of her staff. We can give them their schedule sheets it will save me traipsing around with them, why have a dog and bark oneself. I am going to take these films to the cinema staff in readiness for tomorrow's showing."

"Bill! don't forget your bleep."

At the cinema he explained to the staff of the sequence of events which would take place.

"The last time when you held a similar occasion it went like clockwork and there is no reason why it should not do the same this time sir, you can rely on us not to let you down."

He returned to his office and said to Barbara. "I am wandering around like somebody lost and waiting for something to happen."

"That is because you are too well organised. You must accept that everything that needed doing has been done so you must sit, relax and clock watch until 3pm. She said laughing."

"Now what is the point of preaching to me then telling me to clock watch?"

"That was just to cheer you up sir."

"Then cheer me up with something worth while like…a brew!"

When she brought it he asked, "Have you made yourself one?"

"Yes sir."

"Then bring it in here and let us have a chat." When she did so he asked. "When you go to the UK for a break I presume you do fly but by which airline?"

"Being employed by the military I use the same aircraft as you do but I do get a good concession on my ticket."

"Can a non- government employee use that airline?"

"No they have to use a private company airline. They are very good but it is like a bus route with too many stops."

"Talking to Fred on the way here this morning he said something that must have triggered something off in my head because I said to him. "You know Fred when my Military career comes to a close I will seriously consider living here permanently. You have lived here a few years what are your thoughts on permanent residence would you recommend it Barbara?"

"I love it here Bill, you know how friendly the people are, the cost of living is low and with your government gratuity and pension you will be able to afford a nice Villa similar to what you have now. I don't know about the style you live in at present that would depend on the government's generosity for services rendered. Personally I think you could live here quite happily in real comfort."

"Thank you very much Barbara I appreciate what you have told me. It gives me something to mull over. Both Tommy and I like it here, Tommy really loves it but does she love it enough to make her want to stay here permanently? I will keep this knowledge to myself Barbara and see if she changes when my contract comes up for renewal or ends as the case may be."

"It will definitely not end Bill because you are needed here."

"Is it time for lunch yet Barbara?"

"In another hour it will be why are you hungry?"

"I am, do you think I will have time to nip home for a Bacon Butty I could just murder one right now."

"Do you mind if we change the subject because you have got my taste buds going now."

"Did I ever tell you about the young airman who was always so late that he had no time to finish his breakfast? He had a pal who worked in the cookhouse who would invariably make him a Bacon Butty when he was on duty then the airman would run to join the work parade with the rest of his mates with the Bacon Butty hidden on top of his head underneath his headgear. He would then eat it when they had arrived at his place of work. One day the airmen were being inspected for haircuts by their Squadron Officer. When he came to inspect this lad he sniffed then peered at the nape of his neck. You want to change to Brylcreme airman the hair cream you are using is running down your neck and it smells bloody awful."

"Yuk! How awful, fancy eating it after being on his head for goodness knows how long."

"Young recruits in any of the Armed Forces when they are getting plenty of forced exercise develop a tremendous appetite and will eat just about anything. Speaking of appetites I am ready for my lunch."

At the Luncheon Box Alfred and Dot were already tucking into their meal.

"Have you had an industrious morning?" asked Bill.

"Not really, we introduced ourselves to the respective housekeepers and spent a little time with them checking the accommodation to make sure that all was in order."

"Well don't worry when you see me lurking in the background this afternoon I will just be watching the reactions of the recruits."

At 2:30pm Alfred and Dot were waiting to guide the coaches as near as possible to their respective accommodations. They had not long to wait before four coaches made their appearances then Alfred and Dot took charge by stepping on each coach in turn to tell the occupants to form up in three ranks and to stop any congestion by the second coach waiting until the first one has emptied but please take your time and care stepping down from your coach. When they had formed up in three ranks with their baggage which invariably consisted of two large holdalls they were addressed by their Officer i/c. Alfred and Dot both worked with a similar pattern. "Raise your arms the ones who would like their friend if you have one who you would like to occupy an adjacent room to you. After some confusion Dot finally sorted them out. "In fifteen minutes I want everyone outside formed up in three ranks."

Meanwhile Alfred was getting more co-operation from his airmen. They were quicker on the uptake and in a matter of minutes each one entered his own room. "You have five minutes then I want you outside in three ranks. In the five minutes they were all there in three ranks facing Alfred. "Stand easy and relax but no talking until I give you permission. I am Lieutenant Deacon your Drill Instructor for the entire time you will be on this course. First and foremost at all times I am with you I expect you to converse in English, you have no excuse for not speaking English because it is your second language. That is the only advantage you have over me because I do not have a second language and for you to disregard that request it would mean you would be acting in a discourteous manner towards me. I would like you to think about that. You are expected to keep your rooms neat and tidy according to regulations, on Monday I will demonstrate what that means. The Sergeant Housekeeper cum Security means just that, he is not a servant. In the Ablutions especially you will clean your own mess; any single person not doing so will result in a collective punishment where you all will clean the place thoroughly in your own free time. Tomorrow morning you will parade for inspection at 8:30am. At 9:45am you will be sat in the cinema to be addressed by the Station Commander, followed by a film show. I will now dismiss you are and you will perform your first piece of drill, which is, you make a right turn, salute, pause, then break away. I advise you to read the notices pinned on the noticeboard. From now on you will be addressed as a 'flight' for training purposes. You should now be stood easy – that means your body is relaxed your hands held together behind your back. I will call 'Flight!' That is called the cautionary command, which means other commands will follow; you then brace your body, waiting for the next order, which will be 'Atten...shun'. You bring your feet together at the same time, bringing your arms down by your sides. I will demonstrate what I mean," which he did. "Do you understand?"

He got a very little response some even just nodded their heads. He then shouted. "DO YOU UNDERSTAND?" The response was a weak 'yes sir'.

"FLIGHT! Come on wake up. I told you to brace yourselves. So I will start again. FLIGHT...Atten...Shun! Right, we might be getting somewhere. You are now alert to the next order or are you? FLIGHT... DIS...MISS!"

Some turned left some overbalanced and some did it right by saluting.

"Go on, fall out and practice. I want you shaping up better than that in the morning."

When they dispersed he went to have a word with the Sergeant.

"Do not stand any nonsense from them, but we cannot expect much at this early stage. Let me have a report each morning, please."

Dot was having a trying time with her brood. Her address to them was pretty much on a par with Alfred's. The difference was that many of them decided not to listen but talk to their neighbours in their native tongue. When she got their attention she reminded them that she had requested them not to speak in their native language when she was present.

"Unfortunately we have amongst us some very ignorant people who have no idea what discourtesy means or even care. To them I say 'your disgusting behaviour will not be tolerated here so you had better get it out of your system right now or it will lead you into a lot of trouble'. Tomorrow morning you will parade here at 8:30am for an inspection. At 9:45am you will be seated in the cinema for a welcome address from the Station Commander." She told the eight girls who had caused the disruption to "come out front; the rest of you return to your rooms. You eight follow me." She took them to Captain Fahima's office. "Wait there," she ordered, while she went in to report their conduct to the Captain.

"Bring them in then please. Wait outside, because I can really give them a good roasting in their own language. You don't mind do you Lieutenant?"

"Not at all Ma'am." Dot saluted, then brought in the girls.

It took a good ten minutes before the Captain had finished with the girls, who left the office in tears. The Captain beckoned Dot to come in. "I do not think you will have any more trouble from them Lieutenant, I have ordered them to make a public apology to you and the rest of the girls tomorrow on your first parade. Thank you for bringing this nasty incident to my attention; we do not want any more incidents like that. I have made a note of their names for future reference."

"Everything appears to have gone well Barbara, it is now home time, will you ring for Fred please?"

"Are you ready for home sir, after having a busy time at the office?" Fred asked, giving Bill a salute and a wry smile.

"You are not wrong there Fred. On the whole it has been a boring day and I'm glad it's over."

"I don't think you are the only one to think that; not a boring day but glad it is over."

"Sounds interesting, tell me about it."

"Your Lieutenant Dean had cause to take eight of the girl recruits to Captain Fahima where apparently they received a real rollicking and left in tears. Your Lt. D had requested them not to speak in their native tongue when she was present and apparently they just ignored the request."

"Thanks for that info Fred, they were getting that request in my talk to them tomorrow, now I can stress it."

"Another thing, the Captain has ordered them to make a public apology to Lt. D. and the rest of the girls on their first parade tomorrow."

"And I thought everything had gone well for them."

"Your Lieutenant Deacon is going to have fun with his lot. He gave them a right turn, some of them turned left and others lost their balance. Who would be a Drill Instructor?"

"Take a look at them in a week's time Fred you will not recognise them as the same recruits!"

"Here we are, home sweet home, I will see you tomorrow Fred, Salaam and thanks for all the info'."

"Salaam sir."

Tommy greeted him with a kiss. "Your beer will be waiting for you when you get changed love.

When he returned he asked what kind of a day she had had.

"Nothing much, I just did a bit of titivating around the house, I tried changing some things but it was just a waste of time. I am going to phone Viv later to see if the magazines have arrived. I am dying to hear their reactions."

"It is probably too early yet I would think it could be nearer weekend."

"Well I want a chat with her anyway."

"Dinner is ready Ma'am called Leila."

"Coming Leila."

"And how are my favourite Chef and housekeeper today?" Gushed Bill.

"How many Chefs and Housekeepers have you got" demanded Tommy.

"Only the one more which is you my love but with Thomas and Leila I get two for the price of one."

"There is no answer to that Bill Barrett" said Tommy as she shook her head looking at a laughing Thomas and Leila. "Give him his dinner Thomas to shut him up then I can have mine in peace."

Over coffee Bill asked Tommy. "Everything is under control now that the Training School has opened officially, what do you say we take some leave and go visiting our friends?"

"Oh Bill, that would be lovely when are you thinking of us going and for how long?"

"Can you get packed up to leave on Monday morning for four weeks?"

"You just try and stop me, come here let me give you a kiss."

"I have been making tentative plans. We spend a couple of days with the Jacksons then some time with Jackie then a few days with Nessie returning to stay with Jackie and concluding with two days with the Jacksons. What do you think of that?"

"Yes, I think that sounds fine Bill but we will have to let Jackson know now."

"Ring Ella and ask her if she had to pay airfare when she went to the UK."

"Ella, Tommy here we are taking some leave to the UK tell me will I have to pay airfare?"

"No Tommy, it is in Bill's contract that his next of kin travel free. All Bill needs to do is contact the airport to inform them that you both will be travelling whenever and giving your return date. If you have pen and paper handy I will give you the telephone number to ring. When are you thinking of going Tommy?"

"On Monday for a month,"

"I wish I was coming with you."

"Thanks Ella I will be in touch before we leave." She then told Bill and explained what he must do, by ringing them love you can get the proper procedures. Go on give them a bell!"

He rang the number Ella gave them. A voice asked in English Hello can I help you?"

"Good evening I am Colonel Barrett." He got no further…

"Colonel Barrett this is an honour your exploits precede you and you are held in very high esteem with all the staff here. How can I help you sir?"

Bill explained his concern over the procedures with not having previously taken leave of absence from duty and taking his wife with him.

"All you need do Colonel is give me the date you wish to travel and the same for your return journey, then all you and your wife need do is show your I.D cards to the staff at check-in, your flight leaves at 5am."

"Thank you very much for your help and for living up to the tradition of Aljibia being a friendly country Salaam."

"It is a privilege to have been of some help to you Colonel Barrett, have a safe journey and enjoy your leave I am sure you have earned it. Salaam."

"That was easy peasy, all we need do is tell them when we want to fly, show our I.D.s at check-in and everything is done for us."

"Now phone Jackson and tell him?"

Bill got on the phone and rang the number. "Hello Jackson speaking." "Hello Barrett speaking."

"Bill, how are you old friend? It is great to hear you again…'Joyce it is Bill calling.' We were only talking about you this morning about your magazine; yes we got it this morning Hey! What a belter it is too thanks very much and for the CDs I have shown them a number of times at the club, and I have earned more Brownie points by doing so."

"Jackson I haven't much time because Tommy wants a word with Joyce but have you got room for two lodgers on Monday for a couple of days?"

"You both can stop for two bloody years if you want Bill"

"That's all I want to know for now here is Tommy, you get Joyce."

"Tommy explained to Joyce the reason they were coming to the UK., after they had a little chat Tommy said she had to do some more phoning but we will make up for it when we see you, love from us two to you two."

"Tommy, Jackson said he will pick you up at Heathrow. Bye.e.e."

"Jackson is picking us up at Heathrow, Bill. So they have got the magazines it should be interesting when we speak to Viv. Now how do we break the news we are coming on leave, do I say nothing but phone Jackie to say when she can expect us or what?"

"Say nothing then phone Jackie tomorrow she will tell them. If we tell Viv tonight it will spoil it for Jackie seeing that we will be staying with her."

"Yes I think you are right. She then phoned the Sergeant Mess."

"Sergeants Mess" said a female voice.

"I would like to speak to Warrant Officer Anderson please." Is that you Tommy?" said an excited voice, "this is Marion Maken." They chatted a bit until Tommy asked her if she would get Viv. A minute later Viv came to the phone. "Hi Tommy she said panting from hurrying. "I should have known you would ring after our huge mail delivery this morning. Reception was overwhelmed never having had so much bulk Mail before. Jackie, Bless her said 'I hope there is one waiting for me at home'. There is talk of nothing else but Bill in the Mess at present because everyone who received a magazine was thrilled to bits and more so because you had remembered them. You should see Roy he is like a dog with two tails and so is everybody else Tommy, but isn't it a lovely magazine the front cover has captivated everyone and I am so proud of Dot and Alfred."

"When we did the proof reading Bill was not over pleased to see just him on the cover so he helped the artist to include Alfred and Dot and had them positioned just how he wanted and what a difference it made. How is Anisa getting on Viv?"

"Absolutely fine I have never met anyone who is so enthusiastic in what she is doing and I think most do like her because she is so friendly and easy to get along with and she is beginning to enjoy our food too. Can I send mine and everyone else's thanks to Bill he is so considerate and can you blame his staff for saying all those wonderful things about him in the magazine and I for one agree with them all. Salaam Tommy. See I am learning a bit from Anisa."

Tommy laughed. "The next time you want her to understand something you say, finish off with Mashy? Which means Okay? You will have her in hysterics; she will not expect that coming from you, Salaam Viv, Mashy?"

"Mashy Tommy" she replied giggling.

She looked at Bill who was in a deep sleep and at peace with the world; I might as well go and get supper ready first before I waken him.

.

CHAPTER 43

"Good morning sir" said Fred with his usual salute and greeting.

"Good morning to you Fred" Bill replied then returned the salute. "Have you anything fresh from the grapeviners?"

"I certainly have sir; you are advised to keep an eye on those eight who caused disruption yesterday."

"I would like to use the car phone Fred."

Dot, Bill here, watch those eight girls I have it on good authority they are out to cause more disruption. What time are you parading them?"

"8:30 sir, thanks for the warning."

"Drop me off at the side of their accommodation Fred they will have their backs to me when they parade then I can get nearer to hear what goes on." Fred did as he was told then drove off leaving Bill in what he hoped was a concealed position. At 8:25 Dot appeared on the scene and waited for the girls to turn out. By 8:30 they all had formed up in three ranks except the eight girls. Dot waited for five minutes then she and the Sergeant Security woman went to investigate. They knocked on all the doors with no response so Dot told her to use her master key to open the doors. When she did they found all the rooms empty and each one had been trashed. Bill saw Dot come out looking frustrated and thought he should show himself. He came out of hiding and went to Dot who explained what had happened.

"Have you got their names?"

"No sir but Captain Fahima has."

He addressed the parade. "Do any of you know anything about the eight girls who have apparently absconded; did you hear anything at all?"

One girl said she thought she heard movement about 3am but thought it was someone going to the toilet.

"Thank you. Right Lieutenant, I am off to see Captain Fahima you try and carry on as normal…if you can" he said with a smile.

He entered Captain Fahima's office. "Good morning Captain, no don't get up, can you give me the names of those eight girls you chastised yesterday please?" He then told her what Dot had found this morning. "Obviously they have absconded and I need their names for security to find and arrest them but first I must report the incident to the Station Commander."

"Tell the Station Commander I must see him immediately it is an emergency" he told the PA.

"Tell the Colonel to come in straight away" he told his PA.

Bill knocked, entered and saluted.

"What is this emergency Bill?"

When Bill told him the tale Eric contacted security giving them the girls' names. "Their I.D.s will be held in the Administrative building, very good thank you. It is now in the hands of security have you any idea what could have brought this on?"

"When Bill told him he replied. Thank goodness we did not waste our time training them. I think I will get an official photographer to photograph each of those rooms they may come in useful at their trial." He ordered his P.A. to get him the security person in the Airwomen's accommodation.

"You are through sir."

"Sergeant this is the Station Commander, the eight rooms from which those eight girls absconded must be kept secured. A photographer will be coming to take pictures of those rooms check his I.D. then open each room for him to do his job. Do you understand? You do? Good."

"That is taken care of Bill so I will see you about five to ten Mashy?"

"Mashy sir."

"Good morning Barbara and before you rap my knuckles I am not late for for my work Parade and I have not got a Bacon Butty under my headgear."

"Silly beggar! What was the hold up?"

"When he told her she couldn't believe it. Why the horrible little creatures what will happen to them when they are caught?"

~ 286 ~

"For their absence or they might call it desertion here, plus the damage to their living quarters they will have to face a trial which could result in a prison sentence.

Anyone who does wrong should be punished that is the creed here so the Emir told me."

"Are you coming to the cinema Barbara?"

"I would love to."

"Then we have time for a brew before we go."

On the way to the cinema Bill said. "You know that chat we had which included holidays and airlines, well on Monday I am taking a month's leave and we fly out Monday morning to the UK. Tell me would you get pay for a month's leave?"

"Oh yes that is in my contract."

"Isn't free air travel included in your contract?"

"Not that I am aware of."

"When you get home today get your contract out and have a good shufti at it."

"This leave of yours is a bit sudden don't you think?"

"Everything is organised here and all the staff know what they are doing, at present I am just excess baggage, so I say let them get on with it."

When they entered the cinema they saw that all the ones who had to be there were. He chatted with them for a little while then he excused himself, "I want to see the new intakes marching here."

Outside he watched them some distance away trying their very best to look smart. As they got nearer he smiled to hear the coaxing words from Alfred and the smooth words of command coming from Dot. The flight of airwomen swung round to be brought to a halt then turned in line to face the cinema with the Airmen following suit. They entered the cinema in single file and were ushered to their seats by a member of the cinema staff. Bill went and had a word with Alfred and Dot. "For their first time of marching together your flights did well, well done both of you."

"What is happening about the runaway eight sir?"

He told them what action had been taken. "You had better get to your places now the CO will be arriving any minute."

When Eric pulled up in his chauffeur driven car and stepped out Bill threw him up a very smart salute. "Good morning Colonel are we all ready for the fray?"

"We are as ready as we will ever be sir" Bill replied.

"Then as they say in the movies Colonel, let's get this show on the road."

On entering, Bill who had entered first bellowed "Station Commander Present" and everyone rose to their feet. When the Station Commander went on stage he faced them and said. "Please be seated."

He began. "Ladies and gentlemen for the benefit of our new arrivals, permit me to introduce myself. I am Brigadier Khaleel the Station Commander. I would like to welcome you all to my station. You are very fortunate to be the No.1 Entry in a brand new School of Recruit Training, in years to come you will proudly boast that you were in the No.1 Entry. My staff who will introduce themselves shortly are all hand picked and selected for their expertise and professionalism. I wanted the best instructors for you and a search was made both near and far to get the best and we succeeded. We have adopted a saying from Colonel Barrett which I hope you will all take on board, it goes like this, 'If you give respect you will get respect'. Thank You."

He received a good round of applause as he made his way to his seat.

Bill took centre stage and introduced himself. "I am Colonel Barrett." Immediately he got a burst of enthusiastic applause. Thank you what a wonderful welcome I hope you are as enthusiastic when I have finished my little chat but please no over ripe tomatoes they leave such terrible stains on my uniform." He knew he had got them in a good mood from the loud laughter. I am responsible for your training at all levels so if anything does not meet with your satisfaction…blame me. I cannot visualise any of you complaining because you have got some very dishy looking instructors of both sexes." He got giggling from the airwomen and wolf whistles from the airmen…"My sentiments exactly" this also brought lots of laughter. *He thought to himself carry on Bill you have them eating out of your hand.* I apologise for now bringing a spot of doom and gloom just when we were enjoying ourselves but it has to be brought to your attention. This morning eight airwomen decided that this was not the life for them, instead of seeking help they took matters into their own hands by trashing their accommodations and absconding during the night. I deduce that what triggered it off was after their Drill instructor Lieutenant Dean had requested that in her presence they should not converse in their native language but in English knowing of course it is your second language and my second language is also English. But what a coincidence, English is my first language as well." That caused an uproar of laughter, when it had died down he continued. "However, almost immediately the 'runaway eight, began conversing in their own tongue in defiance. Naturally the Lieutenant had no option but to take them to a higher authority namely Captain Fahima who took a dim view of the incident. By trying to bring it to an amicable close she ordered the 'runaway eight' to publicly apologise to the Lieutenant and the rest of the airwomen in the flight on their first parade. The result was as I have already told you. The Station Commander has placed the matter in the hands of the Security Police and I can assure you it will be sooner than later before they are recaptured and placed in a cell to wait for trial. It was a serious offence and they will be sentenced accordingly. What I say to you is, if you have a complaint or need advice please come to see us especially the lady who offers her shoulder for you to cry on but she will charge you to have her tunic dry cleaned." That brought another roar of laughter. "All we ask of you is…come on say it the Station Commander has already given you a clue, now altogether after me "If you give Respect you will what? In unison they all shouted "GET RESPECT" in the midst of their laughter they applauded him. "That was good I think we are friends now, what are we?"

"Friends sir."

"Now let us get down to some serious business. It is my privilege to introduce my staff, my second in Command, Major Khatib. The Major can be found in our Training Offices where he will welcome you airmen who do not want to cry on a female's shoulder unless she is in the same age group as yourselves. He will listen to your complaints and your troubles in fact he will act as a stand-in father to you." More laughter and applause for the Major. Next is the lady you are all dying to meet who will give you a kiss and a cuddle…if you are lucky, the lady who has now had her tunic shoulders waterproofed…Captain Fahima." The Captain got a good round of applause amid laughter of course. Next is the man you have already met, you girls have that pleasure to come. Your male Drill Instructor Lieutenant Deacon." This time the wolf whistles came from the girls. "He is an expert in Drill which you will find as you progress and if you want to make him a friend for life ask him about football."

"Next is Lieutenant Dean our Queen of Drill another expert who can make you girls think you are ballet dancers when you are drilling to her commands. I will let you girls into a little secret; she will hate me for telling you this. Her prowess spread to a Television advertising company who approached her and wanted her to make a TV advert of her drilling Airwomen to the tune of the Nut Cracker Suite. She refused of course saying 'Do you think I'm Nuts?' Dot shook her fist at Bill in mock anger amid a great roar and applause intermingled with wolf whistles from the boys.

"It is now my pleasure to introduce the fittest people on the station, the Physical Education staff. These are the men and women who are sure to find muscles you did not know you had, they are led by Captain Rasheed" who then introduced his staff. "His staff" continued Bill "specialise in most sports from basket ball to football and gymnastics. Finally, Lieutenant Amina Head Teacher and her staff of masterminds of the Education Section otherwise known as School Teachers. That of course is the old fashioned name for Education Teachers." Lieutenant Amina introduced her staff then Bill continued. "You will find that they teach Adult Education for character building and you will be amazed at what you did not know of the world at large. Thinking about it, when you have finished this course you will all leave here as muscle-bound robots marching around spouting quotations from an encyclopaedia. I should go home if I was you. Thank you for your attention…End of Broadcast!"

The audience rose to their feet laughing and giving him a great ovation. When it had quietened down he said. "Thank you once again you are very kind. We will have a few minutes respite while the station staff who want to see the film show come in."

The staff congratulated him for such a laughable experience. When the Station Commander beckoned him over he greeted Bill with a big smile and a handshake. "I do not know Bill when I last laughed so much, but you really had them eating out of your hand and they loved every minute of it, thank you it has made my day."

When a cinema staff member began ushering the people in he was constantly asked. "What has been going on in here all we could hear were roars of laughter?"

You missed a treat you should have heard the Colonel he had everybody almost rolling in the aisles. He was so funny."

When everyone had settled down Bill went back on stage to receive another round of applause. "I wouldn't applaud just yet If I was you because you never know what is going to happen. Welcome to all you late comers to the Aljibian Mad House. You are lucky by just being allowed in; these people were not so lucky they were a captive audience and could not get out." I will show two films, the first being The Royal Air Force Drill Team known as the BlueBelles versus the women's Royal Navy team the WRENS and the favourites to win the WRACS of the Army. I will not tell you the result I will leave you to judge who will be the winners. First may I give you the history of the BlueBelles and how it came about? I don't care if you don't want to know because I am going to tell you anyway because I was responsible for their training." That caused some laughter. "He began right from the beginning with the challenge between them and a team of airmen. He had them laughing by telling of the antics and incidents that took place such as the de-bagging of Mr Teeny Weeny the Knock -out Kid and the Wibbly Wobblies, they laughed their heads off at that. He progressed to BlueBelles 2 and told them how the competition came about. I would like to stress that the members of the BlueBelles 2 Team had only been in recruit training for three weeks the exception were two members of the team who had been in recruit training for only two weeks. My task was to produce a winning team in six weeks; shall we have a shufti to see what happened? Incidentally for most of the time no commands were given to the BlueBelles."

He gave the signal to the projectionist to commence then went and sat with Barbara.

She whispered "You were wonderful."

It was relatively quiet during the film until the BlueBelles marched on to perform their routine then the murmurs of encouragement increased as they were shouted to the screen in support of the BlueBelles. When the team automatically switched to their specialised programme then the tempo of excitement increased in the auditorium. When the BlueBelles finished their routine and marched off singing their signature song the applause from the audience was terrific. When it came the time to declare the winner there was deathly silence as they listened for the announcement. The winners of the Three Services Challenge title are…The RAF BlueBelles. The auditorium erupted with shouts, cheering and applause; it was deafening which carried on for what seemed minutes. Bill got on the stage to shouts of 'Well Done Colonel'. Bill held up his hands to quieten the audience down. On behalf of the BlueBelles Team I would like to thank you for the wonderful reception you have given them it was quite something and I think you will agree with me they deserve every bit of the recognition and applause you have given them. The next film to be shown is nearer to home, it is the Passing out Parade of our last intake. The success of the performance was due to Lieutenants Deacon and Dean who were recruited to train them to a high standard of drill for their Passing –out Parade in just two weeks. Previous to this the same Airmen recruits had very little training due to an incompetent Sergeant whilst the airwomen did very much better with a Female Sergeant so you can appreciate that the two Lieutenants had quite a mammoth task facing them, but their expertise and skill won. You will see from the film the result of their dedication to bring out the best in young people. I will leave you to judge the outcome." He signalled the projectionist to commence.

As soon as the two flights came marching onto the parade ground the audience began to applaud and so it continued throughout the film until the recruits began their specialised routine then the applause turned to cheers until Bill appeared on stage with Alfred and Dot to receive a standing ovation who then bowed solemnly to the audience.

Bill then addressed the new intakes. "You have seen all the good that comes from dedication which is brought about by hard work. The young people in the film have shown you young people what can be done, I am not asking you to emulate their skill and success but there is no reason why you cannot. Your instructors will work you hard and they will not mollycoddle you but at the end of the course you will leave a different person to when you arrived. For your own sakes do not make it difficult for yourselves, do as you are told and keep your noses clean. Thank you for your attention and Good Luck."

He received a standing ovation for the wonderful show he had put on. He saluted them then left the stage. He escorted the CO out to his car. That was some show you put on Bill you have won the intakes over."

Bill saluted him as he was driven away. While he was waiting for the recruits to be marched away he spotted Fred who gave him a salute and held up both thumbs at the same time wearing a big smile. "There is Fred, Barbara"

She looked over and they both waved to each other.

"Shall we go straight on to lunch?" Bill asked.

"I want to go back to the office I want to freshen up first." was her reply.

On entering the Luncheon Box they were escorted to their table to loud applause from the diners who had been to the cinema." A little while later Alfred and Dot entered to applause which they acknowledged with mouthing thank you's and a lifting of their arms in response. They greeted Bill and Barbara. "You were wonderful Bill I had no idea you had so much talent hidden away. The audience's sides must have been aching through laughter I know mine were." said Dot.

"Yes it was some show you put on" said Alfred "it was like a Sunday night at the Palladium. What are you going to come up with next a vanishing trick?"

Bill winked at Barbara. "As a matter of fact Alfred I am going to do just that, funny you should mention it. Tommy and I are doing just that at 5am Monday morning."

"WHAT?" they both shouted startling the diners. "Obviously you are going to the UK with taking that flight how long are you going for just a few days" he was asked.

"A wee bit longer than that."

"Two weeks then."

"Put them out of their misery Bill" said a smiling Barbara.

"We are only going for a month."

"A MONTH! They both shouted.

"Keep your voices down do you want us to be asked to leave?" He said smiling apologetically to the other diners.

"So what are we supposed to do while you are away?" he was asked.

"You carry on as normal and if you can't I will have you replaced it is as simple as that."

"Please don't get us wrong sir" pleaded Dot "we did not mean it in that sense. "What we really mean is we are going to miss you for a whole month, what about our Saturday morning shopping trips to town and lunch out, you are gong to miss that."

"Dot please you are bringing tears to my eyes but I will strike a bargain with you. If you can persuade Tommy not to go then I will stay here and hold your hands."

"That is not fair you know Tommy will not give up a trip to see her friends."

"It will soon pass Dot perhaps more quickly for us than you; you will be too tied up with your young charges to notice time passing by. By the way we spoke to Viv last night, all the magazines arrived and everybody is chuffed to bits with the front cover I don't think they could have noticed you two, but Viv is very proud of you and Alfred. Well shall we go and have coffee? Then this afternoon Barbara we can just sit back and take it easy."

Later in the day when Bill was being driven home Fred said. "What a show you put on today sir the grapeviners could not stop talking and laughing all day about the jokes you made. The CO made a nice little opening speech."

"Hang on a minute Fred you weren't in at the beginning of the show you came in after I had addressed the recruits so how could you know about the CO's speech?"

Fred laughed. "We have a friend on the cinema staff who sneaked us upstairs into the circle and we watched the whole proceedings from there."

"Have the grapeviners got any gen about the runaway eight Fred?"

"Not yet sir but we are working on it."

"What do you mean you are working on it?"

"We have our ears to the ground, sir."

"I have some news for you Fred."

"It is old news now sir, if you are referring to taking leave for a month it is going to be quiet around here then. What are you going to do for a month appear on a West End Stage?"

"No I am going where I can get some peace and quiet away from people who know what I am going to do before I do."

"Then it is an early morning run for me on Monday morning."

"It certainly is and I will tell Mrs Barrett to carry a box of tissues in case you need some. Well here we are I will see you in the morning for my last day at work for a while. Salaam Fred."

"Salaam sir."

"Hello love" said Tommy giving him a kiss, have you had a good day?"

"Yes, it has been very interesting, what have you been up to?"

"Getting all my things that I am taking together then I will not forget anything I hope. I have told Thomas and Leila we are going on holiday and to use the food in the fridge we will replenish it when we get back. Tell Fred I will need him tomorrow at the same time, I want to buy a present for Jackie."

"We will have to go to the bank anyway on Saturday morning to change some money and don't forget you have to phone Jackie tonight."

"Dinner is ready Ma'am" called Leila.

"Good evening Thomas...Leila" greeted Bill as soon as he entered the kitchen. Something smells fishy in here, what have you been up to Chef? I am not sure but I think you are cooking a good old fashioned British Dish and I am not wrong in saying it is Fish and Chips and my taste buds are acting accordingly." When it was placed in front of him he never said a word until he had cleaned his plate. "Thomas, that was excellent thank you, I was going to say that I would recommend you to the Emir but if I did he would probably steal you from us."

After they had coffee Bill switched the Television on and within two minutes he was away with the fairies fast asleep. *It never fails Tommy said to herself.* After Thomas and Leila had gone back to their flat Tommy passed the time waiting to phone Jackie by seeing which clothes she was taking with her on Monday. Bill was still asleep when she went to the phone. "Hello Mum" the reply was a scream of delight from Jackie. They soon got into the non-stop chat routine which carried on for an hour until Tommy had to excuse herself, it will probably be Thursday when we come to you if there are any changes I will let you know. Bye Mum yes, love you too." She then went and got supper ready for when Noddy wakened up.

CHAPTER 44

"Good morning sir" greeted Fred as he saluted. "This is Happy Smiling Face Day."

"I hope somebody is going to make me happy how about the grapeviners?"

"Yes, they can do so on this auspicious occasion for you sir. The runaway eight have all been recaptured and are now languishing in a cell each in security feeling very despondent with them-selves."

"How is absconding classed here Fred, absconding, absent without leave or desertion?"

"Absent without leave sir, I believe over twenty eight days is classed as desertion. They will of course get hammered for damage to Government property."

"What will you do while I am away? By the way can you chauffeur Mrs Barrett tomorrow? Same time please."

"No problem sir it is always a pleasure to be of assistance to Mrs Barrett she is so appreciative. I will be found jobs working in the motor pool for that month."

"Is there anything you are wanting from the Arsenal F.C.I can get for you while I am in London Fred?"

"We the grapeviners would appreciate it if you would get scarves with the word Arsenal on which we could wear when we are watching them on Television. There are eleven of us sir!"

"That is no problem it will be my pleasure Fred."

"Here we are and I will see you later Salaam Fred."

"Salaam sir."

"Good morning Miss Battle anything new in the pipeline?"

"Those girls have been caught and apart from that nothing else, I think we are going to have a quiet day. The recruits have been stood down until Monday haven't they?"

"Ah, that reminds me I must go and have a word with Major Khatib he will be deputising for me. Incidentally did you check your contract appertaining to you qualifying for free travel?"

"I did and would you believe it I do qualify and in your parlance I was quite chuffed."

"Good I am pleased for you, how long is it since you were in the UK?"

"I have never been back since I came here."

"Will you be taking leave while I am away?"

"Yes I might as well otherwise I would find it very boring."

"Good for you I think you are doing the right thing. Well I will go and let the Major know he will be in charge, and I have my bleeper with me."

"Good morning George, is everything alright?"

"Good morning Bill, yes and we have no problems here."

"Why are Deacon and Dean not working in their office George?"

"They asked me if they could stay where they are because they get on so well with the other staff they have all become firm friends so I gave them permission. Now we have an empty office to spare."

"Now I like that George I support young people getting together in friendship. What I have come to see you about is to tell you that as of Monday you will be deputising for me for a month while I take a leave."

"That is no problem Bill, I hope you enjoy it, we will miss you though. You know I still keep laughing at the way you put those recruits at ease and they loved it and so did we."

"I'll go and have a word with Mother Fahima now." George had a good laugh as Bill was leaving…"Mother Fahima, that is a good one."

"Good morning Captain, how are you?"

"I am fine thank you sir."

"Do you know the runaway eight have been recaptured?"

"Yes I have heard so and now they are to be punished for being very silly, there was no need for that kind of behaviour it was contemptible."

"Indeed it was but they are now going to pay the price for that behaviour."

At that moment his bleeper showed he had to report to the Station Commander.

"Sorry Captain I am being paged."

He reported to Eric's PA who informed him that Colonel Barrett had arrived. Bill was told to go in. "Sit yourself down Bill; I would like you to stay here with me while I take the charges of the runaway eight."

"Won't you need Captain Fahima and Lieutenant Dean as witnesses' sir?"

"Yes, you are right I had better have them here just in case."

He told his PA to ask Captain Fahima and Lieutenant Dean to report to my office.

"Have you decided on their punishment sir?"

"Well seeing it is simply a cut and dried case. Yes I have and I shall sentence them all together."

"Captain Fahima and Lieutenant Dean are here sir." his PA informed him.

"Go and put them in the picture Bill and I had better have Captain Fahima in here as a witness to everything being conducted in a proper manner with all the accused being females."

"Very wise sir." he went to put Captain Fahima in the picture and please will you go and be witness to everything being conducted in a proper manner seeing that the accused are all females."

"I understand sir and that is a very wise decision."

"Lieutenant Dean you will wait here in case you are called as a witness."

"Very good sir."

There was a knock on the PA's door and a female security guard entered to say she had the accused outside.

"Line them up outside the Station Commander's door Sergeant he will take the charges with all the accused together, when he is ready I will call you in."

"The accused are outside sir waiting to be called in."

"Thank you Colonel I am now ready, call them in please."

Bill opened the door and opened his mouth to call them in. *My God he thought what a sight.* He saw eight frightened looking girls faces tear stained dressed in civilian clothes which looked like they had been slept in all the time they had been in the cells. They were escorted by two female Security Guards who would not have looked out of place in a wrestling ring. "March-in" he ordered. The girls not knowing any different walked in and lined up facing the CO.

"Why are you not wearing uniform?"

"We threw them away."

"Very well, I shall read out your official numbers and names and I want you to identify yourself as your name is called." That was carried out without a hitch. "Now I will read out the crimes you have committed and are being charged with. Damaging Government property your accommodation, absent without leave and now on your own admission destroying Government property your uniforms. How do you plead guilty or not guilty?"

Each in turn pleaded guilty.

"After great deliberation and taking into account your ages I award each of you Twenty Eight days Detention and on completing the sentence you are to be discharged from the Air Force, March them out."

After they left he told Bill and Captain Fahima "I was tempted to give them a longer sentence but did you see the wretched state they were in, they needed some pity. Thank you both."

They both saluted and left. Captain Fahima went to report the findings to Major Khaleel and Bill went to ask Major Hassan to repair the damage to the Airwomen's accommodation and to Lieutenant Hikmat to remove all bedding but not to replace it.

When Bill returned to his office it was time to go for lunch. "Are you ready for your lunch Barbara?"

"I am always ready for lunch about this this time but you are a little later than usual."

"I am, I have been with Eric and he has had the runaway eight before him to receive their punishment. Come on I will tell you all about it as we go along."

When she heard the whole story she said. "They got off very lightly for what they did the CO has a very kind heart."

When Fred came to take Bill home after work he saluted. In the car he said. "Those girls got off very lightly don't you think so sir?"

"I don't know Fred I was ready to see the book being thrown at them but you should have seen the state they were in. They were dishevelled and the clothes they were wearing looked as if they had been slept in since their arrest and they had a scared look in their eyes it made me think they might have been mistreated while in custody. You should have seen their two female escorts they were built like brick out-houses."

"How did you get on this morning did Mrs Barrett find what she was looking for?"

"I would not know about that but I had to help her in the house with her purchasers."

"Have you got anything special on tomorrow Fred?"

"No sir, do you want me to run you into town?"

"Yes please I have to go to the bank and no doubt Mrs B. will have forgotten something and the two rebels will want to come, Dot calls it a Saturday ritual but we like having them with us. So we will see you at the same time and at the same place.

Salaam Fred."

"Salaam sir."

Tommy greeted Bill with a kiss. "How has your day been love?"

"Quiet yet not a very pleasant one."

"Well go and freshen up your beer will be waiting and I will show you what we have bought Jackie."

When he returned and had a long drink of his beer he said "I believe you have had a nice little spend."

"Just one or two items I really needed but this for Jackie is something special which I think she will love." She took a necklace of multi-coloured semi precious stones from a jewellery box and showed it to Bill.

"Oh yes that is nice and I think that was made just for her, as you say she will love it. I have booked Fred for morning no doubt the two rebels will be coming along."

"Dinner is ready Ma'am said Leila."

"Good evening Thomas … Leila; are you both well?"

"Yes we are both fine sir."

"What culinary delight have you cooked for us today Thomas?"

"Something I have never tried before but with Mrs Barrett's supervision I think you will be pleased with it."

"Very well Chef, I am ready when you are."

Leila brought his plate with his meal under a cover. When she removed the cover his face wreathed in smiles. "I do not believe it, Steak and Kidney pudding! Thomas you are a star." He got stuck into it immediately and they never got a word out of him until he had devoured it all, revealing a very clean plate.

"You will have a good sleep after eating all that, as soon as you get sat in front of the television." Tommy said. "He is so predictable Thomas; when he has had a good meal he pays it a compliment by having a sound sleep."

And so it proved, because Tommy had to waken him up when it was bed time. Would you like some supper love?"

"No thanks, it will only spoil my dinner."

"Here comes Fred and he has got the dynamic Duo with him Bill"

"Did you expect them not to be? If they had not been in the car you would have been phoning them to ask why."

"Well, wouldn't you?"

"Good morning Fred," greeted Tommy. "Has my husband been treating you well this week?"

"Answer that at your peril," threatened Bill.

"Oh and what pray will you do to him, Bill Barrett?" spoke up an indignant Tommy.

"I will not let him drive us to the airport on Monday morning."

"You daft beggar," she uttered, amidst the laughter.

"Do you want me to pick you up at the same time as usual Mrs Barrett?"

"Yes please Fred."

"Where are you going Tommy, anywhere special?" asked Dot.

"I think I would like to have a shufti at the Souk this morning for a change."

"Oh that is a good idea; can I come with you please?"

"What about you Alfred?"

"No thanks, I want to have a shufti at the sports and camera shops."

"Can I come along with you Alfred?" asked Bill. "The Souk is not in my line."

"Of course you can, no problem."

"We will meet up at the usual place for lunch, Mashy?"

"Mashy Ma'am," said Alfred with a grin.

"Souks are never Bill's favourite shopping place Dot I think they are very interesting and so colourful."

"If you think about it Tommy and look around you, what is there here to attract a man? It is aimed primarily at us women, household and kitchen equipment, dresses, blouses, gaudy scarves, as you say it is very colourful and the sellers ply their art of sweet-talking us females. As they were walking past a stall selling books and magazines, the stallholder confronted them with The Aljibian Magazine, but printed in Arabic. Pointing to Dot on the front cover he asked, "You buy lady?" They paused in astonishment and that was what he wanted, he had their interest. He quickly opened the page which showed Tommy. He pointed at her and the picture and in perfect English said. "What a pleasure to meet you Ma'am but this picture does not do you justice; you are more beautiful to see. Would you care to buy a magazine as a souvenir?"

"But it is in Arabic, which I do not understand. Besides, I already have one in English."

Dot said, "I would like one as a memento, especially with it being in Arabic and I will buy one for Alfred. It will make quite a good talking point. If I buy one for Anisa will you take it to her, Tommy?"

"Of course I will. I will buy one for myself as well. We want four; what price are they?" When he told her the price Tommy said, "that is far too much, come down quite a bit". He dropped it a little. Still she was not satisfied.

"That is my lowest price Ma'am; I cannot afford to go any lower."

"In that case I will go and have a word with the Chief Editor of the Newspaper that printed these he will give them to me free."

"OK lady, you drive a hard bargain, but I have some hungry mouths to fill at my home." He offered her a price she could not refuse.

"Thank you" she said, giving him a gracious smile as she offered him the money. Her parting shot was, "remember young man, money does not grow on trees."

"Thank you Ma'am for your advice, but if you look around my stall you will not find a sign which states 'This is a Charity Stall'."

They got out of earshot before they could have a good laugh.

Alfred guided Bill to a sports shop. "I want a pair of training shoes for my work-outs in the gym." He chose which he wanted and at the cash desk he was told. "It is my pleasure to give you a good discount sir."

"Thank you very much, that is most kind of you, but I did not see anything that said there would be a discount."

"No sir, you wouldn't..." He pulled out from beneath the counter a copy of The Aljibian Magazine "...but *this* said it."

"May I borrow your pen sir?" Alfred asked. He then promptly signed his name in the magazine. Bill then took the pen and signed it. They all shook hands to the absolute delight of the shopkeeper, who was profuse with his thanks.

"Well that was a kind gesture. What do you get when you give respect Bill?"

"You get respect," he replied with a smile.

A similar incident happened when Alfred bought his camera. The shopkeeper also pulled The Aljibian Magazine from under his counter saying. "This is your private discount book gentlemen."

The shopkeeper could not believe his eyes when both Alfred and Bill signed the book. He shook their hands saying. "Thank you so very much I will really treasure it."

"It looks like we will need to take a pen with us in future when we go shopping Bill."

"You know what will happen now Alfred; we will have to accompany the girls in the shops when they want to buy something."

They met up with Tommy and Dot, who were sat with a drink each, waiting for them. "You took your time. Didn't you know we have been here ages waiting?" complained Tommy.

"You cannot just walk into a shop to buy a camera, point at one then say 'I will have that one', pay for it, then walk out," Alfred told her.

"Alright, you have made your point. You don't deserve the presents we have bought you."

"That sounds very interesting," said Bill. "When can we have them?"

"Here you are dear, and this one is for you Alfred, from Dot." When she handed them the magazines Bill and Alfred burst out laughing.

"That is gratitude for you!" snorted Tommy.

"Hang on a minute love, while we tell you why we are laughing."

Bill then unfolded the tale. Tommy saw the funny side of it and the boys were forgiven. She then told her tale of how they had bought them, which caused another bout of laughter.

"Thanks anyway, they will definitely be a talking point. Do you think you will be able to pronounce your names in Arabic?" asked Bill. "Come on let us go and have lunch…"

Back in the car they gave Fred a good laugh when Tommy told him about her and Dot's adventure in the Souk. When they arrived at the Villa Alfred and Dot were asked if they were coming to the club with them tonight.

"No thanks Tommy, it really is not my scene, but I will pop in to see you sometime tomorrow."

"You will be watching your football Alfred."

"I will, but I also will come and see you tomorrow."

When they got inside Leila told them that Mrs Whittaker had phoned.

"I had better phone her back, she will want us to go to the club, I expect. Hello Ella… but of course… right then… see you about 8pm… Salaam."

Bill went into the kitchen. "Hello Thomas. Have I time to have a beer before dinner?"

"Yes sir, dinner will not be ready for another hour."

Bill then went off to freshen up and when he returned there was a beer waiting for him. "I like the service in this hotel," he said, taking a good long swig. He settled himself down and within a couple of minutes was sound asleep, only to be awakened by Tommy when dinner was ready.

When John and Ella arrived, the first thing Ella asked was, "When are you going on leave?"

Tommy told her. "And we are going for a month, which looks like we will be having a hectic time visiting this body and that body. I expect we shall be glad to get back here for a rest."

"Did you contact the official at the airport, Bill," asked Ella.

"I did, and he was charming. He could not do enough for me."

On entering the club the duty member welcomed them. "Enjoy your evening with us."

They found a table and ordered drinks. Members passing by greeted them but did not encroach on their company. John pointed out people who were of some importance and Ella did the same for Tommy by pointing out the women. They spent a quiet evening talking about various amusing incidents that had happened. They had a good laugh about Tommy's incident in the Souk today.

On returning to the Villa John and Ella were asked if they wanted to come in for a bite to eat and a nightcap but they decided not to.

"Have a nice holiday and we will look forward to your return in a month's time. Goodnight."

Tommy made themselves some sandwiches for supper and they sat with them talking about the packing and what they wanted to do and who to visit until it was time to turn in.

CHAPTER 45

They spent Sunday morning by the pool topping up their tan to impress their friends in the UK.

"We are going to miss this in the UK we will probably be well wrapped up instead of relaxing in our swimming costumes Bill."

"And being waited on hand and foot, you know love when I think about the schedule we have set ourselves we are going to be glad to get back here but it will be good to see our family and friends again I expect Jackie will have told them we are coming. I am going in for a dip, are you coming?"

"What! To get this swim suit wet I should think not."

"Then why did you buy it?"

"Not to get it wet, I have an old thing I use for swimming."

When Bill had dried himself after a few minutes in the pool Leila brought them cool drinks. Would you like the Newspaper to read sir?"

"Yes please Leila that would be nice, thank you."

They stayed by the pool until lunch time after which they began to do some serious packing. Bill soon finished his but Tommy was making hard work of it by putting items in her case then replacing them to such an extent she began to get frustrated especially with knowing Bill had finished his packing. She was glad to leave it and have a break when she heard Dot and Alfred arrive. "Hello you two, aren't you offering them a drink Bill?"

"We are not stopping thanks Tommy we are going back to see a film someone is showing of a trip into the desert so we came here first knowing you would be busy packing your cases and having an early night. Dot then gave each of them a kiss and to give our love to everybody. Alfred shook Bill by the hand and gave Tommy a kiss. We don't want to hear that you have asked for an extension to your leave either."

"There will be no fear of that" Bill assured him "we have come to like this place too much to want to be away too long, we will be in touch anyway."

After waving them off Tommy said, "I am not doing any more packing until after dinner then I may be in a better frame of mind."

And so that was the case, "it went like a dream" she told Bill.

I am glad about that because I was going to suggest that any warm clothing you might need just take the minimum you can buy what you would need in the UK. You need not bring them home you could leave them at Jackie's she has plenty of wardrobe space."

"Bill! I am not going to repack again so if need be I can still leave some I am taking with me with Jackie, end of story!"

"Have you got your carry-on bag sorted out?"

"Yes and I have put my handbag inside it as per regulations. If you are now satisfied I shall make supper then we will go to bed. Mashy?"

"Mashy."

"Good morning Ma'am greeted Leila" with their early morning brew.

"Morning Leila" replied a sleepy eyed Tommy "is it that time already?" She shook Bill awake. "Come on Noddy it is Wakey-Wakey time, rise and shine."

Bill stirred and grunted "What?" much to the amusement of Leila.

"Do you want hot tea or iced tea?"

"What are you on about woman?"

"If you lay there any longer Leila is going to get frostbite in her fingers holding the mugs."

"He sat up in bed and looked at Tommy, "You are mad! He then saw Leila. "Good morning Leila "

"Good morning sir" she replied with a huge smile breakfast will be ready in half an hour."

"Please make it an hour Leila, have a word with Thomas he will do it for me."

"Thomas said if you want a later breakfast I have to tell sir it will be Brunch.

"Well spoken Thomas" laughed Tommy "now you had better get your skates on, sir!"

When they had finished their breakfast Tommy asked Thomas if he could have a Bacon Butty and a brew ready for Fred when he arrives.

When he arrived Tommy told Bill to let him in while I go and tell Thomas.

"Come in Fred and sit yourself down you have time for a brew haven't you?

"Oh yes sir, we have plenty of time."

Leila came in with his breakfast on a tray.

"Get that down you," Bill said. "It should help you to drive better."

"Just leave him alone and let him enjoy it. You have had your breakfast, now leave him in peace."

"Thank you Mrs Barrett."

"Thank you Mrs Barrett," mimicked Bill. "Would the little old Blue-Eyed boy like anything else?"

"Carry on like that with my chauffeur Bill Barrett and you will be in big trouble."

Thomas and Leila were having a good laugh listening to Bill and Tommy while Fred was sat eating his bacon butties with a smile on his face.

"He happens to be *my* chauffeur and it's only because I am so kind hearted that I lend him to you, otherwise you would be using Shankss' pony."

"Right, that does it. I shall report you to my friend the Emir."

"Excuse me," said Fred "What is Shanks's pony?"

"It is what you will be doing if your driving does not improve… Walking! What were we saying dear?"

"You wanted to know if I wanted the window seat."

Poor old Fred spluttered in his mug of tea, slopping it onto his trousers.

"I would love it dear, and can I have it on the return journey too?

Fred vanished into the kitchen where Leila, with tears of laughter in her eyes, gave him a dry cloth to wipe his trousers.

"I don't believe it Leila, but there is a song written by an Englishman called Noel Coward – 'Mad Dogs and Englishmen Go Out in the Mid-Day Sun'. Now I *do* believe that."

"No, they are not mad, they are very funny. Both Thomas and I get such a lot of enjoyment from listening to them. At times we think are they being angry with each other and we have come to realize they never are; it is their way of showing their fondness for each other. Thomas and I are really going to miss them while they are away."

"I shall too Leila, they are a wonderful kind couple."

"How long is it going to take you to mop up a tiny drop of tea asked Bill? We are going to the UK for a holiday not to the airport to do some aircraft spotting."

"Do you realise, sir, I nearly scalded my leg?"

"Pity it wasn't one of your hands, you might have driven better with one hand."

Fred heard Leila giggling behind his back. "Right then, I am ready when you are sir. Let me carry your bag Mrs Barrett."

"Bloody creep!" snarled Bill.

Fred turned to a giggling Leila and gave her a wink.

They all said their Salaams and Leila's tears were not from laughing as she and Thomas waved them off.

At the airport Bill said. "Well Fred you are now going to have a month of peace and quiet."

"I would prefer to have you here even with the agro sir."

Bill shook him by the hand gave him a hug saying. "You take care of yourself."

"Look after yourself Fred said Tommy giving him a kiss, we will miss you too. Mashy?"

"Mashy Mrs Barrett. Salaam.

"Salaam Fred they both replied.

As he waved them off he mouthed…

'May Allah Bless You and Keep You Safe.'